Friends, Lies, Booze ...and Magpies

... a crime story...

Barry Woodward

A Blum Gatley Book

Lydiate Series Two

My wife found the old lady's body in her greenhouse. She lay on the brick path between the tomatoes, an overturned watering can beside her. Anne had planned a walk around the market, lunch for two at the Plough Horse on the canal, then a visit to a garden centre. To find her dead, yet wearing lipstick and a summer dress ready for their day out, added to her shock.

I took the tearful call at the office that hot morning, drove straight there. I sweated, in shirt and tie, the metallic smell of tomato pollen in my nostrils, stared at her body. I should've been shocked myself, upset at the death of someone I'd known all my life, but those emotional reactions, were pushed aside by unease – and fear. Year after year, I'd dreaded this day, now it was here.

Anne felt we should carry her inside, but I knew enough of official procedures to leave her as she lay, to call the police. We compromised, found a laundered bed sheet to cover her.

While Anne tidied the kitchen and washed-up the old lady's final breakfast dishes, I went into the front room of the small, semi-detached Victorian house, stood at the bay window to watch for the police car. My eyes strayed to a collection of framed photographs on a mahogany table. I had met or known all of those people, their smiles frozen in time. I stared at them in turn, remembered.

Anne interrupted my thoughts. 'Are you all right?'

I turned, nodded.

'Shouldn't we tell someone?'

'There's nobody left, not now'

'Yes, but the vicar, people at the church…'

'I'll call him and put a notice in the paper.'

'What about the funeral?'

I snapped, 'I'll see to it.'

Initial shock had lessened, my wife was agitated, 'Has she left anything to pay for it, though? Has she got a will? What are we going to do?'

'I'm sorry,' I said, 'Let's just get the police stuff done with, shall we?'

The questions had started. There would be more – a lot more. How could I answer them? How could I explain that for thirty years I'd lived a lie? How could I explain the events that had brought me to this state of anxiety? If I told the truth, would I still have a marriage?

The old girl's doctor and a constable, a coroner's officer, visited the house. We were told her death was not suspicious, caused by a stroke. A death certificate was issued and I phoned an undertaker, then the office to arrange time off. My wife interpreted my mood, my silence, as shock and grief, but my mind was in the past – and how to cope with the immediate future.

There was too much to tell to sit down with her and talk. For me, as a newspaper man, the best way was to write it down. When Anne went to bed, I went to the kitchen and opened a bottle of her red wine. It was the first alcoholic drink I'd touched in more than 30 years. A single glass calmed me, focused my concentration at the computer, as I thought about my friend, Blum Gatley.

I wanted to write the truth about those events before I even met Anne; as well as that hidden part of my life after then -- to tell her everything, no embellishment, no lies, most of all, no lies.

The place to begin was a cold morning in January 1970.

Chapter 1
Plums and Road Tax

IT WAS MY best friend Blum's day in court and I was late. I should have reached Preston before ten o' clock, but I'd spent half the night drinking, and in bed, with a girl whose passion had started to obsess me. I didn't do what any trainee reporter should -- double-check facts, in this case the railway timetable. It was quarter to eleven when I made my uneasy entry to the public gallery. The feeling I'd failed Blum didn't lessen, even when he turned in the dock, offered a brief smile.

I whispered my apology to his girlfriend, Viv. Her eyes left Blum for my questions on his mood earlier that day, the state of his nerves. Yards away, a young man wearing a checked sports jacket and scarf wrote in a spiral-bound notebook: a reporter. Viv pulled a face when I pointed him out, speculated where he might be from. For Blum's mam's sake, I'd hoped this minor case might slip past the newspapers. We were startled by the boom of the judge's voice, 'This is a court, not a street corner.'

Recorder Judge Hernshaw glared at us. The comical horsehair periwig perched on his great head failed to diminish his aura of power and authority. The probation officer reading out a report on Blum's background floundered, startled at the interruption.

'Yes, you,' His Honour said, his eyes locked on us, 'If you wish to tittle-tattle remove yourselves from my court. Otherwise, remain silent.'

Should I reply, apologise? But the Judge turned to the probation officer, a flick of his big hand an instruction to carry on. With the Judge's gaze averted, Blum glanced at us, risked a grin. Ten minutes later, a prison officer escorted him down the dock steps to the cells and Judge Hernshaw's words resonated in the oak-panelled Court of Quarter Sessions.

'I sentence you to nine months' Borstal training. Take him down.'

*

I was shocked.

The bustle of Lancaster Road and the nearby market flowed past me, un-noticed, on this bitter, windy day outside the grimy, Victorian court building. It took three matches to light a No. 6, even with the sheltering lapels of the reporter's mac my mother bought me for my newspaper job.

I paced and smoked. Blum sent down for nine months. It was always possible he'd be locked up for his thieving, but I'd convinced myself -- tried to convince him -- he was perfect for the new suspended sentences, or probation. I felt foolish, guilty, I'd nurtured any spark of hope.

In a way I was glad Viv alone had been allowed to see him in the cells beneath the court. False hope of a suspended sentence, my lateness, my missed chance to wish him luck; it combined as dereliction of duty on my side of our friendship.

But this wasn't about me.

How would Blum cope in a regime of humdrum routine, hard discipline, designed to break individual spirit? Would months locked away destroy him as the lad I knew? How would his mam and her half-brother, Uncle Walter, take it? Since Blum's arrest, Walter had ignored him. His mam carried on as normal, but Blum confided his torture at the tears he heard from her bedroom. She wanted to attend court, but Blum forbade her. It was his crime, he said, he would deal with the consequences alone.

The reporter exited the court entrance, tightened his scarf against the wind. I stepped towards him, 'Excuse me…'

He stopped, smiled. 'Yeah?'

I hesitated, waved my hand, 'Sorry, nothing. It's all right.'

He moved off, glanced back at me. I turned away, flushed, ashamed. I wanted to ask him to keep Blum's case out of his paper. All young reporters were warned about intimidation, even bribery, outside courtrooms for that purpose. Though I wanted to protect Blum and his mam from publicity, I was glad I'd stopped that stupid impulse to embarrass a fellow reporter.

I was still cursing myself when Viv, in her Afghan sheepskin coat, green crushed velvet trousers, came out on to the busy pavement. Her hair, grown long since she met Blum, blew in the wind. She clutched her coat closed at the collar, looked for me. I waved, dreaded an angry message sent by Blum. I could see from her eyes, she'd cried. Would she now be angry, scornful, over my lapses?

'Have you got a cig?' she said, 'I gave him mine to keep him going.'

I scrabbled out my fags, surprised at her ordinary words. I might have dreaded Blum's scorn, but I'd also expected upset from a girl deprived of her boyfriend for almost a year. She seemed calm, not as I'd imagined.

I shielded her lighter with my mac. I was tentative, 'Are you all right?'

She sucked in smoke, nodded.

'Sure?'

She blew out the smoke, cupped her right elbow in her left palm, like she often did.

'He said I should keep my mind on the Marjorie plums and the road tax on the Chev.'

I laughed, 'You what?'

She smiled, tears glistened at the corners of her eyes, 'The tax on the Chev's paid up 'til the end of September. That's when his mam's best plums'll be ready and that's when he'll be out.'

I took it in, 'That's one way of looking at it.'

Viv giggled. 'Only Blum'd say something like that, eh?'

She knuckled the corners of her eyes, sniffed. I didn't want her to cry, I was straight in with questions.

'How's he taken it? Is he alright?'

Viv inhaled, blew out smoke, 'He says he'll be fine, to tell you don't worry. He'll let us know about visiting times and that.'

'What about his mam? Someone's got to tell her what's…'

'The solicitor said he'd ring her, explain everything.'

'Oh, right… Good.'

I was ashamed at my relief it wouldn't be me who told her of Blum's sentence. I'd taken a couple of days off from my job on a newspaper in a small Lancashire cotton town. I'd have to visit her.

Viv said, 'I promised I'd go and see her as soon as I could.'

'I will, too, as soon as poss.'

I caught the smell of food, then coffee, on the wind. I was hungry, needed a hot drink. 'Do you want something to eat?'

'Do you know anywhere?'

I did a course in Preston as part of my training, knew Booths' café at the top of Fishergate did hot pot with red cabbage for two shillings.

'If hotpot'll do?'

She nodded. We walked, not speaking, through dinner time crowds.

It had been three months since I heard of Blum's arrest.

*

An autumn afternoon in the newsroom of a hundred-year-old, twice-weekly newspaper; the location of the job I'd started a year earlier. My A-levels could've found me a place at a college, but I was sick of formal education, tired of no regular money, bored. I tried a dull office job with a shipping company, but I'd convinced myself I wanted to work in newspapers. After an interview, I could start straight away, but it meant living away from home.

I was excited by the chance to forge my own life. In 1968, the Sixties were still swinging. Youth clamoured to be heard, post-war austerity was a memory. Higher wages, pop culture and the rise of commercial television injected colour, frivolity, hedonism and materialism into working class life. It was a period of protest and upheaval, turning-on, tuning-in and dropping-out; all happening according to the Press, radio and television, but not in the pages of my newspaper, nor in my life. Except for a girl called Sandra.

Now, in 1969 I tried to write-up an interview with a married couple who worked all their lives for the same mill, soon to celebrate their Golden wedding. Despite the stimulation of four pints of bitter, I struggled to find a clever intro paragraph. I was alone, but for our news editor, Geoff Sillitoe, sprawled in his chair, feet on the desk, half-asleep after his own liquid lunch at The Boot, the office nickname for the Wellington Arms.

One of his three phones rang. With the minimum energy needed, he lifted the receiver, 'News desk.' He listened without expression, put his hand over the mouthpiece, 'For you, cocker.'

'Who is it?' I mouthed.

He shrugged, another phone rang. I was surprised, intrigued. I didn't have many contacts, other than bread-and-butter ones. Had someone remembered my by-line, wanted to entrust me with an exclusive story? I jerked my head to indicate to Geoff I'd take the call in one of the sound-proof booths which ran along one side of the newsroom. He pressed a button and the 1940s Bakelite phone in Booth 2 rang, Hollywood-style, as I picked up my notebook, biro, cigs and matches and, a bit pissed, assumed the persona of a big city newsman.

Viv's voice, on the edge of tears, dumped me back into reality. Blum was arrested by detectives at his mam's house, May Bank View, that morning. Two jacks with a search warrant went through the house, the sheds, greenhouses and outbuildings. Blum was taken from Lydiate, in west Lancashire, to the police station in the market town of Ormskirk. His mam was shocked and worried.

'What have they got him for?'

'Something to do with stuff missing from work.'

'Work? Shit, have they charged him?'

'I don't know. He just said to let you know.'

'Is there anything I can do?'

'Don't know, I don't think so.'

'Tell him I'll be over at the weekend. Should be there Saturday dinnertime…'

Pips signalled the connection would soon to be cut. I changed my mind, 'No, no! Tell him tomorrow night, in the Soldier.'

She'd gone.

I leaned back against the wall, lit up. If Blum hadn't been charged, they'd have to let him out after twenty-four hours. If he was, he'd go before the magistrates. Then it was a remand in custody, or out on bail.

*

While my second pint was poured from a tall pewter jug, Blum proved he was on bail when he arrived at the Scottish Soldier, clapped me on the shoulder. 'Don't forget the jailbird.'

I ordered another bitter and we took them along the black-beamed passageway to the fireplace in the back room, chose an ancient settle seat.

'Do you think it'll come to that?'

'Jail, you mean?' he shrugged, laughed, 'I blummin' hope not.'

He told me he'd been charged with theft of goods on various dates over two years, all from a firm that supplied tools, seeds, outdoor clothes and hundreds of other agriculture-related supplies. From day one as a delivery driver who visited dozens of farmers, growers and smallholders each month, he'd noticed the firm's lackadaisical approach to stocktaking and paperwork. He helped himself to items from the stores and sold them; on the quiet, on the cheap, for cash, a lot of it to the company's own less honest customers. He could pick out in minutes those he could corrupt, he said.

'You idiot.'

'If anyone's an idiot, it's Bryan Daltry.'

I laughed, 'Why? -- He owns the place.'

Blum lowered his glass, 'Ha, managing director, owner and idiot. Too mean to pay-out for a proper company accountant, book-keeper, whatever you call it. Sooner have posh holidays and play blummin' golf than run the place proper. So I helped meself -- and I bet I weren't the only one. I whipped loads.'

'How did they find out then?'

Blum laughed, 'Daltry got married again, didn't he? Some bird with a couple o' them boutique places in Southport. She started poking her nose in, made him bring in a feller called Singleton to shake the place up. He did that alright, talk about mustard.'

'Did you stop?'

'Too right, I did. He had auditors go through the place with a nit comb. Least I got a bit of time to move things. By the time CID turned up the other morning, me mam's was clean as her kitchen floor. Thought the Chev might look a bit, you know, flashy... so I shifted it to Viv's.'

'How come they've charged you, then?'

He looked at me, a short laugh, 'Made the mistake of flogging things from loads I'd signed for, didn't I? I got a bit cocky, a bit lazy, like. I'll give it you -- I was a blummin' idiot to do that.'

I pondered a moment, 'You're saying you got away with more than you've been charged with?'

He lit a cigarette, blew out a ring of smoke. It shivered, slid away in the pull of the coal fire. 'That's why I admitted everything they chucked at me. Don't want them digging, do I?'

'What if they check back with all these farmers and everyone else who might've got cheap stuff?'

'They're happy with me admitting what I have done, so they won't bother. Too much like hard work. Can't prove I helped meself to owt else either. Blummin' place was all over the shop before Singleton.'

I took my fags from the oak table, 'They must've asked you where you sold the stuff, what you did with the money.'

'Flogged it in pubs in Liverpool, I told 'em.' He tapped his head, 'Had a list of 'em up here in case I ever got asked.'

'What about the money, though? Did they ask what you did with it?'

He stood, 'Told 'em I spent it on ale for me mates.' He grinned, 'What you having?'

When he brought back the pints, he invited me pike-fishing next day. He talked little about his case after that. Out of work, he did casual farm labour, helped his mam's cousin's husband, Ted, a gamekeeper, until the magistrates took his guilty plea and committed him to be sentenced by a judge at Preston.

*

Booth's cafe was crowded with shoppers and office workers. The clatter of cutlery on plates and chatter was deafening under the high ceiling of the old-fashioned dining room. Our own conversation was minimal, Viv ate her hotpot. I thought about Blum's evasive attitude over the money from his thefts. Judge Hernshaw mentioned the sum of two hundred pounds as the value of the stolen goods, but the essence of his brief verbal flogging of Blum was about breach of trust, not money.

Two hundred quid was almost three months' wages for me as a trainee. Blum earned more than I did, but not by much. I'd not noticed him spend above his means on beer, clothes or anything else. His single extravagance was his old American Chevrolet, but I know it cost thirty quid, owing its poor state and I was there when he paid for it. I recalled his remark about shifting the Chev to Viv's before detectives showed up, but its renovation had been completed through called in favours, bits from scrap yards and his Uncle Walter's talent for metal fabrication. Viv spent hours refitting the engine, wangled a re-spray through her brothers at her family's garage business. I was sure the Yankee car's renovation wasn't financed with Daltry's money.

I acted daft about Blum's thefts. 'Did they say he pinched two hundred quids' worth?'

She put her knife and fork together on her plate, picked up her cup, 'Yeah, wasn't worth it, was it?'

'What did he do with it?'

She laughed, 'Well he didn't spend it on taking me out, did he?'

I had no idea, I was away so much. But Viv supplied the answer.

'I've never expected him to take me out. I like things he likes. I'm happy with my job and the flat, my bike, what we do.' She paused a moment. 'We don't need more money. I don't know why he did it, the soft sod.' She paused again, 'I don't know what I'm going to do.' Her voice cracked. 'I'm going to miss him.'

She held back her upset.

'If you want to go, I'll see to the bill.'

'I should, I've got to get to work.' She blew her nose, wiped her eyes. 'You got to get back?'

'I took two days off. I'll go home, I suppose. And I have to visit Blum's mam.'

'You staying at Elaine's?'

I shook my head. She lived with her parents, anyway and my girlfriend didn't know I had time off, would be home. 'No, my mum and dad's.'

I was so pre-occupied with clearing work, Blum's court case, I hadn't thought much about what I'd do. I expected Blum to come out of court on a suspended sentence, perhaps probation, so we'd have a day to go fishing, drinking, or to help out at Ted and Marion's place on the Tarlscough estate.

Viv made a move. 'Well, if you can get yourself to your mum's from the hospital, I'll give you a lift.'

She waved away my offer to pay for her hotpot. I followed her to a narrow street behind Fishergate. Blum's Chev was parked in the entrance of a derelict print works. She started up. As ever, it didn't start first time. I pulled out my cigarettes, offered her one, realised she'd started to cry. I had no idea what to do, but made an attempt to cheer her.

'Remember what he said, eh? -- Plums and car tax?'

This triggered a sob. She leaned forward over the wheel, her shoulders shook. I wondered what to do, say. Moments later she apologised, 'Will you drive?'

'I still haven't passed my test.'

'Who cares? It'll be your last chance for a while.'

'Why's that?'

'I'll put the Chev away 'til he gets out. I'd sooner use the Norton, to be honest.'

We swapped places and I drove through busy streets, across the bridge over the Ribble at the foot of Fishergate Hill, and south to Ormskirk. We didn't speak much. She smoked my fags, stared at bleak winter fields. In the staff car park at the hospital, she locked the Chev, agreed to keep in touch. I set off in a sudden shower to catch a bus, she called me back.

'I forgot to give you this.'

She pulled a creased manila envelope from her tapestry shoulder bag, held it out.

'What is it?'

She pulled up her collar against the rain, 'Blum said to give it you if he got sent away.'

It was more a package than a letter. My name was scrawled on the front, it was reinforced with Sellotape. I looked at her as she checked her watch.

'Did he say what it was?'

She moved away, 'He said something about things he wanted doing.'

'Like what?'

She shouted back, 'Why don't you open it and see?'

I squeezed, shook the envelope. I started to pick at the tape, but hailstones pelted me. I pushed it into my mac pocket, hurried to the bus station.

The Roper's Arms was still open as I passed. I took a few steps back, went in, ordered a pint and a small whisky, to warm me up. I sat away from the bar in case the publican started a conversation.

I stripped the tape off the package. I'd seen Blum over Christmas. He seemed to have no worries, other than his mam's upset at the theft charges. He gave no hint of anything he might want me to do if he were locked up.

I tipped out the contents; a folded piece of cardboard and another envelope. Taped to the cardboard were three keys. Two were new, the other older, bigger; tarnished brass, heavy, with a long shank. The envelope was sealed with tape. Inside was a sheet of lined paper from a student's note pad, covered in Blum's careless handwriting, a sprawl of biro-ed block capitals, not the cursive writing our teacher, Hetty Hothersall, once demanded we perfect.

I started to read.

Chapter 2
The Still Room

ON THE BUS, I read it again. Blum started with a jokey paragraph and multiple exclamation marks, said I wouldn't be reading this unless he was locked up. It went on with instructions: the Chevrolet would stay with Viv until I could sell it. *'I want you to give mam the money you get.'* His mam depended on his earnings more these days as fewer wanted her to make dresses, or mend and alter clothes. She'd lost income, too, from her job as part-time housekeeper for her near neighbour, Captain Westbrook, when ill-health forced him to sell up to live down south with his sister. Blum said he trusted me alone to do what he asked as soon as I could.

He came to the keys. *'Take these keys and go to the old farm. Look behind the red door.'*

I didn't understand at first, but he meant Pygon's Farm. I had memories of the place, but it was years before I looked into its history. I knew it was empty and the last owners lived like hermits. The farmer hanged himself in 1962 after his wife died. Years ago, it was said, his father was eaten alive by his own pigs.

When I reached home, the weather was bad, I didn't want to go anywhere. I spent the evening with my family, made an excuse about not going to see my regular girlfriend, Elaine, decided for perhaps the tenth time not to confide about the other girl in my new home town, watched a play on television. I woke early, thought about Blum. How would he cope with his first days inside? Would he behave himself, or rebel against authority? I picked up the envelope on the bedside table. Had he expected me to go to the farm last night? I hoped not.

I hung around until my mum went to work mid-morning, stepped outside into freezing fog. I walked a quarter of a mile to the canal bridge and the shop my grandmother once owned, went in for a packet of fags. The man who served me in the modernised shop had no idea of my identity, even though my grandmother sold the place to his mother. The doorbell tinkled as I left, crossed the planks of the swing bridge. I lit up, idled. A couple of hundred yards away, through fog and skeletal trees, was the frosted slate roof of Pygon's Farm.

Blum was fascinated by the place. I could remember the farmer who hanged himself. I would often see him in the shop when I was a kid, but Blum was always irritated he didn't recall him. Several times as boys, we'd explored the outbuildings, peered through the windows of the farmhouse. Nobody had lived there since the suicide. We'd spent hours in the few remaining fields and an old pasture bordered by goat willows was a favourite place to build sand dams in the stream, or have catapult 'wars' with lads from a new housing estate. Blum told me most of the land was sold years before the suicide. The rest was rented by the pervert farmer, Cyril Clegg, but who owned the farm buildings now, yet left them to rot, I had no idea.

I felt the keys in my pocket as I walked to the farm. Curtains still hung in the front windows. The gate was adjacent to the end of the house. I noticed a padlock and chain between the post and latch. It was tarnished, but not old. I climbed over the gate, heard a cough. A man with a corgi dog appeared from the fog, head down. I stepped back behind the thorn hedge, stood still, as he continued down the lane. When he disappeared, still coughing, I moved down the cobbled slope to the yard.

Puddles in the cobbles were covered with cat ice. Between the three-storey house and the barn and cowshed opposite, the fog seemed thicker. Hoar frost crusted the goat willows behind the tractor shed. '*Look behind the red door.*' The only doors I could see were the porch door at the back entrance of the house and the rotten barn doors. I knew the front door was black. None of the others, including the cowshed door, were red.

Further along the house where the cobbles ran past the tractor shed to the remnants of the pasture gate, rusting, corrugated iron sheets nailed to lengths of timber leaned against the house wall between two big, now leafless, elder trees. Undisturbed for eight years, in sparse earth between house walls and cobbles, the elders had thrived. There seemed no reason why the sheets should be there. Could 'red door' mean 'red,' as in rust? Unlikely, but I moved across the cobbles. Awareness of the suicide, a farmer eaten alive by pigs, didn't help my nerves.

Behind the iron sheets there was a door, but I didn't recall it from past visits. I pulled at the heavy sheets and moved one end away from the house wall. The door was weathered, bleached like driftwood, but when I squeezed between the corrugated sheets and the house I made out traces of red paint in the grain of its boards. There were two locks; one an ancient mortise, the other a new version with a round lacquered plate surrounding the keyhole. I felt in my pocket and pulled out the long-shanked key, too big. I tried one of the two smaller keys in the newer lock. It turned.

My heart beat rose when I pushed open the door. In the gloom were whitewashed walls and shadowy shapes. I struck a match. In the flare I saw another box of matches on a shelf by the door, beside it a new tin paraffin lantern. I reached for the lantern, shook it. There was oil in it. With cold hands it was fiddly to raise the glass, wind up the wick, but I lit it, stepped inside

I raised the lantern. The smell of the paraffin took a few moments to dispel the odour of stale cigarette smoke, mustiness. It must have been the farm's still room; a cool place where bottled fruit, pickles, apples, pears, cheeses and hams were stored. It would have been the place where pork was salted, drained off, re-salted, and hung as flitches of bacon; where, even on the hottest July day, the temperature would never be high enough to spoil hoarded foodstuffs.

Now, the hooks and sandstone slab shelves preserved a different harvest. What Blum had stolen from Daltry's filled a space as big as most living rooms. I found outdoor clothing, tools of every sort, wellington boots, work boots, drums and sacks of agri-chemicals, farm machinery spares, chain saws, tractor and lorry batteries, saw blades, rope, lanterns, boxes of nails and bolts, tractor spares, rat-traps, cases of shotgun cartridges and much more I couldn't identify.

What I did identify was my name on an envelope on the pine table against one wall. Beside the table was a safe, green with brass fittings. It was old, but newly concreted into the cobbled floor. I had to squat to make out embossed lettering that read 'Copplestone and Son, South Castle Street, Liverpool.' I put the lantern down, shifted a crate to sit on. I ripped open the envelope. Another jokey introduction to three sheets of student's notepad reminded me I wouldn't be reading it if Blum were a free man.

I lit up, settled to read, glad of small warmth from the lantern. Blum explained that keeping the stuff he'd stolen at May Bank View had been a problem, even before Singleton's arrival at Daltry's. In need of a 'warehouse' he'd thought of the old farm, commandeered the still room. He'd obtained and installed the safe, fitted locks to the door and yard gate, knocked-up the corrugated iron screen.

I couldn't contain my curiosity at the mention of money, rooted out the long-shanked key from my pocket. When I turned it in the safe lock the internal bolts clunked, slid aside. I dragged the lantern across the table for more light and what I'd just read about was there. I took out the red tartan shortbread tin, prised off the lid with my thumbs. It was full of half-crowns and two-shilling pieces in close piles. I didn't count it, but what Blum had written, I'm sure, was correct; the tin contained more than a hundred quid.

I took the second, a toffee tin. There was more money in it than I'd ever seen -- bundles of pound notes and one of ten shilling notes, each with an elastic band. I pulled off the bands and counted it all. I was always useless with figures --

and money, at that time -- so I counted twice. Blum was correct, twelve hundred and forty pounds. There was more than £1,300 in the safe; about three years' wages for me, perhaps two for Blum, at least when he still had the job at Daltry's.

Blum repeated he wanted enough from the Chev's sale to cover his weekly 'tip-up' to his mam if he were locked-up. I felt the bundles of money. Why did I need to sell the Chev when these tins were stuffed with cash lying idle?

I put the tins back in the safe, went back to the letter. Blum wrote that he'd put the Signalman's four-ten shotgun and his air rifle in Ted the gamekeeper's hands. At the back of the still room were other guns, but these were for sale. I took up the lantern and behind a stack of boxes and a clothesline-like arrangement on which hung dozens of donkey jackets, waterproof and thorn proof coats, I found a shroud of greasy hessian in a corner. Beneath it was a bundle of guns, smeared with Vaseline to protect them from rust, about fifteen in all. The types were familiar, ordinary single and double-barrelled shotguns, but one stood out. I pulled it away from the wall. The odd Germanic profile of the rifle was unmistakeable. It belonged to Captain Westbrook, who had employed Blum's mam. Blum once used it to settle a score with a man who wronged his family.

Blum had too much respect for Captain Westbrook to steal his old muzzle-loader rifle. Perhaps the old boy had given it him before he left Lydiate, but where the hell had the others come from? Blum had always loved guns; shooting them, swapping them, searching for those he fancied, but I'd no idea he had so many; I was sure I'd seen none of these shotguns, most he acquired were neglected, old things with rusted barrels, battered stocks. Quite a few of these seemed to be in good order, one or two looked expensive, like those I'd seen used by game shooters on the Tarlscough estate. I returned to the table and open safe, read further. He told me to look in the bottom of the safe.

I got down on one knee, peered inside, pulled away a piece of oily sacking. I stared at five pistols on a tin tray. Shotguns I understood, but where had he got these? I picked up the nearest. I'd no real knowledge of pistols, didn't even know if they were loaded, but I did know the difference between a revolver and an automatic. It was a Webley service revolver and there were two more like it, all oiled, one pocked with rust pits, I imagined, from the trenches of Flanders. The other two were automatics. I picked them up in turn, the muzzle pointing away from me, my fingers away from the triggers. One was a German Luger, I'd seen them in war films, the other a small Beretta, made in Italy. On the tray was a Terry's chocolate box and inside were perhaps a hundred brass cartridges, different sizes, I presumed, for the different pistols. I replaced the pistols and ammunition. The letter said no more about them.

I read further. Blum apologised, told me he was sorry he'd put me to such trouble when I was living away from home, but it was important I knew what he'd done, and that someone he trusted should keep an eye on his secret warehouse while he was 'inside.' He asked me to destroy the two letters, to speak to nobody about what I'd seen. It saddened me when I read the underlined sentence, *'I don't want you to tell Viv any of this!!!'*

I couldn't understand that statement. I'd spent a fair bit of time in Viv's company, liked her. I'd been with Blum to her family home, next door to which was the garage business owned by her father, who employed her two elder brothers. The father was a tough nut, her brothers each cut from the same block. Her mother, too, was equal to her husband and sons in her confident and forthright manner. If anything, outside the garage, she ran the family. Viv had the makings of a similar character. With her mechanical skills, it was a mystery to me why she wasn't fixing cars and motorbikes, instead of nursing. It would be better paid with no shift work.

I asked Blum about this once and he said, 'It's what she wants to do.' To me, that showed her strength of will inside the Jarvey household, where their god was the family business. I'd seen her stand up for herself as well. Lads on mod scooters once spotted her sitting side saddle on her Norton outside the Scottish Soldier, having a pint with Blum and me. A few snidey comments came from the mods, but she ignored them. Blum bristled, but we were outnumbered.

A tall lad in bleached Levis, Lotus loafers and a purple polo shirt, was their obvious leader. He nodded to Viv, sneered, 'Look at her, skinny little tart. If she dropped that bike, she'd need a friggin' crane.'

The Mod swigged at his pint. His mates laughed. Blum stood, ready to confront him, but Viv stilled him with a look. She strolled over to the leader, stood beside his Lambretta with its front rack of knock-off spot lamps, multiple wing-mirrors. Hands on her hips, she asked, 'What did you say?'

He lowered the pint, grinned, 'You heard, love.'

His mates sniggered.

In an instant, Viv's leg shot out. With her light, but total, weight behind the strike, the sole and heel of her right boot struck the edge of the Lambretta's fairing and the scooter toppled. A crunching noise was followed by the tinkle of glass from half a dozen wrecked mirrors and spots. The lad stared at his fallen machine, open-mouthed. Viv stepped forward, snatched the pint from his hand and lashed beer in his face. He looked at her in shock as she raised the glass, dashed it on the ground between him and his scooter.

'See if you can lift that, soft lad,' Viv said, 'No-one calls me names.'

Blum was delighted, I was amazed. So were the Lambretta lad's mates. The laughter and remarks started. Their leader couldn't stomach merriment and cat calls at his expense. A biker girl, five feet four, had robbed his credibility -- and they let him know it. With Burtonwood's bitter soaking the front of his shirt and jeans, he was desperate to keep his dignity. He dragged upright his damaged machine, swung a leg over it. He kicked the engine into life, raced in first gear as he slewed out on to the main road. Beeping their horns, grinning and waving at Viv, the others followed, left a cluster of half-drunk pints on the forecourt. Blum was nearly helpless with laughter.

Why he didn't want Viv to know about this store of guns and stolen gear, I didn't know. Of the girls I knew, I'd pick Viv as least likely to make a fuss. Elaine would be mortified; Sandra, I couldn't say.

It was cold and I forced myself to get on with what I'd been asked. To sell the Chev would take time. Surely, it would be better to take money for Blum's mam now. I knew Blum tipped up four pounds a week, so I multiplied that by the length of his sentence and came up with £144. If I upped that to a year, it would be £208. But there was so much cash in the tins, it seemed mean. I counted out £250 and put it in my inside pocket. When the car was sold, I could pay the tin back. If the car didn't fetch £250, Blum couldn't begrudge his mam the difference, not with so much stashed away. I put the banknotes tin back in the safe, blew out the lantern, locked the door of the still room.

Back in the fog, I pushed the corrugated iron screen back against the wall. Did anyone other than Blum visit this quiet, decayed farmyard? I set fire to both letters, dropped the sheets, watched them turn to ash on the frosted cobbles, dreaded what might happen to Blum if the police discovered the still room's contents.

Chapter 3
Money and Lies

BY THE FIRE in the Plough Horse warmth returned to my feet. With a hot-pot pie and a pint inside me, I fancied a whisky. Fat Cyril Edensor looked up from the Thursday *Advertiser*, took my order and pushed the newspaper towards me, swivelled it for me to read the front page right way up. He dabbed his forefinger on the newsprint, 'Seen this, la'?'

It was a two column headline just above the fold, 'Delivery Driver sent to Borstal.' A strap line added, 'Spent money on drink for friends.' In the first paragraph, the sum of £200 was mentioned.

Cyril pushed the whisky towards me, took my ten-bob note, 'Pity he isn't here to treat you, eh?'

I said nothing, stared at him, tried to make him uncomfortable.

I saw his uncertainty. 'He was a mate of yours, wasn't he?'

My eyes stayed on his, 'He still is.'

Cyril broke eye contact, tilled my note. I pocketed my change, swiped the newspaper from the bar, took it to the fireside. That reporter I almost buttonholed was likely an agency man, supplying papers throughout the north-west with court reports. I read his piece, bare facts with Judge Hernshaw's comments on Blum's 'betrayal of trust.' Cyril glanced over again. Angered at his snide comment, I chucked my whisky back in a gulp, pushed his newspaper on the back of the fire. It blazed wildly and I feared it might set the chimney alight. I wanted him to protest, so I could tell him where to get off, but he said nothing. I regretted my actions seconds after I left.

I re-crossed the canal bridge. Home was attractive, but I'd told Viv I'd visit Blum's mam, owed it to Blum to see how she'd taken the news. To leave it any later with word of her only child's crime on the front of the local paper would be callous. I changed course for the mile walk to Blum's home, May Bank View.

A hundred yards from the gate the front wheel of a motorbike advanced from the driveway. A car passed and the big Norton swung out into the road, coming my way. It was Viv, nose and mouth wrapped in a black woollen scarf, a matching hat pulled down over her ears. I raised a hand as she accelerated. She braked, turned off the engine.

I crossed the road, 'How is she?'

Viv pulled the scarf down, 'A bit down. I wasn't there that long.'

'Did the solicitor tell her everything?'

'Except why he did it. She asked me three times.'

'What did you say?'

She was irritated, 'What could I say? I don't know. Do you? '

I shook my head, 'I wish I did.'

She blew out, exasperated. Her breath condensed as clouds in the cold air, 'All this upset for money he didn't even need.'

'Do you know where he's gone? Is it far?'

It was a place called Havershawe, out on the Fylde, somewhere between Preston and Blackpool.

'So when can we see him? What day can we go?'

She told me she'd phoned Blum's solicitor. Any individual prisoner had to send a prison visiting order inviting each named visitor. To turn up on spec wasn't possible.

'He told me Blum'd get these VO things posted to people he wanted to see in the next few days,' she said, 'Visiting's on Saturdays.'

'Do you think he'll ask his mam to go?'

Viv shrugged, 'He told me he wouldn't.'

Would being locked up change his mind? I didn't think it would.

Viv re-arranged her scarf, ready to go, and it occurred to me there was no need for Blum to lose the car at all.

'Did his mam say anything about the Chev?'

Viv frowned, 'No, why?'

'In that letter he said he wanted me to sell it and give the money to his mam, you know, to make up for what he can't give her for his weekly tip-up.'

'Ah, no…He wants to flog the Chev? He loves that car.'

'I know,' I said, 'So…I thought I could buy it then his mam gets some money quick. He can buy it back when he's on his feet again.'

'You haven't passed your test. What use would…?'

I cut in, 'I don't need to drive the bloody thing, not yet. I just want to help.'

'I could see what I could get through the garage. It'd save you shelling out for something you can't even… '

'Would you get two hundred and fifty quid for it?'

'You'd pay that?'

I nodded, saw a resemblance to her old man, the car dealer, as she tipped her head to one side, moved her bottom lip back and forth along the upper, 'Bit toppy for the Chev. Sure you can afford it?'

It seemed a neat solution to help Blum's mam, so I lied. I had next to nothing in a savings account, but I spoke with confidence, a pocket full of ill-gotten cash, 'It's not all my savings. And I know his mam'll miss Blum's wages coming in.'

'It's up to you and Blum, might take him a while to pay you back.'

'We can sort that out. For now, you just use it when you like, alright?'

She seemed bemused, 'If that's what you want.'

'Solves the problem for Blum, doesn't it?'

'What else did he have to say?'

She caught me on the hop. I lied again, 'He… He asked me to get his gun down to Ted and Marion's 'til he gets out.' She must have felt the weight of the keys inside that bulky envelope, another lie, 'He's even given me a bottle of oil, tools and that, to clean it.'

She smiled, 'Him and that flaming shotgun, eh? He's forever cleaning it. God knows why it's so special.'

I wanted this conversation over, 'Well, I'll look after it.'

Viv pulled her scarf up over her nose, kick-started her bike. She shouted over the 650 engine, 'Keep in touch about the visiting. Have you got my number at the flat?'

I stuck up my thumb. She nodded, rode away. I watched until she turned out on to the road to Ormskirk. It didn't feel right lying to her. Why was it so important she didn't know about the room at Pygon's Farm?

May Bank View's big garden was blanketed in fog. I waited for a reply to my knock at the back door of the semi-detached Edwardian house. A missel thrush perched on the roof of a tarred black shed, its feathers puffed against the frost. Nancy Gatley opened the door, interrupted jumbled memories of times spent here.

'Hello, love. Come in.'

I hadn't seen her for more than a year. She'd changed so much. I remembered a young mother embarrassed by Blum's behaviour on our first day at school, later when so many times she treated me almost as another son, always ready to laugh and gossip with us lads. Now her face was careworn, her skin pale, dark Grey hair traced by grey. Her eyes seemed no longer bright. She was in her mid- to- late- forties, but looked older, almost an old woman.

She moved aside, 'You've just missed Vivien.'

I wiped my feet on the familiar rag rug, 'Yeah, I saw her.'

I followed her through the kitchen into what an estate agent would call a breakfast room, but the Gatleys called the back parlour. It always seemed an old-fashioned place, it's only concessions to modernity a television set, an electric fire in the cast iron hearth. The Thursday *Advertiser* lay on the oil-cloth that covered the table. Then I saw Uncle Walter.

'Hello.'

But he ignored me, lifted his lanky body from the armchair and, without a glance my way, shambled out through the door to the front hallway.

Blum's mam protested, 'Walter!'

She was embarrassed, but he ignored her, closed the door behind him.

She tutted, 'He did the very same when Vivien came in.'

I said nothing as she pulled out a chair at the table for me to sit.

'He says he's ashamed of David.' She picked up the newspaper, 'Being in the paper makes it worse. Have you read it?'

'I have, yeah.'

She put it on the sideboard, pulled out another chair, 'Our Walter, he thinks David's been led astray.'

I looked at her.

She shook her head. 'No, love, I know he's wrong. Walter blames Vivien, and you as well, but I know he's wrong. I know my lad. He's too strong-willed for anyone to lead him anywhere. If he stole things and sold them, it was for something else, some other reason. It certainly wasn't to buy drink for his friends.'

'I think you're right.'

She met my eyes, 'Well, did he buy drink for you?

I shook my head. 'No more than I ever bought him.'

'I thought not. And what Walter thinks about him spending on Vivien…well, I'm sure he's not right about that either.'

'Viv wouldn't accept it, I know she wouldn't …She's not like that.'

She nodded. Despite what she'd said, she seemed relieved to hear my confirmation. 'I can't understand why he said that about drink, mind. Why tell the police that? Why did he steal things in the first place?'

I said nothing. She picked up a skirt from a chair back, started to unpick the stitching in its hem. 'From the minute the police turned up, he wouldn't talk about it; wouldn't tell me anything at all.' She looked at me, 'Did he tell you why he had to steal?'

I shook my head, 'To help you? ...I don't know...'

She turned back to her work, a blush of colour on her neck, 'I wondered about that,' she said, 'The winter before last we had a gale that damaged the sheds. It ripped the felt off three of them and a couple of slates off the house roof were blown through the top greenhouse. I was worried sick-- we can't afford insurance-- but David got a chap in to fix everything and told me he'd take care of the money side. Heaven knows what it all cost, then just a few weeks after that when the outside pipes burst, he paid for a plumber ...'

She looked at me, 'Do you think all that might've cost two hundred pounds?'

I said I supposed it could.

'I don't know what his father would've said about all this. Eric wouldn't steal a crust if he were starving to death.'

I leaned on the kitchen doorpost while she made tea. She asked about my work, living away. She put the tray on the back parlour table, opened the hall door to call Uncle Walter. 'I don't know why I'm bothering. He'll not come down 'til you've gone. I'm sorry.'

To be polite, show I held no ill-feelings towards Walter. I asked about his garden work. I was surprised at her reply.

'Oh, he's not worked for near twelve months. Dr Grey's orders -- it's his heart.'

'I'm sorry, I didn't know.'

'He'd like to go back, never stops saying so, but he's well past seventy now -- he's worked more than enough for one lifetime. Not that we don't miss the extra money he used to bring home. I wish me-laddo'd thought how we'd manage before this stealing and getting himself sent to prison.'

She sighed, unpicked the hem quicker.

'I wanted to talk about that.'

She looked up, 'The prison? He won't let me visit him, you know.'

'I, erm, I meant about managing without his wages. He told me to sell his car and give you the money.'

She came straight back, 'He's no need to do that.'

'It's what he wants. He wrote me a note before he went to court.'

I dug into my inside pocket, pulled out the bundle of pound notes. 'Thing is, I've been looking for a car, so I bought it myself.'

I put the money on the table in front of her, 'There's two hundred and fifty pounds there.'

She looked at the bundle of illicit banknotes.

'I won't say it won't be useful, love, but are you sure?'

'I'm sure, yeah.'

'Seems an awful lot for that old thing.'

I insisted, 'It's a fair price and he wants you to have it.'

'Thank you, love.' She put her work aside, put the money in the sideboard drawer.

'If he wants, I thought he could buy it back when he gets …when he comes home.'

She looked at me. 'He's fouled his nest, love, as Eric used to say. When he comes home he'll have more important things to think about. Like how to find work with all this bother behind him.'

*

Blum's future and what he would do when he was released were in my thoughts two weeks later when I caught a train, then a bus, to H.M. Borstal, Havershawe for Saturday afternoon visiting.

Free weekends in my job were a luxury, a rarity, but I didn't begrudge time to visit Blum.

It was a different story with Elaine, who knew I was off that weekend, made plans for shopping, a Chinese meal and a film. I was already the focus of her anger when I didn't tell her I came home after Blum's court case. If I'd stayed away from the Hare and Hounds the evening I went to see Blum's mam, she wouldn't have known. I should've apologised to

Cyril, at the Plough Horse, but took the easy option, was spotted by a nosy cow who worked at the bank with Elaine.

Back at my grotty flat, next evening, I picked up a call on the staircase pay phone when I rushed out to meet Sandra. Elaine made no attempt to engage me in conversation, catch me out. It was a surprise attack, prompted by information from the nosy cow. She ranted quotes from the Thursday *Advertiser*.

'"Delivery driver sent to Borstal," "Spent money on drink for friends." "Nineteen-year-old David Gatley, of May Bank View, Back Moss Lane, was given nine months Borstal training…" Do you think I'm stupid? You went to the court, didn't you?'

'What's wrong with tha…?

She wouldn't let me speak, 'You can get time off to hold his hand, but when it comes to spending it with me…'

I shouted, 'Elaine! He's a mate. We've been friends since we were kids. How could I not go -- not support him? I had to come home and see his mum and uncle and…'

She wouldn't listen, 'He's not worth the effort. He's a thief! You keep saying you're working on your career and you spend your time with someone who stole money from his employers and got locked up. How do you think it'll look to everyone, hanging-out with a criminal? What's up with you?'

I lost my temper, shouted down the phone. 'He's my friend for Christ's sake!'

The receiver at her end crashed into the cradle a microsecond before I smashed mine onto the hook of the pay phone before me.

'Take not the Lord's name in vain,' said a voice behind me. I turned to my landlady, Mrs 'Caernarvon Kitty' Williams, a clean towel for my upstairs bathroom in hand, 'Break that bloody phone, *Bachgen*, and kipping with the Sally Army, you'll be.'

I stepped aside to let her pass, tried to calm down, 'Sorry, Mrs Williams.'

She didn't move. Upstairs was almost a foreign country to her, her legs, she said. Any cleaning up there was my problem.

She dumped the towel on me, gave a whisky-fuelled grin, 'There's nice, *cariad*. Put me a Bells in the pipe at The Packet after.'

I nodded reluctant agreement. She was in the pub on the canal next to her house seven nights a week, plus Saturday and Sunday dinnertimes, rarely had I seen her pay for a drink. Extortion was her middle name. I hated her calling me boy, even in Welsh. And I certainly wasn't her sweetheart.

It seemed pointless to ring back Elaine. Ten minutes later I was in the back room of The Packet, swapping a smile with Sandra, tipping a bottle of Babycham into her brandy. Her note for us to meet up was slipped under my typewriter that afternoon when I was out of the news room.

I spotted Sandra in her first week at *The Sentinel* early the year before. She was fresh from a business course in Bolton. I was attracted the moment I saw her. She wasn't a conventional good-looker; slim, blonde hair, a mouth perhaps too wide, almost a Roman nose. I liked her personality from the start. She was irreverent about senior colleagues. She could cope with the unwanted comments of male colleagues, often with sarcastic, withering effect. She could be coarse in her language, but it wasn't off-putting, not to me. She was a laugh, a girl who said what she thought, did what she liked. I'd hoped she was an addition to editorial, but she was the new trainee rep in our advertising department.

Sandra had an enviable ability for getting on with people, even those she'd put in their place with a barbed comment. She was first with a kind remark to anyone who'd suffered illness or bad luck. She was popular, but there was a slight barrier between her and other staff, for Sandra was the daughter of one of *The Sentinel's* directors, P.S. Heaton, also the company accountant; to Sandra, 'Daddio.' She'd known our chairman and owner, A.S. Henty, since childhood and referred to him, often at work, as 'Hentypops.' In quiet asides, Geoff Sillitoe, our National Union of Journalists' rep, warned male reporters to stay away from her. He didn't trust her for being in the 'bosses' camp.' I ignored his advice. I'd become obsessed with her, her body, excited by our secret liaison; feelings that grew month on month.

Elaine had calmed down when she wrote a couple of days later. I wrote straight back to say I'd come home and see her that next free weekend. When I received my VO from Blum, I phoned to say I could make the Chinese meal and pictures, but not the shopping. I was determined not to lie, invent an urgent job, told her I was off to visit Blum. I should've lied. It was easier. I held the news desk phone away from my ear, got a funny look from Geoff Sillitoe on his return from The Boot as Elaine's loud suggestion on what I should do with our day out escaped the receiver. When it came to hanging up, again she beat me to it. She didn't ring back, nor did I.

Chapter 4
Havershawe

HAVERSHAWE WAS A former country house, set in woodland, at the end of a long drive. From the road, it was impossible to see the high fences and the gates with spiked tops. I walked with other visitors in a raw February wind. With Elaine, even Sandra, far from my thoughts, my focus was on Blum. I needed to put his mind at rest about the money for his mam, but most of all, I needed to know what the stash of cash, goods and firearms at Pygon's Farm was all about. My big fear was discovery, Blum facing a longer term inside, at Walton or Strangeways.

I joined the queue to show our VOs to the prison officers at the main gate. Most in the queue appeared to be the mums and dads of young men on the inside, but there were a few lone girlfriends, perhaps wives, one or two with babies or toddlers. A prison officer searched the blankets of a baby in a pushchair.

Viv visited Blum for the first time the previous week, rang me at work to give me the run-down. Wrapped sweets, toiletries and cigarettes could be taken in, but most other items would be confiscated. Prison officers made random searches for contraband like weapons and drink.

When I asked after Blum she sounded more cheerful than I thought she was, told me he was doing okay. 'He says he can't wait to see you.'

'Did he have anything else to say? Any news? What it's like in there?'

'He was more interested in what's going on here. I told him his mum seemed a bit down, but not too bad.' She laughed, 'Don't worry, you can get an exclusive interview with him on Saturday, all the details.' If only she'd known how close to the truth she was. I had plenty of questions.

When I asked if she'd be there as well, her tone changed. I could tell she was upset when she told me she couldn't swap shifts to get Saturday off. I felt for her, but it would be impossible to discuss what was hidden at Pygon's Farm if we visited together.

The prison officer gave the all clear on the baby, the queue moved forward. I was nodded through when I showed the officer forty Player's Cadets and Blum's favourite Bourneville chocolate. I had to show my VO again on entry to the modern extension to the old house that served as the visiting hall with tables and chairs.

Blum looked tired, gaunt, as a door was unlocked and he was let in to meet me. I raised my hand. He came over, smiled as we greeted each other

'Sorry I was late for the court.' My guilt was still there. I hadn't planned to say anything; but that uniform, his long hair cut short, somehow diminished him, and I had to apologise, 'I'm really sorry.'

He grinned, 'One of your famous hangovers, eh?'

I laughed, 'Sodding train timetables, more like.'

I pushed the cigs and chocolate across the Formica table, watched by a young prison officer who patrolled in short steps, up and down between the tables, his eyes everywhere. 'Thought you might like these…'

'Just the blummin' job, ta…' He pocketed them, looked furtive. He laughed, 'Well, you've got to watch it in here. Some of 'em'll pinch owt.' We both laughed. 'Thieving bastards everywhere, I'm not kidding.'

The place was fogged with cig smoke, so I pulled out mine, offered him one. He lit them. his hands looked red raw, sore. 'What happened to your hands?'

He looked at them, touched inflamed skin, 'Scrubbing floors and stairs all day.'

'Is it, you know… really bad?'

'The screws keep telling us, it's Borstal, not Butlins.' He leaned forward, lowered his voice, 'Don't worry. Like I said to Viv, I can manage. It's just counting the blummin' days, that's all.'

'Good.'

'Never mind all that, is mam alright?'

'I phoned her last night. She seemed fine. Said to look after yourself, keep out of trouble.'

He laughed, 'Could've blummin' guessed that.' He paused, then, voice down, 'What's all this about the Chev? Viv said you bought it yourself to give mam the money.'

So Blum's mam had told her.

'I just thought it was the best way. I won't touch it and I told your mam you could buy it back off me if you wanted.' Blum frowned, 'I thought it was a good idea.'

'I didn't know you had the dosh.'

I hissed back at him, 'That's what I told Viv. Where would I get the money for a car? It came out your bloody toffee tin at the farm.'

He seemed shocked, 'What?'

Now I was unsure, 'Have I done the wrong thing?'

He shook his head, his voice quiet, 'Nah, nah, it's fine.'

'All that money, it's just lying there doing nothing, isn't it?'

His mood seemed to change, he was chirpier, 'So mam's got the money and we keep the Chev an' all? That's good, bob-on.' He paused, 'How much has she got then?'

'I worked out your tip-up for a year and added a bit on. So I gave her two hundred and fifty pounds. Is that all right?'

He paused, 'That's fine. Good idea.'

'That's what I thought.'

I sensed what I'd done wasn't part of his plan, whatever that was, but I was more interested in the still room.

'You never told me anything about the farm. I couldn't believe it when I read the letter. Two hundred quid in the court charge and there's more than a thousand in those tins, as well as the knock-off stuff, those guns. Not just shotguns, bloody army pistols. What are you playing at?'

Blum was calm,' I told you I'd got away with more than the jacks thought.'

'Christ, it's like a warehouse. You could set up in competition to Daltry's.'

Blum laughed, 'Never thought of that.'

His airy remark annoyed me. My voice was strangled, aware of dozens of people in the room, 'For God's sake, if anyone found that stuff you'd get more than nine months in here.'

'Nobody's going to find it. When I'm out it'll all be sold. If I do it right, it'll bring in a couple of thousand more, easy. Some o' my old customers'll snap it up.'

'You mean all those who've read about the driver from Daltry's getting locked-up for theft?'

'They won't care.'

'Don't kid yourself.'

'Ha. I'll do it.'

I checked for the officer, but he was in the far corner, drinking tea. Around us, the Borstal lads and their loved ones were intent on each other. The room hummed with conversation, the fag smoke thicker, 'What about the guns?'

'I can sell them an' all.'

'I'm not stupid. You need a police licence to have pistols -- and to buy and sell them.'

'Depends who you sell 'em to.'

I checked again for the prison officer, faced Blum, 'Christ, you're not telling me you'd sell them to…criminals?'

He snatched up his cigarette packet and pulled out another, 'I mean the shotguns, not them. I know plenty of people who do a bit of shooting. Or a gunsmith's shop'd take 'em.'

'Are they knock-off as well?'

He shook his head, 'Nah. None of 'em are. Not them pistols either.'

'How did you get them, then?'

'They've changed the law, Ted told me a while ago. You need a police licence just to have a blummin' shotgun now.

And to buy and sell 'em. You have to write a form and the coppers come and interview you. See you've not been in any trouble. Then you need a reference off a magistrate or an army officer, someone respectable. Without a clean record and a reference, you don't get a licence.'

Blum lit his cigarette.

'That still doesn't explain where you got them.'

He blew out a stream of smoke, 'I started asking my customers about it. Couldn't believe how nervy these farmers and growers were about this licence business. Some of 'em even chucked their guns in the cut or the local pit'ole, just so they didn't have to have coppers round. Most didn't have anyone to ask for a reference either. Talk about blummin' panic…'

I butted in, 'All they had to do was ask the police for help, surely?'

Blum laughed,' You know blummin' farmers, what they're like. Writing forms, no. Having a police car in the yard, no; telling anyone their business, not in a month o' Sundays. When I offered to take their guns off their hands for buttons, they couldn't get rid quick enough. One ex-army bloke, grows tomatoes over in Banks, he even give me a Sten gun, a flaming machine gun, for nowt…'

'You're joking?'

Blum grinned, 'Two full magazines of ammunition and all. I wanted to fire the bugger, but I didn't have the nerve, like. So I chucked it in Altcar Delph.'

He took another drag, 'It was the same with the Army pistols. It was stuff from the War. They were shitting themselves about having them without licences and the thought of the coppers coming round just because they had a twelve--bore or a four-ten, never mind revolvers and automatics …'

'You should've chucked them in the Delph as well.'

He grinned, 'I like 'em, though. I shot that Nazzy automatic in the barn at the farm, blummin' fab.'

'So, how are you going to sell all those shotguns? You haven't got a police licence and you won't be able to get one now, will you, not with a record?'

He looked awkward, hesitant.

'Well?'

He tapped ash into a tinfoil pie dish on the table.

I pushed him, 'Ted said you can't have a gun if you've been inside. So you've no chance of getting a licence.'

He didn't answer. His fidgeting, chewing at his cheek, took me back to his dumb insolence before our headmistress on our first day at school.

'You might as well chuck the bloody lot in the Delph.'

Blum leaned forward on the table. His voice was low and urgent. He didn't even check the prison officer's position, 'I'm not throwing blummin' cash away. Some of 'em are worth good money.'

'You've got no choice.'

His hand went around the back of his head, his fingers played against his scalp. 'But in your job you know people like magistrates and that, for a reference, like...'

'Me? Jesus.'

'You could sell 'em for me. It'd all be dead legal, as long as you've got the licence. It costs about thirty-bob, I'll pay.'

'Why the hell are you dumping this on me?'

Was it so simple? Was it all legal? If the police found out he had that stash of guns, he faced more time and I didn't want to join him inside. But our disagreement couldn't be aired in, of all places, this prison visiting hall.

Blum was insistent, his voice urgent, 'I need the money.'

'Viv reckons you don't.'

He was curious, 'What did she say?'

'She talked sense. She's happy how you are. She says neither of you need money. For God's sake, you made a mistake, leave it at that. If I have to, I'll get shut of everything at the farm, chuck the bloody lot. Make sure none of its connected to you. You can do your nine months and come out and... and make a fresh start.'

Blum fidgeted, 'It's not like that. I was only…I hadn't finished what I wanted to do. I need money for mam...'

'She's got enough to keep going. I'll get more from the farm anytime you say. Your mam'll be fine.'

There was a hint of anguish to his voice, 'You don't know, nor does Viv. It's summat more than a bit of tip-up…'

I cut in on his flow,' Why won't you tell Viv? I thought you two were together and you won't even…?'

I hesitated. What was he about to say? What hadn't he finished? In my irritation I'd pushed on, ignored what he was going to say. His hand was behind his head, tapping his scalp; an old mannerism that told me he was thinking hard, agitated.

He jiggled his leg, flicked non-existent ash off the end of his fag.

'Tell me then. Why you're so desperate for money?'

Blum exhaled; a long sigh.

Chapter 5
A Promise

WITH HESITATIONS, SILENCES, as the prison officer passed, Blum told me why he started to steal from Daltry's. It was all about May Bank View.

Blum often mentioned the house had been in the Gatley family since his grandfather's time. I thought the family owned it outright. In fact, it was on a lease from the original, long-dead owner of the land, managed by a solicitor in Southport for the beneficiaries of the owner's estate.

In 1911, Blum's grandfather had paid the large sum of three hundred guineas for a lease of sixty years. He, and those who came after, were responsible for the upkeep of the house and yearly rates to the council. Each year a 'peppercorn' or nominal annual ground rent was payable. This was two guineas a year, the old term for two pounds and two shillings, which was little in recent times. Blum's mam's problem was the lease was due to run out on the last day of 1971, less than two years away.

'Mam told me when I started work,' he said, 'She wanted to know how much it'd be to buy another lease, renew it like, so she wrote in. This solicitor bloke wrote back and said he couldn't be sure, but perhaps summat like seven thousand pounds.'

My mouth opened at the sum.

Blum shrugged, 'She hasn't got that sort of money and Uncle Walter's only got his pension and burial fund. She never stops worrying over it.'

He screwed out the cigarette in the tinfoil dish. 'If we can't pay up mam'll lose May Bank.'

I knew nothing of this, never had even a clue.

'So this is how you're going to save your mam's house? By thieving?'

Blum grinned, 'I'm not bad at it.'

'So good you're stuck in this place, even more for your mam to worry about?'

He took another fag, 'Next time, I won't get blummin' caught.'

'There can't be a next time. Next time it'll be real jail.'

He blew out a stream of smoke, carried on as if he'd never heard my last remarks 'I reckon I can get about three thousand with what's left, if I find the right people.'

I was incredulous he'd risk further time locked up.

Blum leaned towards me, 'Well, can you think of any other way to get it?'

'Me? I spend everything I earn. What do I know about money? I'm hopeless with it.'

I struggled for a suggestion, side-stepped.

'Have you talked to Viv? She's good with money.'

'I don't want her to know.'

'That's daft,' I said, 'She's got a good job, her own place. Her family's business-minded as well. They might be able to give you advice.'

Blum was sharp, 'I told you, no.'

'She must've asked why you robbed Daltry's.'

'Said I did it 'cause I felt like it.'

I shook my head, tried another tack.

'She's asked me why you did it, you know. She doesn't think it was worth it for two hundred pounds.'

'I can't tell her.'

'Do you want me to tell her?'

'Christ, no,' said Blum, 'Don't tell her. I mean it, I can't...I just...She mustn't...

His leg jiggled faster. He shifted in his chair, fiddled with his fag packet.

'I thought you two were together. What you've said about her. It seems like a lovejob. You even said it was a couple of times. I know you'd had a few pints and that, but...It seemed like the truth to me.'

Blum's face was earnest, 'I want us to get married one day. I blummin' do, but...Don't tell her anything. I mean that.'

I exhaled in frustration. I was the last one to talk about honesty in relationships, but I'd talked with Elaine about marriage and trust and knowing everything about each other, all that stuff. I was pretty well-up, I thought, on what girls look for.

I tried another angle, 'I bet if you asked Viv what's the most important thing about being together, getting married, she'd say trusting each other.'

He looked at me, waited for more.

'Well, it means knowing everything about each other for a bloody kick-off.'

His face was the picture of misery, 'Her older brother's building his own house before he gets married, and the other one's already bought his own flat. Both of 'em'll be partners in the garage. They want to set up a car showroom. When Viv's mam and dad retire, the brothers'll have a business. I've nowt to offer her 'cause I've got nowt. I can't even do what me dad would've done and keep a roof over mam's head.'

The bell for the end of visiting rang, but I ignored it, let him talk.

'I don't want her to think I'm some nobody. I've got to keep a home for mam. If I don't I'll never be able to hold me head up. Or ask Viv to marry me.'

He looked me in the eyes. His hand rested on my forearm, 'I don't care what I have to do to get the money for mam, but I'll do it. I mean anything.Will you help me?'

It had been a couple of years since I'd done anything illegal and I was reluctant, but he was my friend. And he looked so desolate. I nodded. 'I will, yeah.'

His fingers tightened on my arm, 'Promise?'

For the first time I saw tears in Blum's eyes.

I promised.

Had I known what it would lead to my answer may have been different.

*

I went over and over what he'd told me when I left Havershawe. I had three pints in Preston Station buffet. I didn't want to go back to the grotty flat, or The Packet. Sandra knew about my arrangement to see Elaine that weekend, but not that it had disintegrated. She had night school work to catch up on and I didn't fancy being cajoled by Kitty to subsidise her night in the pub. I thought about Elaine, what she might be doing. I had nothing else to do, so I went back to Lydiate. At least I'd have next day at home with my family.

Two hours later, I walked into the Hare and Hounds and stood at the public bar with a drink. In the roar of noise before closing time, I couldn't hear who was in the long room, but I saw one or two of the group of people Elaine knew as they visited the bogs, or came to the far side of the bar. Maybe I hoped word would get back to Elaine I'd turned up, despite our tiff, maybe I didn't. I drank more, my mind on Blum and his intentions, my promise.

A hand ran across my back, went around my shoulder. I detected a combined scent of make-up and Bacardi rum. It was a tipsy, affectionate Elaine. 'Did you see him?'

I nodded.

'How was it?'

'Shit,' I said.

'How is he?'

'Shit.'

We moved to a corner and Elaine talked about our relationship. I made suitable comments I struggled later to recall; most of the time I dwelt on my promise, what it might entail. I walked her home. She told me her parents were at some Masonic ladies' night do. I stayed too late, before I knew it we were back together. If that's what I wanted, I had no idea. I was drunk.

*

On my first day back at the paper, I called into the police station to check the incident book for newsworthy events. The copper on desk duty was Neil Posset. Neil had been at grammar school with me, by chance posted to the same town. We were never mates, never even in the same form, but here we had a sort of camaraderie, like colonial officials far from home in a primitive land.

Pickings from the incident book were scant -- theft from a garden shed (a lawnmower), a minor road collision (no injuries) and three missing sheep (possibly stolen). While I noted the details, Neil leaned his rugby man's bulk over the counter, his voice low.

'Who was that blonde bird you were with the other night?'

'Me?' I looked at him, all innocent, 'When was that?'

He grinned, tapped his chest, 'Don't deny it, mate, I'm a reliable witness. Tuesday, eleven forty p.m. The accused was in company with a female leaving The Packet public house a full hour after permitted drinking-up time. She was wearing one of them trendy placcy macs, shiny red. Medium-length blonde hair, crackin' legs...'

I laughed. 'Where were you?'

He winked, 'Other side of the cut, checking works premises.'

Though I laughed, I was a touch rattled. To save talk in the office, Sandra and I kept our relationship quiet, not easy in a town you could spit across. It was exciting. We carried on like MI5 agents, even adulterers; speaking little to each other in *The Sentinel* buildings, messages left under my typewriter, quick, cryptic conversations on the paper's internal phones. This breach of our secrecy was unwelcome. Neil wasn't known to the office crowd, but anyone could've seen us leave The Packet for my grotty flat.

'So,' he said, 'Who is she?'

'That'd be my colleague from advertising.'

'Doing a turn, then, are we?'

'She's one of the bosses' daughters.'

'Ah, so it's all on the QT? All after-hours nightcaps, what-have-you, eh?'

I shook my head, 'Like I said we're colleagues.'

'Well, if you're not interested you can put in a word for me with your "colleague." It'd be easier to find a decent bird in a monastery than this dump. Hope it gets better when they put me on Panda cars.'

I changed the subject, asked if he had an application form for the new shotgun certificates.

He went to a cupboard, looked back at me, 'Nothing to do with shotgun weddings, is it?'

'Jimmy Tarbuck's got bugger-all to worry about, has he?'

He chuckled, closed the cupboard, 'A shotgun, eh? Worried about the natives up here in Gobbinland?' He grinned, 'Or just that boss whose daughter's getting a seeing-to from one of the lower classes?'

I laughed, 'My mate at home does a bit of shooting, thought I might have a go.'

He slid the form across to me.

'Don't rob any friggin' banks, eh? We couldn't cope with the excitement.'

Later, I sat down in front of the electric fire in the flat with a ten-bob bottle of British sherry, filled in most of the form. I could provide all it asked, except for a reference from a person of standing in the community. I poured a second glass, thought who I might ask. The pay phone on the landing rang.

Caernarvon Kitty shouted, 'For you, *Bachgen*, phone!'

As usual, Kitty left the receiver balanced on top of the coin box on the half-landing. Below me, she swayed as she shrugged on her coat, ready for evening shift at The Packet, snatched up a glass of whisky from the hall table. She swigged it back in one, slammed down the glass.

She headed for her private part of the house and the back door, shouted, 'If it's falling out with her again, don't take it out on my bloody phone.'

I picked up the receiver, 'Elaine?'

It was Viv, laughing, 'I heard that. Was that your landlady?'

'Yep, she's well-gone, already.'

'Sorry to bother you. I tried yesterday teatime, but no answer.'

'I didn't get back from my mum and dad's 'til late and Kitty's usually unconscious after Sunday dinner at the pub. Never makes it to *Songs of Praise* on telly, but wakes up miraculously for seven 'o clock opening.'

She laughed again. It sounded forced, 'Did you get all the answers in your exclusive interview?'

I remembered her joke, 'Yeah. Yeah, I did thanks.'

'I don't suppose being in that place has made him come up with any reason for doing what he did?'

She caught me off-guard, but I didn't hesitate too long. 'He's more bothered about how you and his mam are doing.'

'I wish he'd thought about us before he started nicking stuff from work.'

We talked for a few minutes about Havershawe, how I got there, what it was like, talking around what she wanted to know.

At last, she said, 'How is he?'

I couldn't tell her the truth. I lied, 'He's fine. He seems to have got the hang of the place. He...He was in a good mood. We had a laugh.'

I felt the relief in her voice, 'That's great. I'm glad he's okay.'

Viv and I visited as often as we could. The months that followed were hard for Blum, his mam and Viv. Blum stuck to his decision not to allow his mam to visit, but I phoned her after every visit to Havershawe. Blum's mood wasn't always bright; often I embroidered my reports for her. Meanwhile, my secret relationship with Sandra continued to excite me. Work went well and my news editor Geoff Sillitoe trusted me to take more responsibility in the newsroom than was usual for my trainee status. For me, at least, time passed quicker. Yet on my trips home to Lydiate I missed Blum, as well as our regular natters on the phone. Winter became spring, summer arrived. Blum's release was imminent -- and so was the time for him to call in my promise.

Chapter 6
A Rotten Bastard

I HEARD THE rumble of Viv's motorbike before I saw her. I loitered outside *The Sentinel* office, where I'd knocked off at noon, to start a fortnight's holiday. I'd told Elaine we were too short-staffed for me to take time off before late autumn. Sandra felt obliged to accompany her parents and their friends on holiday in Penzance and I had no real plans what to do with my time off. I had a half-baked plan to write a play set on a northern newspaper, soon forgotten with the arrival of a Borstal visiting order, plus a note from Blum.

His note was apologetic for the short notice, yet insistent. It was vital I should visit him at Havvy that Saturday afternoon, Viv would be there. Viv rang soon after, said she'd pick me up outside the office. I was intrigued by this urgent summons. Blum was due for release that month, but early in August, he'd said I needn't bother to come again. My promise to him hung heavily. Soon, it would require action on my part. Could it be Viv was now included in our efforts to find the cash to save his mam's home?

Or was it about the stolen gear in the still room at Pygon's Farm as well as the money and guns, untouched for months? I'd checked the place as often as I could, but not as many times as I might have done. Viv wasn't supposed to know anything about them, so why ask to see me in her presence? Had he told her? It was a mystery.

The Norton 650's throb came closer along the busy high street as the 'front office' door opened behind me. It was Geoff Sillitoe. I could tell he was off fishing, his elastic-sided chukka boots swapped for black wellies and over the sports jacket he wore most days, his angling anorak.

He pushed his quiff back, plucked an Embassy tipped from his lip, 'Thought yer'd've done a bunk by now, cocker.'

'Er... not quite.'

'If yer've nowt better to do, yer can come and watch yours truly win a match.'

I was running out of excuses. It was a mistake to tell him I did a bit of fishing, he was forever inviting me to some of the many fishing matches he attended. Like Blum, I disliked competitive fishing, but didn't like to tell him. He was my boss, one day I knew I'd have to accept.

Geoff could be a bore about his sport. He lived, breathed and wrote about it in our weekly 'Down the Banks' feature. It was called a 'column,' but Geoff abused his influence over the paper's content and over ten years it expanded from five hundred words a week to fill a couple of full pages between the squashed-in soccer, rugby and cricket reports and deaths and funerals. Few weeks passed in the open season without a photograph of 'yours truly' and a full keep net, or yet another trophy. It was a worn-out *Sentinel* joke the paper should be re-named *Angling Times*.

'Ah, sorry, Geoff,' I said, 'I'm meeting someone.'

On cue, Viv throttled back, slid her bike across the street to halt by us. In this little, grey town she cut an exotic figure straddling her Norton in full leathers and giant-sized, hoop ear-rings. She smiled at Geoff, flicked back her long hair, turned to me, 'Are you right?'

'Yep,' I turned to Geoff, shouted over the Norton's engine 'See you in a fortnight then.'

Geoff was immobile, mouth open. I could only guess at his thoughts. There was a publicity photo on the newsroom notice board of Marianne Faithfull from the film, *Girl on a Motorcycle.* Perhaps for the moment the image of Viv overshadowed thoughts of hook size and ground bait in Geoff's one-track mind. One thing was certain; I'd be the talk of the The Boot when it got out I'd been picked up by my own girl on a motorcycle. I felt my face flush as I swung a leg over the pillion, nodded at a gawping Geoff. It wouldn't do my reputation any harm, though. If Sandra heard, it might cause a spark of jealousy.

Minutes later, with Viv's hair blowing in my face, my hands on the pillion rail, we raced out of town across sunlit moorland, heading for the Fylde. It felt good to be free of work, off to see Blum.

We parked the bike by the gates of Havershawe, joined the line of visitors to show our VOs to a prison officer. I offered Viv a fag, 'Do you know what this is about? He told me not to come anymore, now it's all urgent.'

She lit hers, passed me a brass Zippo. 'I thought you'd know.'

I shook my head, 'Not a clue. You don't think he's in any trouble?'

'God, I hope not. He doesn't need extra-time, not now he's due out.'

We walked past the Victorian frontage of the old house, well-kept gardens. Viv paused by a lad of about sixteen. He wore Borstal uniform shirt and trousers and, with precise care, dead-headed summer's last burst of colour; crimson dahlias and Michaelmas daisies. She paused to admire them.

'Do you look after all these?'

The lad turned to look at her, smiled, at least I thought it was a smile. He said something, but I couldn't make it out. His hare-lip exposed twisted top teeth and gums. His speech was distorted by what I guessed was a cleft palate. He said something else, but I was unable to follow his speech.

Viv smiled, touched his arm, 'They're beautiful.'

We walked on.

'Poor kid,' Viv said, 'He should've had that surgically corrected yonks ago.'

'I didn't catch what he said.'

'Me neither. Sad, isn't it?'

Even though I'd been here a dozen times, it still seemed strange to be close to the little dramas played out in a single room. Joy, jealousy, aggression, remorse, despair; it was all on show in the visiting hall. Yet most of it hushed, tense and suppressed, while a prison officer patrolled between the rows of tables.

An inner door opened, Blum was allowed through. He scanned the room, grinned, and moved between crowded tables to join us. He radiated good health, as tanned as a Greek peasant, so different to my first visit.

We caught up on each other's news, passed the cigarettes across the table.

The patrolling prison officer stopped, 'More coffin nails, Mr Gatley?' Then to us, 'I've told him he'll ruin his health, but will he listen?' We laughed; polite chortles in the presence of authority. Blum's face clouded over as the officer moved away. I knew when he'd taken against someone. Blum opened his Caddies, we lit up.

He apologised for asking me to visit. 'I know you're busy.' He laughed, 'You must be with two girls on the go.'

Viv turned to me, 'You haven't?'

'Oh, yes, he has -- Elaine at home, another'un in Gobbinland.'

A touch flustered, I said, 'She's just a friend.'

Blum spluttered out smoke, 'Ha.'

Viv laughed, 'Oh? Do they know each other?'

I gave her a quick, sarcastic smile, changed the subject, 'Why am I here then?'

Blum turned to check the prison officer's location. I saw him take, without thanks, a mug of tea from a young officer. He was a touch overweight with a fat backside, but narrow shoulders, the makings of a double chin beneath a small, petulant mouth. Above that was an army-type moustache. He was fifty, or so.

Blum leaned over the table, voice down, 'I've got a bit of a job to see to before I get out of this place.'

Viv was alarmed, her voice a whisper, 'What do you mean? You can't take any risks, not now.'

'Look, there's no risk for me, but…Well, before you two say whether you'll help, or not, let me tell you about him.' He jerked his head to indicate the prison officer who folded open a copy of the *Daily Mail*.

I watched the officer sip his tea, turned to Blum 'The bloke who just spoke to us?'

'Yeah, him, the senior officer, Bert Travis, he's called.'

'He seems all right,' said Viv.

Blum was blunt, 'He's a rotten bastard -- I need to teach him a blummin' lesson.'

*

With an occasional glance at Travis, Blum took us back to the start of his sentence in January. His long hair was cut short. And as a new inmate, he was given the despised job of scrubbing floors; no mop, just a scrubbing brush, bucket and a drum of Ajax. The work was like painting the Forth Bridge, only the time scale shorter. It took eight hours a day, on hands and knees, next morning he started again.

Blum kept his head down, avoided any action that might get him into trouble, but on his second night he was bullied by a lad called Vince Doe, who stole his suppertime cocoa, tried to goad Blum to fight over it. Doe harassed him with insults, called him names, but Blum wouldn't allow himself to face-up to the bully. Even though he longed to batter Doe, he valued a good record with no extra weeks for bad behaviour; a public fight would be a disaster.

Blum waited, watched. Doe seemed uneasy about the cockroaches seen at night. The lads delighted in cockie-splattering hunts, or tried to organise cockroach races, but Vince Doe never joined the fun. Blum observed the bully's casual check around his bed before lights out, a routine he never altered. He even put his shoes on to go to the bogs after dark. Blum acted on his suspicion, collected cockies in a treacle tin. He fed them on bread and kept them in a brush cupboard. Doe still harassed Blum, tried to make him fight, but he played a long game.

While he sipped his cocoa a fortnight later, Blum, enjoyed the spectacle as Doe got into bed with dozens of cockroaches. The bully shrieked like a little girl, a shower of cockroaches fell from his legs and Doe wet himself in front of the dormitory's other occupants.

Doe's ruthless hunt for the perpetrator overlooked Blum. Perhaps he thought Blum was too scared of him to attempt a reprisal for the bullying, the theft of his cocoa. A dozen cockroaches were saved for two nights later. Blum ambushed Doe on his way to the bogs, gave him a good hiding, threw him in the brush cupboard, tipped the insects inside Doe's shirt and wedged the door shut. When Blum released him half-an-hour later, Doe came out like a whipped dog. He never spoke to Blum again.

With the arrival of new Borstal boys, Blum was moved to work in the kitchen. He hated peeling spuds, chopping vegetables and scrubbing greasy cooking trays with red raw hands, but it was the warmest part of the old house and he could pinch extra food. But by late February as days grew longer, he hankered to be outside, to experience the arrival of spring.

His passport to escape the kitchen was unexpected. While Blum chopped red cabbage for pickling, Alan Delamere, a car thief from Burscough, lugged a two-foot long metal dish of meat and potato pie to the ovens. Delamere, who wore deaf aids, had become the target of Doe the bully after the cockroach incident. It took a single stare from Blum to make Vince Doe look elsewhere. Delly stuck close to Blum after that. When that morning senior officer Travis came in to the kitchen from outside, everyone but Delly tensed at his arrival.

'Get me some tea,' Travis told Delly. Whether Delly didn't hear in the noise of the kitchen, or was too intent on his work, he didn't respond. Travis grabbed Delly's ear and yanked him round. The tray fell with a clang and its contents erupted through the uncooked pastry top. The kitchen came to a halt. Half-a-dozen inmates and staff stared as Travis kneed Delly in the thigh. The blow was so violent Delly's lanky frame reeled against the oven range. The impact knocked him breathless and he fell to the floor.

Travis kicked Delly's ribs twice, followed up with another to his buttocks, 'Don't ignore me, you cloth-eared shit.'

Delly gasped for breath. 'I didn't hear you, Mr Travis.'

Travis ignored the excuse, 'Get me a mug of tea. Now! And clean-up this fucking mess.'

Travis glared at staff and inmates alike, 'Back to work, the lot of you.'

Travis retired to a corner of the kitchen, pulled what looked like a magazine from his pocket. Delly brought Travis a mug of tea and soon after Blum went to fetch the tin plates for dinner from the shelves near Travis's chair. Travis was studying a seed catalogue, open at a page of cauliflower varieties. Blum glanced at the page, then at Travis. The senior officer seemed thoughtful.

On impulse Blum remarked, 'Me mam always says Snowball's best for our ground. Doesn't seem to pick up diseases, either, she reckons.'

Before he knew what he'd done Blum jabbed a finger at one of the photographs in the catalogue, 'That's the one -- dead white, never yellowy.'

Travis stared at him. Until now, Blum had managed to avoid Travis. He regretted his impulsive remarks.

'What's your name, lad?'

'Gatley, sir.'

Travis sneered, 'Your mother a farmer, or something?'

'No, sir. She's got a big garden, mind, nearly two acres.'

Travis was surprised, or impressed. His tone changed, 'How much of that's down to vegetables?'

'Most of its borders and orchard, but about a third of an acre, I'd say.'

'Does she manage all that herself?'

'Me and her half-brother, me Uncle Walter, we muck in.'

'She'll be missing your efforts then, while you're washing pots, humping out pig swill?'

'Yes, sir.'

Travis folded the page of the catalogue, put it aside. He shifted in the chair. Blum feared he was in for the same treatment as Delly, but Travis took a sip of tea.

'What are you in for?'

'Theft, sir.'

'What sort of theft?'

'Stealing from the firm I worked for.'

'What?'

'Stealing from the firm I worked for… sir.'

He leaned towards Blum, his voice harder, 'I hope you're not taking the piss, Gatley. What did you steal?'

'Just stuff I was delivering, sir. Work clothes, tools, seeds, farming stuff.'

'You know something about agriculture, horticulture?'

'I know a bit.'

Travis picked up the seed catalogue, rolled it up. Would it be a makeshift weapon against him? But Travis tapped it on his left hand, 'Looks like you know more than a bit. Snowball's your choice for caulis, then?'

'Ground here's on the sandy side, just the job for 'em, sir'

Travis nodded, 'I might just try them at home.'

Travis stood up, jerked the rolled catalogue towards the outside door. 'The deadbeats I get out there, no interest. Only thing they're interested in growing is their bastard hair. I might just find a place for you on the farm.'

Before Blum could say anything, the S.O. turned away, 'Back to work, Gatley.'

*

Ten days passed and Blum lost hope he might be transferred to the Borstal's 'farm,' in fact a small-holding of 15 acres with a modest pig unit, poultry runs, glass houses and arable land that provided grain for the hens and pigs and seasonal vegetables for the inmates. Blum started to wash up after breakfast when the officer in charge of the kitchen approached him.

'Leave that, Gatley. Go and report to S.O. Travis at the glasshouses.'

'Me?'

The officer nodded towards the door, 'Get moving, son, if I were you, I wouldn't keep that twat waiting.'

Blum's only time in the fresh air since Quarter Sessions had been the weekly cross-country run through the woods and five-a-side football on alternate Saturday mornings. Outside the cricket season, nobody was allowed outdoors on Sundays. Blum relished the familiar smells of pigs, provender and poultry as he hurried to meet Travis.

Travis was genial and Blum was pleased his first job was to propagate seeds. He'd always helped his father with that job, continued to help his mam. He felt a touch of guilt she'd work alone this year.

'You might like to know I've got some snowball caulis spritting already,' Travis said

Blum looked around.

'In my own greenhouse,' said Travis. 'Gardening's the best way I know to forget the hours I spend in this shithole.'

Blum was shown the compost supply, seeds, seed boxes and other equipment. A written list stated how many boxes of each vegetable had to be sown for eventual re-planting outside.

'Nice work, a blummin doddle after scrubbing floors and washing pots.' he told Viv and me.

Blum was surprised when Travis lingered, worked with him as they sowed shallow boxes with seeds, tamped the surfaces, damped them in. Travis was talkative, asked Blum about his upbringing. He explained how the farm operated and said the governor was keen to sell surplus produce to subsidise Havershawe's running costs. Blum took a barrow for more compost and Travis went with him to the large composting bays. A lad shovelled finer compost towards the finishing bay from the piles of rougher matter. Travis shouted, 'Put that skinny back into it, Jackson. I want all the decent stuff out today.'

A second, younger lad spaded finished compost into a barrow, 'You and all, Foster. I want all the flower beds down to the gates mulched up pronto.'

The lad looked at Travis, said something, but it was unintelligible. Blum had never spoken to Foster, but had seen him, noticed his hare-lip, twisted teeth.

'None of your lip, lad,' Travis laughed, winked at Blum, to make sure he got the joke. Blum pretended not to get it.

'Bugs Bunny here!' Travis, jerked a thumb at Foster, 'Fucking midwife must've used a plumber's wrench that day, eh?'

I butted in on Blum's story, 'Christ, what a lousy thing to say?'

Viv looked across at Travis, 'Horrible man.' She turned to me, 'It must've been that boy on the way in.'

'That'd be Fozzy. He doesn't get any visitors,' said Blum.

Viv said, 'Did Travis really say that to his face?'

'Told you he was a bastard,' said Blum. He looked up at the clock, 'I'd better blummin' get on with it.'

He continued the account of his first day at the farm…

Travis laughed at his nasty joke, told Foster, 'Do us all a favour, Foster, keep your disgusting trap shut.'

Travis moved away from Foster, but turned back to him. Blum noted Foster's flinch. Travis pointed, 'Make sure there's six sacks of compost by the big glasshouse before tea bell.'

Travis led Blum away, 'Wicked little whore's get, is that. Set his grandparents' place on fire and killed the pair of them. Should've been fucking topped, never mind done for arson.'

Blum was shocked, glanced back at Foster, 'He did that?'

'Little freak pleaded not guilty, but the jury didn't fall for it.'

Travis left, Blum worked until dusk. When the tea bell sounded, he walked to the main building and saw a pale blue Ford Cortina reverse near the big glasshouse. Blum hid in shadow, watched S.O. Travis fill the boot with sacks of H.M.Borstal, Havershawe's compost.

Chapter 7
Foster's Story

BLUM HATED BORSTAL and its relentless routine, but found a release in work on the farm. Spring came and with it the results of his work in the glasshouses and fields. Blum found Travis trusted him. No day passed without an appearance by the S.O, but Travis seemed happy to let him work on his own initiative; sometimes he took Blum's opinions in preference to officers who oversaw the farm work.

Blum didn't miss the irony he was inside for stealing from his employer, while his jailer, Travis, did the same. He noted when timber, horticultural chemicals, glasshouse equipment and the like disappeared. To test him, Blum pointed out three automatic greenhouse window openers had vanished. Travis made a show of going to the office to check and told Blum there had been an ordering error; they'd been returned. Travis's promised replacements never arrived.

Foster was one of the farm's most reliable, workers. When cabbages, cauliflowers, beetroot and other vegetables needed pricking-out or planting, other inmates were transferred outside to help. Like Travis said, most lads disliked the work, considered it worse than the workshops, a form of punishment, and often slacked. But Foster was a diligent fixture on the outside work detail. Blum saw his natural talent for tending plants, his patience and affection caring for the hens, ducks and pigs kept at Havershawe.

Foster was wary of Blum, made few attempts at conversation. Blum put this down to self-consciousness over his deformed lip and palate. He heard Foster was ridiculed and bullied over his appearance and speech since his arrival and was shunted out of the workshops to work outside. Blum treated Foster with respect and he began to talk. Blum found the knack to follow Foster's distorted speech. He was curious about Travis's view Foster should have been charged with murder. One day they shared a cigarette in the field and Blum spoke of his thefts from Daltry's. He answered Fosters questions, turned the conversation.

'What about you? What are you in for?'

Foster handed back the fag, turned away.

Blum persisted, 'You in for thieving an' all?'

Foster glanced at him, shook his head, 'Arson.'

'Arsin' about with matches?'

Foster snorted a laugh that turned to a snigger, in a flash, anger. 'I didn't do it. It wasn't me.'

'Ha! Half the blummin' lads here say that.'

'I told yer I didn't do it.'

'All right, then, what didn't you do?'

Foster scratched out chickweed and groundsel between the leeks.

Blum pushed him, 'I told you everything I did, why won't you tell me?'

Foster said nothing until later when they had a brew. Blum made a fire-starter joke when he passed Foster his matches.

'It weren't me who did it.'

Blum said nothing. Foster drew on a dog-end, 'It were our Chris,' he glanced at Blum, 'Me brother.'

Foster hesitated, launched into his story. Foster and his brother, eighteen months older, lived with their widowed mother in Blackpool. Their father was killed in a factory accident. To support her family, his mother took work at a fish and chips café on the Golden Mile. Foster was a similar age to Blum when his own father suddenly died.

In the school holidays both brothers stayed at their paternal grandparents' bungalow in a village near Garstang. Foster loved the countryside, the dairy farm next door, but Chris hated it. He wanted to be in Blackpool with his friends, not stuck with two old people in the middle of nowhere. His frustration caused friction with both grandparents. Rows blew-up when Chris started to sneak off to catch a bus back to Blackpool, sometimes staying away overnight. The day before his grandparents were killed, Chris got up early and went to see his friends. This time he stole three pound notes from his gran's purse.

Grandfather Foster challenged him over the money on his return. Chris denied the theft. Then he admitted it, told his grandparents he was sick of Garstang, shouted he was 'dropping out,' announced he'd leave that minute and never wanted to see his grandparents again. His grandfather lost his temper, grabbed Chris's shoulder length hair. Chris swore at him, grappled with the old man. When Chris began to overpower his grandfather, the old man snatched a skillet from the stove, laid into his grandson.

Chris screamed in pain, Foster rushed to intervene. Alarmed at the violence, he pleaded with his grandfather to stop, but the old man turned on him. The skillet blade slashed a long cut across Foster's cheek. Chris screamed and swore at his grandfather, told him he'd regret the day he beat them. His grandmother berated his grandfather while Chris shot out the back door. His grandmother hurried after him, but Chris ran away across the farm's pastures.

Foster was packed off to bed, the blood dry on his face. He woke after dawn, when Chris climbed in through their bedroom window. Chris dragged a frightened Foster from his bed, took him to the kitchen. He threatened him with violence if he called his grandparents.

Chris muttered and cursed. Foster told Blum his eyes looked funny. He told Foster to sit at the kitchen table and then went to his grandfather's chair by the fireplace. He took old copies of the *Daily Express* from beneath it and shook them open. He draped the pages over the chair then pushed it against the curtains. He held up a souvenir Blackpool lighter, clicked a flame.

Chris stared at it with mad eyes, 'He'll fuckin' regret what he did to me.'

'No!' said Foster,' You can't.'

'Shut up! He's had it coming!'

Chris put the flame to the newspapers, fire took hold.
Foster made a dart towards the burning paper, but Chris
grabbed him, pulled his brother across the kitchen and
opened the back door. Foster struggled and shouted. 'Put it
out! Chris, please...'

His protests were ignored. Chris bundled him out into the
garden and slammed the door behind them. Foster wrenched
himself from Chris's grip, turned back to the door, but Chris
again grabbed him. While Foster struggled, Chris opened the
door, reached inside for the key. He pulled it out, closed the
door, locked it and pushed Foster away. Through the kitchen
window, Foster saw the chair and curtains engulfed by fire.

He shouted, 'Grandma, Grandma!'

Foster grabbed for the key, but Chris evaded him, hurled
the key across the garden. It clinked against the wall, fell into
a flowerbed. Foster ran to the back door, hammering it with
both fists, screaming for his grandmother. He turned to plead
with Chris, but his brother had gone. Foster knew the front
door was always bolted. He ran to the window of his
grandparents' bedroom, shouting, hammering on the glass.
The curtains were drawn, but he glimpsed the light of fire
within, heard the crackle of flame. He looked for something,
anything, to smash the window, but there was nothing.

Foster was frantic. He ran back to the garden, the wall,
where Chris had thrown the key. He scanned the flower bed.
Glass in the kitchen window exploded outwards. He was
almost unaware of the arrival of the farmer from next door
followed by his cowman, ready for milking. Foster whipped
around to see the farmer try to push open the back door. It
wouldn't budge. Swearing and blaspheming, the farmer and
cowman put their shoulders to the door and rammed it once,
twice...

Foster turned back to his search, pinpointed the long key
stuck in a clump of aubrietia and grabbed it. He rushed to the
kitchen door as the combined force of the two men splintered
the lock surround and the door crashed inward. The farmer
and cowman jumped back as a maelstrom of smoke rolled

out and flames ten feet long clawed over the gutters, ravenous for oxygen.

The farmer swore like a drunken soldier as he told the cowman to run and phone the fire brigade. Foster shouted, upset, urged the farmer to go inside.

The farmer shouted, 'Are Arthur and Edna in there?'

Foster was frantic, tried to tell him what had happened, but the farmer ignored him and attempted to duck inside the bungalow, but he couldn't get in for heat and smoke.

The farmer was distraught, 'I can't do it. I haven't got a bloody chance.' The farmer pointed at the long key Foster twisted in his fingers, as he gabbled incoherently. 'Is that the key for...?'

Foster spoke louder, but it was even more distorted in his anguish.

'How did you cut your face?'

Foster waved his arms to mime the violence of the night before.

'Your granddad?' the farmer repeated, 'He hit you?'

Foster continued to gabble and jig, seethed with anger and frustration at his own incoherence, his inability to tell what happened.

The farmer stared at him, his thoughts in overdrive, as he took in the gash and dried blood on Foster's face, his manic jigging that seemed to the farmer like some triumphant victory dance.

The farmer's voice was sharp, suspicious, 'That door's never locked. Did you lock it?'

Foster keened and whimpered, shook his head, in denial of the question and frustration he couldn't communicate. 'It wasn't me. It wasn't me.'

The farmer's face distorted, in a false realisation, 'You little bastard.'

A back-hand fist to Foster's face sent him sprawling across a flower bed as the roof timbers of his dead grandparents' home collapsed inwards, released a rage of flame.

Foster stayed quiet perhaps half a minute, stared out over the plot of leeks. Blum smoked, considered Foster's story. Foster turned to him, 'I never did it.'

Blum nodded, 'I know.'

He could imagine Foster's progress through the courts; no witnesses for a defence and a boy who struggled to make himself understood before a jury. He pictured Foster's fear, helplessness, as a judge sent him down the steps at Lancaster Assizes.

'What about Chris? Where is he?'

'Me mum said he's gone to India with his mates. They've got a van. They're sort of like hippies and take drugs, pot and stuff. He sent a postcard from somewhere foreign.'

'Does your mam believe you?'

He shook his head, 'She doesn't want to see me no more.'

'Are you sure about that?'

Foster nodded, 'She wanted me gran's house to sell – she were waiting for them to die. Now she says she'll get nowt 'cause there's no insurance and it's all my fault. She won't write me letters, won't visit.'

From then on, Blum looked after Foster. With the guilty brother gone, vital witnesses dead, he could see no way Foster could fight his conviction, find justice. Blum urged him to do his time, look forward to release, helped widen Foster's skills in gardening and farming, so he at least had experience to build on when it came to the day he left Havershawe.

But Blum couldn't protect him from Travis.

Chapter 8
Click and Strawberries

FOSTER CARRIED SOMETHING close to his chest as he
ran along rows of cauliflowers and shouted for Blum. It was
a young magpie. Foster was close to tears as he told Blum
he'd found the bird injured by the blackcurrant bushes behind
the big glasshouse. He didn't know what to do, was scared
the bird would die.

Blum took the magpie. It protested with hoarse mews, but
made no effort to fly. Blum took it to the tool shed, folded a
potato sack. He placed the magpie on the pad, examined it
while Foster hovered, fretted.

'Daft bugger must've crashed into the glasshouse,' said
Blum, 'It's bust a wing.'

Foster was anxious, 'It won't die, will it?'

'To be honest, I should twist its blummin' neck and put
the little sod out of its misery.'

Foster was appalled, 'Nooo…'

Blum laughed, 'Better see what we can do, then, eh?'

Blum rooted out a roll of insulation tape, split a piece of
bamboo cane. In ten minutes he fashioned a splint and taped
the magpie's wing in position against the side of its body.

'You'll have to hop wherever you're going for a few
weeks, me laddo,' Blum told the bird and taped up its healthy
wing as well. He presented the trussed up magpie to Foster.
'And you'll have to look after him.'

Foster spent his spare time foraging food for his new
companion. Scraps of meat and fish were saved from his own
meals and no caterpillar, worm, slug, or cockroach was safe
from imprisonment in his old cough sweets tin. The magpie
was put to roost in the rafters of the tool shed, but in work
hours hopped everywhere at Foster's heels.

He demanded food by the minute and would stand and
stare at Foster, his head cocked to one side, black eye

gleaming, and utter a metronomic click until he was handed a dead fly, or wriggling worm. Inside a week, he was named Click. Inside a month his wing was healed and he could fly short distances. Foster was anxious the young bird might desert him, but Click stuck with Foster every minute he was at the farm.

Travis continued to trust Blum in his work on the farm. Blum made mistakes, but not many. Even when he did, he never fell victim to Travis's notorious temper and suffered only the S.O.'s know-all lectures. Travis continued to be surprised at Blum's knowledge of horticulture and agriculture, passed on by his parents and uncle. He asked if Blum's family ever entered flower and vegetable shows. Blum told him they never had. All their produce fed them, or was given to neighbours and friends.

'You're missing a lot,' Travis told him, 'Look at me. Never less than half a dozen "First in Class" gold cards in our local show, mostly more. Year on year, I get that; known for my gold-rated veg the breadth of the Fylde. In the local rag every year, photos and write-up, the lot. It'll be my twentieth year come the next show.'

'What do you enter, then?'

'What don't I enter, more like?' He tapped his forefinger on those of his left hand as he listed, 'Marrow, cabbage, leeks, onions, runner beans, carrots, beetroot, herbs, apples, red currant…You name it, lad.'

'Must take a lot of time?'

'You wouldn't believe the hours I put in. Not to mention skill and patience. Mind you, you must've realised by now. I like things just right, a stickler for it.'

And a thief, Blum said to himself. And it wasn't only farm supplies. Blum had seen inmates carry boxes from the workshops, deliver them to Travis's waiting car. Blum kept a mental note, but was content that Travis's regard for his abilities meant he had an easy time at Havershawe as his release date drew closer.

The year advanced and the farm became busier. Travis drafted boys from the workshops to pick strawberries. Havershawe's farm had never grown them before and the Governor had earmarked the whole crop to be sold to a dealer at Preston market. Travis announced to the pickers anyone caught taking even a single berry would answer to him. The first two days, he patrolled the acre plot like a chain-gang guard. Delly was the first he spotted nicking a few strawberries. Travis stopped work and made an example of him, punched him black and blue before the frightened eyes of the other boys. Another lad avoided punishment in public when Travis saw strawberry juice on his chin and ordered him to wait by the pig unit. The lad never returned to work that day and was found on the manure pile, sobbing, covered in bruises from Travis's truncheon.

When the fruit dealer's wagon was loaded in the late afternoon of the first day's harvest, Blum watched the driver hand over a bundle of pound and ten-shilling notes to Travis. Blum had witnessed Travis's dealings with suppliers before and paperwork was taken straight to the bursar's office near the kitchens. This time, Travis went to his car before heading for the office, now carrying a piece of paper. Blum couldn't swear the bundle of banknotes was now slimmer, but he had his suspicions. Blum made sure he was around the second, third and later days when the wagon took delivery and again saw Travis take money to his car. With other transgressions by Travis, he filed times and dates in his head.

Strong sunshine and nightly drizzle produced an abundance of fruit. The Borstal boys struggled to keep pace with the crop. Travis even allowed some fruit to be taken into the kitchen for Saturday tea, but the gesture was spoilt when he announced no cricket would be allowed on Sunday until the day's order for market had been picked. Blum urged the lads to pick faster, so the cricket could go ahead.

When eighty boxes of punnets were loaded, Blum asked Travis if they could be released for the match. Travis checked the boxes on the handcart, told Foster to take them down to the kitchen yard to meet the fruit wagon. The pickers were released. Foster enjoyed cricket, hurried off at speed to get his last job done, followed, as usual, by Click, who rode on top of the handcart.

Forty minutes later, Blum was bowled out for a duck. He stuck up two fingers to the jeers and went to sit under a chestnut tree in the evening sun. He could take or leave cricket. He ached for the autumn and freedom; to go piking, or potting a mallard on the ditches and ponds as dusk covered the stubbles. It was a while before he realised he hadn't seen Foster arrive. Where was he? Blum sloped away, avoided the notice of the duty officer, who dozed in a deckchair.

Blum walked through the deserted farmyard. He was startled to see strawberries littering the dust of the yard by the pig unit. A pile of damaged, red-stained fruit boxes were piled by its door. A few feet away a whole box lay on its side. He became aware of a noise. It was Click. His familiar sound came from the tool shed. Blum entered, tripped on a four-foot length of rubber hosepipe. The agitated magpie was perched on Foster's shoulder clicking for food, or attention. But Foster could offer neither. He lay in a foetal position, minus his shirt, his ribs and back a mass of lacerations. His body jerked as he gasped, sobbed. Blum knelt and touched the wounds, glanced over his shoulder. Blood covered one end of the hosepipe. Someone had used it to flog Foster; it could only have been Travis.

With the pressed help of a reluctant Delly, Blum raided the medical room for aspirin, gauze, iodine and anti-septic cream. Foster's wounds were painful, but there was no need for an ambulance, or doctor. Blum and Delly sneaked food to Foster in the dormitory for days, kept the wounds clean. Each held him upright for twice-daily roll-call.

Foster regained his strength, told Blum how Travis had gone berserk. His rage was sparked when the handcart turned over minutes before the fruit wagon arrived. Foster was keen to get to the cricket match, careless as he turned the corner on the steep slope down to the kitchen yard. A wheel struck the edge of a flower bed and the handcart tipped over. The piled boxes of fresh-picked strawberries were crushed, or catapulted across the dusty yard below. The wagon driver declined to take even salvageable fruit.

Travis forced Foster to manhandle the ruined boxes and strawberries to the pig unit. Travis wouldn't let him rest for a moment as Foster carried box after box to the pig troughs. Foster was parched, sweating, but Travis wouldn't relent. Stripped to the waist, he kept going until the final box, but collapsed from exertion in the hot sun. Travis dragged him to the tool shed, lashed him until he fainted.

Blum waited, day after day, for Travis to ask why Foster was missing, but he said nothing; even in the presence of the magpie, confused by its keeper's disappearance. It was as if, to Travis, Foster did not exist. Blum simmered with anger, but he knew any form of official protest would be futile. Travis would block a complaint to the governor, or make life miserable for all the lads; or both. To get Foster well was Blum's priority. His next was revenge.

Chapter 9
Dead James Bond-ish

BLUM'S STORY SICKENED us. Viv and I wanted what he'd planned. With one eye on Travis as he patrolled the visiting hall, I asked why he'd never mentioned any of this. Viv asked the same. Neither of us heard negative points about Havershawe on our visits. In hindsight I realised he tended to steer our talk towards events on the outside.

Viv said, 'But why? You could've told us.'

He grinned, 'Ha. If you'd known all this, you'd worry I'd do something daft.'

Viv and I swapped a look, he was right.

Blum was serious, 'Won't say I wasn't tempted to do something straight away. But I've thought it out. This is summat that has to happen with me and Fozzy tucked up in here -- I don't want blummin' coppers coming for me.'

The bell for the end of visiting rang, farewells started.

Blum stood , 'I know there's not much time, but what to do didn't come to me 'til the other day. Reckon you can manage it?'

Again, Viv and I looked at each other. I nodded, he shook my hand. Viv hugged him. 'Course we'll do it.' Over her shoulder, Blum grinned, winked, as I felt the folded wad of paper in my palm. I felt a thrill at the prospect of action.

Viv scanned the grounds when we left. She was looking for Foster, I knew. On children's wards she'd seen young victims of adult violence, worked with fellow nurses to help repair their minds as well as their bodies. Across the lawn, Foster lifted the shafts of a wheelbarrow.

She made a move, but I caught her sleeve

'I need a quick word. Just to tell him he's...'

'You know what Blum said. Foster doesn't need to know anything about us. Blum's minding his back.'

She sighed, lingered, watched Foster cross the grass.

'Come on, if we miss Travis now it cuts down our time and we've only got 'til Friday.'

Ten minutes later found us astride the Norton, in a lane off the road past Havershawe. Blum had seen Travis drive in and out of the gates and knew he came to work from the northern side of the Borstal. We had a description of his car.

'What's his car number?' said Viv.

'For Christ's sake, we're supposed to have memorised all this. It's NPT 451D.'

She turned, grinned, 'Just testing!' She held her fag packet over her shoulder for me to take one. 'Dead James Bond-ish, this, I like it.'

Would she enjoy it when it got to the illegal stage? For that matter, would I have the guts to go through with the plan, without Blum? I focused on Blum's account of Travis's ill-treatment of lads in his charge, hoped our outrage would carry us through. Viv tensed, threw her cigarette aside, when a pale blue Cortina passed the lane end.

She booted the kick-start, shouted, 'There he goes.' She shot the bike to the junction. A quick look both ways and she arc-ed out of the lane to catch the Cortina. 'Number's right,' she shouted, dropped speed, hung back.

Travis might live in Blackpool, or even Preston. It worried me. If we lost him in a built-up area we'd waste forty-eight hours and have to loiter in the lane again on Monday. We reached a main road, Preston one way, Blackpool the other. No signal from the Cortina and it crossed into another country lane. Two wagons lumbered past and we lost sight of the Cortina, but Viv powered across into the lane and we caught up after a few hundred yards. In the Fylde countryside, cattle pastures contrasted with stubbles, the mixture dotted by clumps of trees, some starting to change into autumn colours. On the flat horizon to our left was the spike of Blackpool Tower.

We passed through a block of woodland and as the Cortina approached a bend, it signalled right. Viv slowed as the car travelled turned on to the gravelled frontage of a pub called The Twa Ducks. I glimpsed the September red leaves of Virginia creeper on its white walls and the driver's door of the Cortina opened before my view was blocked by a parked van. Viv rounded the bend and pulled into the gateway of a field.

'What the hell do we do now? What if he's there 'til chucking-out?'

Viv's thought was in my mind as well. 'We'll just have to wait.'

'Yeah, but where? I could murder a Coke, but we can't go and sit in the pub with him.'

I looked back. I could see the front of the Cortina's bonnet parked nose to the pub wall, most of it obscured by the van. I pointed at the gate to a field a few yards away. 'I'll open the gate and you stick the bike behind the hedge. We'll see him when he leaves.'

The sun was dropping, but it was warm behind the field hedge .It stank of cattle and we were persecuted by flies where we sat, surrounded by pats of drying cow muck.

Fifteen minutes passed. I read the notes contained in the folded paper Blum passed to me. Viv was restless. 'Are you thirsty?'

I was, but there wasn't much I could do about it.

'If I nipped down to the pub I could see what he's doing and get us a couple of bottles of pop.' She paused, 'Or I could get a couple of bottles of Double Diamond?'

Beer was a temptation, but, 'He'd recognise you. We can't risk that.'

Five more minutes ticked away. I was curious what Travis was doing. We had no idea where he lived. Was it possible he lived at the pub? Common sense told me otherwise, but he could be married; his missus could be the licensee. I felt I had to make sure. At least I might be able to gauge how long he might be in there. Was it a pint on the way home? Or did he join a Saturday night booze-up with regulars?

I stood, 'Right, I'll go and get some pop.'

She made a move, 'It's okay, I'll go.'

'No, I won't be as…as obvious.'

'What's that meant to mean?'

'How many blondes in full leathers does Travis see in one day? How many do they see in that pub? At least I might just blend in.'

She laughed. 'You'd better stick a straw in your gob then.'

'No need, I already ronk of cow shit.'

I took hold of the gate latch.

'What if he comes out as you're going in?'

'If he leaves, follow him.' I laughed, 'I'll wait in the pub 'til you come back.'

She rolled her eyes. I opened the gate, headed for the pub.

The Twa Ducks was smaller than I'd thought, narrow tap room on the right and a larger best room to the left of a cramped bar. A passage led to the toilets, living quarters and, I presumed, the back yard. I scanned the place for Travis, but there was nobody except a middle-aged woman with red hair putting pies in the bar-top heater. I ordered a pint of bitter and two small bottles of lemonade to take out. I wondered if she was Travis's landlady wife. If he did live here would it make things more difficult for Viv and me?

I stuck the bottles in my jacket pocket, necked half the pint in one swallow. The woman went out into the living quarters so I moved to the back window. I expected a dismal back yard, but there was a cottage garden with a central area of sandstone flags with cast iron tables and chairs. Not ten feet away from me, sat Travis and another man in overalls, two half-drunk pints between them. I stepped back. The other man finished counted banknotes from a bundle. He passed what he'd counted across the table to Travis, who slid them into the pocket of his uniform jacket. I wished I had a camera.

I sat out of their view, drank the rest of my pint. I was about to leave when the back door opened. I lowered my eyes, looked to one side with my peripheral vision. Travis led the way in, followed by the other man, who wore oil-stained work boots. I was terrified Travis might look my way, recognise me, afraid they'd linger, order more drinks. Pint pots clunked on the bar top, but moments later the front door opened, both men had gone.

I checked the woman was still round the back. I was touched by panic now. What if Travis drove off and Viv didn't see him leave?

I went to the front window, peered out. Travis and the man moved boxes from the boot of the Cortina to the back of the van. Print on the boxes read, H.M. BORSTAL, HAVERSHAWE. I shifted to read the lettering on the side of the van: E.J. Hart Engineering. The address was 81, Turnstone Road, Blackpool. I stepped back, snatched a beer mat, wrote down time, date, location and the van's reg. number; I had enough to remember from Blum's instructions to challenge an elephant's memory. I glanced outside as the van doors closed and Travis dropped the Cortina's boot lid.

Travis started to reverse. I panicked again, in case he turned back the way we came. But he turned towards the field where I hoped Viv still kept watch. Travis accelerated away and I dashed out of the pub like a whippet from a trap. I legged across the lane. Viv kicked open the gate, revved the bike, turned out onto the tarmac. The Cortina was out of sight as I ran, pop bottles clinking, and hopped onto the pillion of the waiting Norton

Travis was in no hurry and we settled a hundred yards behind him as he drove along more country lanes. I was pleased with what I'd witnessed at the pub. It added to Blum's plan; yet spying on a corrupt, violent prison officer seemed a long way from that promise to help Blum save his mam's home.

Fields and isolated farms fell away and we entered a village called Prenterton. Travis drove under a railway bridge, past a pub called The Rose and Crown and two or three shops, turned right at a crossroads. A short distance on, the Cortina indicated right, slowed. Viv passed the Cortina as it turned into the driveway of a red-brick 1920s bungalow. We left the Norton in a close of semi-detached houses, walked back to the bungalow.

On foot, it seemed almost hidden by the high hedge which fronted it. We peered through it. The house and garden were neat, well-kept, with a close mown, narrow lawn and flower beds with perfect edges. You could almost smell fresh paint. Joined to the house was a garage, a recent addition as the bricks didn't quite match those of the bungalow. On the gatepost was the name, 'Stella Maris.'

Opposite what we as yet only presumed was Travis's house, was a playing field. Lads were playing football. Viv pointed out a wooden bus shelter about twenty-five yards from the bungalow gate backing on to the field. We crossed over, sat inside. From one end of the bench we could see the bungalow's driveway. Beyond what seemed a sizeable back garden with several trees was a railway embankment.

Viv prised open her pop bottles with her fag lighter, while I told her what I'd seen at the pub, how to achieve Blum's aim, how we might divide the work. I speculated about the railway embankment when a movement caught my eye. Stella Maris's front door was now open. Travis's head and shoulders appeared above the parked Cortina as he pulled the front door shut.

'He's going out again.'

Viv leaned across me to look and Travis came past the Cortina. He paused at the foot of the drive, something in his hand. He whistled and an Alsatian dog lolloped to join him. Travis clipped a leash to its collar.

'Shit,' I said.

Travis walked away from us with the dog, I looked at Viv. We had a problem.

Chapter 10
Tea with Trixie

VIV PICKED ME up outside the Plough Horse on Monday to re-visit Prenterton, this time in the Chev.

The day after we visited Blum was Sunday and Viv had to work. In an attempt not to waste time, I tried to find out about the railway that passed Travis's house, but all I could consult with the library closed, was my dad's road atlas. I was so preoccupied my mum convinced herself there was something wrong with me. Was it something to do with work? Was it something to do with Elaine? How could I tell her I was running over and over in my head a plan to seek revenge on a prison officer I didn't even know?

Viv and I needed a base and I suggested the car park of the Rose and Crown pub in Travis's village. Minutes after morning opening we parked the Chev behind the pub. I had a couple of pints, I was on holiday, I told myself, but Viv stuck to orange juice. With a few questions and a bit of chat, we convinced the landlord we were staying with relatives while we explored the local countryside. From my holiday pay, I ordered a whisky and asked him if we could leave the Chev in his car park. 'Be my guest, sir' he said, in his otherwise empty bar. I felt better with the Chev tucked out of sight.

A detailed look around Travis's place was vital to Blum's plan, but I couldn't think of a low-risk way to do it, thought it might be best to keep thinking while we took a look at the railway embankment. Whether the line was active, or a victim of the Beeching rail closures that destroyed much of the country's railways in the 60s, I didn't know. We were across the road from the Rose and Crown checking a route to take us up on to the embankment when Viv announced she would leave that job to me.

'What are you going to do?' I said.

She picked up on my indignant tone. 'No need to be shirty. I'm going to see Travis's wife.'

'But…We don't even know if he's got a wife.'

'I saw the curtains in the front room window. The driveway'd been swept. The house is just so-- I know he's got a wife.'

'Look, I've thought about this. It's not that easy if she's at home, we need a … a cover story.'

I'd thought of half-a-dozen 'cover stories' from posing as a doorstep sales team to masquerading as council inspectors, all too risky without knowledge, or proof of identity. Now I worried this lack of a cover would sink the whole venture. Travis's Alsatian was an unwanted complication too.

'I've got one.'

I was too busy holding down my fear of failure, panic, Viv's statement didn't at first sink in. I looked at her. 'What?'

'Noticed the change of image today?' She indicated the length of her body. I had noticed, but didn't see any significance. Her hair was piled up, pinned in place, instead of loose. The hoop ear-rings had gone and she wore one of those maxi-coats, 'in' that year. She opened it to display her nurse's uniform.

'I'm a nurse!'

'I know, so what?'

She pointed past me, her finger at a high angle over the frontage of a haberdasher's shop, its windows full of wool, cardboard cut-out models advertising knitting patterns. A sign in the upper window said, 'Flat to Let.'

'Saw that on the way back the other night.' She put on a sad expression and a soppy voice, 'I've just moved in and I've lost my poor little cat on my very first day.'

She thrust a snapshot of a tabby cat in my face. 'My Nan's moggy, she's called Tilly. She'll do us. Not like she has to make a personal appearance, is it?'

Door-knocking sales people could be ignored, most kept council officials on the doorstep. But who wouldn't take pity on a young nurse, a new neighbour, who'd lost her pet cat the day she moved in? I was impressed. I grinned. It wasn't just the drink that boosted my confidence.

*

Viv and I went our separate ways. It was a pincer movement. Viv approached from the road, I made my way towards the rear of Stella Maris from the railway. To get up there, I went up a narrow passageway alongside the shoe repair shop next to the railway embankment. There I could step up on to a low wall, reach the top of the embankment through a thicket of elder and hazel bushes.

I was glad to see the railway had fallen to Dr. Beeching's cost-cutting 'axe.' Rails had gone, the sleepers were covered in brambles and weeds as nature took back her property from British Railways. Both sides of the embankment were a riot of scrubby trees that meant little chance of being seen from houses either side of the track.

I reached the rear of Stella Maris, pushed through willow herb and birch scrub, settled behind a clump of bramble. The back of the house was as neat as the front, the window frames seemed new, all painted glossy white. French windows opened into a lean-to sun lounge of glass and white woodwork, which also appeared to be new. There were two small sheds and a large greenhouse on the right-hand side. At the bottom of the garden, closest to me, were a pear tree and two apple trees, all in fruit. Most of the garden was laid out to vegetables, but for a small square of lawn. There was a door in the lean to, but it was closed. The only open door was in the angle of the house and the built-on garage I'd noticed on our first view of Travis's home. Near the door was a dog kennel. Sprawled in sunshine on the flagstones by the open door slept the Alsatian.

It woke, sprang up and barked, hurried inside the door at the back of the garage. I guessed Viv had arrived. I crouched in shadow, waited. I saw Viv while she was on the property, but it was more than an hour before she could tell me the details.

Uniform on display, snapshot in hand, Viv rang the doorbell at Stella Maris. Straight away, came the Alsatian's response, barks growing louder, more aggressive. The barking became frantic. A woman's voice shushed the dog. The door opened to reveal Mrs Travis, a woman in her late forties. Viv noted her wedding ring, plus the lavish jewellery she wore for a Monday afternoon.

Mrs Travis appraised Viv as well, 'Hello?'

'I'm really sorry to bother you, but I've lost my cat.'

Before Mrs Travis could react, Viv held up the snapshot,' Have you seen her. She's called Tilly.'

'I'm sorry, I...Do you live round here?'

Viv had rehearsed, she gabbled, 'I've just moved in this morning. I tried to keep her in, but I must've left the door open and next thing I know she's gone. I'm terrified she'll get lost, or run over, because she's not used to busy roads. I've asked everywhere, but nobody's seen her.' She forced out the tears, 'I've been knocking on doors for hours. I think she'd be scared of roads so she must've gone down the back gardens or on the railway line...' She sobbed,' I don't know what to do...'

'Don't upset yourself, lovey, you'd better come in.'

The Alsatian growled as Viv was ushered inside.

'Go on Trixie, shoo,' said Mrs Travis as she guided Viv across the hall, pushed open the living room door, 'Don't worry about her, she's a good guard dog, but soft as anything once she knows you.'

Viv wiped at her eyes with a hanky as Mrs Travis guided her to an armchair. Trixie growled again, 'Oh, don't be silly, Trixie. This is a friend.'

She turned back to Viv, 'Did you say you just moved in? Today?'

Viv sat, nodded, 'The flat over the wool shop, round the corner.'

'Oh, I heard Mrs Birstall was renting it out now she's married again. I heard he's a bookie in Cleveleys. Don't suppose she'll keep the shop on much longer either, they say he's made of money.'

Mrs Travis perhaps thought she was saying too much to Mrs Birstall's new tenant, 'Er…Shall I make us a cup of tea?'

Viv nodded, 'Please, if you don't mind.'

'I'll bet you've had no lunch either, looking for your poor cat.'

She left the room, 'Won't be a minute, lovey. I'll find us some biscuits as well.'

Inside, Stella Maris was as neat and well-maintained as outside. The furniture was new, G Plan, fashionable. Viv noted a Grundig TV she thought might be a colour model, an Axminster carpet. She shifted position to see more, Trixie growled.

Viv dug into her coat pocket, pulled out loose dog biscuits. She held them out to Trixie. Masked by the whistling kettle, she made encouraging sounds. Trixie approached with caution. Viv wiggled her fingers, lowered her hand. Trixie snuffled up the biscuits in an instant. The dog eyed her, licking its lips, Viv produced more. They went in one gulp, she was rewarded with a wagging tail. Viv stroked it under its chin, risked a pat to its head. The dog came closer and Viv provided a few more biscuits. Viv petted Trixie while she imagined the costs of the Travis's well-appointed living room.

Mrs Travis came through from the kitchen with tea on a tray, a plate of garibaldi biscuits. 'I told you she was friendly once she got to know you.'

It was obvious Mrs Travis welcomed this break in routine. She spotted Viv's uniform. Viv told her she'd moved to Lancaster Royal Infirmary from a hospital in Liverpool. This prompted a monologue from Mrs Travis which tried to cover the hospital experiences of everyone she knew. Viv waited for a lull to bring talk back to her missing cat.

'Would you mind if I had a look in your back garden? I've looked in all the others this side of the railway.' Mrs

Travis seemed put out at this intrusion on the conversation. Viv applied pressure, 'I'm terrified I won't find her before it goes dark. Anything could happen …'

'Yes, well, I suppose we'd better have a look.'

Mrs Travis led Viv through a modern kitchen, via the back door into the garage. 'I'm sorry about the mess in here. Bert clutters it up with all sorts. He hoards everything.'

'Looks like you're stocked up for a world war.'

'I know, he's always bringing stuff home from work.'

Viv noted the boxes and cartons. There was tinned food, cleaning materials, new garden tools, toilet rolls, as well as other boxes with no clue to what they contained. One pile of boxes were marked HMP, HAVERSHAWE. She also took in the long, wide bench which ran down one side of the garage. One end was a home workshop with an array of power tools. She noted the rear window, which was a solid pane of frosted glass with a transom.

Mrs Travis stood back at the rear door and let Viv go ahead into the garden. Viv started to 'Tch-tch-tch' and call for 'Tilly.' Mrs Travis made a half-hearted attempt to follow her example. Viv ranged across the garden memorising the layout, followed by Trixie. When Mrs Travis looked away, Viv slipped the Alsatian another biscuit. Viv covered the whole garden, pretended to give up.

'I'll just have to look somewhere else.'

Mrs Travis was confident, 'I'm sure she'll turn up.'

Viv nodded. 'Have you lived here long?'

'Just ten years.'

'You've got it lovely, the house and the garden.'

'Oh, that's all down to him.' She regarded the bungalow without expression, 'He even chose the furniture and curtains. Everything has to be just so. He said when we bought this place, he'd have it all finished in ten years, not a penny owed on mortgage.'

'Really?'

'That's why he does so much overtime. Sometimes I think he cares more about this place and his boys than anything else.'

'You've got sons?' Viv hadn't noticed any signs; no photographs, even a bike, or football, in the garage.

Viv noticed a look of regret. Mrs Travis shook her head, 'I meant his boys at work. He's a senior officer at a Borstal, you know, bad lads in trouble. He spends so much time helping them, trying to put them back on the straight and narrow.'

Viv almost laughed, but prompted, 'Looks like he's done what he said about the house.'

Her voice was flat: 'I suppose he has.' She paused, 'It's too quiet, though. I'd swap it all for a flat in Lytham-St.Anne's, or Morecambe.' She continued to stare at the house. Viv had to interrupt the silence.

'Thanks for the tea. I'd better keep looking.'

Mrs Travis and Trixie showed her out. Trixie wagged her tail.

Chapter 11
Inside Job

VIV HAD TO work a shift each day the following week. Back home, I spent my time between my parents' house and the library. I had a letter and dossier to write up on my second-hand Olivetti portable, using dates and the written information palmed to me by Blum at Havershawe. I had to check up on one or two other things, buy a couple of items. My holiday was turning into work, but by Thursday evening I'd done all I needed. At Pygon's Farm I checked everything was in order in the still room, before a drink at the Plough Horse with Elaine, not telling her I'd been home for days.

She was pleased with my surprise appearance, but it didn't take long before the conversation turned to why I didn't come home more often. I countered with airy talk about cultivating contacts, getting on, getting promotion, aiming for a job on a London national. Then she announced we were both invited to a out the following night. It was her work friend's twentieth birthday, a booze-up at the Hare and Hounds.

I panicked. 'I can't, not tomorrow.'

She almost screeched, 'Why not?'

Closing time came, the hushed argument continued. I told her I'd promised to do a few things for Blum before his release. I should have told her it was work. I lied, told her I had to see someone who might be able to give Blum a job. Questions came, I lied more.

We left the Plough Horse, crossed the bridge over the cut. She was angrier, cursed Blum, cursed our friendship, told me I was wasting my time, my life, on a no-mark and criminal. This was too much. I was livid with self-righteousness in defence of my drunken lies, 'You expect me to go to some party for a girl I don't even know, let my best friend down over his future? Christ Almighty!'

She sneered, 'Is it him who's your best friend, or that Viv one?'

The effect of the drink lifted. Now I was clear-headed, but I hesitated in my shock at this allegation. She struck again. 'You've been seen with her--On the back of her motorbike. All lovey-dovey, is it, with him locked up? Does your best friend know about that?'

I started to laugh. Her face was twisted in anger, fuelled by unfounded jealousy, in turn fuelled by Bacardi and Coca Cola.

'Sod you,' she said, 'I'll go on my bloody own.' She moved away, walking backwards, 'Make the most of her before your precious mate gets out of jail. Then we'll see if you're still best friends.'

She turned, hurried away. Drunkenness descended and I started to giggle. I suspected Sandra in advertising might be a touch jealous of Elaine. I was sure she'd soon be jealous of the Girl on the Motorbike. Elaine knew nothing about Sandra, but it looked like she was jealous of Viv. But Viv was a friend, nothing else. She was Blum's girl and I was her pal. And none of them knew about some others, not that any of them were ever important. The whole thing was mad. I went home to a sleeping household, drank whisky my father never touched, stupidly told myself I wasn't interested in Sandra, Elaine, or anyone else -- certainly not Viv. For the moment, my anxiety about the day ahead had vanished. I was too drunk for that.

*

When I met Viv outside the hospital the following evening the hangover that produced a morning headache had morphed into a delicate stomach, aggravated by nervousness. I leaned against the Chev with what was needed for our mission in a potato sack. She crossed the car park, changed into jeans, dark jumper and the maxi coat.

'Got everything?'

'Yeah.'

She looked at me, unlocked the driver's door. 'Are you alright?'

'Too much last night.'

'Bloody hell.' She got into the car. I joined her.

'It wasn't planned.'

'You know what we've got to do. It'll be hard enough without you feeling rough.'

'I'll be fine.'

'So why did you get drunk?'

I exhaled, 'We had a nark.'

She turned, grinned as she put the Chev into drive, 'Oh, yeah, Elaine or the other one?'

I had to laugh and on the way up to Prenterton she tried to get the details of my duplicitous personal life. I gave away as little as possible. The few times she'd met Elaine, they didn't get on. Elaine couldn't accept Viv for what she was, thought her a freak for not sharing interests like clothes and the ultimate goal of marriage, 'getting on.' I imagined it would be much the same if Elaine were to meet Sandra.

I changed the subject to Travis and his brutality. I needed to, owing to my anxiety. I was psyching myself up in my usual way in an attempt to justify doing something illegal, so I questioned aloud how Travis could commit such acts of violence, condemned him. I thought it would help Viv to keep focused as well, as I feared she might lose her nerve. Viv told me she was concerned for Foster's safety once Blum was released.

'Keep thinking that Travis won't be around. And at least you'll have Blum back.'

She smiled, 'Yeah.'

We didn't speak much until we reached the Rose and Crown at Prenterton. The pub was busier than it was on Monday. It was a squeeze to park the Chev. While she locked the car, Viv must have seen me stare at the open door, where the sound of drinkers mixed with the jukebox, Bob Dylan singing *Lay, Lady, Lay*. For me, it meant Sandra, the earliest stage of my attraction to her. I played it in The Boot when she came in those weeks before we got together. I bought the record, played it night after night on my junk shop Dansette. Viv's voice snatched me back from a daydream: of Sandra, her tanned legs, blonde bobbed hair, facing out to sea from a Cornish cliff.

'How's your stomach?'

'Er...Not so bad now.'

She headed for the pub's back door, glanced back, 'A quick drink won't do us any harm, then. Come on.'

I gave silent thanks. She opted for a half of Bass, I pushed in at the crowded bar, added a double whisky. The landlord recognised us, asked how our holiday was going. Viv gave him a smile, I said, 'Very nice, thanks.' He was too busy to ask where we'd explored. Five minutes later, I retrieved the spud sack from the boot of the Chev.

We checked for watching loiterers, crossed the road and went up the side of the shoe repair shop. With Viv behind me, I pushed through the bushes up on to the railway embankment. We walked in silence. It was warm, the voices of children carried from the gardens. We ducked down, froze, when an errant householder appeared above his back fence, tipped grass cuttings on railway property. Different soundtracks of TV programmes drifted from open windows.

Darkness was close when we reached the back of Travis's bungalow. Lights were on, one a fluorescent strip in the sun lounge. I led the way through the scrub to the slope of the embankment. I was terrified Trixie might bark an alarm, but we managed to reach the place where I'd hidden four days ago. I couldn't see anyone, but Viv pointed out Travis, bent over a piece of ground, in shadows, beyond the greenhouse.

Moments later, Mrs Travis came out, followed by Trixie. She plonked a mug on a garden table, turned back to the house. She said nothing, Travis made no attempt to acknowledge her, continued to work. He made several trips to the garage with a large tray. Trixie sat on the flagstones by her kennel. It seemed an age before he finished outside. He closed the greenhouse doors, lashed the untouched contents of his mug across the lawn, went inside the garage. A light came on inside. Mrs Travis appeared in the sun lounge, switched off the strip light. Trixie remained outside, head on paws, asleep.

Eleven o'clock had passed before we saw any movement. A light came on, then was switched off, in what we supposed was the main bedroom. It was chilly now and I wriggled into a jumper I'd brought in the sack. I expected Trixie to bark, but she remained quiet. I craved a fag, pulled my packet from my jeans pocket. I passed one to Viv, was about to strike a match when the garage door opened wider. A wedge of light crossed the garden like a searchlight. We froze as Travis came outside. It seemed to stare straight at us, but there was no reaction. He raised his right arm. I caught the glint of cut glass as he drank what looked like whisky from a tumbler. He belched, drank more.

Trixie stirred, moved towards him, wagging her tail. He ignored her, but she sat beside him, looked up at him, whimpered. Travis took another mouthful and looked at her, deftly kicked her in the ribs. Trixie yelped. 'Get in that bloody kennel.'

I felt Viv tense. She whispered a string of swearwords and I put my hand on her arm to warn her. Trixie slinked into the kennel, Travis went back inside the garage.

Viv cursed again. I willed the bastard to leave the garage door open to make our job easier. But he didn't. Five minutes passed and he closed the door, turned the key. The garage light went off. We were able to light up.

'Did you see what he did to that poor dog?'

'What are *we* going to do about the dog? It still worries me.'

She told me to leave it to her. We finished our smoke.

Viv made a move, her voice low, 'When I say, climb over the fence after me.'

The bedroom light was still off, but there was at least one other light still burning. 'He's still up, you know.'

'He's had a drink, locked up. He won't come out now.' She seemed more confident than me.

Viv picked her way down the railway bank, went to a place where a gap showed at the foot of one of Travis's fence panels. She was in deep shadow. She made clicking noises with her tongue, stopped for a few moments and then repeated them. Trixie loped across the garden. Viv talked to the dog in a crooning voice, as if to a fractious baby, telling it what she was doing as she did it. She sounded so calm, but I was all but paralysed by nerves.

I hadn't mentioned it to Viv, Blum had only small knowledge of my phobia, but I was terrified of Alsatians. I had to scramble over a fence to escape one when I was nine-years-old, but it had still managed to bite my leg. I shuddered.

Viv, still crooning to the dog, pulled herself on top of the fence. I expected Trixie to go berserk, but all I could hear was a soft whimper. Viv continued to croon as she lowered herself into Travis's garden.

Viv petted the dog, asked if she wanted biscuits. In the same voice she used to address Trixie she told me to climb slowly over the fence to join them. My legs shook as I picked up the sack, heaved myself up on top of the fence. Viv continued to croon, warned me not to make sudden movements.

'Come down now,' Viv said. I paused a moment, trying to forget talk I'd heard that dogs smell fear. 'Don't look in her eyes, just ignore her. Then I'll pass you some biscuits and you can feed her.'

I sweated as I lowered myself into the garden. Viv talked to the dog, fussed over her. Her hand came out and I took the biscuits without any jerky movement. She continued her instructions in the same sing-song voice and I offered Trixie the biscuits in my hand. Trixie didn't seem at all wary, took them without wariness, or. thank God, aggression.

'Now pat her head,' Viv said, 'Go on, you'll be fine. You want him to pat you, don't you Trixie?'

I reached out, patted the dog's head, her tail wagged. Viv gave me more biscuits and as my pulse rate lowered, I summoned the courage again to feed Trixie, to stroke and pet her head and shoulders.

I latched on to Viv's technique, we spoke to each other as though all our remarks were directed at our now amenable companion. 'For Christ's sake, don't run out of bloody biscuits, will you?' I crooned. We sat on the ground together, each petting and stroking the Alsatian. Within half an hour the bungalow was in darkness.

Speaking low, including Trixie in our hushed conversation, we stood, moved to the back of the garage. We both put on woolly gloves I took from the spud sack. Next I took a rubber sink plunger and a length of wire fastened to a glass cutter. I slipped the looped end of the wire over the handle of the plunger, then gobbed on the rubber cup, licked around its circumference.

'I don't know if I'm going to fit through,' I crooned.

'Don't be soft, you're like Twiggy.'

I crooned, 'Do you mind?'

'Just hurry up, eh?'

I forced the rubber cup against the glass of the transom window at the top of the garage's rear window. I waggled it until it stuck fast like a toy arrow. I wrapped the surplus length of wire round and round the glass cutter until it was about four inches in length. I set the tip of the cutter against the glass, scribed a circle around the central sucker. Holding the plunger's handle, I repeated this three times, waggled the handle, felt the splintering of glass.

I pulled and lifted out the circle of glass stuck to the plunger, passed them to Viv. One thing I'd not thought about was the height of the window. 'I need something to stand on.'

I looked around, but couldn't see anything.

'Wait,' Viv said. Crooning to Trixie, she moved along the house, took hold of a chair from the outside seating area, put it under the window. I stepped up on to the chair, put my arm through the hole in the glass. I pulled the latch up, raised the transom.

This was it, the illegal part. If I was discovered now it would be police, courts, no job, a future wrecked. For a few moments, I forced myself to focus on why I was here. Then stepped up on to the window ledge and raised my other leg over the transom bar. With a slow roll of my body, I felt downwards with my left foot inside the garage. I shifted my weight on to the transom bar, praying it would support my weight, not give way, drop me on to a sheet of glass that would crack, split me in half with shards like razors.

My foot found the inner window ledge. I was able to insinuate my body and head through the transom. More important was the fact I could now bear most of my weight on the inside sill.

'Are you okay?' Viv crooned.

'Yeah,' I gasped. 'Just hold the window up.'

'Don't forget the sack.'

She held up the transom and pushed in the sack. I had no free hand, took it in my teeth. With Viv holding the transom clear I raised my right leg, pulled it over the transom bar and down on to the window ledge. Holding the transom bar, I lowered myself to the garage floor.

My heart hammered as I dug into the sack for my brand new torch. Viv whispered, 'Are you all right?'

'Yeah.'

I'd feel even better if I were at Elaine's work friend's birthday do, knocking back pints, I thought. Then I heard a metallic clang and Viv's stifled blasphemy. Trixie barked twice. There was a scrape as Viv righted the chair she'd knocked over. I cringed as Trixie barked again. I heard Viv make a hushed fuss of the Alsatian. There was a noise inside the bungalow.

'Quiet. Someone's coming!'

A light came on in the kitchen. A key turned in the kitchen door. In panic, I slipped behind a pile of boxes about four feet high. I doubled over, the sack and torch clutched to my chest. The kitchen door opened. In a flood of light someone came in to the garage. Quiet footsteps crossed the garage, the back door was unlocked. I prayed Viv would stay in shadow.

'Trixie?' said Travis. I peered round the boxes. Trixie tried to come in, but Travis repelled her with his slippered foot, 'Back in that kennel.'

He stared out into the garden for a few moments, then pushed the door shut and turned the key. I held my breath, lowered my head. I couldn't look, but sensed him checking the interior of the garage. I risked a look. From my position I could see the neat circular hole in the top of the window. The night sky was overcast, but it seemed so obvious. Travis shuffled a few steps, still checking around. What if he found me, did what he'd done to Delly, Fozzy and others? Or worse; he could beat me and Viv to death and nobody need know.

Travis moved again and went to the kitchen door. He stepped inside and closed the door behind him. The key turned and I let out my breath, waited for the chink of light under the door to disappear. A minute later it did and I crept to the window to check with Viv. For a moment, I was ashamed to think she might have legged it. She hadn't.

Viv crooned, 'She's getting jumpy. We've got to get on with it.'

I moved to the back door, turned the key to leave the door unlocked, switched on my torch. I flashed the beam towards the opposite wall. I put down the torch and working as fast as I could, put everything I could find into the sack. I didn't care about damage; just piled it all in. The sack weighed heavy and I shook down the contents before pulling string from my pocket, tying up the top. I put it over my shoulder, pocketed the torch.

I stepped outside, expecting Trixie to go for me. Instead I found her sitting as Viv fed her biscuits one at a time. Again, she crooned, told me to go to the back fence. I set off across the lawn again expecting Trixie to re-acquire her role as a guard dog, but all I could heard was Viv whisper to her as they followed me. I trembled as I heaved the sack up on top of the fence. Viv steadied it with a hand. I climbed over the fence, dropped on to the foot of the railway embankment. Now the dog couldn't touch me, I felt a hell of a lot calmer. I took the sack down and Viv climbed on top of the fence, still whispering to Trixie.

I was impatient, 'Come on.'

With a finger to her lips, she rooted a bloodied, paper from her pocket and dropped a scrag-end of lamb into Trixie's clutches. She jumped down and we walked as fast as we could back along the railway track, where Viv lobbed the window cutter into darkness. I crouched in the bushes alongside the shoe repair shop while she brought the Chev from the pub car park. I dumped the sack in the boot.

We were in hysterics by the time we'd driven a hundred yards. Even more so when I pointed out a roadside notice -- Prenterton Annual Flower and Vegetable Show. Across the date was pasted a slip of paper -- TODAY.

I was exhilarated at what we'd done for Foster, all Travis's victims.

*

Nine months to the day since Blum was sent to Borstal, we picked him up at the gates of Havershawe at eight in the morning, several days after our burglary at Stella Maris. We'd called at a local newsagent to buy stamps, envelopes and two copies of the *Fylde Gazette*, the local weekly paper for Prenterton.

Blum was exultant at his freedom on a glorious September day. Eager, too, to know if we'd achieved his aim. I passed him a copy of the *Gazette*, told him of my anonymous tip-off to their news editor.

'We made the front page.'

Blum whooped when he read 'Thieves rob Gold Medal gardener of 20 year ambition.' He slapped the dashboard, laughed and hooted. He read out phrases of local sensationalism, '"Mr Travis blames jealous rivals for daring midnight raid."'

'Ha!' said Blum, 'He can't point the finger at me! Or Fozzy and Delly! Any of us!'

He quoted again, '"Police suspect raiders tranquilised guard dog."'

'No we didn't!' said Viv.

'Don't care what you did,' said Blum, 'You two played a blummin' blinder, don't know what to say…'

He wiped his eye with his sleeve, a crack in his voice, 'I mean it.'

Viv lightened the moment, 'Next time give us a bit more time, eh?'

I laughed, 'Seconded.'

We stopped for a fry-up breakfast at the lorry drivers' cafe on Preston Dock.

I'd prepared the letters, copied the dossier I'd written with information from Blum. And I told him what I witnessed at The Twa Ducks. He was impressed how Viv conned her way inside Travis's house, how she controlled Trixie.

He reached out and squeezed her hand. 'Haven't I told you she's scared of nowt?'

Blum smoked as he read the dossier.

'Is there anything you want me to change?'

Blum tapped our copy, 'No, no, this is bob-on. I want Travis up to his neck in trouble. If I were mam I'd blummin' pray for it.'

That night I posted copies and covering letters. One envelope for Fozzy contained a copy of the *Gazette* for his personal enjoyment. On the list were the County's Chief Constable, the Home Office, the Minister for Prisons, the *Fylde Gazette*, all the Lancashire evening papers, all MPs in Lancashire, the governor of HM Borstal, Havershawe, and the TV news desks in Manchester. Though the letter was unsigned, we hoped the litany of violence and theft would convince the Press and authorities that Havershawe needed looking at in general -- and Travis in particular. If it didn't work, Blum declared, at least the destruction of Travis's flower and vegetable show ambitions meant he had some measure of revenge on behalf of Fozzy. But he was emphatic; if it were possible, he wanted more.

To celebrate Blum's release we went fishing on the sluice that crossed Tarlscough estate; made a day of it with food, beer and a bag of grass Viv said would make a beautiful afternoon last forever. It didn't, but it was good to try. We lay on the bank in warm sun, talked of, Blum's time in Havvy, our concern for Fozzy and the burglary of Travis's place.

Viv said, 'I feel a bit mean thinking back, what we did to him.'

I was in first, 'You what? You know what he did. Even if the papers won't touch the story, I'm sure the coppers will.'

'I mean his prize vegetables. Just stealing them and...It seems tight.'

It had to be the dope affecting her head. I turned to Blum. He threw his joint in the water, picked up his beer bottle.

'I mean, conning his poor wife. It feels kind of...of nasty.'

'Nasty?' Blum let the word hang in the air, 'I'll tell you summat nasty.'

He continued, 'The day before I sent you both VOs I'd just about given up getting back at Travis for beating Fozzy. Then I walked into the big glass house. Fozzy was crying, pleading. I watched from behind the water tank. Travis had Fozzy's magpie. He taunted Fozzy, Click was screeching like mad. Foz was beside himself. I thought it was just some sick joke to get him going, but it wasn't...'

Blum mimed the movements. 'He twisted the magpie's head off and chucked it on the ground. It flapped to death in front of Fozzy. Then he threw its head in the poor lad's face.'

Viv gasped, I felt sick. Blum drained his bottle.

'Fozzy ran out and I went in to Travis. He just kicked the bits of magpie under a bench -- didn't say a word. Went on about his fruit and veg show, how he'd win everything, like blummin' nowt'd happened. That's when I had the idea. I wanted him to know how it felt to be hurt, sick, empty inside...'

Blum stood the empty beer bottle in the grass.

'Fozzy's lost everything and Travis did that to him. That's nasty. None of us need to lose sleep over that bastard.'

None of us knew that lovely afternoon how Travis's callous treatment of Fozzy and his pet magpie would lead us into more breaking and entering -- and real danger.

Chapter 12
Not for a Million Pounds

FIFTY FEET ABOVE the ground in frosty night air, Blum and I crouched in silence. It seemed it lasted forever, yet it had been no more than a few seconds. Everything happened so fast. First, the grating noise as the big, earthenware ridge tile shifted. Then Viv's shriek as she lost her balance. She grabbed for the adjoining ridge tile, but failed to grip it as the dislodged tile tobogganed down the moonlit slope of the roof. Viv scrabbled at the slates as she started to slither downwards. Her scream coincided with the thump of the yard-long tile hitting the flagstones three storeys below us, was obliterated in the echo of its impact.

In slow-motion, mouth open I watched her slide, full of horror, the dread she'd follow the ridge tile over the roof's edge in a long fall to instant death. But it didn't happen. Viv's sliding figure came to an abrupt halt. I gasped in disbelief, heard Blum's drawn out, 'Jeeesuss…'

Viv's arms stretched wide, her woollen gloved hands pressed the slates. Her right knee was bent and the edge of her motorcycle boot below it was inches from the void, but her left boot was braced against the inside edge of a gutter. She was stuck, thank God. But the pitch of the roof was too steep for her to raise herself, creep back up, not with the rucksack and rope on her back. And the slates glistened with the frost that caught us out. If she moved, she'd fall, die.

Twenty-five feet from us, her face, encircled by the black, woollen balaclava, was pushed against the coil of rope between her left shoulder and the slates. At an awkward angle, her frightened eyes looked up towards us.

Her gasp misted in freezing air, 'I can't get back up!'

Blum's voice was hushed, but urgent,' Don't! Don't move at all.'

I swapped a look with Blum. Between us was the yard gap where the absent ridge tile once lay in its bed of crumbled mortar. We crouched on similar tiles, no idea how safe either of them now were. I feared we might roll down, dislodge Viv from her precarious position, the three of us falling to our premature deaths.

My guts somersaulted.

'Get the rope down to me,' Viv said.

Blum came straight back at her, a tremor in his voice, 'You won't able to tie yourself on. I'm going down for help. We need the fire brigade.'

Viv was emphatic, 'No!'

'Don't be daft. I'll be as quick as I can.'

She was even more insistent. 'No!'

I could see Blum's anxiety. His hand went behind his head, feeling at his scalp as his mind raced, sought a solution. 'I've got to. We can't do it. Not with me like this. I won't be able to…'

Viv snapped, 'Listen!'

Blum eased himself upright, winced with pain, 'I've got to get help.'

'No. We have to do it on our own.'

Blum was ready to go, 'It's no good.'

Viv was angry, 'For Christ's sake, listen!'

*

That was all to come. They were the most frightening minutes of my life and I'd never go through them again, no event for a million pounds.

In the weeks after Blum's release, I was excited at the reaction to our dossier on the wrongdoings at H.M. Borstal Havershawe. The police had confirmed to the Press they were making inquiries. Questions had been asked in the House of Commons by two of Lancashire's MPs. Prison reformers wrung their hands in articles over the shortcomings of the Borstal system.

To Blum, Viv and me, though, more important was the news that Travis had been suspended from duty and now helping police with their inquiries. The police investigation was two pronged: his violence to young inmates and the theft and sale of Borstal supplies, some of it valuable workshop equipment and machine tools, disposed of at cut prices to the engineering firm in Blackpool. Of course, there'd been no police progress over the burglary and theft of a sack full of prize fruit and vegetables at Travis's home...

We learned more detail about Travis's troubles from our visits to Fozzy. Travis took time off with an unspecified illness following the theft of his vegetables. On his return, there were detectives at Havershawe. Word was that Travis would never again work at Havershawe. And a rumour Mrs Travis walked out on him, with Trixie, when she heard the allegations of violence.

Lads at 'Havvy' were interviewed by Lancashire CID. Tales of Travis's ill-treatment started to seep out. Once frightened lads made statements, and, after the publicity, a number of ex-inmates went to the police to make allegations. Fozzy was buoyed by Travis's removal from his daily life. He told detectives about his beating in the tool shed, lesser assaults. Fozzy, Delly and other lads were examined by a police surgeon.

Fozzy had another medical appointment. Viv's opinion when she first saw him was correct. He'd never had any corrective, surgical treatment, it was overdue. Blum was delighted, I was impressed, when Viv approached Mr Farid 'Freddie' Roop Singh, a specialist in such conditions at her hospital, aroused his interest. She told him about Fozzy's wrongful conviction, his difficulties making himself understood.

Freddie Roop insisted he examine Fozzy at Havershawe. Fozzy was intrigued by his crimson turban, the discovery he carried a Sikh dagger in his sock. An unsure Fozzy said Mr Roop told him he used his gold-trimmed dagger to do operations. We laughed, but poor Fozzy was nervous. Mr Roop arranged X-rays and Fozzy was escorted to Preston Royal Infirmary by two officers. Despite his unease over surgery, the prospect of correction for his disability did wonders for his confidence. It focused his mind on his future rather than his fractured past. Useful, for he'd heard it was possible his release on probation might be approved the following year.

On the day Fozzy's news came, I heard Travis had been committed for trial on charges of assault and theft, already dismissed by Her Majesty's prison service.

In the months after Blum's release, I came back to Lydiate as often as possible. The job took more of my time as Geoff Sillitoe entrusted me with stories needing more 'nous', as he put it. He was pleased I volunteered to help him on press nights to learn how the paper was 'put to bed' for printing. Sometimes I stood in for him on the news desk, so he could nip off fishing, or cover events for the angling press, often as a stringer for the Manchester tabloids.

Elaine was studying for banking exams, which could mean promotion, so our spats over the little time I spent with her were fewer, but she never missed a chance to disapprove of Blum, my time spent with him. Often I lied to conceal visits home, told her I was chasing non-existent stories for *The Sentinel* when I was with Sandra, or drinking.

Sandra and I met as often as we could. A quarter bottle of Bells scotch for my landlady ensured a blind eye was turned when my '*cariad*' opted to stay overnight -- if we couldn't contrive to spend the night together without Kitty's knowledge. But Kitty didn't often miss a trick, got to expect her whisky to share over late morning tea with her next-door-neighbour, Mrs O'Carroll. When we weren't in bed together, Sandra and I would drive out to pubs in her white '66 Mini Cooper S, remoter ones in the West Pennines, sometimes the Ribble Valley.

Now and then, if I had a 'night job' to cover some evening diary event, she'd come with me. It was often a good way to get free drinks. I regretted it sometimes when tipsy after buckshee glasses of plonk, she'd spice-up talk with strangers, invent stories about me. One night I had to accept the congratulations of an amateur dramatics producer, delighted my girlfriend was expecting twins. And she told the chairwoman of a parish council my dad was a member of the House of Lords. Often, I'd return to Quinn Street to find she'd checked Kitty was in The Packet, sneaked in the back way. I'd find her in bed reading, listening to radio, the bed warmed by hot water bottles. I loved to come back to her at the flat. There were a lot of laughs, a lot of sex. Secrecy added to our excitement.

Elaine hadn't repeated her mad allegations about me and Viv and the single time Sandra asked me about the girl on the motorbike, I told her it was Viv. She laughed, told me about Geoff Sillitoe's vivid, exaggerated description of the encounter to *Sentinel* gossips.

Blum split his time that winter between helping with the game-shooting season at the Tarlscough estate, working with Ted, the gamekeeper, and flogging, bit by bit, gear from Pygon's Farm. Uncle Walter died. At the funeral, Blum told me his mam had been hit hard by the loss of her half-brother. He felt obliged to try to make up for the loss to their household of Walter's pension.

My anxiety over Blum getting caught, locked up again, persisted, but he assured me he kept away from former customers, sold stuff away from his old patch. He used the Chev for transport, but soon spent some of his illicit cash on a Bedford Viva van from Ormskirk motor auctions, in the interests of petrol costs, to be less conspicuous than the driver of a turquoise Yankee car. I asked how he could afford the van. I was uncomfortable when he admitted he'd told Viv I'd lent him the money. I hated his lies to her, but let it go. I couldn't think of a better way he could explain the outlay. In a few months he'd made up the money spent on the van, added several hundred pounds to the fund to help his mam stay at May Bank View.

To help him to raise cash for the renewal of the lease, I became the holder of a little white card not much bigger than a library ticket called a shotgun certificate. My respectable reference to get it was a conservative town councillor called Harold Fairbrass. I'd been introduced to him by Geoff Sillitoe when I started to cover council meetings. Fairbrass, a champion of small business, was one of Geoff's contacts, the chairman of the parks, gardens and leisure committee, a regular at The Packet, owner of a timber yard in the next street to mine.

On the evening a police officer was due to interview me about my certificate application, I gifted Kitty a generous half-bottle of scotch. Rather than share it with Mrs O'Carroll, I encouraged her to sample it straight away. I didn't want any interruptions during my time with the copper. And I wanted my licence to possess, buy and sell shotguns kept quiet. When the bobby turned up, Kitty was spark out on her sofa downstairs, Hughie Green's *Opportunity Knocks* blaring up through the house.

The officer was matter-of-fact, asked few questions. He asked how many guns I had a mind to buy. I had a mad urge to declare I had maybe a dozen I could lay hands on. 'You can add five army pistols if you like and I know where I can get a Sten gun and ammo if you lend a police frogman's outfit.'

Instead, I said, 'Just the one.'

He asked where I would keep it if my application was approved, seemed happy with the security of the lock on my 1930s wardrobe, Kitty told me had been made at her grandfather's cabinet maker's workshop in Caernarvon. Two weeks later, the certificate arrived by post.

One morning, at Pygon's Farm, Blum and I took to pieces and cleaned three of the smartest double-barrel twelve-bore guns and he drove me back to my flat in the van. In an almost Dickensian gunsmith's shop in a ginnel behind the town hall, I unloaded my old cricket bag, sold all three for £680. We were delighted.

At the end of January, to mark the game-shooting season's end, Blum, Viv and I were invited to stay at Ted the gamekeeper's place. It was a good weekend with Ted and

Marion, but a small incident led to that night I would never repeat for any money you cared to name.

Chapter 13
Throddie and Memory Gaps

BLUM, VIV AND I arrived at the head keeper's house on Tarlscough estate on a Friday night. After a fish and chip supper and a couple of pints at the Scarisbrick Arms, Marion chased us off to bed ahead of an early start. Next day was the last pheasant shoot of the season. The three of us would join others beating through covert after covert on a 'cocks only' day, where the number of male pheasants was reduced ahead of their breeding season.

The occasion was the traditional day for regular beaters to shoot the landowner's birds while regular syndicate shooters left their guns at home and spent the day beating. Ted needed us three to replace the selfish shooters too mean, or lazy, to give up a day so their loyal beaters could have the perk of a day's shooting

A bright, cold morning found us assembled in the yard at Home Farm for Ted's informal gun safety and batting order address. To laughter and encouragement, stood on the midden wall, he mocked the absentee shooters who'd sent apologies for not turning up.

'Norman bloody Tisdall phoned to say he couldn't turn out. "Oh, why not, Norman?" I said. "Pressure of work," he said. "Sorry to hear that, Norman," I said. "Take it easy, la'. It's not bloody fair expecting you to prop up the bar at the bloody golf club all on your bloody own seven days a bloody week."' Ted grinned, waited for the laughter to fade, '"Bloody hell, Norman," I said, "Christ knows how you find the bloody time to count your bloody money."'

With a few character assassinations notched up, he specified what could, and could not be, shot.

'Cocks only means what it says: cocks bloody only. Any of you bloody cowboys shoots a bloody hen bird, he buys everyone a bloody drink. No bloody excuses. And leave any rabbits and hares a-bloody-lone -- I don't want any bugger's bloody legs shot off, not that it'd make much bloody difference when it comes to the way you shape your-bloody-selves... So, no bloody four-legged ground game. And talking of four legs, anyone sees a bloody fox, shoot the bastard. If you bloody nail it, everyone buys you a bloody drink!'

Half-way through the day, Marion drove Ted's van out with a crock of her celebrated hot-pot and an urn of stewed tea. The last shot was fired when the sun started to sink towards the Irish Sea and we trekked back to Home Farm to count the bag. Miraculously, not a single hen pheasant was shot. No foxes, either, to Ted's disappointment. By dusk we settled in for the boozy end to beaters' day at the Scarisbrick Arms. We sat with Ted by the fire. He pulled up a high back chair, pulled off his wellies, toasted his feet before blazing coals.

Neville, the scouse under keeper, came over with a tray with the first round paid for by Ted. He thrust a tumbler of Cutty Sark whisky into his boss's hand. 'E'are, chief, get that down yer.'

Ted gave a sigh of satisfaction, raised his tumbler to the flames, 'To the end of a bloody good bloody season...'

Marion appeared at his shoulder, 'You go easy on that stuff, Ted Crossman.'

Everyone, but Ted laughed. He turned to her, 'Christ All-bloody-Mighty. Me bloody lips 'ent bloody touched it. First time I've put me bloody feet up more than a bloody minute since bloody October. Don't I deserve a bloody night off and a lay in -- Bloody Norah!'

With a huff of displeasure, Ted turned back to the fire.

Marion leaned over the back of his chair, 'I don't want you lying stinking drunk in bed in the morning. I need you for something.'

'Ooooh!' said someone.

'Aye, aye!' said another.

'She don't want yer with that brewer's whatsit!' jeered a third.

Other ribald remarks and merriment ran around the company.

Marion turned to them, 'You can keep your remarks to yourselves and all, you mucky sods.'

Ted grinned, again raised his tumbler.

Marion winked to the company, 'I meant after that.'

Laughter erupted.

Ted turned back to her, 'You bloody what?'

'I'm still waiting for you to knock up that new aviary. You know, the one you were going to make last August Bank Holiday; the one you were definitely going to do New Year's Day -- before you wrapped yourself round a bottle of that stuff.'

'Bloody hell, love, it can wait a bloody day or two, can't it?'

'I've waited long enough. So have my birds.'

She pecked him on the cheek, 'Enjoy your drink, love. I'll come back after for them who need a lift home.'

She headed for the door, Ted swallowed his whisky in a defiant gulp, 'Bloody birds. Bloody hell. Whose bloody round is it?'

*

I had only sketchy recall of sharing the back of the van with the other drunks as Ted sang rugby songs. It seemed I heard Ted's loud tuneless voice from the van's passenger seat, the next minute that same voice bellowed up the stairs of the head keeper's house and daylight pushed through the curtains.

'Get your bloody arse downstairs, or I'll scoff your bloody throddie.'

'Throddie?' What? I peered at my watch on the bedside table. It was ten past eight. Ted was an early riser, but was this his idea of a lie in? I got out of bed, dressed, and after a quick trip to the bathroom, went downstairs. Despite last night's skinful of bitter I was only a touch hung-over. For once I'd resisted the hard stuff, but Blum and Viv'd joined Ted's efforts to empty a bottle of Cutty Sark.

I was surprised to see Viv, Blum and Ted, heads together at the kitchen table, sketching out something on a sheet of paper. Fag smoke and bacon fumes filled the kitchen. Marion turned away from mixing poultry mash, gave me a smile.

'Sleep well, love?'

'Great, thanks.'

Blum looked over, 'Hope you're sober enough for a bit of woodwork.'

'Me?'

Viv laughed, 'We talked about it last night.'

I bluffed, 'Oh, yeah, that.'

Looks were swapped. Blum snorted a laugh, '"Oh, yeah that?" -- Ha.'

Viv said, 'You don't remember a word, do you?'

'We had to put you to blummin' bed. Can't you remember?'

I realised I couldn't. I hated the memory gaps -- I was defensive, 'It wasn't me on the whisky.'

'Ale gets you drunker than bloody whisky any bloody day of the bloody week,' Ted winked at me, jerked his head at Marion, 'Been telling her that since the bloody day I bloody met her.'

Marion scoffed. 'Fiddlesticks!'

He grinned at me, turned to Marion, 'You believe what you bloody want, love, but its scientific bloody fact.'

Blum put his arm around Viv.

'He had a fair bit to tell us about that girl of his up in the hills, didn't he?'

I felt a sudden embarrassment. What had I said?

Blum went on, 'Sounds like you're smitten to me.'

Viv protested, 'Don't be mean.' She turned to me, 'You talked about her a bit, that's all.'

Blum laughed. Marion said, 'I was the only one sober in this house last night, love, and you've nowt to be embarrassed about. Sounds a grand girl to me.'

I'd thought a lot about Sandra and me in recent weeks. How far from the truth was Blum? There was a growing intensity about my feelings for her, I wished she were here. I'd known Ted and Marion since I was a boy, felt easy with them. I knew Sandra would have reached that stage in an hour or two.

Marion smiled at me and, cloth in hand, opened the Rayburn stove, took out a dish. 'Let's get some breakfast down you.'

Ted pulled the roll-up from his mouth, jabbed it towards me, 'If you don't bloody fancy it, la', push it my bloody way.'

'What is it, again?'

The dish was lined with a Greyed substance. Laid across it were half a dozen rashers of crisped fat bacon.

'Bloody throdkin,' said Ted, 'Best bloody thing that ever came out of the bloody Fylde; that bloody-scrag-end-bloody-bit of the county of bloody Lancashire…'

Marion was straight in, 'I beg your pardon.'

Ted smiled, 'Apart from that bloody missus o' mine, o' course.'

'Don't let my brothers hear you knocking God's country, Ted Crossman.'

Ted snorted. Marion pulled her tongue at him as he turned back to his sheet of paper.

I stared at my dish. Marion slid a knife and fork to me, 'Fat bacon on a bed of oatmeal, plenty of pepper. Salty bacon fat seeps right through.'

My stomach rumbled at the smell of bacon, but I preferred mine with eggs, especially after a heavy night. I was polite, but wary. 'Sounds nice, smells nice...'

Blum noticed my hesitation as I picked up the knife and fork, 'Best blummin' hangover cure going is throddie.'

Viv added, 'Too right. Why are we so full of energy and raring to go?'

'If that's the case, love,' Marion pointed at the door, 'Get yourself and them two lummox out o' my kitchen and get cracking on that aviary.'

Ted, Blum and Viv sloped outside. My Throddie was tasty. Ten minutes later, I joined them in Marion's huddle of sheds, wire runs and aviaries that housed her ever-increasing collection of poultry and fancy birds. Restored by my fatty breakfast, I was ready to help. We built up the new aviary from a base of planks. Ted and Blum measured and sawed to length the uprights, braces and top pieces. Viv and I nailed them together. While Blum and Ted bickered over the pitch of the aviary's roof, we used fence wire staples to cover the frame and door with chicken wire. We all mucked in to secure the final compromise of a roof by tacking on a sheet of bitumen felt. To finish, we covered the floor with shavings, installed low perches, filled feeders and drinkers with water, seed and grit.

Marion came out from making Sunday dinner to inspect our work. Ted appeared with a cardboard box as she moved round the new aviary and we awaited her verdict.

Ted was impatient for approval, 'What do you reckon, love? Not bloody bad, eh? They'll be snug as bloody bugs in that.'

Marion considered, nodded, 'Aye, it'll do.'

Ted beamed, presented her with the box. She opened the door of the aviary, stepped inside. She set the box down and released, one by one, a dozen dainty painted quail.

'At least these little lovelies won't have to share with my budgies anymore.'

*

Talk at the Crossmans' dinner table covered the game-shooting season gone and its highlights. Ted had a marvellous grasp of the characters that came to work, shoot or beat at Tarlscough Estate; a huge knowledge of their private lives, foibles and secrets-- stories about them all. In another time, place, he could have been a comedian, or a gossip columnist, perhaps a blackmailer. His stories had us helpless with laughter.

When talk turned to the year ahead, it was Marion who silenced the table when she reminded Blum his casual work on the shoot ended with the game season. He couldn't be kept on for the coming months, 'What will you do, Davy?'

Blum's pudding spoon stopped midway to his mouth, 'Ha, don't worry about me, Marion.'

Marion was blunt, 'You're big enough to look after yourself, lad, but what about your mam? Our Nancy'll need you to bring in a decent wage, more so now Walter's gone.'

Blum took time that weekend to remind me of his concern for his mother, the lease at May Bank View. I knew more than Marion and Ted, certainly Viv. There was an awkward silence. Blum's glance met mine for a moment.

Whizzing through my mind were my worries about the stolen goods at Pygon's Farm. I was committed to their early sale, if only to get shut of them, keep Blum from being locked up, and I'd made that promise to help. Clearing the lot for whatever we could safely sell it for was overdue; the lease on May Bank expired next New Year's Eve.

Blum's spoon remained in mid-air, 'I've saved some money working here. Now I've got the van I'll take anything, anywhere, for payment. Kind of a one-man transport company, like.'

He looked at Viv. She nodded her support. Perhaps they'd discussed it, I didn't know. But I knew he still hadn't told her the truth of his family situation.

Ted pointed his roll-up at Blum, 'Bloody good idea, la'. I'll see what I can do with the bloody boss,' He looked to Marion, 'You can put the word in at the bloody chicken farm, can't you love?'

''Course I can.'

'That's good of you, both of you, thanks.'

Marion looked unsure, 'That's all we can do, mind, Davy. Are you sure you can make a wage?'

Ted was expansive, 'Give the lad a bloody chance, love, you bloody know he'll bloody do it.'

'Don't worry, Marion,' Blum said, 'I'll make enough to look after mam.'

'That'll do me, love.'

She stood, 'Now, who wants a glass of my damson gin?'

Ted raised his hand, glanced at the shelf clock. 'We'll have a walk down the belts first, love. Then have a do at them bloody woodies. The dogs'll be ready for it.' He stood up, 'We'll bloody shift the damson bloody gin when it's dark.'

We put on coats and wellies. Ted explained we'd walk the belts of trees that led to a twelve-acre wood of mixed deciduous and fir trees. We'd take any chances to pot the vermin every gamekeeper waged war on each day. Then wait in the lee side of the wood to shoot woodpigeon as they slipped in through the tree tops at dusk to roost.

Ted took two boxes of twelve-bore cartridges from a kitchen cupboard, tipped the contents into the pockets of his tweed coat. He took his old Greener double-barrelled gun from the assorted firearms propped behind the kitchen door, broke it open and passed the Signalman's four-ten shotgun to Blum. I couldn't help staring at it as the day he stole it flashed into my mind.

Ted picked up a single-barrelled version of Blum's shotgun, addressed me, 'How about you, la'? Another bloody four-ten here.'

I recalled that dream-like July day, deafening gunshots inside that tiny cottage, before Blum destroyed all traces of the Signalman's existence. Was his memory of that day as vivid as mine?

Ted thrust the single-barrel gun at me, 'Too much bloody puddin', eh? Wake up, la'.'

'Er, sorry…I'll just watch, thanks, Ted.'

'Take it, have a shot,' said Blum.

'I'm fine just watching.'

'You get blummin' loads coming into that wood? Sure you don't want a go?'

'Deffo. I'm just a spectator.'

Ted laughed, 'In that bloody case,' He picked up a game bag from the kitchen floor, dropped in an extra box of cartridges, 'You can bloody carry this and whatever we bloody shoot.'

I took the bag from him, caught his eye, grinned, 'Bloody fine by me.'

He laughed, turned to Viv. 'You want to take the bloody thing, love?'

She took the four-ten from Ted, 'Yep. I don't mind.'

Blum nodded to Ted, 'Give her a chance, she'll outshoot you.'

Viv laughed.

Ted winked at her, 'Aye, she might bloody outshoot you as-bloody-well.'

*

Ted's two Labradors and cocker spaniel romped around us as we strolled out on to the estate. Blum potted a grey squirrel as it scampered up an ash tree, Ted pulled off a long shot at a crow, but missed a second. When it flapped away squawking, he matched its ill-temper with a splenetic torrent of all the swear words. For a moment, he thought our merriment was judgement on his shooting, until Viv had him belly-laughing when she mimicked word-for-word his foul-mouthed outburst.

When we stopped for a smoke, Ted was telling us about the habits of carrion crows when there came the 'chack, chack' of a magpie. In a fluid movement, Ted stuck his roll-up in his mouth, spun towards the sound of the bird, closed his gun. I glimpsed it slipping away through the tree tops on the other side of the belt, as Ted mounted and swung the twelve-bore, fired. The magpie checked, but didn't drop, fluttered to a lower branch. Ted was about to use his second barrel, but Blum shouted, 'Don't shoot!'

A bemused Ted turned to Blum, his gun still pointed up into the air, 'Why the bloody hell not?'

But Blum pushed through dead bramble and rhododendron bushes in the direction of the tree where, that moment, I saw the magpie flutter down. It looked like Ted fluffed the shot, only a few pellets or less had struck the bird in a non-vital place.

'Is there someone bloody in there, or summat?' said Ted.' I'm buggered if I bloody saw anyone.'

Viv called, 'Blum? What're you doing?'

Blum came back through the with the Signalman's gun in his left hand, the other against his chest, holding a flapping magpie.

'God in bloody Heaven, I could've bloody finished it with a second bloody barrel. What you bloody doing cuddlin' a bloody magpie?'

Blum thrust his gun into my hands, 'Here. You lot crack on with the woodies. I've got to get back.'

He turned to an open-mouthed Ted, moved away. 'Sorry, Ted. I need to see Marion.'

He trotted across the stubble towards the head keeper's house.

'Has being locked up sent him round the bloody bend? What's he bloody doing bloody nurse- maiding bloody vermin?'

He shook his head, whistled the dogs, set off to the roost wood.

Viv and I guessed in an instant. I looked at her.

'For Fozzy, you reckon?'

She laughed, 'Who else?'

*

The roost-shooting was successful. Ted's dozen, Viv's seven and my own three plump woodpigeon weighed heavy in the game bag. The bulkhead lights at the back of the house lit up the yard when we returned soon after nightfall. Blum and Marion stood talking by the new aviary. Its appearance was transformed.

Ted marched into the yard, approached what now looked like a big, wooden packing crate, 'What the bloody hellfire have you bloody done to it?'

Three sides of the aviary were now covered in sheets of plywood and hardboard. One side facing the field was open mesh. The door now included a hatch like those in prison cell doors with a wide ledge. Peepholes were drilled through the plywood at face height.

Ted turned to Marion and Blum, 'If you said you wanted a bloody Punch and bloody Judy show, I'd've bloody made one. God All bloody Mighty, where the bloody hell are the bloody quail? Bloody...

Marion cut in, 'Stop fussing, Ted Crossman.'

Ted bellowed, 'Don't bloody tell me it's for that bloody magpie.'

'Of course it's for the magpie. No need to shout.'

Ted blustered, 'Bloody hell…Christ, Almighty…Bloody Norah…Have you bloody taken leave of your bloody senses as well as…?'

He pointed at Blum, but Marion took his arm, steered him to the back door.

'Stop getting yourself in a state. Have a whisky and I'll tell you all about it.'

Viv looked at Blum, I could see she was taken with the idea, 'It's for Fozzy, isn't it?'

Blum smiled, 'It's his birthday, seventh of March. I wondered what we could get for him, a present, like.'

She clapped her hands together, 'Brilliant. Great idea.'

I laughed, 'It's a cracking plan, but…' I was already seeing problems.

'We're doing it,' declared Blum.

He pulled a woodpigeon from the game bag, fished out his pocket knife. In a moment, he opened it, fingered out its guts and internal organs.

Viv was at the hatch, ready to open it, look inside. 'Will it survive, though?'

With a bloodied hand, Viv stopped her opening the hatch.

'If anyone can blummin' make it right, it's Marion,' he said, 'She says it'll be fine. But it's got to be kept shut up. It can't even see who feeds it.'

'Why not?' said Viv.

'Not much fun for the magpie,' I said.

Blum picked out some piece of the woodpigeon guts, chucked it aside. 'It can't get used to any human until Fozzy gets hold of it. With a bit o' luck, it'll take to him soon enough.'

He opened the hatch, dropped in the woodpigeon's innards, snapped it shut.

Marion saw us off in the Chev. Blum and Viv were to drop me off at the station to get back for work next day. Mellowed by a few drinks, Ted had fallen asleep on the kitchen couch, but not before Marion relayed to him what Blum had told her about Travis, Fozzy and Click the magpie.

Blum said, 'If you and Ted change your minds about the bird, I'll find somewhere else for it.'

'You're all right, love, it'll be fine here.' She kissed us all goodbye, 'That Fozzy lad deserves a bit of light in his life and we're glad to help.'

Viv looked confused, 'Is that what Ted said?'

'No, love, that's what I said. His last words to me were, "Tell the bloody three of them -- one bloody word gets out about us giving bed and bloody breakfast to a bloody verminous bloody magpie and I'll shoot the bloody lot of them, bloody magpie bloody included."'

Marion smiled at Viv, 'He's a blathering so-an'-so, I know, but his heart's in the right place.'

Blum and Viv came on to the platform as the train out of Liverpool drew in.

'This magpie, let's keep it a surprise, eh? No blabbing, no blummin' hinting, next time we see Foz.'

I boarded the train. 'Just one thing, if Fozzy's birthday's in March and he won't get out 'til later on, how can we give him his present? We can't just march in on visiting day with a flamin' magpie.'

I closed the train door and pulled down the window as it started to pull away. 'Have you thought about that?'

Blum grinned, raised his hand, shouted, 'We'll get it to him by special delivery.'

Chapter 14
Why the Hell Not?

I THOUGHT IT was a daft joke, a throwaway line, until the next time we visited Fozzy at Havershawe.

Fozzy had no further news about Travis, but we were delighted to hear he'd have the first of his corrective operations in a few days' time. Mr Freddie Roop would undertake the first surgery at Preston Royal Infirmary, Fozzy would be a patient for several days.

When we left, Viv was upset. She'd hoped Fozzy's operation would take place at her own hospital. 'I could've settled him in and I know Mr Roop would've let me go down to theatre with him.'

Blum put his arm around her, 'Don't worry. He'll be right.'

'He's so nervous, though.'

'He's been through worse things than an operation or two, hasn't he? When they've fixed his mouth his life can only be better, eh?'

Since his release, Blum and Viv visited Fozzy most weeks, while I went when the job allowed. All together this time, I suggested a drink at The Twa Ducks pub where I'd spied on Travis and the Blackpool engineer the previous autumn. Conversation continued on the subject of Fozzy's operation.

I bought a round, passed Viv her drink, 'Will we be able to see him in hospital?'

'I don't think so. I've seen prisoners in private wards a few times, but they always have a prison officer with them, day and night, never noticed any visitors. Thing is, he probably won't be able to talk 'cause of the stitches and dressings in his mouth.'

'Best leave it 'til he's back at Havvy,' said Blum.

'Could we hand the magpie over then, when he has the op?' I said, 'What do you reckon?'

'Ha. With him cuffed-up to some blummin' screw?'

'Well, I can't see any other way of getting it to him, unless we wait 'til they let him out.'

'Nor can I,' said Viv

Blum laughed, 'I can.'

Viv beat me to it by a split-second, 'How?'

'Yeah, how?' I said, 'Stick it in a box with a bow and post it?'

Blum exhaled a stream of smoke 'Nah, better than that. I deliver it to him, in Havvy, the night before his birthday.'

Viv and I spoke as one, 'What?'

When he told us, I was amazed. So was Viv.

Too loud, she said, 'Break into Havershawe?'

Blum and I looked round in alarm, but the few locals stood at the bar seemed not to have heard.

Blum snaked his hand around the back of his head, his voice low, 'I can do it all right...' He drummed his fingers on the back of his head, looked straight at me, 'I might need a bit of help, mind.'

The idea attracted me, but the customary response came to my lips, 'Are you sure about this?'

Before Blum could reply, Viv said, 'We've got to do it, Fozzy'll be chuffed to bits.'

Blum faced her, 'No, not you. Sorry.'

Viv bristled, 'You what? Why the hell not?'

'Too risky.'

'What's that meant to mean?'

Blum checked over his shoulder for eavesdroppers, 'You heard what I said.'

Viv was furious. When her voice reached top note with her argument to be included, the locals turned to watch. Wary of information slipping out, Blum slammed down his half-drunk pint, strode out of the pub. Viv went after him like a terrier. I swallowed the rest of my pint, put our glasses on the bar, smiled at the curious drinkers, ''Night.'

Blum and Viv stood by the Chev, faces inches apart. Viv was winning on decibels, but Blum stubbornly repeated his earlier verdict.

'Funny how it wasn't too risky for me to burgle Travis's place when you were locked up.'

'That was different.'

'No, it wasn't.'

'It's a government building, a blummin' prison. If we get nabbed...Do you want to lose your job?'

I butted in, 'Perhaps the whole idea's ...Well, a bit ambitious.'

I was ignored. I glanced back at the pub, where two customers peered out, pints in hand. I snatched the car keys from Blum's hand, slipped into the Chev, started up, rolled down the window.

'Shut up and get in, the pair of you. We're going.'

In the back seat, their argument continued most of the way home. Viv tried every way she could to make her case to be included. Blum wouldn't budge on his view. Each tried to recruit my support, but I declined to ally myself with either. Now and then, they lapsed into sullen silence, then the arguments would be repeated. I spent the interludes asking myself whether I should back out of the venture myself. Work was going well, I felt I had a future, easily destroyed if we were caught, but the truth was the idea excited me. I reflected on the times I'd followed Blum into danger of some sort, or other. Every time I'd been so anxious, sometimes even to the point of shaking with nerves. Always, though, when danger had passed, I was exhilarated by the sheer visceral thrill of what we'd done. I felt that same rush of euphoria when we went AWOL on our first day at school as the night Viv and I burgled Travis's bungalow.

I drove the Chev down the sloping dual carriageway from Ormskirk, asked where we were going.

'The Soldier,' Blum said.

'Home,' said Viv.

115

Like a chauffeur, I looked in the rear-view mirror. I caught Blum's eye and he nodded his grudging deferment to Viv.

Outside her flat she said goodnight to me as Blum made a move to accompany her. She slammed the car door in his face, hurried to her front door.

Over a pint at the Soldier, our conversation was desultory. After a long silence as he tore an empty fag packet into tiny pieces and sprinkled them into the ashtray, he looked my way and said, 'Do you think I'm right? You know, about Viv not coming?'

I lowered my glass, shrugged, stayed neutral, 'It's something for you to decide, not me.'

I was concerned Blum's whim about the magpie for Fozzy, this fall-out with Viv, meant his energies were diverted from the more vital need to save his mam's house.

*

Back on the paper I half-expected a call from Viv. I thought she might try to get me on her side, to lobby Blum to relent. Instead, I was phoned on near a daily basis by Blum at the *Sentinel* newsroom. Of course, I always had to ring him back. Once Blum had an idea in his head it almost always verged on obsession. To get the magpie to Fozzy for his birthday was no different, except for one factor.

He'd often kept details of his plans to himself until the last possible time. Now, he was on the phone , time and again, to talk over every aspect of the venture. I paid little attention to the shifting details. Did he now believe it was too ambitious? Did he want me to find a fault that would give him the chance to cop out?

When I was next home, I tested his commitment in the still room at Pygon's Farm. Blum checked over some coils of nylon rope, a vital part of our planned invasion of Havershawe. I wanted him to concentrate what still had to be sold, but he chattered about the convalescence of the magpie in Marion's care.

Fozzy was in hospital after his operation two days earlier. Though Viv and Blum had spent no time together since the Twa Ducks bust-up, they kept up appearances when they visited Fozzy. Viv rang me at work the day before with news from Mr Roop that everything had gone well and Fozzy was still laid-up. There would be no visit to Havershawe that afternoon, which depressed Blum. He wasn't happy either that Viv had phoned me, not him, about Fozzy's op. It was obvious he missed her.

I interrupted him, 'Look, have you thought about leaving the magpie at the Havershawe farm? Fozzy'll still be working there, won't he? He'd soon find it and it wouldn't be half as risky as getting into the dormitory in the main...'

Blum was tetchy, 'Don't you think I've blummin' well thought about that?'

'No, but it does seem...'

Blum dropped a coil of rope, 'The farm's the weak point in the whole place. That's why it's the only part of Havershawe that's got fences wired up with alarms. The only other alarms are on the offices and that, on the ground floor, and two fire escape doors.'

'Are you sure about that?'

'Dead sure,' he said, irritated, 'We had a lad in Havvy, a factory-breaker from over Nelson way. He spent half his time trying to work out the best way to get out the place. He knew every window -- every blummin' keyhole in that place. It was like doing some sort of crossword puzzle, or something, for him, a kind of hobby, like. He showed me the alarms round the fields and the glasshouses. Try to get through them and you've had it. Same blummin' problem if you tried to get in or out anywhere at ground level.'

'So how are we going to get in?'

'From the woods, on the other side of the big lawn where they have the cricket. Up and over the high fence, in then out, between the patrols. No alarms to worry about, just...' He stared at me for a moment. 'I thought I'd gone through all this?'

'Erm…I don't think so.'

'I did, on the phone to you at work.'

'Yeah? Can't say I remember.'

He exhaled, shook his head in frustration.

I pulled out my Number 6, tossed one to him. I sat on top of the safe and pulled up my feet, my back against the lime washed wall. I wondered if revealing his plan in detail would make him reconsider the obvious risks, 'We'd better go through it again then, eh?'

We sat and smoked as Blum went through his method to get in and out of Havershawe.

'Have you blummin' got it now?'

'Sounds alright to me, that's if you're right about that broken window latch in the bog and everything.'

Blum was defensive, 'I am, dead right.'

He said no more, picked up the end of the coiled rope, twisted it in his fingers, stared at it. He wasn't his usual confident, excited self over the prospect of action.

'You don't seem sure,' I said, 'About the whole thing, I mean.'

There was no response. I tried again.

'Look, if you think all this is too much it doesn't really matter, does it? Fozzy can have his magpie when he comes out.'

He was silent.

I stepped on to thin ice, 'It's a great idea, but all the while you're dwelling on this magpie business, you could be flogging off what's in here and getting more cash for your mam's lease. Time's going on.'

I wanted to give him a good excuse to scupper the whole venture without losing face.

'I'll get the money. You know I will.'

There was another silence.

'What is it then? I know something's eating at you?'

He looked at me. 'I meant what I said to Viv. Thing is, we can't blummin' do it without her.'

'You've just told me how we'd do it?'

'But ... It needs all three of us to do it right. We need someone else with us and Viv's the only one I trust'

'Then tell her.'

'I'm worried about her -- in case summat goes blummin' wrong.'

'You've told me more than once, she's scared of nowt. Give her the chance to say whether or not she still wants in on it.'

He fiddled with the rope.

'Let her make the decision instead of you.'

Blum nodded. He seemed brighter. 'I'll go and meet her from work.'

I don't know what was said between them, but with Viv and Blum back together, the tempo of the preparation stepped up that same day. Viv bubbled with enthusiasm. That night we abandoned our usual, favourite pubs where it was difficult to avoid people we knew, went to The Ship on the canal at Haskayne. A bitter wind sliced across the flat moss land, kept even regulars at home. We had the back room to ourselves. Blum revealed he'd made a reconnaissance trip to Havershawe days before and climbed a tree, equipped with his grandfather's Great War field glasses. We discussed equipment, worked out a timeline, estimating as far as we could how long each stage of the entry and exit of Havershawe might take. My excitement mounted.

Chapter 15
Ice Skates and Fishing Line

TEN DAYS LATER was the evening before Fozzy's birthday. By the light of a near full- moon, Blum and I loaded the gear into the Bedford van at Pygon's Farm. The stuff we took, the rucksacks and balaclava helmets, reminded me of a night at Cyril Clegg's place. This would be another commando-style mission, but far riskier than tipping that despicable farmer into the biggest trouble of his life.

With everything checked, Blum brought from the still room a box which had taken him and Viv a couple of evenings to make. It was about fifteen inches long, ten wide, made of thick card with a hinged top lid and reinforced corners. Two rows of air holes were punched along all four sides. He slipped inside it a folded piece of paper.

'Note for Foz, all anonymous, good wishes, like.'

Pasted to the top of the box was a small card in Viv's neat writing, 'One for Joy! Happy Birthday!'

'Viv's brainwave, that.'

'I don't get it.'

'You must've heard that old rhyme thing? Numbers of magpies?'

I frowned, 'Isn't it one for sorrow, two for joy?'

He laughed, 'It's what she wanted. ' He grinned at me, 'None of that newspaper guff about checking facts, if you don't blummin' mind.'

I laughed, held up my hands. 'Won't say a word.'

'It's just …Now we're together again, like, I don't want to rock the blummin' boat.'

I got the message.

I was pleased they were together again, though I still didn't like the way he kept Viv out of the picture. If Viv was the one and he was keen on marrying her, he needed to start sharing his life and its priorities with her, mainly his mam's lease. I still thought he should tell Viv everything. And he needed to get moving to raise the cash.

Next stop was Ted and Marion's place. I was worried about awkward questions, especially from Ted. Never in a hundred years would he think we planned to break in to a prison, but he'd know you couldn't waltz into Havershawe, present an inmate with a live bird. Blum dismissed my concern.

Marion was on her own watching telly. Ted was out with Neville after a gang of persistent, illegal hare coursers. Marion wanted news of Fozzy's medical progress, but as Blum reported, I sensed his impatience to be off. While he took the magpie from its solitary confinement, slipped it into the box with a few chicken livers, Marion asked the awkward question I'd anticipated from Ted.

'We'll deliver it first thing to the Havershawe farm,' he told her, 'It's all fixed up. Special permission from the boss up there, as long as Fozzy keeps the bird outside.'

She accepted this, 'When will that poor lad get out of there?'

Blum opened the back door of his van just wide enough to place the magpie box inside, careful Marion didn't spot the rucksacks, ropes and other stuff, 'Not sure, yet, but it should be this year.'

Blum turned down Marion's invitation to stay for a bottle of beer. 'We'll see you in the Scarisbrick soon. Hope Ted nabs them blummin' dog men.'

Blum drove across flat, open land to meet Viv from work. We collected three packets of cod and chips on the way and ate them inside the van in the hospital car park. Viv had swapped her uniform for boots, jeans and black leather biker jacket. While we ate, we talked through the plan again, step by step.

An hour later, Blum drove, with lights off, up a cart track behind Havershawe and turned into a clearing between birch and oak trees. Lights shone through the woods, against the sky two close strands of barbed wire ran along the top of tall, chain-link fencing. Before we left the van, we pulled on balaclavas. We all wore gloves. Each of us knew what we had to carry. Blum had a rucksack and two coils of rope; Viv and I each carried a rucksack and single coil. I pulled on my rucksack, dropped the climbing rope over my head and under the opposite armpit like a Che Guevara cartridge bandolier. It was colder north of the Ribble, our breath condensed in clouds against the light from the windows of Havvy, a hundred yards away.

Lights out at the Borstal was at 9.30 p.m. It was now almost twenty-past. Blum's plan presumed the patrol of the exterior of the building's walls was still on the hour, every hour after lights out, until the following morning. It was essential to wait, make sure this had not changed in past months. We moved at a slow pace through the trees, relied on the moonlight rather than torches, settled in the shadows of a wide Scots pine twenty feet from the fence.

'Last chance for a fag,' Blum whispered. 'Keep 'em hid.'

Viv and I sat and smoked, Blum concentrated on the house. Tawny owls hooted to each other across the cricket lawn. Blum pointed out one owl perched on a chimney pot against the moon. It seemed tiny. How small we might look if spotted on the roof of the big, Victorian mansion. The thought caused a shiver of apprehension. I craved a drink to dull my nerves.

Half past nine arrived and lights on the upper two floors went out. Those on the ground floor facing us were also extinguished. Our movement across the lawn from the fence to the main building would be lit only the moon. I started to feel the cold, was impatient to get moving, quell my nerves.

While we waited, Blum took from Viv's rucksack sisal ropes wrapped around slim pieces of hardwood. It was a rope ladder. He showed us the two steel hooks on one end before producing a spool of heavy nylon sea fishing line from his pocket. He wrapped the sea line around the hooked end of the rope ladder, fastened it with two half-blood angling knots, and pocketed the spool. Then, from his own rucksack, he pulled out a pair of old-fashioned screw-on ice skates. The skates differed from normal skates in one way: the blades had been given attention with a grinding wheel and their straight edges had been cut like a saw blade with half-inch, backward facing teeth. Only when he'd screwed the modified skates to the welts of his work boots, did he relax.

Two fags later, he tensed and put his finger to his lips, motioned us to follow his example and crush out our smokes in the damp grass. I heard a gate open. Our eyes followed Blum's across the lawn. Moments later, two figures came from the corner of the building to our right. I caught the glint of metal buttons on their uniforms as one paused, used a fag lighter. The murmur of their voices carried.

There seemed no urgency in their movement. They strolled rather than walked, didn't even glance towards the perimeter fence, as if they'd nipped out of a party for a breath of air. In less than a minute they went out of sight behind the building. Blum checked his watch, whispered. 'Smack on blummin' time. That's it, clear for another hour.'

Blum hobbled on the saw blade skates, us following, to the fence. He laid the bundled rope ladder and sea line at the foot of the chain-link fence and adjacent to one of the tall, steel supporting poles. He gestured for me to turn my back towards him and took from my rucksack a folded, green sleeping bag, a roll of corrugated cardboard and an army blanket. With concentration, he fed the cardboard into the bag, tearing it off to length until there were four layers inside. Then he lined the bag with the folded blanket. He fastened the zip and put the bag over his shoulder.

In a fluid movement, Blum stepped towards the fence and climbed. Despite his load, the saw teeth of the skates made his ascent seem effortless as they clicked into the mesh of the chain-link fence. In moments, Blum reached the top of the fence alongside the steel pole, about twelve feet above the ground. He pulled the sleeping bag from his shoulder, laid it on top of the double strands of barbed wire, bending it over lengthways. Satisfied, he swung his leg over the sleeping bag, took the sea line from his pocket. He hauled on it and the rope ladder snaked upwards, the round tops of its steel hooks clinking against the links of the fence. When the top of the rope ladder reached him, Blum grabbed it and hooked it on to the top of the fence. He looked down, signalled for us to climb the rope ladder.

Viv adjusted her rucksack and rope on her shoulders, climbed the rope ladder to join Blum. When she was astride the sleeping bag, I followed. Any moment, I expected sirens as prison officers streamed out across the cricket lawn, but all was calm. Even the owls continued their duet. I swung my leg over the top of the sleeping bag between Viv and Blum. We had to stiffen our legs against the chain link to keep our balance. I was nervous our combined weight might cause the barbed wire to break, but it held.

Blum was busy. He unhooked the rope ladder, hoisted it up from the woods side of the fence. He dropped the bottom of it over the cricket lawn side and hooked it on for our descent. This time, though, he positioned the steel hooks about ten inches below the top, each hook inside a diamond of the chain links. Then he took the length of sea line and threaded it over the very top of the chain link and dropped the spool down on to the grass. Blum descended the rope ladder first, followed by Viv. As planned, I got on to the rope ladder before pulling the sleeping bag from the barbed wire and dropping it to the ground. As I stepped off the rope ladder, Blum unclipped the ice skates from his boots. He took the sleeping bag, zipped the skates inside.

Viv and I waited, nerves on edge, as without a trace of urgency or nervousness, Blum took hold of the sea line. We looked up as he took up the slack and twitched the line before steadily pulling on it. The line between the rope ladder and the top of the fence ten inches above stretched tight, then the hooks came away from the chain link. Blum steadied the rope ladder with one hand as he lowered it to the ground. Finally, he rolled up the rope ladder and placed it at the foot of the fence. He covered it with the sleeping bag.

Blum signalled us to follow him. We hurried across the cricket lawn until we reached the shadows of the main building. The only noise from us was the clink of equipment in our rucksacks. At the corner of the wall was the gate where the patrol officers had emerged. Blum opened it without a sound, ushered us through. I was amazed a gate inside a prison would remain unlocked, but Blum had told us during our planning it didn't even have a lock; Havershawe's security was to stop inmates breaking out, not others breaking in.

The gate opened on to the yard outside the kitchens, the laundry and the administration offices. All the windows were barred with devices reminiscent of stable hay baskets, which were screwed into the brickwork around the window frames. The devices stuck out some nine inches from the window panes. The upper two floors that housed eight dormitories, each with beds for up to ten lads, had similar barred windows. Blum closed the gate behind us, pointed across the yard to a metal staircase. It was the fire escape for the top two floors where the lads slept.

Blum led the way and stepped on to the steel steps of the fire escape. He turned to us and put his fingers to his lips, pointed at the steps. He moved up the staircase placing each footstep with care. Even with three of us ascending, the steel structure made no more noise than slight creaks. We turned the corner of the metal stairway and arrived on a half landing. Adjacent to it was a stout door which led out on to it in case of fire. This door, if opened, would lead into the dormitory corridor of the first floor. It was also connected to the alarm system. In one of these dormitories, Fozzy would be asleep on the eve of his seventeenth birthday. The fire door was not an option, so we had to go higher to reach his bedside and deliver the magpie, which had remained silent inside its box for more than two hours. Blum led the way up to the next metal landing and identical fire door on the second floor. The easy part was over.

Chapter 16
Don't Look Down

WE NEEDED TO be on top of the roof of the long, main body of the old house. The edge of the sloping gable was still ten feet above us. We watched Blum as he moved to one side of the fire escape platform and tapped a fingernail on a black metal pipe. It was one of the mansion's foul pipes which carried waste from the showers and lavatories on the first and second floors down to the sewers. Blum pushed and pulled the pipe, testing its firmness. It didn't move, but I eyed with uncertainty the rusty bolts which held it to old brickwork.

Between the balustrade of the fire escape steps and the slant of the roof, there were four sets of two bolts in four cast metal brackets which fastened the foul pipe to the wall. The pipe itself went higher than the roof by about five feet and was capped by a perforated finial like a big pepper pot, designed to scatter bad smells to the wind. The top of the pipe was three feet away from the ridge of the roof.

Blum motioned to Viv to turn her rucksack towards him. He delved into a side pocket and pulled out a handful of objects; inch wide strips of mild steel, each bent into a peculiar shape. He kept one and handed the others to me. These, I knew, he'd fashioned from steel he found in the barn at Pygon's Farm. Blum passed all but one of these devices to me. Then he pushed his hand behind the foul pipe and hauled himself up on to the fire escape balustrade. He reached up to the first cast metal bracket and slipped one end of the stirrup-like steel hooks on to the bracket, between the pipe and the wall. It slotted on to the bracket with a satisfying clunk, making a strong and steady foothold. Blum raised his thumb to us then grabbed the new foothold and held out his hand for another. I got up on the balustrade and continued to pass up the other footholds until there were eight of them in position on the four sets of brackets. I waited, my feet on the second to bottom footholds.

Blum pulled himself up on to the sloping roof of Havershawe house's main wing. He leaned forward, then sat astride the ridge. He motioned me to follow. I took a deep breath, hauled myself upwards. Blum grabbed my rucksack strap, pulled me onto the ridge. Viv came up without our help.

I never liked heights, but I remembered my dad's instructions when I was up a ladder helping him replace a gutter, 'Don't look down and you'll be right.' But wherever I looked, I couldn't forget how high we were. The air was clear, to one side the lights of Blackpool, in the other direction, Preston; further south, across the estuary, shone the distant lights of Southport and beyond. My head swam for a moment, so I forced myself to look only at the roof. It was about forty yards long. At its apex ran a strip of flat-topped ridge tiles each a foot or more wide. Several chimney stacks rising through the roof appeared gigantic.

Blum whispered to me to put my socks on. He'd already covered his boots with thick woollen hiking socks. I took out my own pair, pulled the first over my baseball boot.

Our intention was for Blum and me to enter the third floor then go down to the second, where I would listen for patrolling screws, while he delivered the box to Fozzy's bedside. We needed to muffle our footsteps so as not to alert prison officers, or the sleeping lads. The minute my socks were on, Blum and Viv stood up. He led us along the 'footpath' of the roof's ridge. I took a deep breath, followed, my eyes staying on the figures ahead of me, afraid to look anywhere else.

We continued until we drew level with a lesser chimney stacks. It was on the left hand slope of the roof, but we wanted to climb down the right hand slope. Blum produced a mallet and two metal items he'd shown me at the farm. They were for rock-climbing -- one a spike with a loop, the other a carabiner; a metal loop with a spring loaded side section to aid the insertion of a rope without threading it all the way through. Blum hammered the spike into the crevice between the ridge tiles, tested its firmness and clipped on the carabiner. He asked Viv for her coil of rope, tied one end to the carabiner.

'Be careful,' said Viv.

He said, 'Can you start on the block while I'm at it?'

Viv began to unload her rucksack. I took off my rope, knotted one end to the carabiner and watched Blum lower himself, walking backwards down the pitched roof to the smaller chimney stack. He went out of sight. Long moments later I saw him reappear on the other side of the stack. If he lost his grip on the rope, he would fall fifty feet to the ground at the front of the house. Blum held the chimney stack with one hand, the slack rope in the other as he balanced on the steep slates.

I whispered, 'Ready?'

'Go on,' said Blum. He took the first rope between his teeth.

As planned, I let the second coil of rope, now attached to the carabiner, slither down the slates and fall past him. Slowly, he stooped and grabbed it. Within seconds, he was walking up the roof towards us, hand over hand, trailing the first rope from his teeth. When he was back on the ridge, I untied the second rope from the carabiner and coiled it up while Blum took both ends of the first rope and knotted them together to form a big loop around the small chimney stack, which extended to the ridge of the roof. Viv attached to the loop an unused block and tackle set, courtesy of Daltry's. She was familiar with the equipment, having used it many times to lift engines from vehicles. It was a subject of discussion that night in The Ship. Viv said she could borrow a set from her dad's garage workshop, but Blum said he had one already. When Viv queried this, he lied, said he'd been given it by Ted.

Viv laid the block and pulleys on the opposite slope of the roof to the small chimney stack while Blum checked his watch.

'We need the loops now,' she said.

'Right,' said Blum, 'We're a bit ahead. Nearly forty minutes till the screws are out again.'

I didn't follow the finer points of using pulleys, but the plan was that the block would be supported by the rope looped around the chimney stack at its top end. From its bottom end, Blum and I would be lowered on two loops of rope which fastened close to our chests and ran under our arms. On these, we we'd descend, over the edge of the roof, to the window of an out of the way bathroom on the top floor.

I sat and waited as Blum rigged up the loops of rope, tested them and attached them to the block and tackle. Viv would be in control of the pulley system. She would lower us, then, after the magpie was delivered, haul us back up on to the roof. While we were inside, she would shuffle down the roof while roped to the spike in the ridge tiles. In that way, she would hear us when we were ready to come back up on the roof. The pulley system required only modest effort, as the physical force was magnified by the set of pulleys. Or something like that, I never did grasp O-level physics. The important factor was Viv could haul our combined weight upwards with minimal effort.

Blum passed me my rope loop. I took off my rucksack and left it on the ridge, before slipping my loop into position beneath my arms. Blum took off his rucksack, took out the magpie box. He transferred it into a big drawstring school gym bag, put it round his neck, before putting on his rope loop. He checked the torch in his pocket. I followed his example with mine.

Blum looked at both of us. 'Any questions before we get going?'

Viv shook her head.

'Nope,' I said.

To Viv, he said, 'Make sure you keep hold of the fishing line 'til we've got the scrap metal up. We'll do it as quick as we can.'

'Right, 'she said, 'Hey, don't forget it.'

She passed him another spool of sea fishing line and pointed to where it was tied to the rope loop alongside the block and tackle. Blum pocketed the line he would allow to run free from his jacket pocket and nodded to me it was time to move. I copied his actions as he manoeuvred himself on to the sloping tiles. As Viv operated the pulley block, we slithered on our backsides down to the blackness beyond the edge of the roof. As it came closer, I would have given a month's wages for a slug of whisky. I feared the rope snapping, I feared setting off some unknown alarm system. And as we got closer to the edge, I was afraid the rusting iron gutters would be dislodged and crash down to wake everyone in Havershawe. It seemed Blum had the same fear, for as he came towards the edge he reached and grabbed the gutter. He waggled and pushed at it, then repeated the process. He glanced at me, nodded. That was one less worry, but the others remained. I could feel the muscles in my legs trembling.

Blum twisted himself around and sat on the edge of the roof, his thighs over the gutter. He shifted until a single buttock rested on the gutter. I hesitated to follow him, as we'd planned. Now I had to put my trust wholly in the system of ropes and pulleys, any remaining bravado dribbled away. Blum sensed my fear, whispered, 'Safe as blummin' houses. Only thing to worry about is making a noise.'

Still, I hesitated. He swung the magpie box out of his way, wriggled over the edge of the gutter to demonstrate his claim. Now he hung on the rope loop with no contact with the roof or gutter. His head showed above the roofline, grinning in his idiotic way. I moved closer to the edge, forced myself to trust the rope. I closed my eyes and rolled over, feeling at once the pressure of the rope under both arms and across my back as my body swung and bumped against Blum. I heard the magpie scrabble in its box.

'See, blummin' doddle.'

I opened my eyes, my heart hammered, Blum's arm shot up to signal Viv. I saw the brickwork of the building three or four feet in front of me. I realised the rope hung over wide eaves as well as the gutter. It forced our dangling bodies away from the wall as well as from any window. I heard the creak of the block and pulleys as we descended then stopped. In front of us was the barred window of the out of the toilet, our way in. The top of the window was level with our waists. Blum fiddled at his pocket and took hold of the sea fishing line.

He murmured, 'One pull for lower, two pulls for higher. Wait for five seconds, then one, two, three feet.'

We waited.

There was a squeak from the pulleys and, with a jerk, we descended until our knees were level with the bottom of the window. As we swung, Blum reached out, grabbed the bars of the cage which covered its frame. 'Get hold,' he said.

I grabbed hold of his arm and worked myself towards the bars. We pulled ourselves closer as gravity and the width of the eaves and gutter forced our ropes and us away from the wall.

'Keep hold while I check the window,' Blum said. His hand slipped between the bars which were about six inches apart and tugged at the join down the side of the window. The window opened sharply and smacked against the bars. The catch was still broken. 'Ha!' said Blum.

He left the window alone, grabbed the bars over the frame with both hands, tugging hard at it. Our bodies swayed towards the building as Blum murmured, 'Let's see if Billy from Nelson was right about crappy screws.'

I joined in his assault on the ironwork and at once the bottom two corners came away from where they were screwed to the brickwork. The screws were rusted into the bars.

'Harder,' said Blum. I twisted and pulled as the top left corner came away. Blum's voice was hushed, but urgent, 'Hang on, hang on. Take the weight.'

I gripped the bars as Blum swung away, pulling at the sea line running from his pocket. He bit through it and stretched out to tie the end of it to the central bar; three half-blood knots one after another. Satisfied, he grabbed the bars and we heaved and twisted them. The final screw snapped like a stick. The full weight of the barred frame was in our hands. It wasn't as heavy as I'd imagined, but I worried about extra weight on the block and ropes, felt sweat run under my shirt.

'Got to get it the other way about,' Blum said. Switching our grip from one hand to the other, we turned the barred frame so the three intact screws faced away from the building; we didn't want the screws to snag on the gutter or roof tiles. 'Right, that should do it.'

He reached for the attached sea line and pulled on it repeatedly. A moment later, the line tightened and we let go of the barred frame and watched as it rose, Blum reached up to push it to one side of our ropes. We hung in space looking up as an unseen Viv dragged up the lump of scrap iron. I felt Blum tense at the clank as it hit the iron gutter. I watched and willed it not to snag. It didn't, but there was a horrible scraping sound as it crossed the gutter. Then the noise was less as Viv hauled it slowly to the top of the roof.

Now we concentrated on the window. Though it had opened, thanks to the unrepaired catch, the frame and ledge were out of reach without the bars to cling to. Blum raised his leg, angled his foot like a hook to catch the edge of the window frame, but it was still too far away. Blum put his arm across my back,' Get your legs up and swing!' At first, I didn't know what he meant. Then it came to me, remembered from times at the swing park as kids when we competed to see who could swing highest.

I raised my legs, kicked towards the wall. Blum extended his foot, but missed hooking the window frame by an inch. 'Harder,' he said. I kicked both legs forward then forced them downwards, our bodies moving closer to the open window. This time his foot hooked the frame. He let go of me and as I swung back, terrified of even a glance downwards, he grabbed at the leg of his jeans, used his own leg as a rope to pull himself forward, to grab the window frame. Once he had a hold of it he stepped on to the window ledge, ducked through the open window. Then he turned around and reached out to take my hand. He pulled me closer then held my rope as I got my feet on the ledge. I pushed in beside him, desperate to stand on anything harder than fresh air.

'Blummin' eaves. Never bargained for an overhang like that.'

He pulled out his torch, shone it around. We were on an interior window ledge, above a washbasin, about five feet above the floor. To one side were two toilet cubicles. Old, broken chairs and some venetian blinds stood in one corner. The room smelt musty, unused. The red tile floor was covered in dust.

All was quiet, but for the scrape of the magpie's claws inside the cardboard box. I wondered if magpies could die of fright. I envied its ignorance of what was happening beyond the darkness of its box.

I switched on my torch and, took of my rope loop. Blum switched off and pocketed his, passed his rope loop to me, 'Hoick 'em over them taps.'

I did so as Blum shuffled along the window ledge and jumped down. It should've been effortless. Perhaps the woollen socks over his boots combined with dusty tiles didn't help. First I heard the thud of his heavy fall. This was followed by a gasp and a muttered, 'Christ!' I moved my torch. Blum lay on the floor, his hands on his left ankle, his breath rasping. He grimaced in pain.

Chapter 17
I Am the Cockroach

I STEPPED DOWN into the washbasin, sat in it and slid my feet to the floor. Hushed, I voiced my immediate thoughts. 'Can you stand on it? Will you be able to walk?' My mind flooded with the horror of a serious fracture, hopeless surrender to the prison authorities.

'I don't know.' He pulled himself up on to his good foot and pressed down with his other. 'Blummin 'eck, that hurts'

'Do you reckon its bust?'

He put his weight on it again. In my torchlight, I saw him wince.

'I felt summat go, but I don't think so. Not as bad as it was last time.'

A few years earlier when he climbed a tree to retrieve a snagged-up pike spinner, he jumped from a lower branch, fractured a bone in the same foot. He was in a plaster cast for weeks.

'Let's give it a go.' He put his injured foot forward, took two steps. He paused and grabbed my shoulder. 'It's no good, you'll have to help me get down to Fozzy.'

I held back my panic, tried not to think how slow it might be to get to our target area, 'Won't I be quicker on my own.'

'You won't find him. You'll have the blummin' place awake.'

'Maybe we should just get out...'

Blum hissed, 'Don't be daft! We're only yards away!' He threw his left arm across my shoulder, adjusted the gym bag containing the box and magpie, 'It's a wonder I didn't crush this bugger. Torch off. Get that door open.'

I opened the door, listened for noise or movement.

Blum whispered, 'There's steps down just here.'

While Blum leaned on me, we negotiated the steps and, moved along a narrow passage about ten yards long, which joined a wider one at a right angle. That was lit by moonlight from a high window at one end. At the other was the inside of the top fire door, the words FIRE EXIT beneath a dim light. Earlier, Blum told me we had to pass two of the four dormitories on that floor before reaching the staircase down to the lower floor. The dormitories didn't have doors. Wide archways made the inmates more visible to passing screws. As we moved past the first archway, I could hear sleeping lads breathing, or snoring. We froze as a boy in the second bed from the door turned himself over, pushed himself up then threw himself back on his mattress, mumbling. We waited until he settled before we passed the next archway, all quiet, but for a single snorer.

At the top of the stairs, we separated. Blum grabbed the banister rail, hopped one step at a time downwards. I was glad his boots were muffled. I trod with care in case I slipped, twisted one of my own ankles. We shuffled across the half-landing and he hopped down the lower flight of stairs. Blum took my shoulder and we moved past one dormitory, arrived at the archway opening of another. Blum whispered, 'Here. Stop.'

He shone his torch on the outer wall of the dormitory, lowered the beam. Just as I recognised the sleeping Fozzy, he switched it off. He raised the drawstrings of the gym bag over his head and, with me helping him to stand, took out the magpie box. He nodded his head towards Fozzy. Then leaned against the archway so I could let go of him and take the box. I had no idea what I'd do if one of the lads woke. My legs started to shake again. Blum's impatience showed as he again nodded towards the dormitory.

Holding the box like it was an unexploded bomb, I advanced into the dormitory. Moonlight shone through the edge of a window blind on the outer wall. I focused on the corner of Fozzy's bed as I passed sleeping lads. When I reached it I could hear his breathing. I entered the space between his bed and the wall. Fozzy shifted, I froze. For an instant, I thought he'd woken, but he turned over, pushed his face into the pillow. I lowered the box to the floor, bent down, nudged it towards the bedside locker. I jumped, startled, as the bird's feet scrabbled on cardboard, froze again. I dreaded the rattling screech of an alarmed magpie, but Fozzy slept, the bird stayed silent. I stood straight, retreated without making a sound, to re-join Blum. Euphoria at our successful delivery bubbled up over my nerves.

Blum jabbed a finger at his watch, whispered 'Come on, quick.'

Now I had to focus on the practical problems we faced with Blum crippled. How long would it take us to get out? Would he manage? The fear of failure, the humiliation of surrender, returned. I forced myself to remain calm as he threw his arm across my shoulder and we moved, him limping, to the staircase. Going up was harder than going down and I sweated with the effort. We reached the top step and the third floor and I wished us back at the van, our exit complete. Then leather shoes on lino sounded to our right. They stopped. A hesitant voice said, 'Who's that?'

I turned to the noise, alarmed, but Blum turned quicker. He clicked on his torch under his chin, lighting his face, surrounded by the black balaclava. In a deep voice, lilting higher, he said, 'I am the cockroach.'

The dark figure emitted a girlish shriek. I knew at once it was the lad who picked on Blum; that bully, Vince Doe, who'd failed to hide from his ill-chosen victim his fear of cockroaches. Like a startled cockie himself, Doe scuttled away into a dormitory archway. The torchlight had gone and Blum was pulling at me to hurry as he hopped and hobbled past another dormitory towards the old toilet. Now out of sight of the landing, I could hear shouts as boys woke. I almost carried Blum up the steps, twisted the door knob, pushed him inside the toilet. He fell to the floor. As I closed the door, I heard an indignant shout, raised voices, a lad swearing.

'Blum! Get up! For Christ's sake!'

I pulled out my torch, lit up his face. He was shaking, struggling to keep quiet, his shoulders heaving, out of control, with suppressed, hysterical laughter.

'We've got to get out! They'll be after us!'

I flashed my torch to the washbasin and the rope loops over the tap. The window ledge seemed a hell of a height for Blum to manage. I hurried to the corner, pulled away the roll of venetian blind, took a chair towards the window, positioned it by the washbasin.

I turned and grabbed Blum, dragging him up, 'Blum!'

He snorted and giggled as I forced him towards the washbasin. I left him, with one hand on the basin, his other trying to stifle mad laughter, while I stepped up on to the window ledge. I took his hand and pulled as he climbed from chair, to washbasin, to window ledge. It seemed to take an eternity and I could still hear voices from downstairs, but when he put weight on his bad foot and gasped in pain, his laughter stopped. He regained his self-control enough to remind me to replace the chair and blind.

I put them back as I'd found them, got back on the ledge as Blum put the rope loop over his head and under his arms. I put mine on while leaned out of the window and spoke, a harsh whisper, 'Viv?'

She came straight back, 'I'm here.'

'Ready?'

'I'll whistle when I'm back up. Be careful, it's gone frosty.'

I heard Blum's sharp exhalation. I didn't know if it was prompted by Viv's news, or pain in his ankle. But I was more worried what was going on in the dormitory. Voices from there were now louder, like an argument. I dreaded a blare of alarm bells, a search by screws.

When we heard Viv's whistle, Blum told me to go first. I swung myself out, let the rope take my weight. Blum followed a second later, our swinging bodies colliding. I whispered, 'We need to shut the window.'

Blum tried with his good foot, but we were still swinging and he missed. A moment later, as we moved towards the wall, I raised my own foot and swung it back almost into place.

Blum called, 'Pull us up.'

The squeak of the ropes and pulleys sounded louder than before as we jerked higher. In no time, our chests were hard against the gutter and we had to heave ourselves up on our arms to escape the relentless pressure of the pulley block. With the constant upward pull on our rope loops, though, getting back on the roof was easier than I'd imagined. I looked up to see Viv operating the block. In the space between us frost on the slates glistened in moonlight.

Viv's voice was urgent, impatient, 'Have you done it?'

I gave her a thumbs up.

I went up the slope on my hands and feet. Blum tried, but groaned in pain as he put pressure on his injured ankle.

'What's wrong?' said Viv.

'Me blummin' ankle.' He let the injured foot drag and levered himself up with his good foot.

I pulled myself on to the ridge of the roof, 'He slipped going in. It might be bust.'

'Get your boot off, I'll have a look.'

Blum was terse, 'No time. Fifteen minutes 'til the patrol.'

I added, 'We need to get going -- Someone saw us.'

'God, who?'

Blum had started to dismantle the pulley system. 'Nowt to worry about. Tell you later.'

Viv put a hand on each of his ankles, to make a comparison. 'It's swollen. Are you sure you can manage?'

'No blummin' choice, we've got to go.'

'Try to keep the weight off it. You'll need an X-ray.'

As planned, I was about to undo the rope looped around the chimney stack and coil it up. Blum said, 'Wait.'

I looked. He pointed to the iron window bars Viv had pushed along the ridge. 'Before you undo that, we need that scrap down there, between the chimney stack and the roof. Don't want some bugger spotting it.'

I wondered about trying to slip it over the rope to lower it into position, but it would take too long. I had no choice, but to risk the frosted slates, stow it myself. I didn't want to stand, so I crawled towards the bars and dragged them towards me. I daren't walk down the frosted roof, even with one hand gripping the rope. Blum and Viv were distracted; he packing gear into the rucksacks, she trying to examine his ankle above his boot. They didn't notice me moving downwards on my heels and backside, one hand on the rope, the other gripping the window bars. I tried to focus on the brickwork of the chimney stack so I didn't look into the blackness below, or the distant lights. I was halfway down when my sock-covered heel slipped on the slates. I grabbed the rope with my other hand and the window bars clanged on the slates as they fell.

I cringed as they scraped down the slates. If they went over the front edge of the roof they'd fall fifty feet on to stone flags. But one protruding, rusty screw snagged and the bars arced to one side, slid downwards. A tiny miracle happened. They came to rest where I wanted them, in the angle of the roof and chimney stack.

'Ha,' said Blum, 'Fluke.'

My legs trembling I turned, hauled myself back to the ridge. I untied the rope from the spike, pulled it up from the chimney stack and coiled it, before putting it over my body and pulling on my rucksack.

While Blum and Viv packed, I looked along the roof. We had twenty yards to go to the foul pipe. We had to negotiate the foul pipe, fire escape stairs, the cricket lawn and the perimeter fence. Blum would be able to move at only half-speed, less. I turned my watch to the moonlight.

'Only ten minutes to go.'

Blum said, 'Let's see if we can get off the roof, into the shrubberies before they come out.'

I wasn't confident and still fearful of what was going on below. Was Doe telling the others about Blum? Or would he keep such an apparent cock and bull story to himself; hide his secret fear of cockroaches? I felt he would; a bully hates to expose his own weakness, but I couldn't be sure. Would screws bully the bully to tell all? Were they already outside? Could they hear us?

Viv helped Blum to his feet, 'You go first. Take your time.'

Blum put pressure on his foot. I saw pain in his face when he looked at me, 'Okay with you?'

I nodded, tried to look confident.

Blum limped away along the ridge of the roof. Viv followed and I forced my eyes to stay on my friends, not to look down. Blum tried hard to make decent speed and we were within six or seven paces of the end of the roof and foul pipe when the ridge tile fell. Viv slithered after it, screamed.

Chapter 18
All my Nightmares

THAT FEAR IN the minutes that followed Viv's fall is scorched in my memory. It features in my nightmares. I don't know how I managed to do what I did that night. Even to describe it makes me tremble, my breath catch.

From her perilous position, Viv explained: Blum couldn't get down to her with one injured foot. He could, though, help me down with a rope to tie around her to pull her up. I could feel their eyes on me as I struggled to quell this escalation of my fear.

I couldn't speak, even nod my head, my apprehension was so complete. But admission of my cowardice in the face of friends relying on me in this terrible moment was deferred. A man's voice came up from the yard below, 'Bloody hell! Quick, Sid! Look!'

Footsteps were followed by another voice, 'Looks like it fell off the roof. Thank God it didn't hit anyone.'

'Told yer I heard a bump.'

'What are we going to do?'

'Write it in the log. What else? Come on, let's get round quick. It's brass monkeys.'

In these terrifying circumstances, those moments of talk seemed an eternity, ended only when the gate to the cricket lawn opened and closed. For moments, none of us spoke. But the patrol was no longer a real concern. We had a full hour to get out. Or surrender. Or witness Viv's death. My courage, or lack of it, was back at the top of the agenda.

Blum looked at me, 'Reckon you can do it?

What if our positions were swapped? If I were lying down there on the roof, would Viv or Blum be too frightened to help? Would they admit their fear, chicken out, give us no option but to seek help, involve us in trouble with the law, which would ruin our lives? I knew they wouldn't. It was nobody's fault I was in this position, but my own. I wanted the excitement of it all and I'd been willing to take the risks. Pure happenstance had created this ordeal. I had to embrace it.

I nodded, 'Yep.'

'Right,' Blum said. He launched into a rapid explanation of what we would do. His plan was stark. He would straddle the ridge of the roof to anchor the rope. I would slither down to loop it under Viv's arms. Then he would pull up Viv alone. When she was safe on the ridge, he would lower the rope for me and they would both pull me up. I was about to ask if he could bring up Viv and me together, but if either of us slipped or toppled the other, Blum would be unable to take our combined body weight. I said nothing.

Viv called, 'I've got cramp in my leg.'

Blum was brisk, 'Let's get a move on.'

To cover my fear, I lowered myself to sit on the ridge, took off my rope and rucksack. Blum took one of the coils and made the end into a loop. I glanced at the frosty tiles, hurried to pull off my over socks, remove my baseball boots, then my socks. Blum looked as I hurried to stuff them into my rucksack.

This was my decision, 'If I'm barefoot I won't slip.'

He nodded, handed me the loop of rope. I put it over my head and under my arms, stepped into the gap where the ridge tile had lain. Blum shuffled himself into position, gripped the rope. 'Fast as you blummin' can, eh?'

I could see the sweat on his face as I turned backwards, my eyes intent on my feet, on the slates, as I backed my way down. I paused and forced myself to look over my shoulder, to get a bearing on Viv.

'Keep going,' whispered Blum.

I heard a whimper from Viv, 'Oh, God, my leg's shaking.'

'Hold on,' I said. I twisted as I came alongside her, put my backside and heels on the slope of the roof, felt the support of the rope. I budged further down, checking the grip of my naked feet on the slates. I forced myself to blot out everything else, focused on Viv. Sweat ran down my back, chest, crawled like insects through my hair inside my balaclava, as I eased the rope loop off my body. I was now dependent on my own grip and balance. One careless move, a loss of balance, I would fall. Turning as far as I dared towards Viv, I cast the loop over her outstretched arms.

'Slow now,' said Blum.

I didn't need to instruct Viv. She moved one hand away from the roof, put it under the loop. I pulled it down slightly and she did the same with her other hand. The coil of rope over her shoulder and the rucksack were the obstacles to speed. I slid the loop further down, all the time working to one side of me. I pulled the loop further back and over her head. In a moment of near panic I imagined her slipping, pulling Blum and me after her. I took a deep breath, concentrated, as a trickle of sweat escaped my Balaclava, zig-zagged across my brow, insinuated itself, stinging, into my left eye. I daren't wipe in case I lost my balance, so I blinked and blinked, then closed it. Would my right eye avoid blindness from my own sweat?

I eased the loop further down under her arms to give me extra space to get it over her rope and rucksack.

'My leg's going dead.'

Christ!

'One more minute.'

The loop was a tight fit over the rucksack and I daren't pull. I had to reach backward, my hand going under the coil of rope over her shoulder and drawing the loop further down under her chest. I caught the scent of the patchouli oil she often wore, noted her increased rate of breaths. In ideal conditions, I would've untied the loop, made it bigger, but that was impossible. I moved my head so I could see with my good eye, worked as fast as I could. I wiggled the loop lower, managed to pull it over and under the back of her rucksack.

'Is it right round you?'

'Yeah.'

'Blum! Take the weight,' I said. I couldn't look back and up, but I saw Viv's feet move, heard his encouragement. I had to force down my terror, as in my peripheral vision, I saw Viv disappear behind me. I remained in position, trembling, my head wobbling on my neck, my now cold, bare feet flat to the sloping roof, my buttocks just above them. I had no choice, but to face forward, confront my fear. All that was before me was clear air, distant lights -- below me a dark void. I felt like a tiny speck in a universe of nothingness, had to fight a wild urge to scream; both the essence and climax of future nightmares.

Behind me came a scraping noise, a sharp gasp. I twitched with fright. Viv had slipped, Blum was calm, 'I've got you. Take it slow. Keep going.'

I breathed in, tried to calm myself, avoid panic. Blum urged Viv higher. How much longer would I have to wait? It seemed I'd been in this state of apprehension forever, needed to leave it now. If I didn't I might lose my mind as well as my balance. Viv's boots scraped as she scrambled on to the ridge of the roof. Blum's voice soothed her, told her she was safe.

Viv gasped, short of breath, 'Get it down to him'.

'On its way, get ready,' said Blum.

Still I daren't move. The rope skittered down the slates, brushed against me.

'Stay as you are, just pick up the loop and get it under your arms,' said Blum.

I picked up the rope, my movements tiny, slow, as I brought the loop over my head and arms, manoeuvred it into position, felt the tension of Blum and Viv's upward pull.

'We've both got it,' said Blum, 'Roll on your belly. Slow, now.'

My body felt stiff, clumsy, as I rolled over. The pull on the rope was steady. My numb feet pushed me upwards as they hauled me higher. Thirty seconds later I sat astride the ridge of the roof, felt Viv's hand take mine. Blum put a hand on my shoulder. Together, we trembled in silence. Blum lit cigarettes, passed them to us, 'Five minutes, then we go.'

Our exit was slow, yet it seemed easy. Viv and I, perhaps all of us, must have been in shock. But I felt no apprehension now; felt calm, confident, in control.

Blum went down the foul pipe first. He was slow, but his strong arms made up for his injured ankle. I was last off the roof stuffing the steel stirrups into my pockets as I retreated down the pipe. Going down the fire escape required Viv and me to support Blum, his arms across our shoulders. It was the same as we lumbered across the cricket lawn. Thanks to Blum's trick with the fishing line, I was able to haul up the rope ladder. I took charge of getting us and any evidence of trespass over the outer fence, back to the van.

Blum was unable to drive. Viv and I bickered over who was in the right frame of mind to take over. I won the argument when Blum asked if Nurse Jarvey had forgotten his ankle. Blum recounted our chance meet-up with Vince Doe and I drove to a park in Preston. Viv tore the lining out of the sleeping bag, soaked it at a drinking fountain, bound Blum's foot in ice cold rag. Viv spoke to the sister in casualty at her hospital. X-rays revealed no fracture, but a bad sprain. I stood outside and smoked, wished I had a drink. Blum was issued with a pair of crutches. On our way to her flat, Viv and I dumped all our gear in a bus shelter, confident it would find new owners.

Viv plonked a bottle of whisky bought for her dad's imminent birthday on the table in her kitchenette. We sat up late, talked over the night's events, toasted Fozzy's birthday. Any talk of how the night could have ended didn't happen. I feared there might be a row between Blum and Viv of the 'told you so' sort. But they both seemed content; their unspoken thoughts, perhaps, that Viv was still alive; everything else unimportant. I know mine were.

The level of the bottle dropped and a half-cut Blum raised his glass, 'I am the cockroach,' he announced. We had succeeded and the horror of failure, or worse, was now forgotten in laughter. I didn't care about any laws we'd broken, the mad risks we'd embraced, all out of proportion to our wish and whim to give one lad, so badly wronged by life, the perfect birthday present. I sipped neat whisky, felt the rush of exhilaration at what we'd done.

*

Days later, Fozzy threaded his way to us through the visiting hall at Havvy. He was a changed lad. He appeared relaxed, confident. Straight away, we saw the reason. For his misshapen lip had been remodelled. Even the appearance of his twisted front teeth had been much improved.

Viv led the fuss over his new look, but Fozzy brushed it all aside, 'Thanks for my birthday present. I thought I was dreaming.'

We laughed as Fozzy twisted in his chair, checked for the prison officers, then looked at us in turn, his voice low, bursting with curiosity, 'How did you get in? How did you do it?'

Blum laughed, 'How's that magpie coming along?'

Fozzy's enthusiasm engaged us all, 'He's a little bugger. Bright as owt, he is. And he likes things Click used to like, can't get enough worms, the greedy sod. He follows me all round the yard and the glasshouses, even roosts in Click's old speck.'

Blum said, 'How's Vince Doe. Is he still here?'

Fozzy looked puzzled, checked around, leaned forward, 'Some new lad give him a right going over the other night.'

'Oh, aye?' said Blum.

Fozzy grinned, whispered, 'Late on, it were. New lad went mental when Vince crashed into his bed. The argey-bargey woke 'em all up on Two Floor. Vince said he was having a bad dream, or summat, but this new feller still battered him. Turns out one of the lads Vince was pickin' on the other month is his cousin. Bad luck for Vince, eh?'

Fozzy looked at Blum, 'What you asking about him for?'

Blum shrugged, 'Nowt, just wondered, like.'

Fozzy regarded him, his mind ticking over.

Viv changed the subject, 'Any other news?'

Fozzy laughed, slapped his temple 'How daft can you get? I had to see the governor. Don't know what's happened, but it's to do with the operations. He says it's all about medical grounds and I should be on probation now. They're letting me out -- on May the twenty-fifth.'

Viv was delighted, 'Out, out? You mean for good? Released?'

Fozzy nodded, beamed. We congratulated him, kicked up a din. The duty officer barked at us to pipe down.

Fozzy leaned forward, 'Tell us how you did it? How you got him to me bed?'

'Who said we did?' said Blum.

He looked at our deadpan faces in turn, 'You must have…Who else could've…?'

Blum, Viv and I swapped puzzled looks. Fozzy was confused.

Blum laughed, 'We don't want you telling any tales, not a word. We'll tell you when you get out.'

'Fair play,' said Fozzy. He frowned, 'Was it anything to do with Vince Doe?'

Blum laughed, 'When you get out, right?'

Fozzy asked no more, gabbled on about his magpie, 'I'm teaching him to talk. I know he can do it. And I'm going to call him Clicker, if you think that's good? What do you reckon?'

I saw the looks on Viv's then Blum's face as their hands joined on the edge of the table, shared and enjoyed Fozzy's outflow of happiness. Blum turned to me, grinned, just like he always did when he was happy. Despite the risks, despite the dangers of that night on the roof, seeing the changes friendship and a surgeon's skills had brought to Fozzy, it had all been worth it. One for Joy might've been the wrong line of that old rhyme, but for that particular magpie, it was spot-on.

Now Blum's obsession had been satisfied, I was anxious to fulfil my promise to help Blum find the money to save his mam's home. Weeks had passed, he needed to concentrate on that.

Chapter 19
An Evening with Kav and Delly

I STOOD IN the gloom of the Scottish Soldier, watched Noreen the barmaid pour two fresh pints of bitter from the tall pewter jug, thought how good the day had been. It was a warm evening late in May and Blum, Viv and I had moved Fozzy and Clicker into their new home. Tomorrow Fozzy would start his first-ever job.

If there was a single plus to Fozzy being sent to Borstal for a crime he didn't commit, it was the experience and knowledge he gained in the fields and glasshouses at Havershawe. Blum had encouraged his interest and skill tending crops under glass. When Fozzy's release was announced, he knew at once who might put Foz on course to a new start.

Blum met Arnold Sharrock and his wife, Glenys, when he did the rounds for Daltry's. Blum told me the Sharrocks wouldn't steal a penny from a millionaire, so he'd not even thought to tempt them with his special offers. The couple worked a small-holding on the border of Tarleton and Hesketh Bank on the rich, flat land of west Lancashire. It supplied the markets of the north- west with tomatoes, lettuce, radish and more.

The Sharrocks always enjoyed the news and gossip about other farmers and growers brought to their door by Blum. Though they knew why Blum was sacked, they were among only a few former customers who didn't hesitate to give him van work when he put an advert in the paper after his release. Blum hoped the Sharrocks might point Fozzy in the right direction to find a glasshouse job. But, he told me later, it turned out better than that.

Blum spent a Sunday teatime at the Sharrocks' place, told them in detail Fozzy's story. Before Blum even finished his account of the boy's false conviction and his promising talents as a grower, Arnold and Glenys were exchanging glances. Blum suspected they might welcome a youthful addition to their own business.

Arnold tapped a grimy fingernail on the best linen tablecloth, 'Did I ever tell thee I did six months' jail when I were a lad?'

Blum was surprised at this revelation, shook his head.

'Not that he did what they said, mind,' said Glenys.

'That's the truth,' said Arnold, 'Nineteen-thirty-four it were, Ormskirk magistrates. Charged wi' cuttin' a lad's jaw wi' a beer bottle in the Cock an' Bottle. Witnesses were drunk, or thick as pig muck; police too idle to do their job proper. And th'owd feller were too mean to pay a solicitor. Made me say I did it just to get it o'er and done, wouldn't even let me plead not guilty, speak for meself.'

Glenys added, 'He's always said most folk deserve a second chance after prison, guilty or not, haven't you, love?' She glanced at her husband, turned back to Blum, 'He never spoke another word to his father after that, you know.'

'That's why you're sitting there now, lad,' Arnold said, 'That's why this friend of yours can come and work here, if he's minded. If he's a good lad like you say, he'll be welcome.'

Glenys was excited at the prospect of a teenager about the place. Blum knew the couple's only son, Paul, turned his back on a future as a grower after only a year full-time in the glasshouses, preferring a career with the RAF. Glenys was proud of Paul, but hated his long absences. Arnold was proud, too, but disappointed his lad would never work the expanding business the couple built up since they married. Before Blum left, plans were advanced. If Fozzy wanted, he would have a formal apprenticeship and wage. He could have his meals in the bungalow with Glenys and Arnold if he wanted, but he would also have the privacy of his own place to call home. In fact, a room over their big garage once fitted out as a retreat to humour Paul during the long months of sullen behaviour when he daren't tell his parents he'd rejected a future in their footsteps.

Fozzy was on the edge of tears as the Sharrocks welcomed him and Clicker to their new billet. Glenys and Arnold had painted and wallpapered. A bed and furniture had been brought from the bungalow and Arnold had installed a television and transistor radio. Blum rustled up a second-hand Baby Belling electric stove and a battered Frigidaire. Viv stuffed Blum's van with pots, pans, cushions, sheets, blankets and other surplus bits and pieces from her parents' house. I got a delighted laugh from Fozzy when I presented him with a parrot's cage for Clicker. The door was missing, but I decided the magpie wouldn't need one when I nicked the relic from Kitty's junk-filled, garden shed.

I smiled to myself, recalled Fozzy's happiness, carried our pints out into the dying sunshine to join Blum at bench tables under the white lilac at the corner of the Soldier's forecourt.

I was surprised to see Blum with a lad I was sure wasn't local. He was tall, but slightly built, hair, short, unfashionable. When I put the pints down, I noticed he wore a hearing aid.

'All right?' I nodded to the lad. He gave me a glance, carried on his conversation with Blum.

'We all had to tell the coppers everything about him. Give 'em the low-down on what he'd done to us. Havvy was swarming with pigs.'

'I heard,' said Blum.

'I hope they give him twenty years -- more. I wouldn't mind knowing someone in the nick they send him to. I'd pay 'em to work him over, I would, the fuckin' bastard. Give me five minutes on me own with that fu...'

Blum interrupted, 'This is Delly. He was up at Havvy with me.'

'Yeah, I remember the name.' I said,' You're not a member of the Bert Travis fan club, then, eh?'

It was a joke, but Delly didn't find anything humorous in it. He continued with a fantasy about hunting down Travis, doing this that and the effing other to his erstwhile jailer with knives, boiling water, razor blades, the effing four-letter word, and so on.

He seemed intense; stressed, even. I hated what Travis had done to lads in his charge, but I couldn't warm to this victim, Delamere. I didn't like the idea Blum might renew acquaintanceship with those he knew inside, other than Fozzy. It might seem strange, snobbish, considering Blum's own morality, but I felt he was somehow above people like Delly. He had future jailbird written across his face. I'd seen so many like him before the magistrates. I tried to turn the monotonous conversation away from Travis.

I asked Delly, 'Fancy a pint?'

He shook his head, 'Can't. Not stoppin'.'

'You're from Burscough, aren't you? '

His eyes moved to me, suspicious, wary, 'Yeah. Why?'

'Just wondering what brought you down here? Bit old-fashioned, not even got a jukey.'

In the corner of my eye I noticed Delly's foot under the table. His leg jiggled. Delly was anxious about something.

He nodded to Blum, 'Your mate here, up at Havvy, he used to tell us about this pub, didn't you, Blum?'

Blum was mellow after a drink, a good day. He lifted his glass, 'I missed a blummin' pint in there all right.'

Delly's tone became oily, he sucked-up to Blum, 'Used to tell us all sorts of stuff didn't yer, mate? Poachin', fishin', shootin', thievin'… We had a good laugh, didn't we…?' He paused, 'Eh, you still got all them guns?'

My glass stopped half way to my lips. A tiny alarm sounded. I thought Blum might have had the sense not to talk about owning guns in a place full of criminals, more than a few in Borstal for violence.

'Some of 'em,' said Blum, 'Sold a fair few.'

A lad in his twenties approached. He'd left a green Ford Corsair, parked off the roadside. There was another feller of similar age watching from the passenger seat, a fag in his mouth. The first lad was a few steps away, his agitation obvious. 'Eh, Delly?' He poked Delamere in the back, 'We haven't gorrall friggin' night.'

Delly was uneasy, 'Give us a chance. We haven't seen each other for ages.'

The first lad sat on the opposite bench, continued in his scouse accent, 'Never mind sittin' there janglin'. Have you asked him?'

That tiny alarm was now a clanging bell.

'Just doing it,' said Delly.

The lad turned to me and Blum, 'Are you gonna fix us up with some guns, or what?'

'Oh, aye, what are you after?' said Blum.

I spoke over Blum, 'No, he's not.'

Blum flashed me a wounded look. He wanted a deal.

The lad stared at me for a moment, malice in his eyes. To say I hated him on sight was an understatement. Then he turned to Blum, 'Who's guns are they?' he said, 'Yours?' He jerked a thumb at me, 'Or twat-'ead's?'

My loathing of him moved up a notch; his dirty, greasy hair, his unhealthy pallor, the absence about him of anything likeable.

'Mine, but you need to blummin' tell us what you're looking for?'

The lad looked around, checked nobody might overhear. Even before he said it, I knew he wasn't some would-be poacher after a cheap shotgun to lamp roosting pheasants, 'Yer know, a pistol. Norr arsed as long as there's bullets as well.'

'He hasn't got anything like that,' I said.

He leaned towards me,' Worr is this, eh? A fuckin' double act?'

I said nothing, kicked at Blum's leg under the table.

The lad jabbed a finger at me, 'Keep out of it, you. All right?'

He turned back to Blum, 'Well, have you gorrany?'

'Nah, sorry, no pistols.'

The lad turned to Delly, 'Was you lying to me, gobshite?'

Delly looked cowed, 'It's true, Kav. He told me had five.' He looked to Blum for confirmation, 'You did, mate, didn't you? Tell him.'

Blum leaned forward, elbows on the table, 'Delly's right, I did. But some bugger snitched and I had the coppers round. Blummin' good job they were hidden at the girlfriend's place.' He shrugged, 'Had to get rid double quick.'

Kav hadn't lost hope, 'Where are they? Can you put us on to who's gorrem?'

'Bottom of that flooded quarry on the road to Formby.'

Kav slammed his fist on the table top, 'Yer jokin'! Friggin' hell!'

'Aye, a waste of blummin' good guns.'

Delly piped up, 'He's got shotguns though.'

Kav looked at Blum, 'Yeah? How about a coupla double barrels? You know, sawn offs?'

I kicked Blum's leg again. Then I couldn't believe his reply, not to this character.

'You'd have to see to that yourself. You'd only need a hacksaw.'

'Yeah, yeah,' the lad said, 'I can do all that.'

I didn't want Blum back inside and to supply this nasty individual with any sort of firearm seemed a certain way to get there. Kav's obvious short temper, his finger on the trigger of a loaded gun, was unthinkable. I didn't care how menacing he might be. I said, 'Have you got a licence to buy a shotgun?'

'Christ! It is a double act!' A vein in his forehead bulged. 'Do I look like I've got a fuckin' licence, yer gobby get --?'

It must have been the pints I'd drunk that prompted my reckless interruption, 'I don't care what you look like, no

licence, no shotguns. You'll have to try somewhere else…
Right, Blum?'

Blum held up his hands, 'I know you're Delly's mate, but
I'm keeping my nose clean, I have to.' He indicated me with
a nod, 'My mate here's got a police licence and we use that
for any deals we do. We sell the odd shotgun -- anyone with
the right paperwork, like.'

Kav glanced at me with contempt, focused his stare on
Blum. For a tense moment, I thought he might summon the
other tough-looking lad in the Corsair to make something of
this refusal. Instead, he stood, headed back to the car. Delly
glanced at Blum, shrugged, scurried after Kav.

Kav paused at the driver's door as Delly joined him, his
demeanour showing his fear, 'Sorry, Kav, I didn't know he'd
dumped…'

Delly's words were cut short as Kav grabbed his shirt
with one hand, kidney-punched him with the other, then got
in the driver's seat, slammed the door. A doubled-over Delly
managed to get in the back of the Corsair a moment before
Kav fired the engine, pulled away and U-turned at speed in
the direction of Ormskirk.

I turned on Blum, 'Bloody good job I was here, wasn't
it?'

Blum laughed. 'What for? To blummin' frighten him
off?'

'If it wasn't for me you'd've sold a pistol to that shit.'

Blum picked up his pint, 'I might've sold one to Delly.'

'Delly's scared stiff of him. Any gun you flogged to
Delly'd go straight to him. And why do you think someone
like him wants a gun?'

'Nowt to do with me, is it?'

'Isn't it? What if he killed someone?'

Blum was scornful, 'Ha.'

'What if they got caught and told the police where they
got it? That Kav might not snitch, but your mate, Delly, he
would, deffo.'

Blum shook his head. I was annoyed.

'I'd put money on it, that's how lads like him survive. And if he pointed the finger at you it'd be more than nine months in bloody Butlins.'

Blum protested, 'I could've sold 'em a twelve bore. I could've asked ten quid, even for a knackered one. Now they'll get one somewhere else.'

'At least it won't come back on you.'

'You know I need every penny I can get for mam's lease.'

'Then concentrate on selling all the stuff you've got, dump those bloody guns. They're not worth the trouble.'

He swigged at his pint.

'I mean it. Get shut of 'em all.'

Blum said nothing. I was reluctant to turn this into an argument, perhaps Blum felt the same after a pleasant day, but I couldn't resist the last word. 'You should've kept your mouth shut in Havvy and all.'

'Blummin' 'eck, I only told Delly.'

Delly was one too many, but I didn't push it, 'Good.'

I stood, necked the rest of my pint, 'I said I'd meet Elaine. Are you seeing Viv?'

He nodded. 'We'll probably have a look in the Plough Horse if you fancy it.'

'Right,' I said. I knew already Elaine would find an excuse if there was any chance she might have to talk to Blum, or Viv. Blum never showed any animosity to Elaine, but I had no doubt he knew how she felt about him. 'If we don't make it, I'll ring you.'

I glanced back as I left the forecourt on the walk to Elaine's parents' place. Blum sat hunched over his beer. I hoped Delly's appearance with that Kav character had taught him to be more careful in future.

I was wrong.

Chapter 20
Bloody Phone, Isn't It?

NOW IT WAS summer, work was harder. We had to cover for those on holiday and it was a struggle to fill a local paper in the so-called 'silly season' when local government was in recess and schools, factories and mills had holidays and summer shut down.

Extra hours at work didn't help my social life. I hardly saw Elaine, or enough of Sandra. I worked most weekends and evenings. When Geoff Sillitoe went on a two-week fishing trip in Ireland wangled through a Kilkenny tackle manufacturer, I had to do my own job while 'temporary, acting news editor.' Had he not left an acre of pre-written copy singing the praises of the almost unknown Irish outfit and the Republic's angling paradise, we'd have had little to publish.

Weeks passed, it was late July before I spoke to Blum again. When it came, it wasn't a social phone call. It came unexpectedly, on a day already different from usual.

I welcomed Geoff back from his holiday with relief, discovered our news editor was not alone on his trip to Ireland. His fellow ligger on the all-expenses-paid trip was Councillor Harold Fairbrass. Under the influence of buckets of free whiskey and Guinness, the free-loading duo dreamt up a project: the jointly sponsored *Sentinel* and Alumbrook Council Open Angling Match.

I could see the imagined kudos for an ambitious chairman of the parks and gardens committee who wanted to be an alderman on the town council, but didn't think it possible Geoff could squeeze into the season even one more fishing match. The idea was sold to our company chairman old man Henty; remarkable, as he was a purist, dry-fly trout fisherman. With Geoff using Henty's name like a cosh, I was press-ganged on to the steering committee for the event which would take place on the canal at the bottom of my street in September. If only I hadn't told Geoff I was an occasional angler. The only redeeming factor for me was Geoff used the same cosh in the advertising department, Sandra became a dogsbody colleague on our little committee. After many months of clandestine liaison, we now had reason to be seen together.

Earlier on the day Blum phoned, Councillor Fairbrass called our first meeting at his office in the timber yard. I could think of a dozen better places to be on a hot afternoon. When Fairbrass discovered there was only a dribble of whisky in the bottle in his stationery cupboard, it was proposed and carried without dissent, the meeting be relocated to the best room at The Packet.

Talk over the first hour covered everything but the short agenda we'd met to discuss. By the time we'd finished that it was well after four o'clock, I was only a touch less pissed than Geoff and Fairbrass. I knew Sandra was a bit gone herself by the way she looked at me, not to mention her shoeless foot between my shins. Geoff Sillitoe presumed I was going back to the newsroom, but Sandra suggested she and I should 'get our heads together' and 'knock up a joint report' on the meeting. She winked at me, grinned. Councillor Fairbrass considered her offer with due gravity, congratulated us on our enthusiasm. Geoff weaved his way back to *The Sentinel* alone. Sandra and I couldn't get to my grotty flat fast enough.

It was nearly six o' clock when I was woken by the phone ringing on the landing. I thought it was my alarm clock. I was disorientated further when I felt Sandra's warm body next to mine on the green candlewick bedspread. Then Kitty's knuckles rapped a tattoo on my door.

'For you, *Bachgen,* phone!'

Sandra's arm crossed my chest, she murmured something. I pushed it aside, shushed her.

The rapping on the door sounded again, louder.

'*Bachgen*. Bloody phone, isn't it!'

I jumped off the bed naked, grabbed my trousers, pulled them on. I tried to fasten them as I pulled the bedroom door closed behind me, opened my entrance door a crack. If Kitty saw Sandra she'd wheedle for a flask of Bells.

'Gone deaf now, is it? Been ringing ten minutes easy,' she said as I manoeuvred myself to block any possible view of Sandra.

When Kitty turned away, I could smell booze from her panting breath hanging in the warm air. Or it could've been mine.

'Sorry, Mrs Williams, I fell asleep. Did they say who was ca--?'

But she was already trudging downstairs, muttering about her legs. I grabbed my shirt. Sandra raised herself on one elbow, grinned, 'If that's Elaine, you won't be too long, will you?'

She laughed as I clutched my waistband and shirtfront, headed downstairs and snatched the receiver from the top of the payphone box. 'Hello?'

It was Blum.

'Jeeze, you pick your times.' I pushed my backside against the wall to stop my kecks falling down. I couldn't manage to fasten the waist button with one hand. 'Can I call you back in about ten, no make it ...'

He cut me off, 'Listen. I've no more money and I can't hang round. Can you come over now? I need help. Today's been a bit of a blummin'...It's...'

'What's happened?'

'I just need you to pick me up. Get the van from May Bank and come to the phone box by the wide sluice, the one up from Ted and Marion's. Wait there.'

What the hell had happened? 'Are you hurt?'

'No.'

'Can't Viv get you?'

'No!'

The pips sounded. Blum shouted, 'Phone box by the wide sluice bridge -- Fast as you blummin' can.'

I shouted too, as if that would negate the need for more coins, 'Are you sure you're okay?'

The line was dead. I put the receiver back. Sandra appeared at the top of the stairs, covered her nakedness with a pillow. Her voice was hushed, 'What's with the bloody shouting? Who is it?'

I hurried upstairs, ushering her inside, shutting the door. 'Can I borrow the Mini?'

'What the hell for?'

'I need to get home. Quick!'

'Is it your mum and dad? Are they all right?'

'It's not them, it's a friend. I've got to meet him right now.'

'Why?'

'I don't know. He just…He's in some sort of…Look, I'll be dead careful with it. I'll put petrol in it.'

'Are you joking? You're not insured. You haven't even passed your test.'

'It was Blum. He wouldn't call like that if it wasn't serious.'

'I'll drive you.'

'Are you sure?'

She stooped to pick up her clothes from the floor, turned to me, grinned, 'Nowt else to do, have I?'

*

Minutes later Sandra revved her Mini's engine as I dashed out of Dootson's corner shop at the other end of Quinn Street from Kitty's. In my hand were two rolls of Polo mints. Next stop was a filling station. I rooted in my pockets for cash, peered across at the driver's wing mirror, as a long-haired lad with acne practiced for the title of the world's slowest petrol pump attendant.

I was anxious to be on my way to Blum, exhaled with impatience, muttered, 'For Christ's sake, mate, shape yourself.'

Sandra rolled the window down further, barked at the teenager, 'Hurry up, Gordon. You could piss faster than that.'

I offered her a handful of change, including two of the new fifty pence pieces.

'Don't worry I'll stick it on *The Sentinel* account.'

I was startled, 'You what?'

She laughed, 'Don't fret about it.'

'Fair enough, why should I worry?'

I was about to pocket my cash, but she took my wrist, picked out one of the fifty coins, 'Hang on I, need summat for Gordon.'

'Hey, that's a ten-bob piece!'

'Where else can you get a full tank for that?'

Gordon replaced the pump nozzle.

Sandra told him, 'Signed for by my dad.' She flicked my fifty pence piece and he snatched it from the air with one hand, 'Ta, Gordon.'

Gordon pocketed my coin, gave her the thumbs up, 'Good as done, Miss 'Eaton.'

I was amazed at this casual fraud. Every week Geoff Sillitoe had an audience with old man Henty, the sole purpose of which was to examine each reporter and photographer's expense claims, to strike out even genuine items on a whim to satisfy his parsimony. Geoff never defended our claims and my attempt in his absence in the Republic met with a blank stare before Henty settled the matter with a stroke of red ink. Yet here was the advertising's department's junior rep ripping off Hentypops' company to run her nice car. The Mini was an expensive seventeenth birthday gift from her mum and dad. I suppose you couldn't blame an upstanding member of the parochial church council like P.S.Heaton, chartered accountant, director and freemason, for subsidising its running costs from company funds. I wondered if she claimed expenses for work petrol as well.

Sandra rammed the gear shift into first, grinned at me, 'Breathe a word about that little fiddle and I'll chop your cock off.'

I laughed as she swung off the forecourt, on to the road heading south west and home.

'How long have you been doing it?'

She grinned, 'No comment.'

'Does Hentypops know about it?'

'Shit, no!

'Off the record, then?'

'I've nowt to add at this point in time, as Councillor Fairbrass would say.'

I laughed, 'I wouldn't snitch. You know I wouldn't.'

'Oh, yeah…'

'I wouldn't.'

She glanced at me, laughed, 'Drop it, John Pilger. Now keep feeding me Polos. If I get done for drink-driving, Daddio'll stick me in a bloody convent.'

I placed another between her lips, stuck three more in my own mouth in preparation for driving Blum's van. In those days when the breathalyser was new, people put their faith in all manner of methods to protect them from having to blow in the bag. Most drink drivers of my acquaintance relied on mints.

Sandra swore she was fine to drive, but when she switched on the radio, sang along with Cat Stevens, drummed the rhythm on the steering wheel as we touched seventy on the twisting road across the moors, I had my doubts.

I needed to get to Blum, didn't want any unwanted delays.

Chapter 21
Don't Breathe On Any Coppers

WE REACHED THE M6, joined it for a short stretch south
from Leyland. At Charnock Richard services I told her to
turn off. We sneaked out of the car park along a service road,
entered the maze of lanes that would take us through the
villages of Wrightington, Heskin, Hilldale, Bispham Green
and Hoscar, then to Ormskirk. Blum knew these lanes
through his job at Daltry's. Often, we'd driven them in the
Chev. On this summer evening they were at their best; some
like green tunnels through low-hanging trees, head high cow
parsley. Had I been there other than as a result of Blum's
call, I'd've shown Sandra one or two good pubs, perhaps
before a walk through the woods.

I tried to think what could have prompted Blum's call.
Sandra turned off the radio.

'You're quiet,' she said, 'Worried about your mate?'

'Yeah, I can't weigh it up.'

The lane reached a junction, a choice of two other equally
narrow lanes. 'Left here.'

She turned, whipped the fag from my hand, took a drag.
'Did you say he wouldn't get his girlfriend to pick him
up…?'

'Yeah.'

She exhaled smoke.

'Why's that?'

'I don't know.'

She glanced at me, passed back the cigarette, 'You must
have some idea.'

'It's just…I know there's some things he doesn't tell her.'

'Such as?'

Sandra had never met Blum, though I'd mentioned him
often. What I'd told her was innocuous, from when we were
boys, pranks and practical jokes. She knew nothing about our

revenge on Travis, that night on the roof at Havvy. I'd told her Blum had been in Havershawe, but nothing about the guns and knock-off goods at Pygon's Farm, Blum's reason for stealing from Daltry's.

'Just… odd things. Money and that.'

Sandra looked pleased with herself, 'It's another girl, isn't it?'

I was shocked, emphatic. 'No.'

'Sure it's not some boyfriend on the warpath? Or has he got some married one? Is the husband after him and he needs to scarper, hide somewhere? Am I right?'

'He's not like that?'

'Not like you, you mean?'

I looked at her. She was grinning. 'You don't tell Elaine everything, do you?'

'No, he's not like me.'

'Wow, honesty.'

'Since he met Viv he's not looked at another girl.'

'How do you know? You don't see him that often.'

'I just know. They're made for each other. He's told me he wants to marry her.'

Sandra looked, 'Really?'

'That's what he told me.'

She laughed, 'Is he a piss-artist like you, then?'

'Eh?'

She looked at me again, amused, as we joined the main road from Preston to Ormskirk, 'You told me you told Elaine you wanted to marry her when you were drunk.'

I was startled. *How did she know that?* 'Did I?'

'You couldn't remember when she mentioned it next day.'

I squirmed. She grinned at me.

'You must've been three sheets when you told me as well.'

What? 'I told you I wanted to marry you?'

She laughed,' See what I mean?'

The panic lasted only moments.

'You might be pleased to know you didn't. I meant you must've been drunk to tell me about it.' She laughed, 'You're a bloody liability, you are.'

I didn't want any discussion of what I might've said about marrying anyone. Or my drinking habits. I told her, 'All I know is it's a lovejob with him and Viv.'

'A lovejob?'

'You know...'

She glanced at me, 'I like that – Never heard it before. Lovejob...Lovejob, lovejob -- it's nice.'

She took her eyes away from the road, 'Could we be a lovejob?'

I was startled again.

I'd stopped myself from such thoughts for months. Yet when she left me an affectionate note, when she walked into a room, when I watched her getting on so easily with others, when we lay talking in bed; yes, I thought, we might. But I'd left it too long to reply.

'Shit, I'm sorry,' she said, 'That wasn't fair.'

She drove on, it came out, I couldn't stop myself, 'What if I asked the same question?'

She took her hand off the wheel, dug me in my side.

'Hey, that's unfair as well!'

She drove on, smiled to herself. It was a minute before she spoke again, eyes on the road 'Well, if it's not some jealous bloke, what is it? Why's he in a panic?'

I was disappointed she'd changed the subject.

She glanced at me.

My worries about Blum returned. I shook my head, 'I don't know.'

She turned her eyes back to the road.

That was something else I liked about Sandra. She might have asked questions, but she didn't demand answers, unlike Elaine.

We approached May Bank View and I was desperate to get to Tarlscough. I told her she could drop me at the next corner.

She pulled up, turned off the engine, 'I can take you to meet him, if you want.'

'It's alright, he said to use his van.'

'Do you want me to wait? It's up to you.'

'Best you get back. God knows how long it'll take. Wait at the flat, if you want.'

'Just for a bit, perhaps. I could nip through the back door if Kitty's in The Packet. Or I could come and pick you up, if you give me a time?'

'I can't. I'll hitch if I have to,' I said, 'Done it before.'

I leaned over, kissed her, got out. 'Thanks.'

She started the Mini, laughed, 'Don't breathe on any coppers.'

She reversed into a lane, accelerated away with a pip of the horn. I was nervous when I stepped in to the drive of May Bank View to take the van, hoped Blum's mam wouldn't call the police if she noticed it missing.

I peered through the window of the back parlour. The telly wasn't on, so I guessed she'd be in the garden making the most of the warm evening. I could've looked for her to say hello, but Blum would be worried I was taking so long. I opened the van, retrieved the spare ignition key from the slit in the driver's seat, slid a Polo mint in my mouth. I still felt drunk.

*

Ten minutes later, I crunched and swallowed my last two mints. The still warm sun hung over ripening barley fields, I drove as fast as I dared to the rendezvous.

I felt guilty I'd not looked for Blum's mam. I hadn't seen her for months, thought how lonely she must be now. Fewer locals called in with sewing work, she no longer had Uncle Walter for company and Blum often stayed at Viv's. Loneliness and the ever present worry of the May Bank lease must have weighed on her spirits. I felt for her.

A movement in the wing mirror caught my attention, a police car approaching at speed. I cupped my hand over my mouth, tried to smell my breath. I had no idea if that afternoon's whisky still lingered. I'd had nothing to eat since a sandwich at noon, so it likely did, despite the overdose of mints, now making me belch. I dreaded being asked to blow in the bag.

Since I started to drive the Chev, later the van, Blum and I had an arrangement. If I were stopped, I'd give Blum's name and address. If he was in the passenger seat and asked his name, he would pretend to be me. But to use his identity if I were dragged in for drunk-driving was unthinkable. If a breath test proved positive, I'd have to come clean, accept being banned even before I passed my test, prosecuted for no insurance as well. I slumped with relief when the police driver failed to switch on his blue light, hurtled past me towards Southport like he was on more important business.

I wondered if there was an alternative route in case I came across the police car further on. Norman Tisdall from the estate's shooting syndicate once boasted he could drive from the edge of Southport almost to Lydiate and travel 95 per cent of the distance on tracks that weren't public roads. Norman told a tall story, but it was a way to keep clear of any cop car.

I turned on to the next cart track that pointed roughly in the right direction . It ran through wide grain and spud fields, punctuated by belts of trees and isolated coverts of birch, pine and alder. My progress was slower. A tractor would've been more use over the ruts and potholes. I cursed my impulsiveness. For all I knew I'd reach a dead end, have to turn back, but I picked up speed as the track became smoother.

In my rush to reach Blum, I drove too fast. The nearside wheel hit a deep rut. The van bucked, wobbled. There was a clang of metal on metal, a grating noise as I braked. Christ, I couldn't break down here, not now. I got out, hurried to examine the wheel that ran into the rut. Had I bust an axle? Had the wheel been sheared off the bolts? What the hell was it? I stooped down, grabbed the tyre and pushed and pulled at the wheel. It seemed solid, undamaged. I set off again.

Everything seemed fine, but when the van crossed yet another hole, I heard a similar metallic noise, this time from behind me. I braked, pulled aside the curtain that separated the seats from the back of the van. Beyond the pile of hessian potato sacks Blum used to protect furniture from damage were two black objects against the rear doors. I moved forward in first gear, jabbed the brake hard. The same grating noise and the objects had moved. Irritated, I got out, opened the back doors.

Straight away I knew what they were. Two similar blue-black tapered tubes about a foot and a half long; each of the double tubes fixed together with a thin rib of steel. On the thicker ends of each was the ragged evidence of a hacksaw's work -- the discarded pieces of two double-barrel shotguns that had been sawn-off.

I pulled at the sacks, looking for the actions and butt ends of the guns: nothing. After all I'd said he'd kept those bloody guns. Even worse, he'd turned at least two into objects with only a single purpose: crime. I stared at the sets of useless tubes. Had he sold the cut-down, working actions of both guns to criminals? I could've screamed in anger, frustration. Did this have something to do with his call? I forced myself to give him the benefit of the doubt. Perhaps he'd chickened out of a deal to sell guns. But owing to that, was someone after him? Was it that Kav character? He had the makings of a violent piece of work, seemed desperate for guns. Did Blum call me to spirit him away from criminals demanding guns? Christ, I hoped it was as simple as that.

I had to get going, but I was damned if I'd drive around with two sawn-off barrels. I knew being caught with only the cut-off remnants could mean prison. Last winter *The Sentinel* carried a story where a family man tried to intimidate someone who'd cheated him over the sale of a car. In a pub he'd threatened the seller with a sawn-off gun. The sawn-off was never found, but he was convicted when police found cut-off barrels in his locker at work. He was jailed for cutting shotgun tubes down to less than two feet on a separate charge to his antics in the pub. I had to get rid of these barrels now, but where?

Deep water was ideal, but I knew nowhere close. In fact, I wasn't sure where I was. I scanned the acres of cereal awaiting the combine harvester. On either side of the track were deep, moss ditches, each at least ten feet deep. But I knew after recent hot weather, they'd contain little water. Next winter they'd be dug out, anything hidden exposed. I could bury them. I crossed a ditch bridge of old railway sleepers at the opening to a field, kicked at baked earth. I'd no spade to bury them deep and a plough might unearth them after harvest. Then I spotted a cluster of rat holes near the bridge. Blum and I had often shot rats on ditch banks like these. I checked the landscape for farmers, walkers, any witnesses, rushed back to the van, grabbed the tubes, put each in a different rat burrow. I pushed and kicked them until both were out of sight.

I drove away as fast as I could. A long wood on my left with an electricity pylon behind it was familiar. I was almost at the road which led to Ted and Marion's place. I slowed, looked to my right, slewed out left on to the tarmac road, drove towards the end of the wood, where a chevron marked a sharp left-hand bend. I knew I was two or three minutes' drive at most from our meeting point. I dropped a gear for the bend, turned the corner and accelerated. A uniformed policeman stepped forward holding up his hand.

A patrol car was parked at a right angle to the wood edge. I braked hard.

Shit!

Chapter 22
Road Block

BEYOND THE CONSTABLE with the raised hand, a second copper moved away from the car to join his colleague. My hands and shirt cuffs were mucky after manhandling the tyre, burying the sawn-off barrels, I started to sweat. God knows how desperate, how suspicious, how drunk, I looked. I tried to relax, compose myself. The first copper moved to my open window.

'Sorry to delay you, sir,' he said, 'I wonder if you'd mind telling me where you're going?'

Like a ventriloquist, I tried to speak without opening my mouth, doing what Sandra had jokily warned me about. 'I'm, er, visiting a relative.'

'Would you mind telling me their name and address?'

I pondered a moment, chose to give Blum's details if necessary, and, for the moment, Ted and Marion's address. If it came to the breathalyser, I'd confess my true identity. I had no choice.

The copper was impatient, but polite, 'The address, sir?'

'Er, yeah, it's the Head Keeper's House, Tarlscough Home Farm.'

'That'd be Ted Crossman's place?'

Oh, God. How well did this middle-aged constable know Ted?

'Yep. Ted's wife, Marion, she's my mam's cousin, I do a bit to help out.'

'I see. And your name, sir…?'

I hoped this bobby didn't know Blum. 'Gatley, David Gatley.'

There was no sign he did. I was comforted he made no attempt to write anything down.

'You live local?'

'Down at Lydiate.'

'Just routine, sir, but we'd like to check the back of your van. Is it locked?'

I shook my head. The copper gave the nod to his colleague who moved along the van's nearside.

The first copper said, 'Have you been in this area at all earlier today?'

I heard the back doors open, a swishing sound as copper number two moved the sacks.

'No, I've been working.'

The back doors were slammed shut on the place where only minutes ago lay evidence that could've put me inside. If the copper had measured my pulse rate, he'd've had me handcuffed in an instant. Instead he looked to his colleague behind the van and nodded.

'Thank you for your co-operation, sir, on your way.'

My hand shook as I reached for the gear stick. Whether I was playing for time to compose myself, or it was a reporter's curiosity, I wasn't sure, but I asked, 'What's with the road block? What's happened?'

'I'm not at liberty to say, sir.'

He stepped back from the van, waved his hand, obliged me to go. I pushed the gear stick into first and ballsed up the clutch release. The engine stalled. I had to fight to control myself, to concentrate. I depressed the clutch, turned the key. It was sweat, but I felt my pores were pumping out neat whisky; that I stank like a distillery. My foot was a trembling dead weight on the pedal, but I managed to release it, move off. I went up the gears as quick as I could. My hand still shook as I fumbled a cigarette out of my pocket, craved a smoke. A drink would've been better.

I knew where I was now. A crossroads of four single track lanes was ahead. Left led to a scattered hamlet called West Meols. I turned right to an area known as Ninefields. On either side were Perch Pool woods where so often we'd picked blackberries for our mothers. I left the woods, headed out into open, flat farmland. Ahead was the red telephone kiosk, its colour and presence incongruous in this landscape.

I remembered the old A and B button days when Blum and I never passed without a check for forgotten pennies.

I pulled up by the phone box, got out. A few yards away a white steel and wood bridge crossed the big sluice, a major field drain, ten yards wide. I was wary of the police presence in the area, felt exposed. I went to the kiosk, stepped inside. It was like an oven. I picked up the receiver, tried to appear normal, but my eyes raked the place in case Blum had left some message. He hadn't. I couldn't bear the heat, so I left the kiosk. I leaned against the van, looked around. If a vehicle approached in any direction I would see it from a half-mile away, the same for anyone on foot. There was no sign of Blum. I began to worry I was in the wrong place.

On the moss it was silent, bar the noise of grasshoppers, the tinkling song of a skylark. I looked up, tried to pinpoint it, when I heard a voice call my name. It was Blum. I whipped around, but he wasn't there. Feeling foolish, I said, 'Where are you?'

'Under the blummin' bridge!'

I moved towards it, 'Where?'

I grabbed the rail of the bridge, ready to drop down the bank through the man-high willow herb and reed mace.

Blum's voice was urgent, 'Don't come down. Stay there.'

I leaned on the rail, as though enjoying the peace and quiet, but my mood wasn't tranquil, 'What's going on? What are you doing dragging me out here?'

'The police are after me. Have been all blummin' day, but I lost 'em.'

'Christ, what have you done?'

He ignored the question,' I've got to get out of here, right off the moss. Can you get the back doors of the van open and get it started up, ready?'

'Tell me what's going on.'

'I'm on the run from a robbery.'

'What robbery? Where?'

'Get us out of here and I'll tell you.'

'Tell me now!'

'A blummin' cop car stopped on this bridge before. We've got to go.'

Now I knew the reason for the road block. Thank God, I got rid of those barrels, or I'd be in custody, number one suspect for this robbery. God Almighty, what had he got himself into? 'Have you got a gun with you?'

'Dumped it,' he said, 'Just blummin' start it up, eh?'

Drunkenness was draining away. I was resentful at what Blum has sucked me into, angry at what he'd revealed. I opened one of the van's back doors, backed round, so the rear end faced the bridge. I checked either way there was nobody around, feared the police might have binoculars. I started up, leaned out of window, 'Ready?'

In the mirror, I watched Blum hurry from under the bridge, stooped low like a soldier under fire. His jeans and olive tee-shirt were filthy, covered in goose grass burrs, fluffy seed heads and dried duckweed. His hair tangled and greasy, his forearms scratched. His face was blotched with midge bites or nettle stings. His boots scraped on the floor of the van, the door slammed shut. He poked his head through the sacking curtain.

'I'm blummin' parched. Got owt to drink?'

I was terse, 'What do you think?'

'A fag then?' he said, 'Haven't had one in hours.'

I backhanded my packet and matches into his chest, drove back the way I came.

'Turn left at the crossroads in Perch Pool wood.'

'No bloody chance, I've just been stopped at a police road block up there. We'll go straight on, through West Meols.'

'Did they check in the van?'

'Did they find those sodding sawn off twelve-bore barrels, you mean?'

'Blummin' heck, I forgot about them. Did they...'

'Good job I found them first and got rid, isn't it? I'd be nicked and you'd still be under that bloody bridge.'

I approached the crossroads, reduced my speed to a crawl, checked both ways. No traffic, but the police were still where I was stopped, still visible hundreds of yards away on the left. I floored the accelerator, shot over the crossroads, out of their line of sight, into the woods.

My anger and resentment bubbled, I had questions, but my priority was to get on to a busy main road, to avoid police cars. Out here I felt exposed.

Blum asked for another cigarette. 'Stop poking your head out. Try and clean yourself up a bit as well-- That bloody weed for a kick-off.'

My instinct was to drive like the clappers, but I kept the speed down as we passed farms and houses. I tried to stay calm, get Blum and myself as far away from here as I could.

'Where was this robbery?'

'The post office at Meanygate End.'

'Who else was in on it?'

'Three other lads, that's all.'

I almost shouted the question, but I suspected the answer already, 'What bloody lads?'

'It was just…Delly and Kav and another feller.'

'Jesus!'

I pulled the curtain aside to see him cross-legged, fag in hand, picking off goose grass with the other.

I shouted, 'You handed the guns out and all, didn't you?'

'I thought we'd be all right.'

'You stupid sod. I suppose those pillocks got caught?'

'I don't know.'

I was angry, 'So it all went wrong?'

'Nobody got hurt and I've got the money.'

'You've hidden it somewhere?'

'Nah, it's here, down me jeans.'

I was speechless. How much worse could it get?

Then I saw the roadblock. Two hundred yards ahead on the straight flat road through forty acres of barley. A uniformed constable move into position to wave us down.

174

'Christ, it's another road block. Get under the sacks! Keep quiet!'

Blum scrabbled round in the back, bumped the back of my seat, 'Can't you turn back?'

'And have every copper in the world after us?'

My eyes stayed on the constable, 'If they ask, I'll give them your name like the last time, hope he doesn't look in the back.'

It would be a miracle if he didn't search the van. The apprehension flooded through me; soon I would tremble. And, ridiculous as it seemed, despite having an armed robber and his loot behind me, and a police road block in front of me, I still worried I smelt of drink.

Blum piped up, 'Have you got that Press card thingy of yours on you?'

'Yeah, why?

'Stick it up their blummin' noses as soon as they stop you.'

My fingers went into my inside pocket, touched the plastic wallet that held my journalist's union card, complete with mug shot, that entitled me to recognition and cooperation from all police forces in Britain and the Republic of Ireland.

Blum added, 'Give 'em some guff about doing a write-up on the robbery.'

'I can't, I'm out of my area. My paper doesn't cover...' I shut-up. It was a good idea, I had none of my own.

I had no time to rehearse. I slowed, stopped, as the copper approached, hand raised. He was little older than me, with a moustache to make him look more mature.

The copper announced, 'I'm sorry to...'

I didn't shove it up his nose, but proffered it at arm's length, so he had less chance of missing my photo and PRESS in tall, black type – or smelling booze on my breath. I spoke before he finished his sentence, 'I'm following up this robbery, mate. Any arrests yet?'

'Oh, aye?' he said, taking the Press card. I reckoned it was the first he'd ever seen. He examined it for a moment and I felt the sweat on my back, 'It doesn't say what paper you're on.'

I forced a matey chuckle, 'I'm with the *Evening Post* in Preston, pal. The cards are all the same, union cards.'

The copper looked at it again, compared my sweaty face with the card's black and white photo. He handed it back, seemed relaxed, perhaps because I wasn't a robber with a sawn-off shotgun.

'Any arrests, then?' I repeated.

'If you ask me they're long gone.' He laughed, 'Like the Benny Hill Show over there this morning, organised flippin' chaos.' He corrected himself , 'Eh, don't be putting that in the paper.'

'No, no, don't worry, all off the record, mate. So…What makes you think they're gone? My office says one of them's on the run out here. You know, Ninefields way.'

I picked up my fags, offered him one. 'Grand, mate, I've run out. Ta.'

He lit the cigarette. I prompted him, 'So there's still one out here?'

'If he is, I've not seen him.' He blew out smoke with satisfaction. 'About an hour since there was a radio message said he'd been spotted legging it through Churchtown into Southport. I've been told to stand-by in case the borough force needs help.'

'So he's in Southport now?'

'It looks like it. It's where they'll have come from, if you ask me.'

'Have they got the other robbers yet?'

He laughed, 'Bugger-all over the radio, but I'll bet the lot of 'em'll be in some bar on the front by now, bevvying it up with all them Jocks down for holidays.'

'So I can knock-off and go for a pint meself?'

He chuckled, 'Aye, do that, mate. Wish I could. Thanks for the smoke.'

I let out the clutch and drove away, my eyes on him in the wing mirror. He took the cigarette from his mouth, used the same hand for a cheery wave.

Blum laughed behind me, 'He's never going work for Scotland Yard, is he?'

'I'm not laughing,' I said, 'I still want to know why you risked our necks with all this.'

I drove into Ormskirk from the Preston to Liverpool road and pulled up outside the Acropolis, the Greek-Cypriot-owned chippy, away from the centre of town, counted my money. Blum poked his head through the curtain, held out a fiver. 'Here... Blummin' mad, isn't it? Copperin' up to ring you and I've got tons of these.'

'How much is tons?'

'I make it just over fifteen hundred quid.'

'Bloody hell.'

I regarded the fiver.

'I'll pay,' I said, 'I'm not getting done for handling stolen money.'

Blum stayed in the back while I bought pie and chips twice, a bottle of Tizer. I drove out of town, up Clieves Hill. We parked by a bench, ate as the sun began to set over the flat plain below, beyond it the Irish Sea. Down there in the patchwork of west Lancashire farmland was where the robbery happened, where Blum evaded the police all day. I wanted to know everything.

Chapter 23
Mayhem at Meanygate End

AT QUARTER TO nine that morning, and the sun already warm, Delly dropped Blum at the only bus stop in Meanygate End. It was in what passed for the centre of the village, or what passed for a village. The place was no more than a hamlet with no pub, no village hall and no church. It had a couple of farms, about ten private houses, half a dozen council houses and a phone box. Opposite Blum was the village shop and post office.

The post office was the focus of Blum's interest as he sat on the bus stop bench with a folded copy of the *Daily Telegraph*. A more appropriate *Daily Mirror* wasn't big enough to hide a Belgian twelve-bore hammer gun minus most of its barrels and part of the wooden stock. Tucked down the waist of his jeans was a pair of washing up gloves. In his back pocket was a woman's nylon stocking.

Today was old age pension day and to rob the post office when it had the largest amount of cash on the premises was Kav's and then Delly's joint venture. It had been since April when he'd sounded out Delly as an experienced car thief, someone vital in the need to provide two knock-off cars and act as driver. In the run-up to the 'job' Delly told Blum how he became involved.

Delly had no luck finding work as a former Borstal inmate and was keen from the start when Kav bought him a pint and mentioned the car man would get a quarter of the robbery's proceeds; good money as Kav estimated there could be more than a thousand quid in the post office on pension day. Kav already had two more petty criminals recruited and now the only problem that remained was the need for guns. Kav had asked around, but nobody could help. No doubt with a wish to ingratiate himself with Kav, Delly bragged about his 'mate' from Havvy who had five pistols. That prompted Kav and Delly's first visit to seek out Blum at the Scottish Soldier. But in July, one of the petty criminals had been remanded in custody on shop-breaking charges. Kav and Delly made a second visit to the Soldier with an alternative strategy.

Blum was uneasy at their appearance in the back room of the pub. The instant Kav put a pint of bitter in front of him, he told him, 'I'm not selling you anything.'

Kav sat opposite him, 'I don't want to fuckin' buy 'em. Just lend us a couple.'

'Don't be daft. You could still get nabbed with them.'

Kav leaned over the table, 'What if I said lend us a couple for a few hours and you get two hundred quid, maybe two fifty?'

Blum laughed, 'What you going to do? Rob a blummin' bank?'

Delly leaned in, 'It's that post office over at....'

He got no further. Kav swung his clenched fist, backhanded Delly, almost knocked him over. 'Eh, soft lad, watch the gob.'

Kav glanced around, lowered his voice, 'Lend us the guns and we'll let you in on it.'

I interrupted Blum's story, 'Christ, why did you agree?'

'I just did.'

'But an armed robbery. You could get ten years, more.'

'I thought you wanted to know about today?'

'I want to know why you risked everything to get involved in something like that? Well?'

Blum faced me, picked up my packet of fags, 'Do you want to know what happened, or not?

I sighed, nodded. He lit up.

Blum watched the post office as the first customers came and went. Kav had suggested they strike as it closed for lunch to give them more, uninterrupted time; until Blum pointed out the obvious; that by then half or more of the cash would've been handed out to pensioners. The robbery had to be when the post office opened. That was the first of Blum's alterations. Kav wanted them all to be armed, but Blum refused to provide any more than two sawn off twelve bores. Kav would have one to intimidate the post master and his wife. Blum would have the other to bolster his position at the door of the post office where he would admit any customers, but not let them out. Delly would stay at the wheel of the car and the third lad, a none-too-bright seventeen-year-old called Cooey, would act as bag man, make sure every banknote given up by the post office owners went into a spud sack.

In the days before the robbery, Kav pressed Blum to hand over the guns. But Blum was suspicious that once he'd handed them over, Kav would cut him out of the venture to give himself, Delly and Cooey a three-way split on the cash. He wasn't prepared to take the risk that if things went wrong, his fellow would- be robbers might give up the identity of their armourer and Blum would end up in trouble, minus any profit. Kav argued his point, told Blum he needed to practice with the gun, but Blum was adamant he would hand them over only on the morning of the raid.

He used this lever the night before when he insisted that the Ford Anglia and Hillman Avenger cars stolen that day by Delly were wiped clean of possible fingerprints; would not be touched un-gloved by any of them. With everything set, he insisted he would be in position before the others arrived at the post office. If he decided to abort the robbery, his word would be final.

Kav bristled, 'It's my fuckin' job, this. If anyone's going to call it off, it'll be me.'

Blum told him, 'We do it proper, or I don't blummin' bother. You three can do it on your own, or wait till you find someone else, some other guns. It's up to you.'

Blum knew from Delly's indiscreet comments Kav needed the money. He was behind on his rent. From Delly he knew also that Kav was on the fringe of a group of more organised criminals operating in Southport, was desperate for the credibility he needed to get more involved. Delly revealed that he and Kav had been paid twenty pounds by the Southport lot to follow a lorry from the docks in Liverpool to a wholesale company in Blackburn. 'Kav was hassling the bloke from Southport, Frank Pye he's called, to let him in on one of their jobs,' Delly told him, 'Pye said he'd have to have a word with his boss. But he told Kav it wasn't like nicking sweets from Woolies.

Blum laughed, 'Oh, aye. What did Kav say to that?'

'He was narked. Said he'd show the bloke, prove himself kind of thing.'

This was enough to convince Blum that Kav wanted the job done, whatever the terms. He needed to impress this Frank Pye character and the people behind him in Southport. Blum sensed Kav lacked confidence, wanted someone on the job with more nous than Delly and gormless Cooey. He was convinced Kav wouldn't attempt to cut him out of the proceeds.

Blum prompted Kav, 'Well...?'

Kav jabbed a finger at Blum's face, 'Just make sure you're there on time with them fuckin' guns.'

At five past nine, the post office now open, Blum looked east along the road out of Meanygate End for the approach of the blue Hillman Avenger. He pulled the gloves from his waist band, slipped them on. He felt inside the newspaper, levered open the sawn-off. He took two red Eley cartridges from his pocket and slid them into the chambers of the gun. He closed the breech, clicked back both hammers. He'd seen the glint in Kav's eyes earlier that morning when he passed over the other sawn-off and two similar cartridges, watched him load it. He was wary of the combination; Kavanagh and a loaded gun.

When Blum again looked east, the Avenger approached. It pulled up at the kerb a few yards past the post office, a dozen yards from the door. Inside, three faces turned to him; Kav in the passenger seat, Cooey in the back, Delly at the wheel. Blum knew the only customers inside the post office were two old ladies. He raised his thumb to Kav, dragged the nylon stocking from his pocket, pulled it over his head. Inside the Avenger, Kav and Cooey did the same. Blum loped across the road and Kav and Cooey burst from the car. With the sawn-off in his right hand like a giant pistol, Kav launched himself at the door, pressed the handle and shoulder-charged into the post office, Cooey after him with the sack. Blum scanned the vicinity, slipped in behind them.

The two old ladies cowered against a rack of greetings cards. Kav shouted and waved the sawn-off, 'Keep still, or I'll shoot.' He jabbed the gun towards a tall man with the moustache behind the counter, 'Give us the money! Quick!'

The postmaster's face coloured in outrage, 'Get out of my premises!'

'Gerrit now!' Kav roared.

A middle-aged woman behind the counter was already pulling banknotes from the till.

Kav shouted at the postmaster, 'Open the safe!'

The postmaster didn't move, his voice firm, 'Get out.'

Kav pointed the sawn-off at his face. 'Open it!'

The man stared at Kav, stubborn, defiant. Cooey scraped banknotes off the counter into the sack. Blum's attention on the stand-off between Kav and the postmaster was distracted as an old man entered.

'Do it!' Kav shouted.

The postmaster said, 'Get out of my post office.'

Blum took the old man's arm, ushered him towards the old women. 'Stay there, you won't be hurt.

His voice on the edge of hysteria, Kav bellowed at the postmaster, 'Fuckin' do it!'

He tilted the sawn-off upwards, fired. The blast of the gun inside the tiny premises made Blum's ears ring. The postmaster was immobile, shocked, staring at Kav.

'Do it, or I'll fuckin' kill yer!'

The postmaster's wife shouted, 'For Heaven's sake, Arthur! Do what he says!'

The postmaster pulled a key from his pocket, unlocked a small safe.

'All of it, all of it!' Kav screeched.

The postmaster scooped out slim bundles of banknotes and dropped them on to the counter. Cooey stuffed them into the sack.

Kav levelled the gun at the postmaster, 'Fuckin' all of it, I said!'

The postmistress moved to her husband, shouted at Kav. 'Leave us alone. That's it. There's no more!'

'Out! Out!' shouted Blum. Kav backed away from the counter, swung the gun between the postmaster and post mistress, the three pensioners. A door from the living quarters swung open, a young woman stepped into the room.

She shouted, 'You won't get away with this. I've phoned the police!'

Blum saw the panic on Cooey's face.

'Out! Out! Now!' Blum shouted.

Kav moved for the door. Cooey followed. The young woman lunged towards Cooey, snatched the sack. Startled, Cooey let go. Blum fired a shot into the ceiling. The shock of the gun's report froze the young woman. Blum ripped the sack from her hands.

'Don't come after us. Stay there,' Blum told her, hurried out after the others.

The Avenger's engine was running. Kav and Cooey yanked open the doors, scrambled inside. From the driver's open window, Delly shouted, 'Quick! Quick! Get in!'

A Massey Ferguson tractor braked sharply behind the Avenger. The instant it stopped, a heavily-built farm worker jumped down. Blum could see the determination on the big man's face as he rushed for him. Blum turned for the getaway car, but the man grabbed hold of his upper arm, then the other. With a grip on the gun and sack, Blum tried to pull away, but the man was built like a bullock. He swore at Blum, threatened him, told him to drop the gun. Blum pulled and wriggled, but the man was rock solid, immoveable.

'Shoot the fucker! Do him!' Kav screamed from the Avenger.

The farm worker's grip on Blum's arms increased. He kicked at the man's legs, but he yielded nothing in the strength of his grip. Blum saw the spittle at the corner of the farm worker's mouth as he cursed him, noticed the two pension books in the pocket of the man's dirty overalls.

Kav screamed while Delly revved the car, 'Shoot him, shoot him!'

Even had he wanted to, Blum couldn't manoeuvre the gun while his arms were locked in the man's powerful grasp. He took another tack, pulled the back trigger. The sawn-off's second barrel blasted the ground. Simultaneously, Blum twisted his body, booted the farm worker between the legs. The man bellowed in pain, let go, fell forward. Blum turned away to see Delly accelerate away. Tyres screeched as Delly took the Avenger up its gears like a rally driver.

Violent anger towards Delly charged through Blum. All his talk of comradeship and 'the job'; yet the minute a gun fired, he was off, his mate left behind. But there was no time to think of Delly. The postmaster was now outside, the two old women at the doorway behind him. The farm worker lumbered up off his knees. Blum ran.

He tore down the road. When he reached a cul-de-sac of council houses, he put the gun under one arm, pulled off the stocking mask, stuffed it into a hawthorn hedge, turned into the small estate. He ran seventy yards up the road, across a grassed play area, up the path of the house at the top of the close. If he could cross the fields behind, he would be on course to reach the small birch plantation where they'd planned to dump the Avenger, get away in the Ford Anglia. Could he cover a mile of farmland before the whole area crawled with police? Blum tried the latch of the back gate, pushed through. A young woman hung out nappies to dry. Blum ran past her, jumped up on to a rabbit hutch at the bottom of the garden, launched himself over the back hedge into the field. Across early stubble, Blum saw a clump of trees. With the sun on his back, the nutty smell of cut wheat in his nostrils, he ran in a straight line, two hundred yards to the trees.

Sweat ran down his face when, gasping, he reached the shade of a sycamore tree. A moorhen squawked in panic, flapped for the reeds at the edge of a pond hidden by the trees. Blum looked back across the stubble. Meanygate End shimmered in the heat. Apart from the steady clucks of the irritated moorhen, all was quiet. Seconds later, a flash of blue light shot through the trees, from further away, the sound of a police car siren.

He moved for a better view. A police car drove at high speed down the road into Meanygate End in the opposite direction to the Avenger's getaway route. Had that bastard Delly managed to turn off into the lane before the police car appeared? Or had another patrol car intercepted them? He hoped not. If the others got away, his chances of escape were higher. If Delly was questioned, Blum had no doubt he would give up Blum's name if it meant advantage to himself. He felt the surge of anger again. Whatever happened, he would have revenge on Delly. First, though, he had to escape the police, leave no evidence.

He looked at the sawn-off in his hand. He'd wiped his prints off it that morning, but to make sure, he wiped it again with the edge of his tee shirt. With the washing up gloves still on his hands, he took out the two fired cartridge cases and wiped those, replaced them inside the gun, snapped it shut. He took hold of the shortened barrels, flicked the gun into the pond beneath an ancient alder. Two big bubbles came up after the splash, followed by the bad-egg stink of pond mud. He hurried to the edge of the field, looked across to the houses, but saw nothing. He rooted in the long grass adjoining the stubble until he found a cobble raked from the field. He shoved the stone inside one glove, pushed both inside the other. He went back to the sack, lobbed the yellow lump into the middle of the pond. The moorhen squawked its objection from the reeds.

He opened the sack, took out the banknotes. He pushed them firmly into the corner of the sack and rolled it up around the notes. He opened his belt and zip and arranged it across his abdomen, fastened up his jeans. He pulled out his packet of Cadets and matches and lit up. He moved to the field's edge again as he drew on the fag. He heard the sound of a radio voice. Then he spotted a uniformed copper by the road, scanning the expanse of shimmering stubble. Blum squinted against the glare of the sun. The copper was speaking into his Pocketphone radio.

Blum abandoned all thoughts of the birch plantation, the Ford Anglia. He knew the others couldn't, or wouldn't, wait for him. He turned away, nipped off the lit end of his cigarette, put the stump in his packet. He slipped through the trees at the side of the pond, moved at a trot along a hedge that ran away from the pond, heard another police siren. He had to reach Southport -- to lose himself in the seaside crowds.

Chapter 24
On the Moss

OUT ON THE flat mossland between Meanygate End and the built-up coast there was no continuous cover. Houses, farms and glasshouses were scattered. Occasional plantations of trees, pockets of heath and scrub were separated by expanses of stubble, still uncut cereals and fields of potatoes and root crop. Every field was surrounded by a deep ditch. Blum knew if police patrol cars came out in force he would be spotted.

He slithered down into a ten foot deep ditch, squatted on his heels to think. The ditch was almost dry. There were no railway stations out here, no bus stops he could recall. Even if there were, the police would home in on anyone waiting and by now they'd have a description of his clothing. Blum lit the stump of his previous cigarette. It was a frustration he was only a few miles from Ted and Marion's place, where he knew a dozen places to hide around the head keeper's house and home farm, but he didn't want to take trouble to their doorstep. Blum crushed the cigarette end into ditch mud.

He scrambled to the top of the ditch to look across the fields. He could see the high, grey gas storage canister, a landmark on the eastern side of Southport, its outline distorted in heat haze. He needed to reach the minor road across the moss which ran eastward from the edge of town. Then he might manage to thumb a lift. It promised to be laborious, slow, but he knew the flat landscape meant he had to make his way by walking the ditch bottoms. It would be difficult, he'd have to rely on his sense of direction. He scrambled back into the ditch, set off.

Even at the foot of the deep ditches, there was no escape from the heat. Mud in the waterless channels slowed his footsteps. In some places the ditch bottoms were so narrow it was difficult to put one foot in front of another without stumbling. He walked for two hours, frustrated by the right angle nature of the ditches which meant often he walked sideways to his intended direction. Hungry and thirsty, he daren't touch the pockets of ditch water, but stopped to pull two carrots from the edge of a field. Unwashed, they stopped the hunger, but filled his teeth with grit. He passed underneath open, featureless lanes through culverts, most so low he had to get through on his hands and knees.

Blum reached another road, but the culvert beneath it was sealed by a grid of iron bars. There was no option, but to cross the road in the open. He crawled up to the roadside, hidden by tall grass and thistles, looked left and right. No traffic, but the continuation of the ditch on the other side ran alongside some sort of light industrial buildings. Next to it was a large detached house with a front gate and, surrounding it, a high hedge. At the hedge corner was a narrow tarmaced moss road. He could make out the roadside sign, Whimbrel Lane. He knew where he was. He looked beyond the corner of the high hedge. Yes, he could see two distant green grain silos close to a farm he knew alongside the road to Southport. He couldn't risk crossing to the ditch next to the busy yard, opted to cross to Whimbrel Lane and then strike across the fields towards the road, find the cover of another ditch. He checked again for traffic, stood, and crossed the road. He moved past the front gate of the house on the newly cut grass verge, turned into Whimbrel Lane. The first thing he saw was a pile of hedge cuttings, then a set of stepladders he almost walked into; the third was police car driving towards him.

Blum's mind raced. The police car was a hundred or more yards away. To turn back would look suspicious. He took in the grass verge beyond the stepladders. More hedge clippings had been raked into piles. Near a narrow side gate in the hedge was a wheelbarrow and beside it a Raleigh bike, propped against the privet. To his side were an abandoned pair of hedge shears, beside them a rake leant against the thirty yard hedge. The police car slowed as Blum took hold of the rake and started to re-arrange the nearest pile of cuttings. Blum ignored the car, heard distorted voices from its radio set, hoped it would pass. The car stopped, a voice said, 'Have you seen anyone pass here on foot?'

Blum looked up. A young, uniformed copper, his elbow on the edge of the police car's open window, regarded him, 'I said, have you seen anyone go past on foot?'

Blum leaned on the rake, noticed a second copper in the passenger seat. 'Walking past, like, yer mean?'

The second copper leaned over his colleague, 'We haven't got all day, lad. Yes, or no?'

'There was someone, but he were running. In a reet 'urry.'

The first copper swapped a quick look with his mate, 'Which way did he go?'

Blum stepped into the lane and pointed past the lane corner, back the way he had come.

The second copper said, 'You mean towards Ormskirk?'

Blum shook his head.

The first copper was impatient, pointed, 'Did he go right or left just there? To Ormskirk, or Southport way?'

Blum again shook his head., 'Nah. Jumped over the ditch like. Ran across that wheat stubble. Thought it were a bit funny. No footpath across there. You have to go up past the…'

The second copper butted in, excited, 'When was this? How long ago?'

Blum shrugged, 'An hour since, summat like.'

Without another word from the coppers, the car accelerated hard to the junction, paused a moment, turned towards Ormskirk. Blum dropped the rake, moved to the bike in the hedge. He had one hand on the handlebar when a voice, said, 'What do you think you're doing?'

An older, thick-set man in Grey corduroy trousers and flat hat stood at the narrow gateway in the hedge. In his hand was a big pot mug. He bent to put it down as Blum pulled the bike, prepared to scoot off. But it was stuck. The man stepped forward. Blum tugged at the bike again. A padlock and chain ran from the bike's frame into the hedge.

The gardener lurched at him, 'Get here, you,'

With the man in pursuit, Blum sprinted away. Fifty yards along Whimbrel Lane, he swerved into the long grass of the verge, jumped the ditch down into a spud field. He glanced back. The gardener, his hat in one hand, stood on the ditch side, shouted, 'I'll have the bloody police on yer, yer thieving bugger.'

Blum ran further into the field. A covey of grey partridges erupted at his feet. Whirring wings beat hot air and they gained speed before a long glide into another field three hundred yards away. He envied their power of flight as he stumbled between the raised rudges of thirty acres of flowering potato plants, checked his position against the distant twin silos.

With sun hot on his shoulders he dropped, breathless, down the bank at the end of the spud field. A six foot wide field drain, a sluice, blocked his path. His body ran with sweat. He stood up, peered back towards the corner of Whimbrel Lane. He was alarmed to see a police car by the long privet hedge. Beside it was a van. The hair on his neck stood up as he heard a dog's excited bark. Another joined in; police dogs.

Would the dogs follow the scent backwards, lead their masters astray, despite the evidence of the gardener? He didn't know. Blum wanted time to think, but he had none. He had to break his scent trail as soon as possible. The answer was in front of him. The sluice was full of water, even if the ditches were not. Water was the best way to confuse the dogs.

He wasn't too sure how deep it was. Rushing, he unfastened his belt and jeans and took out the sack of money. He folded it lengthways around the banknotes and laid it around his neck, removed his boots, tied the laces together. He put them around his neck, hoped they'd keep the sack in place. He stepped to the reeds at the edge of the sluice, lowered himself into water covered with millions of tiny, floating duckweed plants. The water came up to his thighs before his stockinged feet found the silt and clay bottom. He took a step towards the middle, which was slightly deeper. He started to wade. The cool water on his legs was a relief in the heat of the afternoon sun. Then flopped forward, started to swim. He struck out down the long straight channel between towering reeds. A new escape plan crystallised in his mind.

Twice he was forced to climb out of the sluice to check his direction. Each time, he scanned the landscape for police, listened for dogs, but saw and heard nothing. The sun was even hotter, he was tempted to lie hidden in long grass to rest. He wanted a smoke, but his cigarettes were sodden, along with his matches. He pocketed them, not wanting to leave anything to aid his pursuers, waded back into the water.

An hour later the sluice network joined a wider one he knew crossed the Tarlscough estate. The floating duckweed was sparser where breeze pushed it back against the reeds, so swimming was easier. He was also more exposed to anyone walking the banks, but he knew there were few footpaths in this area and crops had been planted to the edge of the waterway. In half an hour, he was within fifty yards of the road bridge that carried the road near the twin silos. He moved to the side where his feet found the bottom and watched the road. A tractor passed over the sluice, followed by a lorry going in the opposite direction. Then two cars went by. Blum kept close to the reed beds that lined both sides, swam as fast as he could under the bridge, kept going until he was a hundred yards beyond it. He stopped to regain his breath for ten minutes, one eye on the bridge. Only half a dozen vehicles crossed. He reconsidered thumbing a lift to Southport, but knew his latest plan was safer. What clinched the decision was the arrival of a police car, which stopped on the bridge. He edged back against the reeds, waited. A radio voice carried along the water. Two uniformed coppers got out of the car. One stood against the bridge rails, looked along the corridor of water. Blum presumed the other did the same on the other side of the bridge. Had the police surmised he'd made a getaway by swimming? The copper moved back to the car. Indistinct voices carried towards him before both car doors slammed. The police car moved off in the direction of Southport. Blum rested a little longer, before he set off on the next leg of his swim.

When he thought he might find somewhere to sleep off his weariness, his destination came into view. He'd spent many days by this bridge. In summer, fishing for roach and tench, in winter helping the beaters push ducks off the sluice to waiting guns, or live-baiting for pike. Blum swam under the bridge, pulled himself out on to hard earth beneath the planks. He crawled out through reed mace and nettles, checked for movement in the landscape. He rooted in his pockets for coins and hurried to the phone box. He made two fruitless calls to *The Sentinel* newsroom, returned to the bridge to count the damp banknotes, then later reached me at the flat using the last of his coins. He was half asleep when a police car and two coppers parked on the plank bridge, talked about Preston North End's imminent fortunes, had a hurried smoke before they left. Two fag butts sizzling as they hit the water, did nothing to help his need of a smoke.

*

When Blum said I stank of whisky. I thought it was safer he drove us back to May Bank View. I tried to keep the higher moral ground, admonished him for his stupidity joining an armed robbery: had he thought about being jailed for years, did he care about the effects on those in the shop, what about those old folk with no pension money? Yet, inside, I admired his athleticism, the quick thinking that secured the cash, led to his escape. I knew I could never have evaded capture as he had, but I'd love to try. I'd played my part in the venture, but I wished I'd experienced the excitement of it all.

Blum drove down the back lanes from Clieves Hill to Lydiate. It was now dark and I'd planned to see him home, then to hitch back to the flat. When we turned at Our Lady's church, he said, 'Fancy the last pint at the Soldier?'

'Haven't you had enough excitement for today?'

He laughed. 'Don't tell me you've had enough to blummin' drink.'

'Go on, then. You can get some cigs as well -- Even if you buy 'em with knock-off cash.'

Blum tried to pay for the beer, but I insisted. '"Spent money on drink for friends," I don't want to see that headline again.'

I brought four pints on a tray out to the corner of the forecourt. Inside the bell rang for last orders. Blum swallowed his first jar in a few gulps. I wasn't far behind. It was still warm; no breeze and I could feel the sun's stored heat from the cob wall of the old pub.

We went over the day's events. Blum seemed satisfied he'd left no evidence to connect him to the robbery. Fingerprints on the gardener's rake and the Raleigh bike's handlebar were a possibility, but Blum said he was sweating, his hands filthy with ditch mud. I told him that if he were questioned, he'd need an alibi. He looked at me. I raised a hand, 'Any other time, yeah. But I spent half the day with my boss and a council committee chairman. I can't do it.'

Blum nodded. I knew he wouldn't push it.

I picked up my second pint, 'Do you reckon the others got away? You know, the second car and that?'

'That copper seemed to think so.'

'What are you going to do about the money?' Kav had a sawn-off gun now and I knew he wouldn't let Blum get away with keeping the cash, 'Not going to try and keep it all, are you?'

Blum shook his head. 'Nah, I took my share out. I'll get the rest to them. I've a good mind to shove Delly's money down his blummin' throat, mind -- choke the lanky bastard.'

Blum was quiet for a few moment. His fingers tapped the back of his head.

I said, 'Do you reckon Kav told him to drive off and leave you stranded? --Is that what you're thinking?'

'I don't, no. He saw I had the sack o' dosh in me hand,' He lifted his glass, 'I reckon Delly's got no nerve, no guts, that's the top and bottom of it. Soon as he saw that bugger on the tractor having a do at me and I fired that shot, I reckon he shit his pants.'

He slugged down the rest of his pint. Almost to himself, he said, 'He'll be shittin' 'em again when I blummin' see him.'

Blum stared at his empty glass. Noreen the barmaid came outside to clear up. When she put Blum's empty glasses on her tray, I said, 'Any chance of a sneaky one? -- One for you as well…'

She pulled a face in apology, 'Can't tonight.' She nodded back to the front door, 'Boss cashed up on the dot.'

I sighed, drained my pint. Noreen took my glass, smiled, 'Any road, thought you two'd be off somewhere better than here.'

We looked at her. 'You know, with them mates of yours…'

Blum and I swapped a rapid look.

Noreen screwed up a discarded crisp packet, 'Haven't you seen 'em? Came in asking for you, what, nine o'clock-ish.'

Blum and I swapped a look, this time to the sound of alarm bells. Blum was first in. He was casual.

'Oh, aye, what did they want?'

She laughed, 'They were looking for you, you daft bugger!'

I butted in, 'We've got that, Noreen, what did you say?'

'What could I say? You weren't here.' She nodded to Blum, 'Said they should go over to his, ask his mum.'

Blum was on his feet in an instant, moving to the van.

'Have I said summat wrong?' Noreen said.

Chapter 25
Just Tate and Lyle's

WE COVERED THE half mile from the Soldier to May
Bank View like a dragster. The road outside was deserted,
but for a green Corsair parked alongside the front hedge. In
the light of the street lamp opposite, were two faces, Kav in
the passenger seat, another lad at the wheel. 'If they've
scared me mam, I'll blummin' 'ave 'em.'

Blum braked inches from the Corsair's front bumper. He
was out of the van before I opened my door. Kav came out of
the car on the bounce, straight to Blum.

'Where's our money?'

Blum ignored him, looked in the back of their car,
'Where's Delly?'

The lad I presumed was Cooey came around the Corsair
to join Kav. When I joined Blum, Cooey stepped closer to
Kav. Blum repeated, 'Where is he?'

'He couldn't make it,' Kav said, 'Where's our fuckin'
money?'

'I said, where's blummin' Delly?'

'In bed for a week -- I pasted him for doing one this
morning. Where is it?'

Blum stuck his hand down his trousers, dragged out the
cash wrapped in the sack.

Kav eyed him. 'Is thar all of it?'

'We got more than you reckoned, but I've got my share.
It was fifteen hundred and thirty five. Divide by four means
three- hundred- and- eighty- three each. I took three-eighty –
you pillocks can fight over the blummin' change.'

Kav held out his hand.

'Hang on,' I said, 'We need that gun back first.'

'I dumped it.' Kav said, added in a childish voice,
'Sorry.'

But Cooey gave the game away when he looked sharply at Kav.

'You're lying,' I said, 'Give us the gun first.'

Kav turned to me, 'It's fuck all to do with you. Stay out of it.'

Yet again drink boosted my courage. I took a step forward, 'My mate was left high and dry by you and Delamere. By rights he should keep the lot.'

Kav bristled, 'I didn't fuckin' tell him to drive off like that. He lost his arse, good-style. Why do you think he's having a lie-in?'

Blum said, 'That gun was lent out. Give it back and you get your money.'

'Ar, eh, what's one friggin' gun to you? I need it.'

'So do we,' I said.

'Look, take fifty quid out Delly's share and I keep hold of it, eh? More if you want. I'm nor arsed.'

Blum was firm, 'You'll get another soon enough with three -hundred quid, but I'm not selling mine. Let's have it.'

Kav jerked his head at Cooey.

'What?' Cooey said.

Kav snapped, 'Get the friggin' gun!'

Cooey opened the passenger door of the Corsair, took out the sawn-off. Kav snatched hold of it, faced Blum, 'I mean it. You can have all Delly's share if you let me keep it.'

Blum shook his head, 'I'd sooner have it back. Then nobody's going to act the blummin' goat with it.'

Kav pointed the sawn-off at Blum's chest. 'It's still loaded, yer know...'

I was horrified. The left-hand hammer was at full-cock, ready to fire.

Kav continued, '...You might wanna think about me offer, eh?'

'Ha.' Blum scoffed. He grabbed the sawn-off and turned the gun on Kav. Kav stepped back in alarm, falling against the Corsair's bonnet.

Kav's face drained as he leaned backwards over the car. Blum pushed the gun into his face. Kav was scared.

'Eh, eh, it's fuckin' loaded.'

Blum said nothing. Kav raised his hands, 'Come on, mate. I didn't mean anything. Purrit down, eh?'

'Yeah, it is loaded,' said Blum. 'With a blummin' sugar cartridge. They both were. No lead shot, just Tate and Lyle's.'

Cooey sniggered. Kav's mouth fell open. Blum de-cocked the gun's hammer, flung the sack in Kav's face

'We're square now,' Blum said, 'Stay away from me and tell Delly the same. I see him again, he'll get more than a week in blummin' bed.'

Blum watched, not taking his eyes off Kav, as he and Cooey got back in the car, drove away. Blum laughed. I was still too shocked at what I'd witnessed to enjoy Kav's climb down, share Blum's amusement.

'Christ, first a robbery and then you're carrying on like, like some gangster.'

'Ha,' said Blum and went to the van.

I followed, 'What's happened to you? Why did you get involved with him -- with an armed bloody robbery?'

Blum offered me the sawn-off, 'Here, do what you want with it.'

'I don't want it.'

He pushed it against my chest and I had to take it.

'Well...it can go in the cut,' I said, 'Now. Tonight.'

Blum moved to the van, opened the door. 'I'll run you there.'

We smoked, didn't talk. He looked weary, strained. The gun lay across my knees. He pulled up in a lane and we walked to the hump-backed Billy's Bridge, crossed by a farm track. Blum took the gun from me and I watched as he wiped it all over with a mucky hanky to remove fingerprints. He did the same to the fired and unfired cartridges. He tossed the cartridges over the parapet, then pulled the hanky through the trigger guard, swung the sawn-off gun around his head.

When he let go of the hanky, the gun arced through the air, plopped into the cut beneath the willows opposite the towpath. We watched ripples move out from the splash. The first time I stood here with Blum was years before on the last day of school before summer holidays when we watched kingfishers catch jack sharps and he gave me the book I treasure. Blum interrupted my thoughts.

'Come on, I'll run you back.'

'You're knackered. I'll hitch back if you drop me at…'

'I said I'll run you.'

'On one condition, then...'

He looked at me.

'We go to the farm first and all the guns come back with me.'

'Don't be daft.'

'You heard how desperate he is to get a gun. I don't trust him not to come back looking.'

'You mean you don't blummin' trust me not to do another robbery?'

He was right, but I met his eyes. 'I didn't say that.'

He shrugged, 'Got to lock up today's wages anyroad.'

I followed him back to the van. I felt bad I doubted his intentions over those guns, but after today I didn't want to take any risks. I had to get them away from him. And he needed to stay away from Kavanagh.

Chapter 26
They Don't Give a Shit

I HADN'T VISITED the still room at Pygon's Farm for months. It was much the same, but only about a third of the gear from Daltry's remained. By the light of the paraffin lamp, I loaded five double barrelled, three single barrelled shotguns and a set of barrels into a sack. They weighed heavy, so I double-sacked them. Blum, meanwhile, had the safe open. He counted the money in his toffee tin.

The antique German rifle I now knew Captain Westbrook gave Blum when he left Lydiate was still there. It was of no use for criminal purposes, weighed as heavy as two, even three, shotguns.

'I'll leave this here, then?'

Blum looked, nodded. 'Blummin' shame, but I might have to sell it.'

No licences were needed to sell antiques like the old Scheutzen rifle. 'Let me know and I'll find out what it's worth.'

I lugged the sack of shotguns across to him. 'Right, where's the pistols and ammunition?'

Blum took the five pistols and the chocolate box containing the pistol cartridges from the bottom of the safe. He dropped them into the sack.

'You've no licence for pistols,' he said. 'What if you get nabbed with 'em?'

'I'll take a chance. Best they're away from here if him and his mates come looking'.

'How much do you think we'd get for 'em?'

He held his hand up to block any protest. 'I mean selling them legal; to someone with a licence, like, or that gunsmith that took the decent twelve bores.'

'I don't know. I'll have to look into it.' I checked my watch. It'd gone midnight. 'We'd better get going.'

I stowed the guns in the back of the van. Even though we were miles away from the scene of yesterday's robbery I hoped to God the police hadn't connected the two sightings of Blum's van, circulated the number. Blum locked up and we retraced the route Sandra and I took hours earlier.

I struggled to keep my eyes open. I didn't know how Blum kept awake after the day he'd had. I could've slept, but I feared a spot check. Blum became chatty as we drove east, across country, to the M6. He told me he'd been to the Sharrocks' place a couple of times to visit Fozzy. Arnold thought his new worker was 'just the man,' while Glenys had 'never been happier.' To cap it all, Fozzy's facial surgery was now almost complete. Mr Roop Singh needed only to operate once more.

'Viv's made up. He's a new lad, he's changed, ready to show he's as good as anyone. With his mouth and teeth done and the new job and that, he's on cloud blummin' nine.'

When I asked after his mam, his mood changed. I relayed my thoughts earlier when I didn't make the effort to say hello. He agreed his mam's life had become more difficult than when they had a regular income and plenty of work to fill her days. I asked about the renewal on the lease for May Bank View; how close he was to raising the cash.

He kept his eyes on the winding road, stared into the light of the van's beams. I thought at first he hadn't heard me, then feared he was dozing at the wheel. But he pulled out a fag, struck a match, his hands holding the match box against the steering wheel. I asked again.

'You haven't got seven thousand yet?'

Without warning, he steered the van off the road. It bumped up on to turf grazed close by moorland sheep. He turned off the engine, dragged at his cigarette, blew out smoke in a long stream while his eyes stared out at the heather lit by our headlights.

'It's not going to blummin' happen.'

'But...I thought you'd have most of it by now.'

I saw his hands grip the wheel. The muscles in his forearms clenched.

'I'm not earning enough and everything I sell from the farm, the money gets dipped into, just to keep going. Mam's earning next to nowt these days, nobody needs her.'

'You've got a few months yet, though,' I said, 'I've got holidays after this fishing match thing, so we could have a big push -- get rid of what's left.'

He stayed silent. I prompted him, 'How much have you got?'

'I told you, it's not going to happen; it's not just blummin' money, not anymore.'

He turned to me, his face full of misery. 'Mam's had a letter from the solicitors for the bastards who own the house. They won't renew the lease. We'll have to leave.'

I was shocked. I blustered, 'Won't they let you rent it? Or you could buy it. If you and Viv took over you might be able to get a building society mortgage, or something.'

Now his misery turned to frustration, anger, 'Greedy bastards want to cash in on this house-building lark. Demolish May Bank and destroy mam's garden -- just to build a blummin' housing estate. Old Gidlow's place'll get bulldozed and all.'

I pushed for details. Blum rarely swore these days, but the bad language flowed, as he gave me the facts. I didn't know the next door neighbour of the semi-detached houses, old Gidlow, who died weeks before Uncle Walter, had also leased his house from the same landowner. Demolition of his now empty home and May Bank View would free about three acres to cram in more of the new semis built in the parish since Blum and I were kids. The London-based owners had applied for outline planning permission.

Blum shook his head, upset, 'Where's she going to live? It'll kill her leaving May Bank. She's put every spare minute into that garden since the day she got married and that lot, the destroyers --- they don't give a shit.'

I asked again about money. In all he had about £2,750. 'That's enough to buy somewhere, I'm sure. Or she could get a council place.'

Blum shook his head. 'I've looked in the paper. It's not enough to buy a place with a big garden. A blummin' council house won't have one either.'

He wound his window down, chucked his fag end on to the road.

'Is that why you got involved in the robbery?'

'Ha. I thought there might be more in that post office than what we got. I should've blummin' stayed out of it.'

'Have you told Viv? About the lease?'

'No!'

I could feel his resentment at my questions, but pressed on.

'Wouldn't it be better to tell her before your mam does?'

'Mam doesn't discuss our business with anyone.'

'But Viv might be able to help. Like I said from the start, she's well-up on money and...'

Blum started the van, 'It's my blummin' job to put a roof over me mam's head, not Viv's.'

He bumped back on to the road and we didn't speak until he coasted down Quinn Street, pulled up by the overgrown hedge that surrounded Kitty's. He checked all was quiet before he opened the back of the van. Even up here on the edge of the Pennines, it was still warm. Moths fluttered around the front porch light, privet blossom scented the air, a change from the smell from the paint factory.

'Do you want to stay?' I said, 'Kitty'll be out cold 'til mid-morning.'

He shook his head, 'I said I'd be at Viv's when she got home.'

He helped me lug the guns to the front door.

'Thanks,' he said, 'For today and everything.'

'Don't make a habit of it, eh?'

He grinned, nodded. 'See you next time you're home.'

'Keep your head down.'

Blum left Quinn Street before I got the sack to the bottom of the stairs. Only Kitty's snores broke the silence. I cursed the guns as I struggled upstairs. Despite what Blum said about finding a legal way to sell the pistols, I'd decided not even to try. Yet that was before I knew of his mam's eviction, perhaps a few more pounds might help. Now all I wanted to do was lock them in the wardrobe, go to sleep.

I switched on the inner hall light, pushed into the bedroom. I leaned the sack against my legs, turned the key in the wardrobe lock. It jammed. I turned and re-turned it, pulled hard. The door flew open, crashed back against me. The sack of guns toppled, thumped on the floor and a Webley revolver, then Luger automatic, scraped along the barrels of the shotguns, clinked together on the carpet.

'Shit!' I bent to pull up the sack and the set of shotgun barrels fell out, clanged on top of the pistols. 'Bloody hell!'

I could do without this. I wanted to sleep.

Quick footsteps crossed the living room, a bulky figure appeared in silhouette. For an instant, I was alarmed. The bedroom light clicked on. It was Sandra, my reporter's mac around her shoulders.

'Shit, what are you doing?' she said, 'You'll wake the bloody street up?'

It was too late to push the guns under the bed, she'd caught me red-handed. But she showed no reaction, no sign of horror, even surprise.

She picked up the two pistols, one in each hand, 'Where do you want these?'

I stared at her.

She laughed, 'Look at that face! Have you got pissed again?'

'Had a couple of pints, that's all.'

She dropped the pistols inside the sack, picked up the barrels. 'Thank God I wasn't daft enough to lend you the Mini.'

She pushed the barrels into the sack, 'Hurry up, I need some kip.' She took off my mac, 'You do and all. You look buggered.'

She held up the mac, fanned her nose, 'Helped myself to your stinky mac. Dozed off and got a bit chilly. Oh, yeah. I ate your spaghetti hoops -- Sorry!'

I couldn't believe her unconcerned air.

'I would've had toast, but your bread...' She laughed, 'Bloody hell, did you know it was green mouldy?'

'Oh? ... Sorry.'

I heaved the guns into the wardrobe, locked the door. Sandra hooked my mac on the back of the door, scrambled onto my old-fashioned bed, pulling off her clothes.

She giggled, 'I stuck it in the bin, so you don't bloody poison me in the morning.'

She couldn't care less about the guns. Elaine would've fainted, called the police, walked out; or all those things in turn. At the least, the inquisition, the arguments, would've gone on until first-light. Instead, Sandra wriggled against the pillows to get comfortable, 'What was the panic with Blum, then?'

I lied to her. It was the first time.

'He's getting hassle off some lads he was with in Borstal. They want to buy guns from his collection, you know, for the wrong reasons. He won't have it. So he wants me to keep them safe for a bit.'

In every other relationship I'd had, I'd always lied, most often to Elaine. With Sandra, from the start, I'd been open, truthful, about everything. I felt no need to embroider. I hated the idea of being dishonest with her, giving her any reason to reject me.

I sat on the edge of the bed, undressed. I couldn't tell her I'd helped Blum to escape a police hunt, that he committed armed robbery, the tawdry confrontation with Kav. In a way I was as bad as Blum. Yet, I didn't regret it; did it all because he was my friend. And it gave me a kick, though instantly I pushed that thought aside.

I turned to her, 'You're sure you don't mind being here with a load of guns?'

She laughed, 'I'm not Elaine,' she said, 'When my brother lived at home he had that many guns and swords and bloody bayonets he kept half of them under my bed.'

I watched her as she settled. That understanding, without judgement, of my incompatible relationship with Elaine, that easiness about what I'd just brought home; the simple image now of her face against my pillows -- it all added to the list that ran through my head earlier in the Mini when she asked that question and I failed to answer.

I joined her under the covers. She pulled me towards her, kissed me, turned over.

'It was good of you to drop everything, to go and help him. It was. Is he all right?

'Yeah.'

'Nowt to muck up the lovejob, then?

'Nope.'

'Good, that's the most important thing.'

She snuggled backwards against me.

'Is it?'

'Mmm...'

I lay in silence as she fell asleep. I'd longed for oblivion, but now I couldn't switch off as the events of the day, its excitement, ran through my mind, but that soon gave way to worry. Now the owners of May Bank View were set on eviction, Blum had lost both his job and reputation and served nine months in Havershawe, all for nothing. And there was still a chance he could be caught for the post office robbery. With the loss of May Bank View only months away, he was desperate. Only that had made him join those idiots in armed robbery. I wished I could help him, feared what he might do next.

Dawn came before I fell asleep, still worried about Blum.

Chapter 27
A Disgrace to your Profession

BERT TRAVIS WAS a husk of a man in the dock of the same court room where Blum had been sent down eighteen months before. He'd lost weight, his hair was grey, his officious, military moustache had disappeared, along with his former status and authority. He didn't even glance behind him at Blum, Viv and me, sitting in the public gallery. A gaggle of reporters sat at the press bench. Viv dreaded coming face to face with Travis's wife. With relief, she confirmed Mrs Travis wasn't present.

Nor were Fozzy, Delly and others who suffered at the former senior officer's hands. At a late stage, Travis opted to plead guilty. We were pleased, it meant Travis had accepted his guilt. It also spared Fozzy's obligation to accuse him across a similar courtroom to the one where he'd suffered terrible injustice at the hands of the law. Fozzy was anxious as the court day approached, but now he was well away from the process of justice; at work in Sharrocks' glasshouses, rather than re-living his experiences as a victim of Travis. We were there as his eyes and ears.

Blum was amused His Honour Judge Hernshaw was taking the case, speculated aloud if the old boy would remember his face, but Viv shushed him. She and I knew what it was like to be the focus of his displeasure for nattering in his court.

Travis pleaded guilty to seventeen counts of assault and theft. We had little interest in the prosecution barrister's account of the thefts from Havvy, but we swapped surprised glances when he told the court Travis had profited by more than £10,000. But when the prosecution detailed some of the assaults on boys in his charge we were open-mouthed. In some cases, his violence had verged on torture, mental and physical.

More surprises came when Travis's counsel spoke in mitigation. He almost dismissed the thefts as Travis's temptation at the laxity of Havershawe's administration and accounting systems while struggling with heavy responsibilities of his own caring for the young offenders. He blamed the assaults and ill-treatment on his frustrations when boys spurned his efforts to help rehabilitate them, shunned his many kindnesses, provoked him with bad behaviour. Blum, Viv and I swapped incredulous looks. It was complete fantasy, a sick joke.

When Travis stood for sentence it seemed Judge Hernshaw had similar thoughts. He all but said Travis's mitigation was a fairy story. He dealt briskly with the thefts describing them as 'naked greed' and 'a betrayal of an honourable profession.'

When it came to the assaults, he told former Senior Officer Travis, 'Your claims of rehabilitation are wicked lies. Far from being rehabilitated, young men under your care and guidance were subject to casual brutality and almost systematic cruelty, and they will bear the mental scars caused by you for years to come, perhaps forever. You are a disgrace to your profession and it is well rid of you. You are thoroughly dishonest, a sadist and a bully.'

Travis gripped the rail of the dock, stared ahead, not meeting the Judge's eyes. He was jailed for a total of ten years.

Two of Travis's former colleagues prodded him down the dock steps. Judge Hernshaw rose and left. It was anti-climactic for us. We didn't punch the air, rejoice. It was enough to know justice had been done for Fozzy, as well as other boys, who suffered before him.

*

Arnold Sharrock urged us all to think no more of Travis when he and Glenys invited us to their home two days later.

A big table was set on the fresh-mown lawn between the bungalow and the glasshouses. Glenys provided a spread of sandwiches, pies, roast chicken and salad and home-made cakes. Clicker the magpie hopped between us taking tidbits from Fozzy's fingers, chunnering and squawking. When the three of us were invited we thought this picnic was a celebration of justice, but we were wrong.

While we drank pale ale, enjoyed the smell of cut grass and the warmth of late summer sun, Arnold stood. Clicker hopped on to Fozzy's shoulder, cocked his head from side to side, watched Arnold.

'We all know what happened this week, but I'm not going to mention that feller's name ever again. He got what he deserved and that's that. I reckon all of us here think the same. I'll not be celebratin' it. Best thing we can all do is forget him.' He smiled, 'No, this get-together is to celebrate summat else, summat special...'

Arnold smiled at Glenys. I could see the happiness in her face as her husband spoke, 'This week Glenys had a phone call from Mr Roop Singh...'

A tipsy Fozzy raised his glass, like a jubilant football supporter, 'Freddie Roo -- oop, Freddie Roo -- oop!'

Arnold laughed, 'Give over, lad.' He winked at us, 'Talk about a sniff of the barmaid's apron.'

Clicker squawked, 'Feddie Oop! Feddie Oop!'

Arnold rolled his eyes. We all laughed. He pointed at Clicker, 'That means you an' all, you cheeky bugger!'

Clicker hopped up on to Fozzy's head, croaked, 'Eekybugger, Eekybugger!'

Arnold laughed, shook his head as we composed ourselves. 'Any road, like I were saying. Mr Roop Singh phoned and we're pleased as owt at the news...'

Blum and I swapped glances. 'What news?'

'Ssh, listen,' said Viv.

'It's Mr Roop Singh's opinion that the operations yon mon's had have been a complete success. There'll be no need for more. That's right, isn't it, Glen?'

Glenys put her arm around Fozzy, her face showed her joy, 'You're as good as new, aren't you, Peter?'

Fozzy nodded. put his arms around Glenys and Viv.

'Blummin 'eck,' said Blum, 'Great news.'

I added, 'Well done, mate,'

'Well done, Mr Roop Singh and all,' said Arnold, 'But he's not the only one me and Glen'd like to thank. If there were one good thing to come out of Peter ending up in that Havershawe place, it's meeting you three. We can't thank you enough for what you did for our lad. You might think it a bit funny me calling him that, but since the day you introduced us, we've thought of him like that, haven't we, love?'

Glenys nodded, tears in her eyes.

'So thanks to all of you and 'specially Nurse Jarvey there... She knew straight off the treatment that were needed and made sure it were done. You lads have give up your time and supported Peter right through. You've been proper friends to him.'

Blum and Viv smiled at each other. He took her hand. He gave me his usual daft grin, even dafter than usual, before kissing Viv on the cheek. I felt a soaring sense of happiness as Arnold clapped me on the back, handed me another bottle of pale. Like my beer, the euphoria didn't last long.

Encouraged by Arnold and Glenys, Fozzy showed us around the place. I tagged along, held back a little. I felt almost an imposter. While Viv and Blum had actively helped Fozzy, all I'd given was support. When we reached the second glasshouse, I stayed outside for a smoke. Since the day of the post office robbery I'd not spoken to Blum in private. After Travis's sentencing I had to dash back to work. Viv had been present then and on the drive out to the Sharrocks'. Through the glasshouse, I saw Blum look over his shoulder, then move back, towards me, pulling out fags and matches.

I was straight in, 'Have you heard any more about the ...you know, post office?'

Blum extinguished the match with his fingers and blew out smoke, 'Nah, nowt.'

He changed the subject abruptly. I could see excitement in his face. 'Do you know how to go about finding who owns an...?'

But I cut in on him, 'Have Kav and Delly approached you at all?'

'Nah,' He was dismissive, 'There's nowt to worry about. It wasn't even in the papers after the first week -- the coppers are stumped -- it's blummin' obvious.'

Then he was in with his own question. 'How do you find out who owns an empty house?'

'I suppose you'd have to get on to the county records, or something.'

'Can you find out for us? Quick as you like'

'I sort of know an estate agent. I could sound him out, 'I said, 'Why?'

He turned his back to the glasshouse, 'I'm going to buy Pygon's Farm.'

I laughed, 'You what?'

'It was staring me in the face all the time.' He checked over his shoulder, his voice low, earnest, 'I crow-barred one of the windows and had a look round. There's four bedrooms, a whackin' great attic, three big rooms downstairs, as well as the kitchen. There'd be loads of space for me, mam and Viv. Even the old veg garden is plenty big enough for mam, now she's getting on a bit. And with the barn and the yard and that, I could start a haulage business and...'

'Hang on,' I said, 'A month ago you didn't have the money for a house with a big enough garden, never mind a bloody farm.'

'I'm working on it. I just need you to find out who it belongs to.'

I was already suspicious, 'What does working on it mean?'

He was awkward, 'There's a bit of a job coming up.'

'You said you hadn't been in touch with them.'

We couldn't go any further. Fozzy and the others were leaving the glasshouse.

Fozzy called, 'Blum, Blum! Come and see these.'

Fozzy led the way. Blum whispered to me, 'I'll tell you later. Say nowt to Viv.'

While Arnold and Glenys looked on in the next glasshouse, Fozzy showed us a new variety of yellow tomatoes from Italy. All I could think of was this 'job.' By the sound of it, Blum's preparations had already started and I knew from experience once he'd started on a venture, he always finished it. But again, he wanted Viv kept in the dark. He was pushing his luck as well. One more balls up with Kav and Delly would put him up for a long prison sentence.

*

Blum drove us back to Lydiate. When we stopped for petrol, Viv and I were left alone in the Chev. I was pondering how much it might cost to buy, do-up a place like Pygon's Farm when she turned to me in the back seat.

'Is he all right?'

'Sorry?'

She nodded towards the petrol station. Blum was inside, paying. 'He seems….I don't know, like there's something on his mind.'

I felt uncomfortable. Blum had the knack of keeping his pre-occupations from Viv, but this time, maybe things were different, 'I've not noticed. I didn't see him for ages before the court case.'

Her eyes met mine, 'You phone each other, though.'

'Not so much lately. Work's been mad and with Geoff spending time on this stupid fishing match and me having to cover on the news desk as well as being involved in that…' I was gabbling with my nervousness. I took a breath.

I said, 'Is it something to do with work, the van business?'

'I asked him that. He says everything's fine, work's coming in, but I'm not so sure about that. He usually talks about work, but he hasn't, not for a bit.'

I shrugged, 'He seems all right to me.'

She looked away, reached for her cigarettes, 'I couldn't stand it if he was sent away again…'

I had that urge to lie, to reassure her, despite Blum's alarming announcement less than an hour ago about another 'job,' 'I don't think you need to worry about that.'

She turned back to me, took the cigarette out of her mouth, her eyes holding mine, 'Don't you?'

I shook my head, struggled to meet her gaze, 'I don't, no.'

'Sure about that?'

'Yeah, 'Course I am.'

'You'd tell me if he was up to something that might end up with him in prison?'

It was a struggle to hold that gaze. 'I don't want him locked up either.'

She kept her eyes on mine, 'You'd stop him if you found out he was taking a risk?'

'Jeez, you know I would.'

Blum came round to the driver's door.

Viv, her eyes still on mine, nodded, 'Thanks.'

She turned away.

She and Blum were their normal selves, but I was quiet, uneasy now Viv was worried, suspicious even. And I feared she knew I'd lied.

We dropped Viv off at her flat to get ready for night shift. Blum suggested a pint at the Soldier, but I'd arranged with Elaine to meet up for a drink at the Hare and Hounds, so we left the car, walked along the canal towpath.

*

Blum wouldn't answer my questions about the 'job' until we were settled in the long room at the pub. He had a pint, I had a whisky chaser with mine. We were half the room away from the nearest drinkers. Marc Bolan's T-Rex on the jukebox between us covered our voices.

'You said you'd stay clear of Kav and Delly.'

Blum lowered his pint, 'I am, it's my blummin' job, not Kav's.'

'What is it?'

'Summat that'll sort everything out, make sure mam has a home as long as she needs it.'

The jukebox fell silent. A lad from the nearest group of drinkers stood up, hand in pocket. He dropped in a coin and The Stones filled the silence with *Street Fighting Man*. He deliberated what to play next, but I couldn't wait for an answer from Blum.

'What sort of job?'

With a glance at the jukebox lad, he said, 'I don't want to talk about it too much.'

'For God's sake, he's not listening!'

He glanced at me, 'It's …sort of a robbery.'

'What the hell does that mean? It is, or it isn't.'

Blum eyed the lad at the jukebox, said nothing. Eventually, the lad moved back to his mates.

'Well?'

'Kav's got this job coming up soon and...'

I almost shouted, 'I thought it had nothing to do with him?'

'It hasn't. Well, not really, like'

'Make your mind up, for Christ's sake!'

'Let me finish then.' He lit a fag, 'Thing is I won't be working for Kav, or with him. He's in on a proper job and I'm going to rob him.'

'Jesus…'

'He deserves to be robbed.'

'What if he finds out? He's a nutcase. He's dangerous.'

Blum lowered his pint, 'Ha! He's a pillock.'

'And so are you even thinking of taking the risk. What if you get caught? It won't be Borstal next time round.'

Blum snorted a laugh, 'I'll be robbing a robber. What's he going to do, dial 9, 9 blummin' 9!?'

'Things can go wrong! Look what happened last time.'

'Nah. I've got it all planned.'

Frustration filled me. I needed something to put him off this stupid idea. I said, 'Viv's worried about you.'

He looked. I saw his concern.

'She doesn't want you going to jail.'

'She 's said that a blummin' thousand times.'

'Yeah, but she's got a feeling you've something on your mind, that you might be up to something.'

'You didn't tell her about mam, May Bank, or owt?'

'No, but isn't it time you told her?'

Blum said nothing, took another drink. I tried another tack on this well-worn argument.

'You were talking about the three of you living together. If you... you know, pooled your resources you could find somewhere to buy, or rent, and...'

Blum was blunt, 'Live off Viv's wages, you mean? Ha!'

'No, I don't.'

'She'd be putting in far more than me -- or mam.'

'For now, yeah, maybe, but ...well, not long-term.'

He was stubborn as ever, 'I'm not having that. It's down to me to pay.'

'Even if it might mean jail again? What're your mam and Viv going to do if---?'

Blum cut in.'Hi, Elaine,' he called, 'All right?'

She walked towards us from the steps up from the bar. Straight away, I knew she was put-out to find me with Blum.

Her voice was flat, 'Hello.'

I greeted her. 'You're early.'

'So I see,' she said, 'Dad gave me a lift.'

Blum drained his glass, stood, stepped aside 'What you having, Elaine? That Bacardi stuff, is it?'

Elaine took his vacated place on the bench, slipped off her jacket, 'We'll stay on our own, thanks.'

Blum hesitated, then picked up his fags and matches. Viv would be in work now, but he fibbed, 'Yeah, well, better not have another, said I'd meet Viv at hers.'

Blum knew when he wasn't wanted. Elaine made herself comfortable in his place.

Blum's eyes met mine, 'I'll see you then. Give you a ring.'

'Yeah, do that. I'll see you.'

Elaine ignored him as he left. Before he was out of sight, she said, 'You didn't say you were meeting him.'

I couldn't be bothered to explain about our celebration at the Sharrocks'. I'd told her about Fozzy and his operations months and months ago, but she showed scant interest. I gave up reporting on his progress, I wasn't going to start again now. 'He was here when I came in.'

'What are you doing drinking whisky with beer?'

Irritated, I said, 'I just am.'

She rooted her purse from her bag, 'Because he was, I suppose?

'No, he wasn't.'

She produced a pound note, offered it, 'I'll have a Bacardi and Coke. You look like you've got enough.'

I snatched the note, chucked my whisky back in a gulp, annoyed at her pettiness. At the bar, in a moment of spite, I added another pint and a Bells to the order. Earlier with Fozzy and the others, I'd been elated. Why shouldn't I have a few drinks to get that feeling back? I dropped the whisky in one, bought another -- with my own money.

Chapter 28
The Northampton Job

I WAS MELLOW, if not elated, as Elaine chattered about her mates and work while I half-listened. I couldn't push from my thoughts Blum's new ambition to buy the farm, finance it by robbery. Talk about hypocrisy on my part, but it bothered me how he kept things away from Viv. I'd put money on a bet that if he told her his situation, she'd find a way to help Nancy Gatley.

She might even go for Blum's plan to rob Kav.

God, of all the girls who might give robbery a try for kicks, it was Viv. Perhaps Blum should be open about everything, ask her to help him on this job. The main thing was that what Blum had in mind wasn't a conventional robbery. It was about robbing robbers. She might go for that. I could perhaps lend a hand. She'd stuck by him over his thefts from Daltry's, but would she stay with a lad who stole dirty money from men who'd obtained it by robbery with violence? Would she ever consider marriage? It was a stupid idea, drunken fantasy.

Elaine took my hand, 'You know we've talked about getting married?'

The question bumped me out of my thoughts.

'Have we?'

'Loads of times.'

'Not that often.'

She nudged me, laughed, 'I'm being serious. You know we have.'

As I recently discovered I'd told Sandra, I didn't remember the first time I'd discussed marriage with Elaine -- I was too pissed. When she brought up the subject again, it had taken subtle cross-examination to fill in the missing details. I was wary of the whole subject.

'Well we can't afford it yet, can we?'

'What if I got a rise in salary?'

'You've just had one.'

Earlier that year, she'd passed some banking exam, moved up a pay grade. I didn't know how she stuck the job. It wasn't as if banking was some career ambition. When she left school she wanted to do English at university, perhaps teach, but her father was in the same Lodge as the manager of her branch. Whether he wanted to protect his only daughter from a life of debauchery away at university, or the branch manager was some Masonic fixer he needed to suck-up to, I didn't know. But Elaine was offered up as a sacrificial A-level entrant to the bank. Even after the Brotherhood big-wig moved on to regional office, Elaine had continued to do well.

'I know, yeah, but what if I got another one?'

'Is that going to happen?'

'I was talking to Pete the other week and he got me thinking.'

Pete was the assistant manager at her branch of the bank. If I were the jealous type this work friendship might've irked me. He was a twenty-nine-year-old who had transferred from the Midlands to take a position that wasn't usually available to anyone under forty. I imagined some confident public schoolboy with an MG sports car. Our only meeting was in Liverpool city centre one Saturday afternoon. He was prematurely bald, wore jeans with back to front creases, tie, sports jacket and black-framed specs. Elaine introduced me and he regarded my flared loons and long hair like an unworldly judge in a rock world drugs case. I breathed beer on him while he showed Elaine the golf clubs he'd bought. He wasn't her type. Nor mine.

What got Elaine thinking was a staff bulletin vacancy for a chief cashier's job at Pete's former branch in Northampton, the next logical step for Elaine's career. Pete pointed out the chief cashier at their own branch would not be holding his leaving do anytime in the next fifteen years. He urged her to try for the Northampton job, said he could put in a word with the right people.

She took hold of my arm, smiled, 'I've got an interview on September the 15th.'

'In Northampton?'

She laughed, 'Where else, you soft sod?'

When I left home for *The Sentinel*, Elaine cried buckets, to the point of my embarrassment. My long absences had been an issue ever since, 'But it'd mean you working away.'

'Well...? You work away.'

'And get non-stop grief . With my hours and you down there, it'd be--'

She moved closer, 'Not if you were with me.'

'What?'

'You could get a job in Northampton.'

I sat straight, pulled away. 'I can't.'

'Why not?'

'I just can't.'

I took a nip of my whisky chaser.

She was put out. 'Well, I didn't expect this. Not after what you said.'

'Said what? What do you mean?'

'You said when you got a job on an evening paper, I could transfer to a local branch, then we could think about getting married.'

I didn't remember it like that, but perhaps she was right.

'I'd be getting proper wage on an evening paper, that's what I meant.' I laid it on, 'It's all right for you, you get wage rises, I'm stuck on trainee rates for another two years. I can't do it.'

She put her hand on mine, 'I know, but this new job carries a salary of two-thousand, seven-hundred and fifty pounds.'

I looked at her, astounded. I bet Geoff Sillitoe didn't screw that out of *The Sentinel*.

'It's a big step up. We can both rent rooms and I'll cover our bills 'til you're fixed up.'

'I can't just walk out of my job.'

'They do have newspapers down there, you know. One evening paper and a few weeklies -- I've checked.'

She had it all planned,

'But I'm indentured. I've signed papers.'

'Just break them.'

'It's…it's just not done.'

'They can't really stop you, not these days -- checked that as well.'

I took a moral tack, 'But…how's it going to look to some future editor? It'll make me look bad, unreliable, not to be trusted.'

She took hold of my hand with both hers, 'I understand it's a big step, for both of us, 'course I do. But it's what we both want. And we can do it now.'

'You might not get the job.'

She shook her head, smiled, 'Not the message I'm getting from Pete. They've taken him up as a reference already and he had a long phone call from the manager in Northampton.'

Christ, it was like my life was being re-organised behind my back, as if I were about to be marched at gunpoint to a train bound for Northampton. I took a swig of bitter, dropped the last of my whisky.

I faced her, 'I can't …I need to finish my training. Nobody's going to look at me without more experience.'

She put her hand on my leg.' I don't expect to get married straight away, you know. We can share a flat, too, if you want, live together -- I don't care if my dad kicks off.'

'What about my mum and dad?'

'They'd object? To us living together?'

'I mean, I'd never see them.'

'Come on, you hardly see them now.'

'Yeah, but I'm not that far away. Northampton's bloody miles off and...'

'We could come up once a month, visit both sets of parents.'

She piled it on. 'We'll be able to afford a car and save for a deposit on a house. And I'll get a subsidised mortgage after a year in the job.'

I was a fish with the net closing over me. She'd got every last bloody detail worked out.

'I've never put a foot in Northampton, it might as well be a foreign country!'

'It's the same as everywhere else. What's so special about here? -- That backward little hole where you work?'

'I happen to like it -- I like round here as well.'

'What about all that you said, working in London? Move down there and you're half way there -- more than half-way.'

'I don't want to go to bloody Northampton.'

'You said you'd go anywhere, any town, any paper, to get the experience.'

'I know, but--

'So the London stuff was just talk. Beer talk, eh?'

'I'll do it in my own time. All right?'

She almost sneered, 'So it was just talk? All the getting married stuff as well!'

'I...I just feel like, like I'm...I don't know... being pushed...'

Elaine paused, controlled her irritation.

'Okay, maybe it's all a bit quick...'

I stared at the empty whisky glass in my hands; my resentment, stubbornness growing.

'... But give me one reason, just one reason, why you can't leave the life you're living now.'

I didn't think, just said it, 'Friends.'

'I've got friends as well, you know. Do you think I'm going to forget them because I've moved away? Anyway, we'll make new friends. You know we will.'

'What if I don't want new friends?'

'Christ, what's so special about the ones you've got?'

My anger rose,' What's that supposed to mean?'

'You're always telling me about your boring evenings when you haven't got night jobs. So I'm pretty sure you

haven't got any friends over there. Who does that leave? --
David Gatley and the hippy biker girl?'

To pick on Blum, and Viv, was predictable, but she knew
nothing of the others. I'd tried to talk to her about Fozzy,
Arnold and Glenys, Ted and Marion – even Sandra; confined
to some of the outrageous things she said to elders and
superiors on *The Sentinel*. Times I'd mentioned these people,
though, she'd been disinterested, dismissive. Friends of hers
I'd met, to me, seemed dull, uninteresting, all the same age, a
similar outlook on life. I enjoyed the company of people like
Marion, like Arnold, like Fozzy, even Nancy Gatley. To me
they were friends, to me more real than hers. I couldn't begin
to explain to her my feelings hours before when Arnold told
us about Fozzy. Her dismissive attitude angered me.

I snapped at her, 'Leave them out of it!'

'I wish you'd just turn your back on him,' she said, 'If we
had a new life away you'd soon forget him, the pair of them.'

'I wouldn't! Why the hell should I?'

The drinkers by the jukebox looked over.

'They're no good for you. I don't know why she bothers
with him either, she must be mental. You and her, you'll both
get dragged down by him.'

I was furious, 'For Christ's sake! You don't even know
him. You've never even tried to get to...

Her face showed pure contempt, 'He's a thief and a no-
mark. Just you see, one day you'll realise hanging on to
people like that's a waste of time and effort. He's a criminal.'

'He served his punishment.'

'Till the next time.'

From my conversation with Blum not an hour ago, it was
a daft thing to say, but I said it anyway, 'He's learnt his
lesson.'

'Don't kid yourself. He's a no-good, always will be.'

'Don't be stupid!'

She flushed with anger, 'Don't you dare say that!
Apologise!'

The jukebox drinkers smirked, swapped remarks, I didn't care.

I didn't lower my voice, 'It is stupid. Blum's a good friend, so is Viv. You've no right to say all that.'

Elaine half turned away from the spectators. She shoved her purse in her bag, picked up her jacket. She lowered her voice, but she was still angry.

She leaned in to me, 'It's obvious you care more about them than me.'

'It's not like that.'

She stood, 'You know damn well it's like that! If you don't care, neither do I.'

She turned, took a couple of steps.

'Elaine?'

She turned back, her hand chopped the air, 'That's it. It's finished. Over. Right?'

'Sit down.'

'No, I mean it. We're finished. And don't follow me.'

She walked away, didn't look back. I waited half a minute, picked up my fags, and headed for the bar. To save face, I rolled my eyes at the jukebox witnesses of what seemed our final row, headed down the steps to the bar. I ordered another pint, leaned on the counter. Elaine had it right: I didn't care enough to take the chance she'd offered me. In honesty, any feelings for her had gone; I didn't care enough about her. There was only one person I wanted with me at that moment. That person was Sandra.

Chapter 29
Not a Proper Robbery

EVEN AFTER THE spread at the Sharrocks', I felt hungry when I left the pub. I headed in the opposite direction to my mum and dad's for chips. Viv's flat wasn't far away and I didn't fancy an early night, I ordered a second cod and chips for Blum.

When I knocked at Viv's it was dark. The Chev was parked where we left it up the side of the old house, which was split into Viv's place and a couple of bed-sitters. Usually, Blum left the van around the corner, but I hadn't looked on the way, perhaps he hadn't come back here.

I knocked harder, worried I might have to eat two packets of fish and chips. Then Blum opened the door, a bottle of pale ale in his hand, stood aside to let me in.

'Watching the bats out the back. Blummin' loads of 'em tonight.'

I held up the chip packets, 'Hope you're hungry.'

'Just the job,' he said, 'Go through.'

He followed me as I opened the door off the hallway, went into the flat. I sat at the kitchenette table, slid a packet towards him. I noticed there were bottles of pale ale on the drop-down ledge of Viv's Hygena unit, along with a half-bottle of Caernarvon Kitty's favourite whisky.

I un-wrapped my packet, looked at my fish and chips, no longer hungry, perhaps because I'd spotted the drinks.

Blum sat opposite, opened his, 'You're earlier than I thought you'd be.'

'We had a row.'

He laughed, 'Ha! Nowt new then?'

'She says it's over. We're finish--

I stopped, he blew on a hot chip.

'Hang on,' I said, 'What do you mean? Earlier than you thought?'

He grinned, 'Even if you and Elaine stayed 'til chucking-out, I knew you'd end up here.'

'Why?'

'Why? Ha! You can't wait to find out what the job is, that's blummin' why?

'I want to know what risks you're taking.'

'Want to see if you can get involved, more like.'

I laughed, 'Get off. Me?'

'Yeah, you,' Blum stood, moved to the bottles. He took a glass from the kitchen unit, picked up the bottle of Bells, put them by me on the table. 'I were that blummin' sure you'd show up, I got this.'

I laughed, 'Thanks, but, you've got it wrong.'

I unscrewed the top, slopped a good inch of whisky into the glass.

Blum sat, continued to bolt his cod and chips. He looked at me for permission as his hand hovered over my untouched fish. I nodded, he scooped it up.

He spoke with his mouth full, 'It was Viv spotted it first off.'

'Spotted what?'

He laughed.

'What?

'When you did Travis's place you were shit scared of that dog, but you did it. Then on the way back, she said you were on a big high, like on blummin' drugs, or summat.'

'I…Well, I suppose I was, but…That was a bit different to a bloody robbery.'

'Still against the law, mind.' He grinned, 'Same again on the roof at Havvy. Saw you meself.'

'Christ, that was a nightmare.'

'Yeah, but you were flying, after it. I was, Viv was -- we all were. You loved it.'

I said nothing.

'You were narked with me over the post office job, but you loved every blummin' minute when you got me off the moss. Hiding them sawn-off barrels, dodging the coppers at them road blocks, squaring up to Kav over the sawn-off and that...You wanted more of it...'

I blustered, denied it, but saving him from arrest for armed robbery, was a thrill, an antidote to everyday life.

'Even when we were lads it was a big kick. Taking the gun to that old bastard off the cut, remember that? And that other bugger's place in blummin' flames?'

He was right. I remembered it all; every minute. But still, I protested. 'It's different, though. I mean, Christ -- a robbery.'

'How many times...? I keep telling you, it's not a proper robbery, just robbing a robber.'

'It's still robbing someone!'

Blum leaned on his elbows, facing me, 'Nobody needs to get hurt, no coppers chasing us all over the blummin' show. I reckon I could find someone else to come in on it with me easy enough, but I want to give you first refusal, like.'

I topped up my glass, took a sip, then another, delayed my reply. 'Thing is, I'm doing all right on the paper. If I get caught, even if I'm suspected...it's finished. It's breaking the law, it's criminal. I'll get jailed. No career; nothing.'

'You're doing it again!' He exhaled in frustration, 'Getting mixed up. All we'd be doing is robbing Kav and some baddies from Southport.'

'It's still a bloody risk.'

''Course it is. But only if they find out who done it.'

Blum rolled the ale bottle between his hands, 'The risk is what it's all about, isn't it? I had a reason for robbing all that gear from Daltry's, but every time I did it, it was a...a -- a buzz, Viv calls it -- I felt blummin' great. It is a risk. Like a mad bet on a horse; putting everything you've got on the nose. Isn't that why you loved it all?'

I sipped at the whisky. I hesitated to believe his theory, wanted to resist it, but he was right. I enjoyed risk. If I were honest, I always had done.

Blum put his bottle down. 'I'm offering you first refusal. I've got to do this -- for mam. To show Viv I'm not some deadbeat who sees his mother with nowhere to live and does nowt about it. You don't have to do it at all, but we'll still be mates, even if you don't.'

I stared at my glass.

'Another thing,' said Blum, 'When you first came to see me at Havvy, you promised you'd help me over May Bank...'

I looked at him, said nothing,

'I'm not going to hold you to that. You saved Viv's life on the roof. You saved me from getting nabbed on the moss. You owe me nowt– I owe you more like.'

'I just did what I...'

He held his hand up. 'I know what you blummin' did. You've done enough. More.'

I sipped at the whisky. He screwed up the chip papers, my leftovers, pushed them into the kitchen bin.

'If you say no to this job of mine, I'm not bothered. I mean that.'

I nodded. I believed him; he'd still be a mate, whatever I decided.

'No need to give us an answer now,' he said, 'Take the bottle and I'll run you back to your mum and dad's.'

I took another sip of whisky.

'How far have you got with the planning? How did you find out what Kav was up to?'

Blum picked up another bottle of pale ale, clicked off the top with an opener, pulled up his chair.

'I had to make sure Delly kept his gob shut about the post office job, so I thought I'd have a word. Remember I told you Kav was using the Meanygate End thing to prove himself to that big fish in Southport?'

'Yeah.'

'I'd been thinking like mad how to get some decent dosh for mam. It came into me head I could rob Kav if he were in on summat bigger for the fellers in Southport, even for himself.'

'Did Kav come back to you, like with the post office job?'

He shook his head, 'Nah, felt he'd have summat else going on, though. Thought Delly might know, like. An' I'm telling you, it's a good-un an' all, a blummin' cracker, big enough to sort everything, I reckon.'

I poured more whisky.

'Have you seen Delly?'

Blum nodded. His mood became sombre. He looked at me, 'I'm not proud of what I did to him, but I had to teach him a blummin' lesson.'

Chapter 30
Delly's Telly

BLUM DREDGED HIS memory for every bit of information he'd learned about Delly in their time at Havershawe and the run-up to the Meanygate robbery. He knew the name of the road where he lived on a council estate on the edge of Burscough, but not the number. He remembered Delly's mother left home, he now shared the three-bedroom house with his father and elder sister.

Delly's road was a short cul-de-sac off an avenue. Blum bought a pair of false number plates for the van, parked in a side road facing it. From the back of the van, with his grandfather's field glasses, he watched Delly's road, late afternoon into evening. Delly had told Blum his sister was a barmaid at the Railway pub in the large village, his father a night watchman at Westbrook's packaging factory.

The comings and goings were ordinary; kids drifting in from school, adults coming back from shops and work. After an hour, he saw a woman in her early twenties leave one of the houses. She wore a short skirt and high-heeled shoes. He drove behind her, passed her, parked near the A59 road through the village, followed her on foot. She went into the Railway pub at two minutes to five. He returned to the cul-de-sac. Just after six-o-clock, a man in his early fifties wearing a donkey jacket, with a workman's carry-out box under his arm and a Thermos flask in his pocket, come out of the same house. The man paused, irritated, and shouted to someone unseen inside the house. Blum waited a few minutes then drove to the packaging factory. From seventy yards past the factory gate he watched in the nearside wing mirror while the man in the donkey jacket spoke to another man at the gate, went inside.

Blum returned to the Railway pub to check whether the woman was a customer, or actually worked there. He ordered a half of bitter from the woman he'd followed from the house. The pub was empty, but for a couple of old men, three workmen playing darts. He moved away from the bar, avoiding any conversation with her, finished his beer, satisfied she was Delly's sister; close up he could even see a family resemblance, wondered if she was a chicken-heart like her brother. Before leaving, he nipped into the gents' toilets. On his way out, as he went to open the door, he stopped at a familiar voice.

'Come on, just a quid. You'll get it back on Friday when I get me dole.'

It was Delly, talking to his sister.

Blum held the door open an inch.

'I'm still looking for thirty bob that went missing out my purse on Sunday.'

'It weren't me.'

'As if!'

'Ah, don't be tight.'

Blum opened the door a little wider so he could see both speakers

'Go an' ask me dad,' she said.

'He says he's skint.'

'Well that makes two of us. Get lost.''

'How about five bob to get the bus into Ormy?'

'To look for a job?'

'At this time o' day?'

'You're an idle get. Leave me alone.'

'You wait 'til I make some money. I'll remember this!'

His sister laughed, 'Like some day, never? Piss off, will yer.'

Blum waited until he heard the sound of footsteps, the front door open, then close. He came out of the toilet, glanced over to the bar. Delly's sister looked up from the *Daily Mirror*, Blum ignored her, left. Outside, he looked up the sloping road leading back to the main street, watched Delly slouch out of sight, hands in his pockets, before going back to his van. He gave Delly a start, followed. He sped past him as he headed for the cul-de-sac. Then turned round, crawled back at low speed and stopped. He watched as Delly trudged up the side of the same house left earlier by the barmaid and the man in the donkey jacket.

Next day, Blum again watched from his van. He settled-in at half-past four, having done some reconnaissance of the fields behind Delly's cul-de-sac. He waited as Delly's sister left for the Railway and his father later left for night shift with his box and flask. He had no way of knowing if Delly was at home, but he would return, day after day, if necessary. He left for tea with his mam at May Bank View, then clipped a stretch of his father's old yew hedge, killing time, waiting for dark.

*

Blum parked his van in a corner of the vast, derelict wartime airfield behind Delly's home. He put on his army surplus greatcoat. From the van he took the Signalman's folding four-ten shotgun. He pressed the button on the action to fold the barrels under the stock. Earlier, he'd threaded a piece of parcel string through the trigger guard, tied it off to make a loop. The loop went over his head so the folded double-barrelled gun could be carried under the greatcoat, hands free, as well as hidden. He checked his jeans pocket for the pair of two-inch long Eley cartridges.

With a torch to guide him, he walked the length of a cabbage field close to a thorn hedge. The same hedge turned at a right angle along the back of the houses on Delly's side of the cul-de-sac. Blum had marked the position of Delly's house by a poplar tree at the foot of the back garden. He crept to the tree, peered through the hedge. Light from the kitchen shone across a small, neglected garden with a wooden shed, surrounded by un-cut grass.

Blum dropped to his knees, took out a pair of gardener's secateurs. He cut away the thinner twigs with their long thorns, chucked them out behind him. He snipped until there was a space big enough to crawl through between the main stems, without getting snagged.

He pushed through the hedge, stood up, and froze as a dog in the garden next but one yapped. A minute later a woman's voice scolded the dog, ordered it inside and Blum made a move towards Delly's house. He skirted the back wall, turned down the side to the front. He scanned to check the cul-de-sac was clear, moved to the front bay window. He heard the opening title music of *Cannon,* the American private eye show.

He peered around the edge of the window frame. The only light in the room came from the kitchen through the partly open living room door. With his back to the kitchen door, Delly lounged in a shabby armchair, his stockinged feet rested on a coffee table. In one hand he held a mug, in the other a roll-up fag.

Blum withdrew, crept back to the rear of the house. He pulled the shotgun on its loop of string from around his neck. He pressed the button and unfolded the barrels, clicking them into the full length, locked position. Then he pressed the side lever and broke the gun to load it. He rooted out a single cartridge, slid it into the right barrel chamber. He closed the gun, thumbed back the right side hammer. Cradling it in his arms, he pulled on some garden gloves and moved to the kitchen door, turned the doorknob. With his heart beat rising he pushed the door. When it opened, he stopped a few moments to settle his breathing, lower his heartbeat.

Blum moved the door aside with his shoulder. With the gun barrels raised he stepped into the kitchen. American dialogue from the television came from the front room. The place was a mess, dirty dishes in the sink and on the draining board, used pans on top of the gas cooker. The smell of bacon and chips lingered. He crossed the floor to the partly opened door which led to the hallway. The inner, living room door was to his left. In view was Delly's left arm, hand and cigarette. Blum raised the gun barrels to vertical and squeezed through the kitchen door without opening it further. In the hallway with the living room door in front of him, he changed the gun to the other hand, pushed the door more open. He was six feet from Delly as he again took the gun into his right hand. He put the stock into his shoulder, rested his right cheek against its walnut comb. He adjusted his aim as his forefinger found the front trigger. He looked down the barrels.

Private Eye Frank Cannon was driving a white Lincoln Continental down an avenue of manicured lawns and perfect palm trees. Blum's finger squeezed and Cannon, the Lincoln, the palm trees and the TV screen disappeared in an instant at the impact of a thimbleful of lead shot. The ear-ringing report was followed by the tinkling glass of the imploded television tube. Delly leapt out of the chair, his mug of tea and cigarette flying into the air. He let out a shriek of fright.

Blum stepped into the room, the shotgun pointing towards the ceiling. Delly's mouth dropped open when he recognised his visitor. Blum stared at him, not saying anything for half a minute. He needed to listen for any signs the neighbours may have heard the shot. He doubted they had. The house would act like a baffle, a silencer, to flatten the gun's report. But his silence was effective. Delly was trembling.

Blum said, 'I heard you've been talking about me.'

'I haven't. Honest, Blum'

Blum gestured with the gun barrels, 'Close them curtains.'

Delly's eyes flicked from side to side, his fear obvious, 'What for?'

Blum lowered the gun barrels, pointed them at Delamere, 'I don't want anyone to see what's going to happen to you.'

Chapter 31
Not that Bright, is He?

DELLY STOOD WITH his eyes locked on to the gun, blinking like a mesmerised mouse cornered by a snake. His legs shook.

Blum shouted, 'Close 'em!'

Delly's body jerked in fright. Then he moved to pull the curtains together, doing it by touch, not taking his eyes off the shotgun's barrels that followed his movement.

Blum gestured to the coffee table. 'Sit on that.'

Delly moved back towards Blum. He made a crab-like movement, to sit, his eyes still on Blum, the gun.

'Me dad and our Linda, they'll be back in a minute.'

Blum laughed, 'Do you think we haven't checked? One of the lads watched him clock in at Westbrooks and Linda's in the Railway 'til chucking-out.'

Delly picked up on the 'we,' 'Is someone else here?'

'Only a couple, in case you try and leg it.' Blum said, 'Put your hands on your head.'

Delly's hands shot to his head. Blum stepped forward, the gun pointed square on his chest.

'What've you been saying about me?'

'I haven't said nothing, Blum, honest, I haven't.'

Blum moved the muzzle of the gun under Delly's chin.

'Why did you drive off and leave me?'

'I didn't mean to, I just...'

Blum's voice was louder, 'Why?'

Delly's mouth opened and closed silently.

Blum nudged the barrels against his neck, barked the question, 'Why?!'

Delly shuddered, jerked away from the gun. Blum levelled it at his face.

'Why?'

'I…I…It…'

'Why?'

Delly started to sob. 'I…I…The sawn-off fired and I…I'm sorry…'

'Why?'

'I couldn't help it….I lost me arse…I couldn't…I'm sorry.'

'I could've got blummin' caught, couldn't I?'

Delly nodded, 'I'm sorry, Blum.'

'Look at me!'

Delly raised his eyes.

'If I'd got hold of you that day I'd've blummin' killed you -- on the spot. Every day I think about it I get angry, dead angry. I'm going to push this in your gob, right in, and pull the trigger.'

Blum clicked back the left hammer of the now unloaded shotgun. Delly flinched at the sound.

'Don't Blum, please.'

'It won't be here, on the old airfield, somewhere quiet.'

'No…Please, no, Blum.'

'I'll have a fag first, mind.'

Delly looked at him confused. Then, he was eager to appease.

'I've got some. Only rollies, but…'

He made a move. Blum snapped at him, 'Keep still!'

Delly froze. His knees were knocking.

'I've got my own.'

Blum moved away, blocked the door, took out his fags and matches. With the gun under his arm, he struck a match, lit up. He moved back closer to Delly.

'Who have you told about me going on that job?'

'Nobody. It's true. Honest, I haven't said a word.'

'What did Kav say about you driving off and leaving me?'

Delly sobbed, 'He battered me. Kicked shit out of me.'

'Did he give you your share of the dosh?'

Delly shook his head.

'Nothing?'

'He said he had to give it all to you. Said he had to see you right 'cause I left you.'

'He's a liar, as well as a bastard, then? I only got my share, not yours. He robbed you.'

Delly stared at Blum. Blum nodded confirmation.

Blum bluffed, 'I know you've seen him since he battered you. What did he want?'

'I promised I'd keep it to myself.'

'Keep what to yourself?' Blum returned the muzzle of the gun to Delly's neck 'Are you that daft you think it blummin' matters now?'

'I promised, Blum, I swore I wouldn't say anything. He'll do me over, I know he will.'

'You're not blummin' with it, are you? I'm here to finish you off, do away with you,' Blum said. Then he shouted, 'Tell me!'

Delly babbled it out, 'He's hi-jacking a lorry with that lot in Southport, the ones I told you about. It's a load of cigs and booze. He wants me to get the cars'

'Is that all?'

'I've got to get the car, drive them on the job and he said there might be some fetching and carrying after.'

'When?'

'Soon. He said he'd let me know.'

'Did he tell you how much you'd get?'

'He promised me two hundred quid.'

'Not much, is it? A lorry load of fags, booze, it's got to be worth more than a couple of hundred quid. More than the post office job. Why didn't you tell him to stuff it?'

'I'm skint.'

'Oh, yeah, forgot, so skint you haven't got the dosh to get the bus to Ormskirk? So skint you sneaked thirty bob from your sister's blummin' purse?'

Delly looked at him in disbelief.

'There's people working for me who know everything about you. People you see every day. People you know watching you, just to tell me. Everything comes back. That's why I know you've talked about the post office job -- About me'

Delly dropped his head.

Blum nudged him with the gun, 'Who did you tell?'

'Just a mate. I didn't mention your name, honest.'

Blum bluffed again. 'Don't be daft. I know it was more than one. Do you want my lads to work you over before I finish you?'

Delly shook like he was freezing to death, 'I told Chris Ormiston and Trev Millett, that's all. They won't say anything, I know they won't.'

'But they did talk, didn't they? How do you think I knew, eh? Now the pair of them'll be shitting themselves in case I turn up to see 'em.'

Delly stared at Blum, confused.

Blum pushed the gun barrels hard into Delly's neck, 'Do you think I'm a pillock like Kav? Do you think I don't know what I'm doing? Do you, eh?'

Delly was in tears, 'No.'

'Do you know what you've done wrong?' Blum said, but didn't wait for a reply, 'You should've kept your mouth shut. You shouldn't trust people you think you know. That was your big mistake -- not being able to keep blummin' quiet.'

Blum tossed his cigarette end into the fire grate. 'Right, I'll whistle the lads in. They'll take you to a van at the top of the road. I'll see to you on the airfield when I've set this place on fire.'

Delly was distraught, tearful, 'You can't!'

'Stop skrikin'. You won't be here.'

'Please Blum, it was a mistake. I should've kept quiet. I'll do anything you say, honest. Please.'

Blum was almost there.

'How about something to prove you can keep your gob shut?'

Delly looked at him. 'I'll do it, Blum. I promise I will.'

'You do everything I say when I say. You don't make any mistakes. Right?'

Delly wiped at his eyes and nodded. 'I promise.'

'You know what'll happen to you and this house if you don't?'

Delly nodded again.

'Do it right, keep your blummin' gob shut and I'll pay you. More than that bastard Kavanagh's offering.'

Blum tossed his fags and matches to Delly, sat in the armchair to discuss his new role as Blum's inside man on a lorry hi-jack.

*

First light filled Viv's flat. Both of us were now silent. Blum blew smoke rings at the ceiling. Would Delly do what Blum wanted? And would he keep his mouth shut? I was a touch shocked at Blum's treatment of Delly. Blum broke the silence, as if he'd read my thoughts.

'I blummin' hated doing that to him, you know,' he said, 'But time's against me. This could be my only chance to get mam a new place. He deserved a proper fright for dropping me in it an' all.'

'Do you reckon he'll do what you say, though? I've told you before, lads like that snitch to survive.'

He looked at me, 'Thing is he's terrified of me now, not Kav. Remember when he brought Kav to the Soldier looking for guns? You said how scared he was of the other feller. Now I'm the other feller.'

I laughed, 'Oh, yeah, the one with "the lads" and spies all over Burscough.'

Blum chuckled, 'Poor Delly, not that bright, is he?'

'Why did you shoot the telly?'

'It just came to me when I saw him watching it. It was me firing that sawn-off outside the post office that panicked him. I needed him to hear a gun go off in his house to frit him, get his attention, like.' He paused, 'I've posted him a couple of hundred quid, mind--a bit of encouragement, like. Enough to get the telly fixed, leave him a bit spare.'

'What if he does a bunk?'

Blum laughed, 'I'll murder him on the old airfield and burn his house down.'

I knew Blum's regret was genuine, but I knew he wouldn't baulk at a measure of ruthlessness to reach his goal.

I crashed-out on Viv's sofa, not before going over in my head whether or not I should join Blum in this bid to rob Kav and the hi-jackers. I wanted to help his mam, but I was also attracted to the idea of putting one over on Kavanagh, someone I loathed, despised, the instant I met him.

*

I woke up with a blanket over me. Blum was frying bacon and eggs. Viv cleared the table, clanked empty beer bottles on the draining board. I stretched and yawned, craved coffee and fags.

Viv saw me, laughed, 'Wakey, wakey. We don't do breakfast in bed.'

'Sorry,' I said, 'Too much to walk home.'

Blum snorted, 'Too much to walk to the blummin' sofa!'

I made a half-hearted attempt to fold up the blanket.

'Leave that,' Viv said, 'Come and eat something.'

I sat at the table. Blum plonked down plates of fry-up, mugs of coffee.

'How bad is it?' said Viv, 'Should we do you a bowl of throddie?'

Blum mimicked Ted, 'Bloody throdkin, grand as bloody owt.'

'This is fine, thanks.' I poked at my egg, 'Even if the yolk's like a pebble.'

Blum laughed, 'There's still a bottle of ale if you need summat to swill it down.'

It had some appeal, but I shook my head.

'Blum said you'd had a bust-up with Elaine…' She grinned at him, 'Not that he got the juicy details.'

I'd talked to Viv before about Elaine . She knew Elaine had no wish to include her in her group of friends, that she looked down on Blum, even more so since Borstal. Never, though, had Viv criticised her in any way. Over breakfast, I told them about the Northampton job, Elaine's last words to me.

'Hasn't she chucked you before?' said Viv.

I shrugged, 'Yeah, but…Well, I think that's it now.'

Viv put down her mug, 'Better it's over now before you uproot yourselves and move away.'

'I suppose so.' I couldn't even bring myself to feel unhappy, bothered, about our break-up. 'It's a bit of a relief, getting away from all that stuff about the future, her planning everything.'

Viv looked up from her breakfast, 'If that's how you feel, I think Elaine made the right decision.'

'I should have stopped it ages ago.'

Blum said, 'At least you've still got a spare in Gobbinland.'

Viv laughed, 'Is that still going on?'

'Yeah. We have a laugh. We don't talk about careers and getting married. It's not serious.'

Viv stood, picked up her empty plate, 'Sure about that?'

I didn't know what to say. 'I don't know.'

She smiled, 'Maybe it will be …' She turned to Blum, 'I need to get some sleep.'

Viv and Blum cleared away the dirty pots. I smoked while they discussed each other's plans for the weekend. Blum had never mentioned any talk of marriage from Viv. As far as I knew that intention was one-sided, but they appeared more of a together couple than Elaine or I could ever be. I thought about Sandra. Would we ever be a couple, serious about each other? The thought was interrupted by Viv.

'Are we allowed to come to this fishing match of yours?'

'Not mine. My boss's idea – along with some daft councillor with ambitions.'

Blum looked at Viv, pulled a face, 'You want to go to a fishing match?'

'Foz does.'

'It's an open match, no reason he can't.'

'Great. I'll phone him. He'll be made-up.'

Blum said, 'He's never talked about fishing to me.'

'I think he's a bit shy about asking, so I promised I would. I'll ask our Tony if Foz can borrow some of his match tackle.'

'Blummin' eck, he should be coming piking with us this back-end -- Never mind tiddler-snatching for silver cups.'

I voiced my agreement, but I was sensitive about talk of angling. I resented the time Sandra was obliged to spend on the Fairbrass-Sillitoe project, how she'd been overloaded with extra work. I'd be glad when the first, and I hoped, the last, SACOAM was over. I was overdue for two-weeks' annual holiday, ready for it. Covering for Geoff, attending the tedious committee meetings with tedious experts from the town's angling club, weighed on me as well. I was tired, bored.

Most of the weekend at my mum and dad's I spent sleeping and thinking, sober by then, about Blum's offer to join him to rob Kav and the Southport lot. The idea tugged at me, excited me. I feared, resented, the fact, Blum might recruit someone who wasn't up to the challenge, but was I up to it? Blum had released me from my promise, but I felt for his mam faced with the distress, upset, of eviction after all those years at May Bank View. Was I prepared to take the necessary action, the unknown risks, to ensure my friend's mother had a home for her old age?

Elaine didn't phone. If she did, I decided, I wouldn't apologise or bury our grievances like those other times we'd broken up. She'd finished with me, I wanted Sandra -- there was no going back.

Chapter 32
Back on the Moss

A FEW DAYS later, Sandra and I took a late lunch in the Boot. Even then, we didn't escape work. She took me through a check-list of the tasks delegated to us by the SACOAM committee. Sandra had placed ads in the angling press and newspapers as far afield as Yorkshire and Cheshire. I'd backed them up with ready-written articles extolling would-be Alderman Fairbrass's dubious theories about local government's desire to encourage angling to promote business, tourism and a worthwhile leisure pursuit for all ages, especially today's teenagers. Pure hypocrisy; in private, he proclaimed most teenagers needed a haircut and a damned good spell in the army.

Committee members had also lumbered Sandra with arranging a running drinks and 'finger buffet' reception for the Mayor and his guests at, of all places, The Packet, where a marquee would stand on the old barge quay. She had to arrange for a trophy shield to be made and delivered on time. And she'd been put forward to accompany the Mayoress on the day, alongside old man Henty, who would escort His Worship, the Mayor.

The evening before I'd persuaded her to forget all this. We drove up the Ribble Valley, walked along the river from Edisford Bridge near Clitheroe. It was warm in the cattle pastures. From other fields came the smell of drying hay, the final cut of the year. Near Mitton, swifts and sand martins skimmed the river, snatched flies from its glassy surface. We stopped to watch them and I told her Elaine had finished with me.

'How many times have you two split up?'

'I know,' I said, 'This time, though, that's it -- for good.'

She looked at me.

I protested, 'I mean it, it is.'

I told her about the Northampton job; her dismissive attitude to my work on *The Sentinel*, Blum and Viv; how I couldn't be bothered even to tell her about my pleasure, delight, over Fozzy's good news; how I felt she'd tried to manipulate my life.

She was quiet for a while as we strolled back upstream. Then she looked at me.

'Do you hate her now?'

'Of course I don't. No.'

'No?'

'I'm not like that.'

She nodded, 'Good. I thought not.'

'It doesn't mean I'm going back with her.'

'You don't have to say that, you know.'

'It's true. I mean it. I'm out of it.'

She nodded. I wanted to kiss her, hold her, but she moved ahead of me, appeared pre-occupied.

I wanted her to understand it was over for good with Elaine, but what more could I say?

She moved through clumps of nettles, thistles, dying cow parsley. Her fingertips brushed the plumes of tall, seeding grasses. Insects, moths, criss-crossed madly about her in warm, still air. Her figure mounted the steep slope of the field back towards Edisford Bridge. She became a silhouette against sunset colours as a curl of breeze brought again the scent of hay; all a mental snapshot that would remain with me, pin-sharp, undiminished, half a century on.

She was quiet on the drive back. She declined to come to the flat, have a drink in The Packet. I didn't try to persuade her; I was tired myself.

Now, in The Boot, despite being snowed under, weary with work, she made me laugh at Daddio's private, dinner table remarks about Councillor Fairbrass. Like, 'It would be more sensible, and cheaper, for the ratepayers to finance his booze bill than his crackpot initiatives' and, 'Alderman, or not, it'll make no difference – the man's a blasted imbecile. He won't get into the golf club, either.'

I was about to get more drinks, hoped we might skive off for an hour, perhaps at the grotty flat, anywhere to talk to her properly, away from everything, everyone.

Phyllis, the landlord's wife, came over.

'Message from Christine in the newsroom,' She referred to the fag packet in her hand, 'Can you phone Mr Blum at May Bank View. Four o'clock.'

'Oh. Right. Thanks Phyllis.'

Phyllis smiled and left.

Sandra said, 'If he needs you at home, I can't drive you.' She shrugged, smiled, touched my arm, 'I'd love to, but...Sorry...You know...All this...'

'I know.'

My mind was elsewhere; I knew what the call was for. It was time to decide.

Later, I settled into a news room booth, dialled May Bank View. Blum brushed away my greetings. 'Have you thought about it? Are you in on it, or not?'

I yearned to be away from work and SACOAM. I stared out at the newsroom through the glass strip in the door. I needed a break and so did Sandra. I craved the tonic of excitement. And most of all it was for Blum's mam's future. Promise, or no promise, I was committed to help Nancy Gatley.

Blum was impatient, 'Are you still blummin' there?'

'I'll do it. When?'

'You need to be over here about eight tomorrow morning. Bit o' luck, you'll be back with your girl tomorrow night. Sure you can make it?'

'Yep, deffo. Is it all fixed?'

'I'll tell you tomorrow. I'll be at Ormskirk station.'

Blum hung up, I lingered in the booth. Geoff Sillitoe had his feet up on the desk reading *Angling Times*. He wasn't putting himself out to get this bloody fishing match organised. Sandra seemed to be carrying all the weight for him, for Fairbrass. Why should I worry about a single day off? I had to get away for twelve hours, or so, that's all. We were short of staff owing to holidays, what could I tell Geoff to make that possible? I pushed out of the booth, over to the news desk.

'I need to take a day off tomorrow.'

He looked at me, 'Flippin' 'eck. Yer pick your times. Yer know how pushed we are.'

I wanted to say, 'So I see,' but said, 'It's my gran's funeral.'

'Yer could've mentioned it. Give yours truly a bit o' notice.'

The old girl had died five years before. I hoped I'd never revealed that to him.

'I wasn't going to go, but me dad's just told me it'll upset my mum.'

'That's not clever, is it?' He stuck an Embassy filter on his lip, flicked over a page of the big news desk diary, 'Aye, all right, cocker. Suppose we'll manage.'

At his suggestion, I spent early evening with Sandra going through the check list for Councillor Fairbrass's big day. She didn't question it when I told her I was visiting Blum next day, she was pre-occupied with SACOAM detail. In recent days I'd thought about what I'd do on my holidays. I planned to ask her to spend a few days bed and breakfasting in the Yorkshire Dales, perhaps North Wales. But she was worn out by the check list, plus a dozen phone calls needed when the marquee supplier backed out. She was in a frazzled, distracted mood. I never managed to mention holidays.

I went to bed before nine with a big glass of Cyprus sherry to knock me out. My first train was at six o'clock. I couldn't believe my bubbling excitement.

*

Early autumn sun warmed the Lancashire moss. Fields were still in stubble, but most were ploughed and drilled with back-end cereals. Blum and I sat behind a thorn hedge, laced with white bell bindweed flowers. Our feet dangled above a dry ditch, behind us a wood. Lanky nettles and run-to-seed willow herb concealed us on both sides. The ripe stink of pigs, their ill-tempered shrieks and squeals, carried from the farm. Through the hedge I noted the farmyard formed a rectangle. On one side was a higgledy-piggledy row of run-down buildings, on the other a big Dutch barn. At the end, opposite us, was a newish pig unit. We were close to the yard; only the width of the cart track that ran along the other side of the hedge separated us from this open space. Access by vehicle from public roads was from the pig unit end.

We'd entered our hiding place an hour earlier. Blum met me at the station, drove us out of Ormskirk. He pulled off a straight, narrow moss road, crossed wheat stubble alongside a wood about two hundred yards long, a hundred wide. He backed the van across a culverted ditch into bracken and rhododendron beneath sycamore trees. The wood was a shooting covert and I asked if we were on the Tarlscough estate, but Blum told me we were a few miles north of its boundary.

Blum took his grandfather's field glasses, but left the other gear in the van, led the way through the wood. I was so tense, my heart jumped to my mouth when a cock pheasant rose in a mad clatter of wings. With a manic ka, ka, ka it powered up through the trees, burst through the canopy and away.

Blum muttered, 'Bad as blummin' blackbirds for giving the game away.'

Settled on the ditch side, Blum told me the farm belonged to a cousin of Kav's hoppo, Cooey. The cousin had been in and out of prison until he inherited the farm. He'd made his living from agriculture in recent years, but hadn't left the criminal life behind. He kept his hand in ringing stolen cars, didn't mind harbouring knock-off stuff if it meant extra cash.

I was bemused at our location until Blum told me to look at the Dutch barn. 'Just a stack of bales, eh?' he grinned at me, 'Three guesses what's inside it, mind.'

'How about a lorry stuffed with fags and booze?'

Blum stifled a snort of a laugh, 'I couldn't believe me luck when Kav forced Delly to come and help stack them blummin' bales. He's been reporting to me, phone box to phone box, every night since before the hijack. Delly knowing this place's made it ten times easier.'

Blum explained the lorry was on its way from a bonded warehouse in Liverpool to a wholesale warehouse in Blackburn. It was hijacked at a transport café near Chorley. It was a regular trip and Kav and Delly, or Kav and Cooey, shadowed the lorry a number of times. The driver always stopped at the café. On the day, Kav, Delly and a character called Frank Pye were ready with stockings over their heads. Kav stuck an automatic pistol in the driver's chest while Pye took the lorry keys. Pye drove the load of fags and booze to the farm, Kav forced the driver into the stolen car's boot.

I interrupted, startled, ' Christ, Kav's got an automatic?'

'Ha. Only a matter of time, weren't it? Bet the pillock thinks he's Burscough's answer to the Kray Twins.'

'Yeah, but we're about to rob him. Jeeze, we know he's a hothead, a nutter...'

'We're not robbing him, not face to face, remember?' He chuckled, 'Don't worry about the Burscough Scouser having a blummin' gun. What was I saying...?'

Kav and Delly drove west, dumped the driver under a bridge on the Leeds-Liverpool canal, tied his hands and feet. Delly was set to drop off Kav and wait to be paid, but Kav ordered him to help hide the lorry in the barn full of bales. Today the fags and booze would be sold. If we could, Blum and I would rob the proceeds.

'Up to then I hadn't worked it out,' said Blum, 'Thought I might have to rob the fags and booze and flog it meself, but Kav being such a lazy bastard was just the blummin' job. If Delly hadn't come here to hump bales, I wouldn't know the half of it. And this Frank Pye feller's got a bigger gob than Ena blummin' Sharples, by the sound of it, must like showing off to kids.'

Delly kept his eyes and ears open, learned the man behind the hijack was a car dealer called Bill Sutton, or 'Sooty' to his associates. Sooty was an ex- convict with a history of armed robbery. He'd moved from his native Manchester with the proceeds of his crimes and started a car sales business in Southport. He owned a car repair workshop, holiday flats, a bed and breakfast set-up, as well as two shops that sold candy floss and seaside rock to holidaymakers. These days he shied away from getting his own hands mucky. Pye was a Liverpudlian, a former dockworker, dock thief and hard-knock, who'd been in prison with Sooty, but now acted as his dogs body in some of his tax-free activities, usually those that involved mucky hands. Blum was interested to learn via Delly that Sutton had a 'dead smart' house in Scarisbrick, a rural district a few miles inland from Southport.

While we breakfasted on corned beef butties and a bottle of cold tea stowed in Blum's army greatcoat pockets, he outlined how he thought the day would develop. He emphasised to me that after this stage at the farm, events might become unpredictable. We'd have to be ready to think on our feet.

Before Blum finished, Kav drove the same green Corsair from that night at the Soldier into the farmyard. Kav, Delly and Cooey got out, all eyes going straight to the stack of bales hiding the hijack lorry. Delly and Cooey lit up fags. Last out was the man I assumed was Frank Pye.

Blum whispered, 'That's Pye. Looks just like Delly said -- Ugly bugger, isn't he?'

'Christ.'

Pye had curly hair that strayed an inch or two down over the collar of his navy blue boiler suit. His chin jutted beneath a small flat nose and prominent forehead. He wasn't tall, but his muscled bulk, his physicality, was obvious under a navy blue overall. At a guess, he was mid-thirties. His appearance suggested a serious hard-knock, not some delinquent, a man to be feared; in comparison, the others looked like schoolboys. I felt a spasm of unease.

Pye moved towards the others, his thick Liverpool accent carried across the yard, 'Come 'ead, never mind ciggies, get f'ckin' movin' will yer.' Delly was slow to move. Pye pushed him in the back, 'Yous an' all, bollocks.'

For more than an hour, Kav, Delly and Cooey laboured to topple, move and re-stack bales at the other end of the barn. At one point, a man drove a tractor into the yard, glanced at the activity, made no attempt to approach Pye and the others. He took a sack from one of the buildings, drove off. Pye checked his watch often. About quarter-to-twelve, he joined in on the bales, urged the others to work faster.

Soon, their work revealed the lorry, green with gold lettering on the cab door that read, Wm. Hobley, Hauliers, Blackburn. Pye pulled on a pair of leather gloves, climbed into the cab, started its engine, the diesel fumes, harsh, unpleasant, against the autumn scent of the wood. Effing and blinding at Kav to shift errant bales out of his way, he drove out on to the yard.

He jumped down from the cab, left the engine idling, pointed at the lorry, 'Keep ya f'ckin' mitts off that. We don't want no prints, right?'

From the Corsair he took a tin of paint, a large brush. The others lit up, watched Pye paint out the lettering on both cab doors and below the windscreen with green paint. He dumped the tin and brush in a cart shed. Pye opened the lorry's door. Kav, Delly and Cooey drifted towards him. Pye said, 'We'll gerroff now. Need to be at Sooty's at ten to one. No stopping off, right?' He swung up into the driver's seat, pointed at them. 'No f'ckin' speeding either.'

Pye slammed the cab door, drove down the yard to the pig unit, turned right. Kav, Delly and Cooey got into the Corsair.

Blum chuckled, 'Just the job. Let's go.'

'You do know where it is?'

'Where do you think I was at five o'clock this morning?' He grinned, jerked his thumb towards the farm yard, 'Not stinking in bed like them blummin' clowns.'

Back at the other side of the wood, Blum edged the van forward out of the trees, waited. A minute later, the hijack lorry crossed in front of us, a field away. Then the Corsair, Kav at the wheel, followed. When both vehicles were out of sight, Blum took the van over the culverted ditch, drove over the stubble, turned out on to the road, headed for Southport.

He made no attempt to keep up with the two vehicles. We could take our time, choose our own route to Sutton's place; some slack in our arrival time was unimportant. He wound down his window, smoked. With an elbow on the window edge, he seemed relaxed, as if out on an afternoon drive, not the run-up to robbery. In contrast to last night's excitement, my guts churned at the thought of what might lie ahead.

Blum asked if I'd had a chance to look into how he might buy Pygon's Farm. I hadn't, but promised I'd find out as soon as I could. He asked about Elaine. I told him I thought I might have had a letter, or a call, but there'd been nothing. 'Still not bothered about it?' he said. I admitted I wasn't. When he asked after Sandra, I complained of the extra work dumped on her, my plan for a few days away in the Yorkshire Dales. 'Nice,' he grinned at me, 'Bit o' luck, you'll have some decent spends.'

We drove into the central part of Southport, inland from the seafront, with its criss-cross, pattern roads. It was an area of terraced and modest semi-detached houses behind the main roads, where Victorian and Edwardian houses were much larger. We approached minor cross roads. Blum checked his wing mirror, swerved to the right of the road, forty yards back from the cross roads. He drew up behind two parked cars, pointed to a footpath on our right, between two blocks of semi-detached houses. Either side of the path were six-foot high concrete slab walls.

'I don't know how long we'll be here,' Blum said, 'But at some time you might need to run out of that ginnel and check the way a vehicle goes. If we don't know which way, we've had it.'

He put his hand under the driver's seat, pulled out two pairs of gardening gloves, stuffed them into the pocket of his Army coat.

'What's with the gloves?'

In a guttural scouse accent like Pye's, he said, 'We don't want no f'ckin' prints, right?'

I laughed. Blum got out, bobbed his head back in. He grinned, 'Come 'ead, bollocks, get movin.'

Blum locked the van, led me into the pathway. Thirty yards along on the left the path widened. Set back were a pair of small semi-detached houses with tiny front gardens, each with a front gate. Beyond the houses, the path again narrowed. When he reached the gate at the second house, he opened it, entered the front garden. I was confused. He'd not mentioned this. I was about to speak, but he let himself through the back gate. He held it open for me, closed it behind us.

The small back yard had high brick walls that contained only a coal bunker and a washing line that carried two long dried, grubby vests.

Blum pointed to an open transom in the kitchen window. 'Ha, just like I left it,' He took out the gloves, handed me a pair.

He vaulted up on to the coal bunker. His hand snaked through the transom, went down the inside of the larger kitchen window. He raised the catch, swung it open.

My nerves were jangling, 'You never said anything about burglary.'

'Don't be daft. We just need it for an observation post kind o' thing.' He jerked his head, 'Back round the front, I'll let you in.'

He ducked inside the kitchen window, I hurried to the front door. I looked both ways, but the pathway was clear. I lingered like a legitimate caller waiting for an answer to my knock. Blum opened the front door.

'All quiet, nobody home.'

He closed the front door, I followed him upstairs. 'The feller who lives here went out about seven o'clock. Bit o' luck he's at work all day.'

We went into the back bedroom. No bed and a clutter of furniture, suitcases, a roll of coconut matting and a bike minus wheels, a place used to store junk. Blum pulled two metal kitchen chairs from a corner, put them by the window. 'That's Sutton's yard over the wall.'

He opened the window. 'Put your fag ash out here.'

Beyond the wall were a dozen or more derelict cars, oil drums and other scrap. Opposite our vantage point was a long, flat-roofed building. To the left was a workshop with one car over an inspection pit, another with its bonnet open. Any mechanics who worked there had gone for dinner break, or been told to stay away. Adjacent was an office with dirty windows. A sign above read 'New Lane Motor Repairs.'

A man in his early fifties stood by the door. He looked prosperous in a light jacket, open necked shirt, grey slacks. Parked up the side of the office was a big silver car. He took a drag on a small cigar, looked at his watch.

'Going on what Delly said, that's Sutton.' Blum observed the scene below through the field glasses. 'Nice Jag he's got, XJ6'

Sutton smoked, again checked his watch. A minute or two later, Pye drove the hi-jack lorry into the yard.

Pye positioned the lorry alongside the workshop. Then Kav drove in, parked the Corsair by the scrap motors. Kav, Cooey and Delly got out, stood, hands in pockets, awaiting instructions. Frank Pye killed the lorry engine and joined Sutton, who seemed relaxed as he spoke and gestured to Pye.

Blum put down the field glasses, but his eyes remained on the yard, 'This is about following the money.' He put his hand to the back of his head, tapping his fingers on his skull, 'When the deal's finished, Sutton or Pye is going to leave here with a stack of dosh. And let's hope it's Sooty, not that blummin' gorilla, Pye, eh? Even worse, the blummin' pair of 'em.'

He grinned at me, but my stomach somersaulted at the thought of confronting either of them.

'When the money goes – if it goes -- you'll have to leg it back to the road, see what way they go. I'll hang back a sec, check if anyone's following.' Blum sat up straight in his chair, 'Aye, aye, summat's happening.'

Chapter 33
Fags 'N' Booze

BLUM TOOK UP his field glasses. A second lorry reversed into the yard. Pye directed it alongside the buildings, so the two vehicles' tailboards faced each other. Pye moved to the hijack lorry, opened its back doors. A Rover 3500 entered the yard, pulled up behind the Corsair.

The man who got out was tall and thin, older than Sutton, wearing a raincoat and a flat cap. He ambled across the yard, to be joined by the second lorry's driver, a man of about thirty with an old fashioned Teddy-boy quiff, ice blue jeans, white tee shirt and black motorbike gloves. Sutton moved to greet Flat Cap and they shook hands, before Sutton spoke to Teddy-boy, pointing to the hijack lorry. Pye gestured to Kav, who hurried to close the yard gates.

Teddy-boy walked over to the lorry, swung up on to the tailgate. He pulled out a cardboard box at random and Pye stepped forward to take it from him. He turned to Flat Cap, pulled a knife out of his pocket, cut open the box. He put the box on the ground, slid out a yellow paper sleeve of 200 Benson & Hedges cigarettes.

Blum kept the field glasses trained on them, 'Looks like he's checking the stuff,' he laughed, 'Wouldn't want them posh Bennos filled with blummin' Woodbines, eh?'

Flat Cap took the sleeve, tore it open. He took out a packet, passed the rest back to Pye. He opened it, withdrew a cigarette. He held it to his nose, rooted a lighter out of his raincoat pocket. He lit up and blew out smoke, nodded. Teddy-boy passed another box bearing different markings to Pye. Pye opened it, pulled out what appeared to be a bottle of whisky.

'Blummin' eck, it's not the gut rot you drink,' Blum said, 'It's the dead dear stuff Ted goes mad for; single malt.'

Flat Cap took a swig from the bottle. He nodded his appreciation, passed it to Sutton, who took a short pull at the bottle. He laughed, passed it back to Flat Cap, who recapped it, handed it to Pye. I watched these professional crooks, my belly full of apprehension at what was still to come, wished he'd passed the bottle to me.

Pye gave orders to Kav, Delly and Cooey. They began to offload boxes of fags and booze from the hijack lorry to Flat Cap's vehicle, supervised by Pye, and Teddy-boy. The number of boxes seemed endless. Flat Cap watched every one go into his lorry and almost an hour later, when loading was complete, he walked over to the Rover and went out of our sight. Moments later he re-appeared with a large manila envelope, re-joined Sutton, who put a friendly hand on Flat Cap's shoulder, ushered him inside the office.

'There goes the dosh,' Blum let the field glasses down against his chest. 'Now we have to blummin' wait.'

I leaned back in my chair. Blum took out his fags, offered me one, gave me a light, 'You all right?'

I blew out smoke, 'Just nerves.'

'You'll be right once we get going. No time for nerves then.'

I nodded, wasn't convinced, but Blum was encouraging. He recalled moments we'd shared over the years, but, if anything, that made me more nervous. So many times we'd got away free -- How long could anyone's luck last? Though Blum had planned the early stages of this venture with care, from now on, success depended on our wits. If it meant the sort of athletic action Blum rose to after the post office robbery, I knew I couldn't compete. For me, the tension, the waiting, was unbearable. I had to use our unknown host's bathroom.

When we'd smoked a couple of fags apiece, Flat Cap's lorry was closed up by Teddy-boy. While he leaned against his lorry, Pye put on his gloves, spoke to Kav, Delly and Cooey. Kav went to the workshop, returned with a jerry can.

'That'll be petrol for the hijack lorry,' Blum said.

'Won't it be diesel?'

Blum laughed, 'To burn the blummin' thing! -- That's what I'd do any road.'

Kav put the petrol in the boot of the Corsair, waited with Pye and the others.

Flat Cap came out of the office doorway with Sutton behind him. Flat Cap jerked his head at Teddy-boy, who went to the front of the lorry. Flat Cap again shook hands with Sutton, strolled over to his Rover. Delly ran to open the gate while Sutton watched the lorry and the Rover leave his premises then spoke to Pye. After a brief, animated conversation, Pye signalled to Kav. He, Delly and Cooey went to the Corsair, got in. Pye went to the hijack lorry, started up. He drove out of the yard, followed by the Corsair.

The moment was getting closer. 'What if he just locks the money away in the office?' I said, 'Do we go in and rob it there?'

Blum's fingers drummed the back of his head. 'Pray he blummin' doesn't. I don't fancy it in that yard. Any bugger could walk in on us.'

Blum's agitation and this lack of a definite plan were doing nothing for my nerves. It was hard to sit in that stuffy back bedroom, to wait. I wanted to be outside; anywhere I could move, walk, run, burn-off the tension. I was about to suggest we went back to the van, to watch New Lane Motors from the street, when Blum sat up straight.

'He's coming out. He's got the envelope!' Blum stood. Sutton opened the door of the Jaguar, put the envelope under the seat. Blum said, 'Right! Come on! Out!'

He hurried me to the door. I crossed the landing, down the stairs at speed, grabbed the Yale latch. I swung open the front door to reveal a middle-aged man with a door key in one hand, a Sunblest loaf and two tins of Heinz beans clutched to his chest. We gaped at each other.

'Leg it!' Blum screeched in my ear.

I barged past the man, strode across his front garden, jumped over the low wall, turned back. The householder was struggling with Blum, the loaf and beans on the ground. The man grabbed Blum's army coat with one hand, tried to stop him. He shouted and swore. Blum's cry was urgent, 'Sooty's car, Sooty's car!'

I hesitated. I didn't want to leave Blum, but we had to know which direction Sutton would take, or all would be lost. I sprinted back along the pathway to the van, in time to see Sutton's Jag stop at the cross-roads, waiting for traffic to pass. I stepped back, looked back. Blum and the man were now in the pathway, the man heaving at Blum's coat. Blum's hand came down on the crook of the man's arms in rapid, vicious chopping strokes. Blum pushed him, the man staggered back. Blum sprinted towards me, army coat flapping behind him, field glasses bumping against his chest. At the junction Sutton eased the XJ6 out and turned right, drove away from me.

Blum unlocked the driver's door. I rushed round to the passenger side. He started the engine, leaned over to unlock my door. Blum wrenched the wheel, jammed the van into first gear and accelerated. I lowered my head to look across Blum in the offside mirror. Blum shifted up the gears. The man came out of the footpath, gripping his arm, shouting soundlessly, as we drove away.

'Do you reckon he got our number plate?'

'Too far away.'

'Jeez, I hope so,' Blum said.

'False aren't they?'

'I blummin' forgot to put 'em on.'

'You're joking?'

Christ! How could he have forgotten that?

'The false 'un's are in the back,' he said, his eyes on Sutton's Jag, 'If we get the chance I'll change 'em.'

My eyes settled on the Jag, separated from us by a Ford Anglia. Would the householder report the burglary? If nothing was stolen or damaged, he might not bother. I didn't notice a phone in the hallway either. Maybe he hadn't thought to memorise the van's registration number. Christ, I hoped not.

Sutton kept to main roads across town. When he reached the far side of the Kew district the XJ6 negotiated a roundabout, took the road for Ormskirk. Sutton drove at a steady forty miles an hour. Blum hung back, but after a mile or two, the Jag rounded a sweeping right hand bend. Blum accelerated to keep him in sight. We passed the sign for Scarisbrick, Blum slowed.

'Looks like he's going home.'

The Jag's right indicator flashed. Blum slowed right down. Sutton turned off into a road called Blakemere Lane. Blum paused a few moments, turned after him. We passed scattered houses, farms, and after a mile-and-a-half, Sutton indicated right, turned into the gateway of a large modern house, set back from the road. Blum cut the speed as we passed. Sutton pushed open the driver's door to get out. Parked alongside the Jag was a blue Ford Escort.

'Did you see that other car?'

My voice sounded hysterical. Blum glanced at me.

'What if there's someone else there, his wife, kids?' I felt a rising panic,' What about guard dogs?'

Blum was calm.

'Big gob Pye told the others he's parted from his missus.'

'Whose car is it then?'

'There's no blummin' rush. We'll have to find out.'

Blum turned the van into a cart track on the same side of the lane as Sutton's house. We were a field away from the house. Apart from a few ash saplings, scrubby willows, a low hawthorn hedge, there wasn't much cover. The Escort and the Jag were visible to us and if Sutton looked across the field he would see the van. Blum wound down the driver's window, focused his field glasses on the side of Sutton's house.

'Do you reckon it's Pye's car?' I said.

'He's busy elsewhere.'

My nerves showed again, 'Jesus! Whose then?!'

Blum looked at me. 'It's no good getting in a blummin' panic over it'

'If there's someone else with him and...'

Blum cut in on me, pointed to the van's glove box, 'Look in there.'

I was confused, 'What?'

Blum leaned over, dropped the lid. In a clutter of fag packets, Bournville chocolate wrappers, lay an unopened half-bottle of whisky. I stared at it, turned to Blum.

'I got it so you could celebrate on the train home, but it looks like you need some now.'

I didn't reply, embarrassed at his detection of my fear; that he knew drink might control it. His voice was without edge. 'I'd sooner do this with you half-cut than go in with a nervous wreck.'

I looked at the bottle again.

'It's up to you, but get in the back first, get ready, eh?'

In the cramped space, everything was laid out. Two boiler suits, two green woollen balaclavas, each with a nylon stocking draped across them. Beside them were two pairs of Totector work boots. The Signalman's four-ten shotgun lay, folded, the breech open, the shiny brass ends of two cartridges in the chambers. Beside the gun were four coils of thick, sisal cord.

I took off my shoes, struggled into a boiler suit and boots. I put the balaclava on, pushed it down like a collar, put the nylon stocking in the top pocket of my overalls. Back in the passenger seat, Blum passed me the field glasses, 'Keep an eye on the house.'

I focused on the two cars while Blum climbed into the back to put on his gear. A couple of minutes later, a woman in her twenties was followed by Sutton to the cars. In her arms was a toddler, a little girl.

I almost shouted, 'There's a woman there!'

'Has she got the envelope?' Blum scrambled back into his seat. I thrust the field glasses at him, looked back to the house.

'I don't know.'

'If she has, we're in trouble.'

A spasm of alarm passed through me at the prospect of robbing a woman and child at gunpoint.

Blum trained the glasses on Sutton, the woman and little girl.

'No, all she's got is the nipper. She's started blummin' skrikin'.

I was relieved that alternative action would no longer be necessary.

Sutton and the woman tried to humour the little girl, but she continued crying as her mother put her inside the Ford Escort. 'Reckon that's his daughter and granddaughter?' I said.

'Not blummin' bothered, as long as she's going.'

The Escort reversed, swung out on to the road. Sutton stood on the driveway, waved them off. In the passenger side mirror, I clocked the Escort pass the end of the track, go out of sight.

Blum reached into the back of the van, picked up the folded four-ten shotgun. He put it between his legs, butt end and muzzles to the floor. We both put on our gloves. Blum ran through how he saw the situation, what each of us needed to do. 'All right on that?'

I nodded, 'Yeah.'

He nodded to the glove box. 'If you want a swig of that, have it now.'

I was embarrassed again, shook my head, 'No.'

'Right,' he said, 'Let's get that blummin' dosh.'

Chapter 34
Double Bubble

BLUM PARKED UP a little past Sutton's house. We had to wait while two cars going in opposite directions passed. On went the stocking masks and we pulled up our balaclavas. We left the van doors resting on their latches as planned, to avoid noise, to smooth our getaway.

Blum ducked down, moved back along the road, turned into the gateway and drive. I was close behind him. He stepped on to the lawn to avoid noise from the gravel drive. I did the same as we headed for a gate under an archway, covered in blue clematis, which linked a garage to the house. I almost collided with Blum at the arch as he stopped, snatched up something from the flower bed along the house wall. He paused for a moment to push whatever it was inside his boiler suit. Then moved to the gate, quietly raised the latch to open it, nodded me through.

I stepped on to a large paved, terraced area, above a long, well-kept garden wider than the property. Blum left the gate ajar, ducked down. I did the same as we moved under two large windows that looked out over the garden. We approached a porch, entered through its open door. Blum turned to me, held up his gloved hand. His fingers were crossed. He reached for the knob of the inner back door. If the back door were locked, or bolted I could see no way to continue. Blum's hand gripped the door knob, turned it. He pushed. I froze, dreaded giveaway noise, but the door opened without a sound. We stepped into a big, modern kitchen.

Straight away, I heard the voice of Peter O'Sullevan, the television horse-racing commentator. There were two doors leading from the kitchen into the house and both were open. The nearest offered a glimpse of the hallway. O'Sullevan continued to address Britain's race fans as we crept across the kitchen. Blum held the folded shotgun diagonally across his chest. My heart was hammering as we moved to the second open door. Blum stepped into the living room. I was close behind him. The focus of the room was a colour telly in a big wooden cabinet. Sutton sprawled in an armchair, his attention on the screen. Jockeys guided their mounts into the traps, the image overlaid by the race card of horses, riders and betting odds.

For a moment I thought Blum might blast Sutton's telly, but in a rapid movement, he raised the barrels of the gun and snapped them into place. Sutton turned as Blum lowered the barrels to point straight at him. Surprise on Sutton's face turned to outrage.

'What the fuck you doin' in here?'

I could feel the aggression radiating off him as he stood. He seemed bigger than viewed from that back bedroom in Southport. He took a step towards us. Blum thumbed back the hammers, two rapid clicks.

Blum snarled, 'Don't f'ckin' move or yer'll gerrit.'

Sutton hesitated.

'Where's the f'ckin money?'

I was startled by Blum's imitation of Pye's guttural scouse accent.

Blum took a step closer, 'Come 'ead, Sutton, where is it?'

A memory jumped into my mind: the night we evaded capture for poaching -- same gun, same fake accent.

'There's no money here.'

Blum shouted, 'A'll not f'ckin' ask yis again!'

Sutton laughed. I hadn't expected this. He spoke as if we were a mild annoyance, as though he didn't have a cocked and loaded shotgun levelled at his chest, 'What money?'

Blum shouted, 'Tell us, or we'll do yer, take the 'f'ckin place apart.'

He sneered, drawled, 'Fuck off...'

Blum slid his hand inside his boiler suit and pulled out a kid's toy, a grubby, felt penguin. He held it up. Shock crossed Sutton's face. Anger followed realisation, 'If you've touched them I'll fuckin'...'

Blum shouted, jabbed the shotgun at him, 'Gerron the floor! On yer belly!'

'Where are they?'

'On the f'ckin deck, now!'

Sutton didn't move.

Blum jerked his head to me. 'Gerron that phone. Tell 'em he's more interested in 'is f'ckin' money than 'er an' the kid.'

I looked around. It was quick-thinking on Blum's part. I realised the little girl had dropped her toy. Blum had cottoned on to that small incident used it; snatching it up outside, then now. It was inspired, yet ruthless, nasty. I made a move to the phone on a table by the window.

Sutton shouted, 'There's no money here. You've got it wrong!'

Blum snarled -- the accent harsher, 'Do yer think we's f'ckin' soft? It was under the seat, in yer Jag. Yer brought it here an' yer've been nowhere else. On yer f'ckin' belly!'

Sutton said, 'Tell us where Karen is.'

'A said f'ckin' down!'

Sutton stood his ground, didn't move.

'Right,' Blum said, jerking his head towards me, 'Tell 'em to get crackin' on the mother ---Do worrit takes. Ger 'er screamin' down that f'ckin' phone, no f'ckin' 'oldin' back!'

I picked up the phone, planning to dial a random number.

Sutton relented, 'All right! All right!'

Sutton dropped to hands and knees, then down on his belly, 'Touch them and you're fuckin' dead!'

'Put yer 'ands behind yer back. Quick! Move!'

Sutton complied but swore, ranted threats; his contacts, his influence, his hard men, the certainty of awful vengeance.

Blum motioned me to take the shotgun to cover Sutton. He pulled a coil of the sisal cord from his overalls, stepped forward to tie Sutton's hands. My legs shook, my arms trembled. I pointed the Signalman's four-ten gun at Sutton's head. Blum passed the cord behind Sutton's wrists.

Then it happened.

I didn't take it in for a second, perhaps two. With startling agility for a big, older man, Sutton twisted his body in a flash. Quick as a snake, he grabbed Blum's arm. He rolled, pulled at Blum. Blum fell forward. Sutton threw his arm around Blum's neck, pushed himself into a sitting position against the sofa. With his forearm across Blum's throat, he faced me; his head partly hidden by Blum's as he increased the pressure on my friend's windpipe. Blum's face went red as he struggled to breathe. Sutton was using my friend as a human shield, gripping him with arms and knees, choking the life out of him.

Sutton gasped, 'Tell me where they are!'

I stared at him. The gun barrels now threatened him and Blum.

Sutton's eyes blazed in rage. Blum's legs kicked as he fought to escape, to get air. 'Tell us, or I'll fuckin' do 'im!' Snot and saliva covered Sutton's mouth and chin, he roared, 'I mean it, yer scouse cunt -- I'll fuckin' kill him!'

I stared at Sutton. I felt calm, almost serene. My heart was no longer hammering. My hands, my legs, were steady. I stepped forward. The horse race was nearing its end. Peter O'Sullevan's words gabbled faster as it neared its crescendo. Blum's face was redder. I raised the gun barrels high over my left shoulder. It was almost like batting at cricket; eye on the ball as it arced towards the wicket. I stepped forward and swung down the steel-plated butt of the shotgun to connect with Sutton's temple.

Sutton's eyes rolled upward, rage extinguished. A horse called Double Bubble won the three o' clock race at Doncaster. Sutton's body relaxed. Blum untangled himself from Sutton's arms and legs, stood. He gasped, dry-heaved, rubbed at his neck. He regained his breath . 'Blummin' eck! Jeez, thought I'd had it there.'

Blum touched Sutton's neck. A rivulet of blood ran from the wound on his temple.

Blum said, 'It's alright. He'll come round in a bit.' He heaved at Sutton, laid him on the carpet, rolled him on to his front. Blum looked at me, picked up the sisal cord, 'Do his feet, I'll see to his hands.'

I put the shotgun on the sofa, tied Sutton's ankles, knot after knot. Then it occurred to me I could have killed him. Yet, I was still calm, surprised I didn't panic after my violence. Sutton said he would kill Blum and I had no doubt he would have done. His blood dripped on to the carpet. I didn't care. To use violence seemed the right thing to do.

Blum tied a final knot around Sutton's wrists, picked up the shotgun, 'Get looking for the dosh. No talking in case he hears us – Ha! Not unless it's scouse!'

Blum moved to the telephone, pulled tight the wire to the wall connection. With his Totector boot he stamped twice on the plastic junction box, tore the wire from its connections.

Blum stated to pull out the drawers of a sideboard as I went to the kitchen. There was no sign of the envelope in the kitchen. What if he'd taken the banknotes out of it? What if it was hidden? Or in a safe? I went through the other door out into the hallway. To one side was an open door. I went in. It was a dining room with pictures on the wall, carpeted with thick, cream shag pile. A big table with shining wood reminded me of fresh conkers. Around it were six chairs. Then I saw it. The big manila envelope, handed-over by Flat Cap, lay across paperwork on the open flap of a writing bureau that matched the table and chairs. On top of it was a slightly smaller envelope.

I moved to the bureau, snatched the big envelope. I looked inside the open flap. It was packed tight with bundles of banknotes. I couldn't help myself, shouted, 'Here!'

Footsteps across the kitchen tiles, then Blum came in, the now folded shotgun in his hand. 'I said no ...' He hurried to me. I held open the envelope, showed him.

'Ha! Bob-on.'

He grinned as I handed it to him, pushed it inside his boiler suit. 'That's it, let's go.'

'Just a sec,' I whispered. I picked up the second envelope. It was sealed at the flap. I tore off the top, looked inside – more thick bundles of banknotes.

'Jesus,' I laughed, 'Double bubble!'

I held it open to show Blum our bonus haul.

'Blummin' eck!'

I shoved the second envelope inside my own boiler suit.

A roar of anger and frustration, a torrent of swearwords came from Sutton, as we left through the back door.

*

Blum drove the van at normal speed as we left Sutton's house. He was insistent on this even before we went in to rob the money. The moment we got inside the van, we chucked the stocking masks and balaclavas in the back, pulled down our boiler suits to waist level. I stowed both envelopes under the passenger seat, lit fags for both of us. I was trembling again, but exultant, felt a soaring sense of power and vitality, of being alive.

I passed a fag to him, 'Christ, we did it!'

Blum nodded.

'That with the kid's toy was a cracker. Making him think we'd got the woman as well.' I laughed, 'And the scouse voice! – A bloody masterstroke!'

There was no exultation in Blum's voice, 'Just luck that nipper dropped the toy. And knowing the woman had been there, so I could use it to put the pressure on him. If I hadn't got that toy penguin, I might've had to blast his leg, or summat.'

'You got what you wanted, though.'

Blum glanced at me, 'It was my fault you might've done him 'in.'

'For Christ's sake, he would've killed you! I know he would!'

'I was careless.'

'It doesn't matter now.' I dropped the glove box lid, grabbed the half-bottle of whisky, twisted off the top. 'It's done. Have a swig.'

He shook his head.

'Go on, celebrate!'

'I'll have a pint when we've got the money locked up, everything put away.'

'Sure?'

He nodded. I took a pull at the whisky. My stomach was empty. The neat spirit warmed me at once, added more to my sense of satisfaction, wellbeing. 'I can't believe there was another envelope -- Talk about luck! -- Bloody hell!'

Blum said, 'He must've got paid-up for some other job as well.'

I put the bottle in the foot well, reached under my seat for the envelopes, 'Should I count it.'

Blum shouted, 'No!'

Startled, I froze.

'Just a blummin' superstition thing, bad luck, like, sorry. I've said to meself all along. I won't count it till everything's tidied up, the van's emptied...' He grinned, 'Just drink your gut-rot, eh'

Blum slowed and indicated as we approached the end of the road to Sutton's house where it met the main road from Southport to Ormskirk. I picked up the bottle, took a smaller swig.

'Jesus!' said Blum.

He braked.

'It's them!'

A green Corsair turned the corner from the Ormskirk direction into Blakemere Lane. Then it was out of view from my seat. Blum pulled out, turning for Ormskirk, 'Are you sure?'

'Delly driving, Kav in the front -- Blummin' Pye in the back with Cooey.'

'Christ!' My feeling of wellbeing evaporated, 'What the hell are they doing here?'

'Must be going to Sutton's, must've got rid of the lorry.'
Blum accelerated.

'Bet they're taking Pye to Sutton's to get their wages.
Should've blummin' thought of that!'

'Do you think they spotted us?'

'I blummin' hope not. Don't want that lot after us.'

Blum sped into the bend at Scarisbrick Hall, swerved
right on to the road that passed through Halsall and
Haskayne, then Lydiate.

My eyes were on the wing mirror, alert for the Corsair. I
couldn't help it. But there was no reason for Pye and
company to turn and chase us right away. But in minutes they
could be untying a furious Sutton. If they had seen us at the
top of the road to Sutton's, how long would it take Kav to
make the connection between the man on the post office job
with him and his proximity today to the theft of Sutton's
cash?

I tried not to betray my unease, apprehension, 'What if
they do come looking, though?' I said, 'If they've gone to
Sutton's they'll have found him by now. That Kav knows
you've got the nerve for robbery, doesn't he?'

Blum glanced at me, 'We'll have to talk our way out of it.
Make sure they see nowt that might give us away.'

'What did you have in mind?'

He seemed calm, unperturbed. He laughed, 'We'll get rid
of the evidence first, then I'll have to think of summat.'

Blum turned right at the next lane. He was quiet, intent
on driving. Echoing his escape from Meanygate End weeks
before, he took a roundabout route, avoided the main road,
worked his way back to Pygon Lane down narrow roads that
crossed miles of flat moss farmland.

Thirty minutes later we drove up the track off Pygon
Lane which edged the remaining fields at Pygon's Farm and
led the back way to the farmyard. Blum reversed the van into
its usual position between the barn and cart shed, ever ready
for a quick departure. We carried the money, the Signalman's
gun, balaclavas, field glasses, everything we'd worn and

used, into the still room. It felt calm, safe, in there. What happened at Sutton's was already receding from my mind. I sat on the end of the table, looked at the half-bottle of whisky, still minus only a couple of swigs. Blum slid the envelopes along to me.

'Go on, you can count it now,' he said, 'If I do it we'll be here all blummin' night.'

I put the whisky in my inside jacket pocket, 'We should ring Elaine. She'd have it done double-quick!'

He laughed, 'Don't tell us how much we've got till you're all done.'

Blum picked up his van jobs book from the table while I tipped out the contents of the big envelope. It was all in fives and tens. When I tipped out the second I saw the bundles were all twenty pound notes, bound by elastic bands. With mistakes it took ages to count and double-check it all and the first envelope added up to £7,750. That alone would've been more than enough if Blum still had the option of renewing the lease on May Bank. I was bursting to tell him, but left him writing in his jobs book. The spoils from the second envelope topped the first -- £8,360 -- to make total of £16,110. I waited until he stopped writing.

'Ready for it?' I said.

He closed the job book. 'Go on.'

To my surprise, he didn't whoop, or punch the air. He nodded slowly, taking in the final figure.

'Do you reckon it'll be enough?'

'Christ, you could buy this place twice over for that, maybe three times.' I told him about a report we carried in *The Sentinel* last winter. A derelict farm near Feniscowles sold for £5,500 at auction. 'Loads more land with a house and a cottage. I bet this won't cost anywhere near.'

Blum took it in, nodded.

'Right, count out your half. I need to get it locked up.'

I was startled, 'I don't want any of it.'

'Don't be daft. You've earned it.'

I stood. 'No. All this...I didn't do it for money.'

'My half'll sort everything out for mam. You've got to have your share.'

'I mean it, I did it to see what it'd be like -- to help your mam. How many years has she been worrying about that lease? What to do if she lost May Bank?'

'Sutton would've throttled me to blummin' death if you hadn't been there. If you hadn't clocked him one it would've been a right balls-up. Go on, count it out, fifty-fifty, it's yours.'

'I'd sooner the lot went to your mam.'

He slammed his jobs book on the table.

'I said, you've blummin' earned it.'

I shook my head, 'I just want this to make her life better, to make up for all these years -- all that worry.'

'I know you mean it, but...'

'You'll need extra cash to do it up.'

'Not another eight-thousand quid. Take what's yours.'

I rooted out a fag and lit up.

'Look, I'm not arguing. If you've got anything left when you've finished this place I'll split it with you, how's that?'

He pondered, nodded.

'Yeah, but take summat now, on account, like.'

I moved to the table, picked up a bundle of twenties I knew added up to a thousand pounds. 'I don't get my wages till tomorrow. I could do with a bit of beer money.'

I pulled out two twenties, dropped the bundle back in the pile.

He laughed, shook his head.

'I'm blummin' serious -- I want you to have something out of all this.'

'Come on, I'll buy you a pint. Isn't it the in-thing for us robbers to buy drinks for our mates?'

He laughed and together we put the day's profits in the safe. I'd fulfilled my promise, Blum's mam would have her house. I could concentrate on my own life, my imminent holiday -- and Sandra.

Chapter 35
Woolly-Back Knobheads

WE TOOK OUR celebratory pints into the garden of the Scottish Soldier. Blum talked non-stop about his plans, even about transferring his mam's favourite shrubs and plants to Pygon's Farm to beat the bulldozers' arrival at May Bank View.

I enjoyed the sunshine, but felt guilty I was skiving work, pint in hand, while Sandra carried the weight to make Fairbrass and Geoff Sillitoe's fishing match happen. When I got back, I'd take her for a Chinese meal. I didn't care if anyone I knew, anyone from the paper, saw us in the Blue Dragon. I'd committed myself to Sandra, the need for secrecy was over, I needed to tell her how I felt.

Blum was on about farm's potential as the base for a future haulage business. 'What do you reckon?'

'Good idea, yeah, but aren't there more basic things to work out first?

'Like what?'

'For a kick-off how you explain to Viv you've suddenly got the money to buy Pygon's Farm?'

'Ha. Easy. She doesn't know May Bank's on a lease. Mam's blummin' sold it to those house-building bastards. That's all she needs to know.'

'What about your mam? How're you going to explain to her?'

'It's been empty for years, so I tell her I've got it on a dead cheap rent, you know, peppercorn, on condition I do it up, make it presentable, like.'

I thought for a moment, 'To make that look good I think you'd have to buy it and then rent it to yourself. Get some printed letterheads, proper paperwork.'

'Blummin 'eck, that'd be bob-on, fab. Can you do that, all legal like?'

'Pretty sure, yeah, but you'd need a solicitor. And find out who actually owns it.'

'This contact of yours, can you sound him out on all this?'

'I'll see to it tomorrow.'

He picked up his pint, grinned, 'Grand as blummin' owt.'

'There's another thing...'

Blum's glass stopped short of his lips.

'If you and Viv are going to get it together, married and that, when are you going to tell her the truth?'

'How do you mean?'

'We've been through this before. Trust, knowing everything about each other -- You'll be...be living a lie till you tell her. What if she doesn't like the idea of living in a place bought with dirty money?'

He put down his glass, 'Have you ever told any girl, or anyone, anything about some of the things we've done? Would you tell any of 'em what we did today? Admit owt about it?'

'No, but...'

'But nowt. You can keep a secret, just like I can. That's what I'll do. I won't be telling her, not blummin' ever.'

I'd said it all about his dishonesty with Viv and I didn't want any friction, so didn't comment, picked up my glass, 'Same again?'

He looked at his watch. 'Delly's been told to ring me at six o'clock, phone box near the Weld Blundell.'

I checked my own, 'Still time for another.'

He insisted on buying them, pulled his jobs book from his back pocket, 'Here, you can do some homework while I get 'em in, look at today's pages.'

Pasted on the front of the notebook was his regular ad from the Thursday *Advertiser*. Inside were dozens of entries; addresses, phone numbers, appointments, pick-up and delivery times, names and sums of money charged. The entries for today were fictional. They'd taken us to half a dozen places in west Lancashire. Most relevant was our shipment of a washing machine from Birkdale to a Mrs Corcoran's home in Dyer's Lane, Ormskirk. The pick-up in Birkdale was at 2.45pm -- roughly the time we were at Sutton's place helping ourselves to the proceeds of the lorry hi-jack -- and that other enterprise we knew nothing about.

Blum returned with the pints, insisted on testing me.

'Do we have to do this?'

'In case anyone comes asking what we've been up to today, I reckon so.'

'You mean them?'

'If Delly spotted us over at Scarisbrick, he wouldn't say a word. Pye doesn't know us from Adam, so if anyone said owt, it'd be Kav. I might call him a pillock, but he's sharp enough, a bit cunning, like. He's the one who could cause us trouble.'

That made me uneasy, 'Cunning enough to guess Mrs Corcoran's washing machine is made up guff?'

Blum shrugged, 'Could be. He'll be desperate to stay in Sutton and Pye's good books and all, now Sooty's dosh's gone west. Any road, we'll face it if it happens. No harm having a story to stick to if it gets a bit rough.'

Even with that worry hovering, I passed his test on the day's fictitious work. Blum laughed. 'Don't forget, Mrs Corcoran give us blummin' Tizer and fruitcake.'

Delly's call was due and we left. Blum put the van into reverse. At that moment, a vehicle braked hard behind us. Frank Pye's reflection appeared in my side mirror, stepping out of the Corsair's passenger seat.

Blum's voice was low, 'Ha, quicker than I thought.'

Kav's face appeared at Blum's open window.

'Turn it off. We wanna fuckin' word with yous.'

Blum killed the engine, 'A'reet, Kav. What you doing down here?'

Kav was barged away from the window and Pye looked in. His big, ugly face dominated the van.

'Gerrout, the pair of yous.'

Blum said, 'We're just off to get us tea.'

Pye was blunt, 'You heard, soft lad. Out.'

My legs started to tremble as Blum and I got out.

Blum said, 'If you want guns we've nowt left.'

Kav snapped, 'It's norrabout fuckin' guns.'

Pye gestured at me, 'Get round here, where I can see yis.'

I moved round the van to join them.

Kav took a step towards Blum, 'What have you and him been doing all day?'

'Working. Why?'

'Where?'

Blum shrugged, 'Blummin' eck, all over the show. Why?'

Pye said, 'Just answer the f'ckin' question.'

'Let's see,' said Blum, touching the fingers of his left hand, 'Here...Maghull...Ormskirk...Erm...

Kav cut across him, 'Worrabout fuckin' Scarisbrick?'

Pye was annoyed. 'I'll see to this.' He jabbed his finger at Kav, 'Just 'ave a look in that van. Purra move on.'

Kav seemed resentful as he went to open the back doors.

Pye told him, 'In the front an' all, under the seats, in the dash.'

Blum said, 'You're not the blummin police! What do you think you're doing?'

Pye gripped the neck of Blum's tee-shirt, pulled him close.

'What were yous f'ckin' doing on Blakemere Lane in Scarisbrick, three o'clock this avvo?'

'Nowt. Didn't have any work in Scarisbrick.'

'We f'ckin' saw yous!' He jerked his head towards me, 'An' 'im.'

'Blakemere Lane?'

Pye bunched Blum's tee shirt in his fist, shook him, 'Don't act f'ckin' soft with me, lar. The other feller there knows yis number plate. Yous was f'ckin' there.'

Blum said, 'That'd be the washing machine for Mrs Corcoran. Aye, that were the job.'

Kav came away from the van, 'Nothing.'

Pye pulled Blum closer, 'What were you doing there?'

'I've just said, shifting a blummin' twin-tub to Ormskirk. Why?'

Kav sneered, 'Yeah, right.'

Blum was indignant, 'Quickest blummin' way if you're picking it up in Birkdale and it's going to Ormskirk.'

Blum pulled his job book from his back pocket, held it up between his and Pye's faces. 'It's all here, look.'

Pye let go of Blum, snatched the book. He glanced at the cover, opened it, leafed through. He found the entries for that day, pored over the pages, took his time. He looked up, pushed Blum away, lashed the job book at his chest.

Kav said, 'What's it say?'

Blum protested, 'Eh, you've ripped me blummin' pages.'

Pye ignored him, turned on Kav, 'It says coming here's a waste of f'ckin' time, that's worrit says. I'm lookin' for robbers. Norra a pair a woolly-back knobheads who've been fetching and carrying all day for f'ckin' buttons.'

Kav was annoyed, 'You don't know what he can do. You know he was on that job a mine the other week and I saw...'

Now, it was as if we weren't even present.

Pye cut across Kav, 'The peanuts job, the one that turned to shite, you mean? Is that the one?'

Kav took the insult, pressed on, 'Look, you're making a big mistake here...'

'The only mistake here is you, Kavanagh. Sooty wants results, not some f'ckin' half-arse goose chase like this.'

'Yeah, but...'

Pye stepped towards, Kav, 'An' 'e might start thinking why yis was so keen to waste time, eh? Draggin' me down here when I coulda been kickin' down f'ckin' doors in Bootle. He might think yis doin' it for a reason -- Like you mighta been talking too f'ckin' much, eh?'

Kav looked rattled, 'You've got it all wrong.'

'I put the word in with Sooty for yous. All of a sudden, things are goin' sqew-whiff. I don't f'ckin' like that.'

'I'm telling yer.' Kav said. He hooked his thumb at Blum, 'I've seen this feller in action an'...'

Pye poked his fingers in Kav's chest, made him step back, 'You don't tell me nothing, Kavanagh. Right? Gerrin that car. You can tell Sooty why you've wasted my f'ckin' time. See worr he thinks, eh?'

Pye got into the Corsair's passenger seat. He regarded us with what looked like contempt. Or it could've been pity. Kav moved round to the driver's side, glared at us over the car's roof, got in.

Blum and I did our best to look like woolly-back knobheads until the car went out of sight. We looked at each other, started to laugh.

*

The phone was ringing in the kiosk when Blum pulled up near the Weld Blundell pub. I pushed inside behind him, Blum picked up the receiver. I leaned in to listen.

Blum didn't speak, let Delly go first.

'Blum? Is that you?'

Blum said nothing.

Delly sounded anxious, 'Blum? Are you there?'

'What have you got for me?'

'What went wrong? You didn't do the job.'

'Nowt went wrong. I had summat to sort out in Ormskirk, so I needed my lads for that. I had to let the Sutton job go, but I'll have him another time.'

'You're not going to like this, but some scousers with guns did Sooty, got everything...'

Blum grinned at me and winked.

'Scousers?'

'Got the fags and booze money and a load more that come from some warehouse job he set up in Bootle...'

Blum and I looked at each other. Pye's comments now made sense.

'Sutton got battered and tied up in his own house. I was there when Pye and Kav found him. I didn't get it all 'cause there was a load of whispering with Sooty and Pye, but these scousers, I think they were threatening to do his daughter and her kid in, or something, if he didn't give 'em the cash.'

Blum cut in, 'Are you sure they were scousers?'

'Sooty said so. He was on and on about it. Fuckin' scousers this, fuckin' scouse bastards that. I just wanted to warn you. Pye and Kav are looking for you.'

'I know. I've just had blummin talk to 'em.'

Delly was straight in, 'I didn't snitch, Blum, honest. I saw you near Sooty's when we were on our way there, but I didn't say nothing. But when we found Sooty was robbed, Kav said he'd seen you. That's why he got Pye to come after you.'

Blum laughed, 'I blummin' saw you and all. Do you know why I was there?'

'I wondered about that.'

Blum winked at me, 'Helping one of my lads pick-up a washing machine for his nan. Had no idea we'd be anywhere near Sooty's place. Didn't even know where he blummin' lives. That Pye, I think it was him, curly hair, ugly mug, dead scouse...

'That's him, yeah.'

'...He turned on Kav when he found out about the washing machine. Treated him like a kid. Not surprised, mind. Sutton gets robbed by blummin' scousers and that pillock Kav thinks it's me.'

There was a sycophantic laugh at Delly's end of the line. Then, 'The thing is, I'm not gettin' paid and...

Blum butted in, 'I'll be paying you extra.'

There was a pause.

'But...I've not done nothing, like. You didn't do the job.'

'It's future jobs I'm interested in. You'll get even more next time if it's a big 'un.'

'Oh...Oh, right. Ta, Blum.'

'You'll have money in the post Saturday. With a bit of a bonus an' all, four hundred quid.'

'Four? Wow. Ta, Blum.'

I could almost feel Delly's excitement down the line.

'I want you to ring me tomorrow. Same number, same time...'

Delly was eager, 'Yeah, yeah. I will...'

'This is between me and you. I want to know what's said between Kav and that Pye. Even that Sutton feller, if he's around. I don't think Pye would do the dirty on Sutton, but I'm not sure about Kav. I've got a feeling he might've fixed up these scouse fellers to do Sutton. What do you reckon?'

A slight pause, then, 'Er...Yeah. Could've done.'

'Funny he was so keen to come looking for me when Sutton said right from the start it was scousers blummin' done it. Trying to put the blame on me, maybe. I reckon Pye might be thinking the same.'

'Yeah, you might have something there, Blum.'

'Say a word about this and you know what'll happen. Phone me tomorrow at six o'clock.'

Blum hung up. We left the phone box, got in the van.

I laughed. 'That muddies the water a bit.'

'Blummin' hope so.'

'Are you going to pay him?'

'Without him we wouldn't have that dosh. I need him to keep tabs on Kav as well, just to be on the safe side.' He added, 'I might be a robber, but I'm not a blummin' cheat.'

He put the van in gear, reprised the scouse accent, 'Come 'ead, lar. I'll run yis over to woolly-back land.'

I laughed, 'God, no more! Not tonight.'

He grinned, 'Scousers, eh? You can blame 'em for blummin' owt. And some folk'll believe owt.'

Not everyone, though, as we'd soon find out.

Chapter 36
Getting Serious, Like?

IT WAS DARK when Blum pulled up outside *The Sentinel* building, where I'd asked him to drop me. If Sandra wasn't working late, she may have left a note. The lights were on inside, as the presses geared up to print our Friday edition. I'd drunk the rest of the whisky on the drive back. All I wanted was to relax with Sandra, but I asked Blum if he fancied a pint.

'Nah, I'll get back, thanks. I'm going to kip at the farm tonight.'

I was surprised, 'What for?'

'If they come back, I don't want anyone following me to Viv's, or seeing the van at May Bank.'

By now, I'd put Sutton, Pye and Kav to the back of my mind. That meeting outside the Soldier persuaded me we weren't serious suspects in Pye's, thus Sutton's eyes. Though Blum'd cancelled my promise, I'd more than honoured my commitment to help. Now, my thoughts were set on time away with Sandra and no work, or SACOAM, to distract us. I was surprised Blum was taking this precaution.

'Whatever Sutton and Pye might think Kav's still suspicious about us. It wouldn't do him any harm to keep an eye on me. If he could get the cash back for Sutton, he'd be teacher's pet again, like.'

'Just watch yourself then.'

He laughed, 'Perhaps I should go to Scouserland instead, book in at the Adelphi Hotel.'

'Don't spend it all on caviar and champagne, eh?'

'It seems mad -- all that blummin' money. I can't stop thinking what the farm house'll be like when I get it done up for mam.' He tapped my arm with his fist. 'Thanks for today. Couldn't have done it without you.'

I watched him drive off, went round to the back door, upstairs to the news room. I passed advertising, but their office was in darkness. I looked under my typewriter for a note from Sandra. Perhaps she'd call in at The Packet later. Or ring me at the flat. By now, I could feel the whisky's effects. Tiredness didn't help.

I was on my way out when Geoff Sillitoe pushed through the swing door between the compositor's room and the wide sub-editors' table, 'Yer too late, cocker, all put to beddy byes.'

'Oh, right.' I enjoyed pitching in to finalise the paper for the printers, but tonight I'd had no plan to get involved, but didn't miss the chance to appear keen, 'Just came on the off-chance, you know.'

'Many thanks, much appreciated.' He clapped me on the shoulder, 'Fancy a flyer at The Boot?'

I was in no mood for talk of angling matches, 'Already overdone it a bit on whisky, thanks.'

He laughed, 'Aye, it smells like it.'

He led the way out, down the stairs.

He lit up, 'How did it go today?'

'Sorry?' For an instant I thought he meant robbing Sutton. I'd almost forgotten my fib to wangle a day off.

'Not supped that much yer've forgotten your granny's funeral, have yer? How did it go?'

'It was all right, thanks,' I added the old commendation, 'Good turn out.'

'Glad to hear it.'

Out in the yard, he turned to me.

'We've got the cream of northern match angling arriving in town tonight, some of 'em proper professionals. Claremont Hotel's booked solid, so I thought yours truly'd put meself about a bit, late session with some proper maggot maestros.'

'Good idea.'

'Rita's at her sister's in Waterfoot, so it might be a late do for me. No harm in butterin' up some new contacts, eh?'

'Yeah, why not?'

'Yer don't mind looking after the desk in the mornin', do yer?'

I was demob happy, focused on holidays, not work, but, 'Fine, yeah. What time will you be in?'

'Let's say I'll be incommunicado for the duration.' He clapped me on the shoulder again, 'I know yer on hols from tomorrow, just leave us a what's what list for Monday.'

'Right. Fine.'

We said our goodbyes, I turned to walk home. He called, 'One thing, cocker.'

I looked back.

'Don't know the local customs in that place yer from, but here we wear a collar and tie for funerals,' He chuckled, walked away. Either he'd heard the gran's funeral excuse before, or, he'd spotted the opportunity to skive-off to booze and hobnob with 'the cream of northern match-angling.' My bet was both.

In town, the air was close. I was hungry. With the unique luxury of forty quid in my pocket I could eat at the Blue Dragon, but it wouldn't be the same without Sandra. I went into a pub I'd never visited called The Chapmen's Arms, had two meat pies and a glass of bitter. I felt better after the pies, washed them down with a pint and a double whisky. I read the *Daily Express* and its account of thieves tunnelling into a London bank to steal half-a-million pounds. Huge as it was to Blum and me, how small our day's profit seemed in comparison.

A marquee on the old barge quay caught my eye as I walked down the ramp to The Packet, checked for Sandra's Mini. It wasn't there, but her efforts had at least solved the marquee crisis. I wandered over. It was fastened up, nobody around. A big, square carpet of fake grass covered the stone setts in front of the marquee. Troughs that looked like they expected potted plants for Councillor Fairbrass's big day edged the fake lawn. Henty and *The Sentinel* board had chipped-in, but how much were the ratepayers forking out for Fairbrass to host a free buffet and booze-up for councillors and cronies; bloody free-loaders, all of them? I felt the matchbox in my pocket. If it weren't for Sandra's hard work and involvement I might've given in to my unexpected impulse to strike a match, send the SACOAM marquee up in flames.

I moved away, went behind The Packet. If Sandra was there, she'd be in the back room. I stepped up on an old horse-trough, peered through the window. In our usual place, an older couple, not speaking, sat and stared at their drinks. Through the opening to the back room I saw Kitty on a bar stool, glass in one hand, fag in the other, holding court. If I went in she'd make me feel obliged to fill her glass.

A deep voice said, 'Aye, aye, what's going on here?'

I jumped, startled, almost fell off the trough, 'Jesus!'

Neil Posset, in police uniform, stood grinning, fag in hand.

'Christ, you could've given me a heart attack.'

He laughed, 'You must be friggin' desperate for a scoop, peeping through windows.'

I laughed, 'Looking for someone, trying to avoid another.'

'Bit of a mix-up with the ladies, then?'

'Trying to avoid my landlady.'

'Oh, aye, doing the landlady now? Need to check, but I reckon I could book you for that.'

I laughed, 'She's seventy-odd and lives on whisky and fags!'

'Just your type, then? Who's the other one? That boss's daughter, is it? The blondie with the legs -- the one on the sly you won't cough to?'

'Sandra, yeah.'

'Eh, is that a guilty plea? At last?' He patted the pen and book in his tunic pocket, 'Ready to make a full statement?'

I laughed, 'Yep, still seeing her.'

'Going all right?'

'Yeah. I've got two weeks off from tomorrow. I'm going to ask her to come away for a few days.'

He trod on his fag end.

'Very nice. Getting serious, like?'

'Think it might be, yeah.'

'You jammy get. I'm still struggling in this dump. It's no better on the Panda cars. Do their dads lock 'em up when it goes dark? Seems like it to me.'

He declined a fresh cigarette, grinned, 'I'm on duty, mate. So...where is she, then, this bird of yours?'

'Bogged down with work on this bloody fishing match, by the look of it. You must've heard all the fuss?'

'That's why I'm here,' He nodded towards the canal, 'Someone at the town hall bent the Super's ear about that tent. I've got to keep an eye on it, stop the natives cutting it up for blankets, or making war canoes.'

I laughed. It came to mind Neil might've nabbed an arsonist minutes ago had I acted on my drunken impulse.

'What goes on in this place, mate, you wouldn't believe half of it.'

He walked with me up the ramp to Kitty's. Neil drew our conversation back to the lack of female company in the town.

'Maybe we should have a bit of a pub crawl, or something, one night -- see if you can give me any tips for tappin'-off with a local bird. How to find one'd help...'

I liked Neil, knew living away from home, working unsocial hours with only colleagues to talk to, could be dull. I agreed.

'Then I could do you a favour, sign you in at the police club. The boss of county CID's in there a lot 'cause he lives this way. You'd make some shit-hot contacts, guaranteed. Blokes who were on the Moors Murders, jobs like that -- proper coppers.'

It seemed an attractive idea, so I agreed. Neil said goodnight, grinned, 'I'd get my head down if I were you, mate. Sleep it off.'

I watched him turn the corner into Quinn Street, then turned and went in at Kitty's back door. I'd been on the go for seventeen hours.

I swayed my way upstairs. What would Neil and those 'proper coppers' think if they knew I'd clubbed unconscious a hard-knock criminal in his own home, robbed him of £16,000? I put *Lay, Lady, Lay* on the Dansette, flopped on my bed. I tried to relive the day's events; the apprehension, the shaking fear, the excitement, then the strange serenity of action, but all I could think of was Sandra. What I wanted, above all else, was to lie here, together, fall asleep. I stared at the light bulb above me, wished she were here, my arm around her, content. No other girl had ever provoked such feelings. But was what I felt real? I pictured her smiling to herself that time, saying 'Lovejob... lovejob, lovejob.' Were we a lovejob?

Chapter 37

Happy Holidays

FACE SHEENED IN sweat, I was half-an-hour late next morning when I sat down in the news editor's chair. Twenty minutes earlier I'd woken up, still dressed, the light bulb burning, the stylus of the record player bumping at the centre of the Dylan record. I gauged my hangover at low to moderate, remembered today I was Geoff's understudy.

I changed my shirt, brushed my teeth, swilled mouthwash in record time. I had to take my jacket off on the run to work, or I'd've sweated gallons in the muggy air that enveloped the town beneath hazy sun.

Now, with a mug of canteen coffee in hand, fag in the other, I reached for the pile of daily newspapers, topped with a fresh copy of *The Sentinel*. Our front page lead story was another chapter about 'The Pong,' as our sub-editors had christened the stench from the sewage works that plagued one side of the town. Fresh complaints from half a dozen residents seemed the only reason for the umpteenth re-incarnation on the front page of a saga that began a decade before I set foot here. I suspected a last-minute paste-and-scissors job by Geoff as, minus any actual news, he hankered to be away from work, to hobnob with the 'cream of northern match angling.'

The 'cream' invasion was the next biggest, predictable item on the front page. In another re-hash of quotes from Councillor Fairbrass, fabricated from his inarticulate meanderings, the piece attempted to drum-up civic pride among our readers for tomorrow's angling competition and its intangible benefits for local folk, the vast majority of whom would go to the grave without picking up a fishing rod.

Less predictable was a memo to all staff from old man Henty, which, with other clichés, urged us to 'fly *The*

Sentinel flag' and do our best to 'show our faces' at the fishing match. While I doled out the diary jobs, tips to be checked and published items that needed to be followed- up, it seemed most of the news room saw the memo as a royal command for which non-attendance would result in fatal career damage. I was snappy with the whiners. I wanted them out of the newsroom so I could ring Sandra on the internal phone.

There was no note and when the office was quiet I dialled Sandra's extension. With our work on SACOAM, I felt no need to hang up if someone else answered her phone. When they did I was told she'd gone out to collect something for the Mayor. I asked if Sandra could phone me back, 'It's SACOAM business.'

The morning dragged, I sat and smoked, imagined what Blum was doing. I shivered at the thought Pye and Kav might have returned to Lydiate to look for Blum and me, but I was almost sure Sutton's search for 'scousers' would focus on Bootle and that other job; on someone who'd betrayed him, someone more likely than two 'woolly-back knobheads' to dare rob him with violence.

When the wage packets turned up, my thoughts returned to Sandra. With three weeks holiday pay and most of that forty quid, I was able to afford a few days away. I recalled a glossy publicity brochure on guest houses in the Yorkshire Dales, launched a search of the news desk drawers and filing cabinets. I could plan an itinerary for next week. But it'd been dumped, or lost forever in Geoff's chaotic filing system. I was irritated, the stuffiness prompted me to find fresh air. Most times I took care of the desk, I'd have a pie or sandwich while I worked. But by quarter-past-twelve I needed light hangover medicine.

On the High Street, air still, sky overcast, the atmosphere was as oppressive as inside. The first person I saw across The Boot's lounge was Geoff Sillitoe. He'd just detached himself from a group of middle-aged men. With them, glass in hand, was Councillor Harold Fairbrass. Geoff spotted me as he moved to the bar.

'Hair of the dog, eh, cocker?'

'Just nipped out for a swift one.'

He laughed, 'If it's medicinal I'll stick it on my round,' He flung out his arm to indicate his company, 'Go over and introduce yerself.'

His expansive gesture and slight slur suggested he'd topped up last night's intake.

'I'm all right, thanks, Geoff. I'll get my own, get back to the desk.'

He leaned in, jerked his head towards the company. 'I know yer don't fish often, but these lads'll open yer eyes when it comes to technique. Come on, you've got time for a natter.' His voice was reverent, as if royalty were present, 'Maurice Crowcroft from Doncaster's here.'

I lied, 'Thanks, but I'm waiting on a couple of calls.'

He put a hand on my shoulder, 'That's one thing I like about yer, me old cock, always conscientious. Makes a world o' difference, I'm telling yer. I'll get yer that pint, whether yer like it, or not.'

'Thanks Geoff.'

'Yer welcome, cocker.' He signalled to Phyllis at the other end of the bar, 'Ready when you are, love.'

Inside a couple of minutes I finished my pint, took a pie back to the office. I waved across to my boss as I left, but he was too intent on his exalted company to notice. There was still no word from Sandra, so I nipped down to advertising. The only person there was an older woman I didn't recognise taking flack over the phone for a cocked-up display ad in that day's paper.

Her conversation seemed endless. I lit a fag. It was daft, but I seemed so focused on Sandra I felt I couldn't settle until I saw her, spoke to her. Waiting on this woman's phone call fuelled my impatience. The second she put the phone down, I said, 'I need to speak to Sandra Heaton. When will she be back?'

'And you are?'

I almost snarled, 'The acting news editor.'

'She's off this afternoon.'

I was startled. She was buried in extra work when we were last together. I had a horrible thought that all that, the pressure, had made her ill. 'Where's she gone?'

She was prim, 'Sorry, Miss Heaton doesn't tell me what she does in her own time.'

It was ill-mannered, but I turned away, left. I glimpsed her through the glass as I closed the door, saw her grimace, fan away my smoke.

All I wanted was a quick call from her. I could have phoned her at her parents' home, but I'd never done that. It was always a note, the internal office phone, or she would call the pay phone on the half-landing at Quinn Street. I'd have to be patient.

I did a ring round to find out what to expect from our amateur sports reporters from the weekend, then typed up Geoff's requested list for Monday. Every time one of the news desk phones rang, I snatched up the receiver expecting Sandra. I thought Blum might have phoned too. I imagined him wandering around Pygon's Farm making his plans. I reminded myself to talk to him about opening a bank account. I knew he didn't have even a post office savings account. He'd need to deposit money gradually to avoid awkward questions, or suspicion. First of all, he'd need a solicitor to buy the farm. I remembered I'd told Blum I'd check up on how to trace the owners of abandoned property. I flicked through my contacts book. When Blum phoned it would be good to give him some info.

I dialled the number of Edward Barwise and Son, a local estate agent's office that handled sales and rentals throughout the area. The man I wanted to speak to was Barwise senior's son, Denny. Months ago I interviewed him for a feature that marked the 35th anniversary of the estate agency. He'd told me to call him if ever I needed information about the property business. I hoped he'd remember his offer.

'Mr Denny's out on a valuation,' the lady who answered said, 'He'll be back any minute. Can I take your number?'

I needed a favour, didn't want him to have to chase me, 'No, no, it's alright. I'll try later.'

I put the phone down, swore. My inability to get instant information for Blum added to my frustration with the day, the increasing mugginess didn't help. While the reporting staff drifted back in to write-up copy for me to read, I was tetchy and critical. I had to apologise twice, blamed the heat. The subs had started to drift off home and, out of guilt at my mood, I gave those who'd written-up their stuff the nod to knock-off. Some of them would soon be tapping on the back door of The Boot where I'd bet Geoff had persuaded Phyllis his VIP drinking companions merited an afternoon lock-in. I made a few alterations to Geoff's list on the strength of what had come in from the reporters. At ten to five, satisfied everything was in order, I picked up my jacket, dragged off my tie, started two weeks' holiday.

On the street, the air was no fresher. I was tempted to a pint at The Boot, but if Sandra had the afternoon off I doubted she'd go there. If I looked in Geoff was sure to drag me into his company and I didn't want the first evening of my hols wasted on the tales of competitive fishermen. I opted again for the Chapmen's Arms, sipped a pint, scanned the *Evening Telegraph*. It was no surprise our competitor's weekend angling feature failed even to mention tomorrow's SACOAM.

I didn't linger, walked back to Quinn Street, thinking of Blum. Damn! I hadn't called back the estate agent's. I supposed Blum wouldn't mind if I called them on Monday. My plan was a bath and shave, the chip shop, perhaps a call from Sandra, or Blum. I'd stay in to listen for the phone, have a pint or two at The Packet later. And I needed to clean up the flat a bit in case Viv and Fozzy called in next day. I let myself in at the front door, thought about the odds of first-time fisherman Fozzy beating Geoff's cream of northern match angling.

I stepped on to the lower stairs when Kitty called, *'Bachgen!'*

She came out from her part of the house, steadying her progress with a hand on the wall.

'I've had enough, these girls ringing up.'

'What girls?'

'Just downstairs and she rings again. Then says she didn't ring me up first. I can't bloody be up and down with my legs.'

'Who rang?'

She frowned, 'Susannah, isn't it?'

'You mean Sandra?'

'Tell her not to be ringing up. Not when you're not there, will you!'

'Did she leave a message?

Kitty looked blank, struggled to recall. I smelt the booze on her.

'She's coming...' She hesitated. 'No, not that, no.'

Then it came out in a rush. 'She'll wait for you at The Packet, till half-five, in her car.'

I looked at my watch, 5.35, moved for the front door.

Her voice was unctuous, 'You and Susannah, staying all night, is it?'

I slammed the door, ran out to meet her. Forty-eight hours without Sandra and I was desperate not to miss her.

Chapter 38
Sandra at Snapeback Fell

DUST CLOUDED AS Sandra braked the Mini on the clinker ramp up from The Packet. She smiled, gestured for me to get in.

I managed to jump in, shut the door, before she accelerated into Quinn Street.

'Did Kitty give you a bollocking? She went mad at me. Told me to stop pestering her,' she said, 'I only rang the bloody once!'

'She's drunk already.'

She braked at the top of the street, turned left. 'Eleanor in front office said you'd gone, likely be in The Boot. I phoned from there.'

'Advertising said you'd got the afternoon off. Thought you were mad busy?'

She accelerated, swore at a bread van slowing to turn left ahead of us, swerved round it. 'Slow arse!'

She overtook another car.

'I was worried, all this work...I thought you were ill.'

She glanced at me, shook her head, increased speed, heading eastwards, upwards, out of town.

'By last night I'd had a belly full of it. Then this morning I had to wait ages at the place in Blackburn while they finished the bloody trophy and the Mayor's cow of a secretary kept phoning Hentypops, mithering over it. Mum wanted me to run her into Preston, so I thought bugger it...Shit, it's hot.'

I rolled down my window, shouted over the rush of air, 'Let's go for a drink. The Acregate isn't far.'

'Too stuffy.'

'Where then?'

She glanced at me, drove even faster. She swung right into a lane that rose steeply between dry stone walls, powering uphill. I laughed, delighted.

'Are we going where I think we are?'

She nodded quickly several times and followed the lane left where the climb became flatter. Below, the town crouched in its hollow at the foot of the Pennines. Further west it was too hazy to make out the Irish Sea. No prospect of a ten-out-of-ten sunset tonight, not like the first time we drove up Snapeback Fell.

Staff from all departments drank at The Boot on Friday nights. For weeks after Sandra started, I found myself willing her to turn up, but it didn't happen. Then one night she appeared. For weeks I spoke to her little, then it was always in company. I drank more than usual, watched her at a distance. Now and then, I was treated to a smile. Other times she left early, often to give one of the girls from advertising a lift. Sometimes I sensed her eyes on me. Once she smiled and I was aware of Bob Dylan's *Lay, Lady, Lay* on the jukebox. God knows how many times I dropped a coin in the jukey to play the same song in hope of a similar smile, up to three times in a night. I lived for the end-of-week booze-up. When I was due to see Elaine, I phoned and lied to her, saying I was busy, I'd be home on Saturday. When I was with Elaine, I couldn't get Sandra out of my head. A sort of paralysis made me unable to pull Sandra away from the pub company, to have her to myself.

She made the first move.

Geoff Sillitoe asked me to cover a meeting called to protest a planned new road. I wanted to be in the pub for the Friday session, to see Sandra, not sent to a village hall to interview leaders of an action committee. I wrapped up the job as fast as I could and the photographer dropped me at The Boot. Inside, I couldn't see her. Had she given it a miss? Had she gone already?

She was paying Phyllis for a drink. I moved to the bar.

She perched herself on a stool, grinned at me, 'Bit late for you, isn't it?'

I told her about the road protest meeting. Talking to her was easy. All the usual things -- where we lived, came from, our families and colleagues. Half-an-hour passed, I couldn't believe my first pint had lasted so long.

'Fancy another?'

She shook her head.

It flattened me.

'Are you sure?'

She looked at me, held my gaze, 'I'd sooner have a drive. It'd be better if you were with me.'

I didn't know what to say.

She smiled, touched my hand, 'I won't tell Elaine if you don't.'

I was startled. I might've mentioned Elaine in the pub, but I had no idea when, what, Sandra had overheard.

She laughed, 'Think of the money you'll save, as well -- Bob Dylan at a tanner a time.'

She slipped off the stool, moved to the door out the pub's car park. I was immobile. She paused, looked back, smiled. I turned to our *Sentinel* colleagues. Nobody was watching us; all busy laughing, getting pissed. I followed, joined her in the Mini.

Not a word was said as she accelerated out of the pub yard, touched fifty-miles-an- hour down the high street. Out of town her speed increased. She braked, turned right up a steep lane between dry stone walls. She drove with concentration, but, now and then, glanced, smiled, at me. Below us I could see the paint factory and the town hall clock tower. Beyond them, the flatter land of mid-Lancashire and, north-west, the Fylde. Further still, the glint of the Irish Sea as the red ball of sun slid lower.

Near the top of Snapeback Fell, she swerved off the road on to a bare patch of stone and gravel by one of the small reservoirs that dotted the West Pennines. The Mini skidded to a halt, near a Victorian stone pump house at the water's edge.

A long, calibrated rule to measure the reservoir's depth ran down the stonework into dark water. Sandra threw open the door, got out.

She slammed the door, 'Come on!'

I got out, closed the door. She moved to higher ground. She looked out towards the sea and its backdrop of flaming colour. Her white, patterned mini dress was suffused with sunset colour, blonde, bobbed hair tinged rosy-gold.

'Just look at that sky.'

I reached her, she grabbed my hand. 'Let's go higher.'

She tugged my arm and we high-stepped over thick purple-flowered heather. With the summit yards off she stopped, turned towards me, took my other hand. She let herself fall backwards, pulling me down with her. I could smell the shampoo scent of her hair and the dusty heather. I kissed her, but she took the lead. It was urgent, quick, and her passion was unlike anything I'd ever experienced.

'Christ,' her voice was low as we held each other, 'Christ, Christ, Christ...'

She kissed my neck, eyes, mouth, 'Why did you wait so bloody long...?'

'Must've been mad.'

She giggled and we lay, no words, until the sun had gone, a breeze blew chilly.

I kissed her again and I couldn't believe what had happened inside an hour, it was like a complete change to my existence.

She took my hand, 'Shall we have that drink, now?'

Hand in hand, we ran down from the top of Snapeback to the car, laughed in delight at our discovery of each other. In town I bought a half-bottle of brandy and six bottles of Babycham. We laughed more, talked of how we'd fancied each other for ages. How slow I was. How she'd waited for a chance to find me sober -- how I drank in the hope I'd find the nerve to approach a boss's daughter. Showing her into my grotty flat, I was embarrassed, but she was at home in moments, relaxed, warming and lighting it with laughter, her presence. She braved my dingy bathtub and I joined her to drink that heady mixture she said was her favourite. Our agreement to keep our union a secret was forged over brandy and Babycham in beer glasses. She stayed the night and our passion was no less intense at a slower pace.

We visited Snapeback three times afterwards, twice in moorland drizzle. In mid-winter, we left the Mini a mile downhill to climb in crispy snow, joked about a repeat of our first visit. But, shivering in clear, frosty air, our breath small clouds, we laughed, agreed it wouldn't happen again unless weather and sunset matched the perfection of that first night.

Now, that sentiment was with me as Sandra came to a stop by the reservoir pump house. Yet she'd said nothing the past mile or so. Had she planned an encore, I knew she'd have been unable to suppress the words to heighten our anticipation. Anyway, the muggy air persisted up here. And as we left the car I sensed in her a weariness, a strain. She looked out at the invisible sea. I put my hand on her shoulder.

'Sure you're all right, not ill?'

She shook her head. Rested her hand over mine, gazed to the west.

'I wouldn't be surprised,' I said, 'All this pissing around for Fairbrass and the rest of them, lumbering everyone with their stupid ideas.'

'I'm... tired, that's all.'

She took my hand, led the way upward. We didn't go far beyond the pump house. She settled on a patch of turf, arms around her knees. I dropped beside her, lay down, propped with my elbow. I lit up, 'This time tomorrow it'll all be over.'

She didn't look at me, nodded her head, took my cigarette, drew on it.

She exhaled smoke, glanced at me.

'Did you think about that first time? Just now, coming up here?'

I laughed, 'What do you think?'

Her hand reached out, again took mine.

'How about you?

She stared straight ahead, nodded.

I tried to lighten the mood, 'It's the thought that counts.' Added, 'Anyway, I haven't, you know...haven't got anything with me.'

She looked at me, smiled, turned away.

Sandra wasn't a smoker. Only ever took a rare, single puff of my cigarette. This time, though, there was a second, deeper drag, before slowly she let out the smoke.

She continued to stare ahead. I eyed the trace of blue veins in her wrists, the blonde fuzz on her forearm, the curve of her hair under her jawbone; regarded the shape of her nose, her eyebrows, her lips; a neat fingernail when she pushed back her hair with a single finger.

She spoke slower than usual, 'It was so perfect for me that time, so ...lovely. It never meant anything, not to me, not 'til then, that first time with you, up here.'

She looked at me, smiled, passed back the cigarette.

I was surprised. 'You've never told me that before.'

She turned away. I waited.

'I should've done.'

A few moments passed, 'You've always been so kind to me.'

I didn't recall a single action of mine she might consider notably kind, waited for example, explanation.

She withdrew her hand from mine and wrapped her arms around her knees, closed her eyes. A rush of anger flashed through me, almost a hatred, against those behind that bloody fishing match, the strain they'd caused her. It was short-lived, replaced by an odd, unexpected sensation: That, as I watched her, Sandra, this ancient fell, all land in sight, the hazy sky, and me, were, at this moment, a single entity. It was intense, fleeting, replaced inside me, by a wave of powerful, hot, affection; an urgent concern, for her.

'You need to get home. You need to rest.'

I took her hand and we walked down to the Mini.

She put her arms around me. She leaned her forehead against my shoulder. Her fingers pressed my back. She didn't move, didn't speak, for what seemed a minute, more.

Without looking up, she said, 'Always so kind.'

She let go, got in the car, and I wasn't sure if I saw her wipe away a tear. On the way back, I asked her about us having a few days in the Yorkshire Dales -- anywhere she fancied we might go -- the choice was hers. She heard me out.

'I'm too tired to think,' she said, 'Can we talk about it tomorrow? When it's all over?'

Instead of dropping me at Quinn Street, I said I'd walk the last half-mile. When she pulled over, I told her, 'Make sure you get a proper kip, eh?' She nodded, reached out to take my hand. She squeezed it, smiled.

'Promise?' I said.

She nodded, let go.

'See you tomorrow.' She pulled out and drove off towards her family's home near Bolton.

I smelt food from a chip shop I knew was in the next side street. I bought steak pudding and peas, ate leaning on the chip shop wall, spotted a pub called The Spinning Jenny down the street. Next to it was the canal.

I escaped the airless taproom, took my pint to a low wall next to the cut. Tomorrow a maggot maestro might occupy this space. Fozzy might even draw this peg. I was on holiday and I might 'show my face' for old man Henty, but I'd had enough of it all. Tomorrow was for Blum, Viv and Foz, and a few pints. I wanted all three to meet Sandra.

Two more pints and a whisky went down and I wished she hadn't been so tired. I needed to tell her what I felt for her; confirm my relationship with Elaine was dead, that a drift back to her would never happen. One thing bothered me, the robbery of Sutton. Yes, I'd helped Blum on behalf of his mam, but I'd done it for kicks too. I shivered at the memory, my calm deliberation, satisfaction, when I smashed the shotgun butt into Sutton's head. I was in the same position as

Blum with Viv. Yesterday was a secret to stay with Blum and me forever. Nobody else must ever know, most of all, Sandra.

Dusk came and I took my last empty glass to the taproom, used their bogs. On the walk to Quinn Street, I passed members of the angling club knocking in numbered pegs along the towpath for the fishing match. By The Packet, council workmen in a van drove away. Potted plants were now crammed into the troughs around the fake turf. No Neil Posset lurked to protect the Mayor's greenery, but Caernarvon Kitty beetled down the ramp to the pub, so I cancelled my plan for a last drink, sneaked into the side door, where take-outs were sold through a hatch, bought six bottles of pale ale.

In the darkness by Kitty's house someone hissed my name. I whipped round, startled. Blum came out of the shadows of the jungle hedge. Over his left shoulder was a leather satchel; in shadow behind him, the Chev.

'What you doing here?'

I noticed the Signalman's gun, folded under his arm.

He was agitated, 'We need to get inside.'

'What for?'

Blum put his hand behind his neck, massaged his skull. He looked anxious.

'In case Kav followed me.'

Chapter 39
A Picture Postcard

IN AN INSTANT my relaxed holiday mood was replaced with dread. I led the way through Kitty's kitchen door, questioned him as we hurried up to my flat. 'Has he followed you? Or hasn't he?'

'I drove half-way round blummin' Lancashire just in case. I don't know for sure.'

I crossed the little hallway into the living room door, switched on the light. Blum clicked it off, went to the tall windows with their floor-length, tatty curtains. He looked out for a moment, 'Just checking, like.' He dragged the curtains shut. 'You can put it on again now.'

I didn't move, 'What's going on?'

'I had to clear out with the dosh,' he patted what I recognised as his old school satchel, 'Kav turned up at the blummin' farm this morning.'

'Christ, how?'

'Not sure.'

'What did he say?'

Blum nodded at my armful of bottles. 'Got one for me?'

I headed for my grotty kitchen. Blum followed me, dumped the satchel and shotgun on my little Formica table, took one of the two chairs. I opened a bottle each.

I repeated my question, 'What did he say?'

'He didn't see me, just the van.'

'But you're here in the Chev...'

'I had to leave the van at the farm and leg it. Thing is, he might have this address.'

I felt a spasm of fear.

'How the hell did he get that?'

Blum leaned his elbows on the table and sighed.

I was anxious now, 'How, for Christ's sake?'

*

When Blum left me at *The Sentinel* he drove home, pulled up a hundred yards away from May Bank View. He looked for any unfamiliar vehicle parked nearby, but there were none. He waited a while, drove on. He crawled past his mam's house, checked there was nobody there awaiting his return.

He drove to Pygon's Farm, checking again for any follower, locked himself in the still room and made up a bed of clothing stolen from Daltry's. He had difficulty sleeping as he gauged the potential consequences of robbing Sutton. Despite Frank Pye's antipathy to Kav, his insistence Blum and I were guilty of the theft, it was still possible Pye, Kav and Sutton might think again, come looking. By the time he slept he'd decided it was urgent that he got away from Lydiate, at least for a few weeks.

He woke too late to catch Viv at her flat before she went to bed after night shift. He left Pygon's Farm, drove in a circuitous route, parked the van in the gateway of a field. He slipped through the gate, hurried along the edge of the barley stubble to the back hedge of May Bank View and pushed his way through a weak section he'd used since he was a boy. Inside the garden, he kept out of view from his mam's house, made his way to the hedge by the front gate under the Marjorie plum tree. He dropped to the ground to peer through the foot of the hedge. There was no sign of any parked vehicle, any watcher.

He went into May Bank View to have breakfast with his mam, gave her forty pounds, before telling her, that was the last of his money, he was off to work on a building site in Lancaster. He told her work had gone flat; his time would be better spent earning wages as a labourer and he'd be away for a few weeks. He packed a small suitcase and said goodbye.

He retraced his steps back to the van, drove to Fox's sub-post office near The Weld Blundell pub. There he posted four hundred pounds to Delly in Burscough. He bought a bottle of lemonade, biscuits, chocolate, a biro and a picture postcard of the Scottish Soldier, returned to Pygon's Farm.

In the still room he took the picture postcard and addressed it to me. He was half way through writing that the Lancaster job would be a fib to his mam and Viv. In reality, he would be lying low in the Lake District, trying to spend the minimum, and would look for a casual job there, that he'd be in touch in a week or so. It was then he realised. In all the recent planning and action he'd forgotten the fishing match; that he and Viv would be taking Fozzy, we'd see each other before he left.

With hours to go before he could talk to Viv, to announce he was going to Lancaster, he decided on a survey of the farm house. He climbed in through the window he'd forced weeks earlier at the other side, hidden from the lane by the overgrown hedge. He took the pen and a piece of cardboard and moved through the house, noting the work required to put the place in order after the neglect of nearly a decade. He was anxious about the roof, worried it might've let rain in. He left footprints in the dry dust of the attic as he looked up at the undersides of the slates. He was satisfied there were no leaks. Then came the sound of a car approaching at low speed.

It seemed to come from the cart track leading to the rear of the farm. He moved to the slanting attic skylight, ducked down to peer through the grimy glass. He could see down across the roof slates to his van parked next to the old pig sties, long ago converted to a tractor shed. He strained to see more through the dirty window pane. Could it be the farmer, Cyril Clegg, who rented the fields? A moment later, he was shocked as a green Corsair came from the cover of the goat willows behind the cart shed and halted. Christ!

He couldn't see the number plate, but he knew nobody else with a car like that. Blum tensed. The driver's door opened. Kav stepped out. He left the door open, moved away from his car. Blum watched, anxiety mounting. Kav's hand went to the inside pocket of his windcheater jacket and pulled out a small, flat-sided automatic pistol. Kav pulled back the slide to cock it, walked towards the yard, the pistol moving from side to side. He approached Blum's van, peered inside, then moved into the yard, the pistol still pointing, ready. Blum threw aside the cardboard and pen. Kav was armed, he wasn't. And he feared Kav was reckless enough to use that gun, more so with £16,000 at stake. He had to get away.

He hurried to the attic door, went down the stairs as quickly and quietly as he could. He hurried to the forced window in the downstairs room, opened it, paused to listen. Nothing. He climbed over the window sill, dropped into nettles. He pushed the window closed and moved towards the end of the farm house nearest to the cart shed and his van, through the overgrown farm garden. He stopped at the back corner of the house, crouched under a lilac bush, watched, as across the cobbled yard, Kav came out through the rotting high doors of the barn. Blum froze. Kav scanned the yard. Then he moved towards the adjacent cow shed. Pointing his pistol, he entered. Fifteen feet to Blum's left were the two elder trees which covered each end of the sheets of corrugated iron that hid the still room door. Blum took a chance and, stooping, hurried to the first elder tree, pushing through it to squeeze between the corrugated iron and the farm house wall.

With the sickly smell of elder in his nostrils, he crouched, listened, pulled his keys from his jeans pocket. He slid a key into the still room lock, opened the door. Then he moved to the second elder bush. He waited and seconds later, through the foliage, saw Kav come out of the cow shed. With a glance towards the lane, Kav walked across the yard to the porch and back door. Kav was now out of sight. Blum knew the back door was locked, the door swollen, lock corroded. If Kav wanted to get inside the house, he would have to try elsewhere. Seconds later, he heard the sound of breaking glass. Kav must have smashed the kitchen window next to the back door.

Blum shuffled back, went into the still room, shut the door behind him. He loaded the folded Signalman's gun with two cartridges. Then he took his old school satchel from a hook on the wall. He opened it, tipped out an assortment of pike traces, bung floats and plug baits. He opened the safe, transferred all the cash to his satchel. With the money already raised, plus that from Sutton's, it amounted to more than £18,000. He slung the satchel over his shoulder and found a hessian spud sack. He put the gun inside it and rolled it up. For a moment, he forced himself to pause, to think. If it came to confrontation with an armed Kav, was he prepared to shoot Kav to save his mam's future? The police knew nothing of this robbery, but if he shot Kav dead he would be a fugitive in a murder hunt. And if he wounded Kav and it was clear he was responsible for stealing the hi-jack dosh, Sutton and Pye would be after his blood. If Kav confronted him now, the only safe course was to hand over the money. It would mean no home for his mam; that all he had gone through was for nowt. It was unthinkable. No, he had to outwit Kav, here, now, get himself and the cash away. To leave May Bank View and Lydiate, to lie low, was now even more urgent.

Blum opened the door of the still room, locked it behind him. He paused, listened. With sweat running beneath his shirt, he noticed the new green stems of elder, broken and bruised by our recent comings and goings. To Blum they were obvious. Was Kav observant enough to spot them, wonder why, discover the still room? But there was nothing he could do. It was time to leave. He strained to hear any noise outside, pushed out past the elder bush. He went between the garden hedge and the tractor shed, through nettles, stepped on forgotten, sandstone pig slabs and round the back under the goat willows until he reached his van. He stooped and crept to the driver's door, carefully opened it. He peered through the windscreen towards the back door of the farm house. No sign of Kav. He reached over the seats to retrieve his suit case. He gently pushed shut the driver's door closed, wincing at the clunk, checked again for Kav. Loaded down, he moved quickly around the back of the Corsair. For a moment, he thought of letting down one of its tyres, but decided not to waste even seconds.

With a last look up the cobbled yard, he scurried, stooping low, for the cover of the hedge that ran from the barn out into the fields. Blum reached the end of the first field, crossed a brook, followed another hedgeline, passing rows of Cyril Clegg's swede crop. At the end of the second field, he smoked a cigarette at the top of the embankment that carried the canal. From there he could see the far end of the back track to Pygon's Farm. He stayed for a few minutes, but Kav's Corsair didn't leave the farm. Blum pushed through long grass to the canal towpath, set off for Viv's place.

He went down the side of Viv's ground-floor flat. The bedroom curtains were closed. He peered through the kitchen window. Certain she was asleep, he put his suitcase in the boot of the Chev with the four-ten gun. He pondered hiding the satchel of cash in the car, but took it with him. He walked to the main road and caught a bus to the Albany cinema. With the satchel on his knee, its straps twisted around his fingers, he sat through Pearl and Dean, the second feature, and dozed-off ten minutes into *Shaft*.

Back at Viv's he put the satchel in the car and prepared a meal for both of them, told her about his plans for Lancaster.

'Why didn't you tell me?'

He passed her a plate of sausages, mash and tomatoes.

'It's only 'til work picks up again.'

'You never said anything about it going slack. Now you're suddenly working away.'

'I just wanted to make a blummin' go of it – and I will. It's...people are still having holidays, there's no demand. I know it'll pick up in a month or so.'

'Why Lancaster, though? There must be other places, closer?'

'It was a tip from a customer. He's a clerk o' works up there. I could make fifty-five, or sixty quid a blummin' week with overtime, he reckons.'

Viv regarded him, 'It's all so quick. Are you sure you're not running away from something?'

Blum was ready for suspicion.

'Don't be daft.'

'You've said before you'd never work away.'

'I haven't got any blummin' choice now, have I? Not if I want to get some dosh in.'

He looked at her.

'I know what you're thinking and it's nowt like that.'

'You know it'd be longer next time.'

'There won't be a next time. Stop worrying, eh?'

She nodded.

'When do you have to go?'

'Thought I'd drive up tomorrow, when we take Fozzy back to Glen and Arnold's after the fishing. Double time if I can work Sunday.'

They left it there and the talk turned to next day and Fozzy's entry to the fishing match. Viv said she'd take the Norton to the Sharrocks' place after night shift finished, Blum could pick them up in the Chev. Viv gave him match fishing tackle from her brother to stow in the Chev.

Blum left when Viv was ready to go to work. He told her he'd be with his mam at May Bank that night. Right now, he needed to be at the phone box near the Weld Blundell pub to take the call from Delly. He was wary of that location. It occurred to him that it was on the route from Burscough, where Kav lived, to Lydiate -- and so was Fox's sub-post office. Had Kav spotted him there that morning, shadowed him back to Pygon's Farm? That had to be the way Kav was able to follow him to the farm. In the Chev, on the way to take Delly's call, he thought of something else: he'd left the picture postcard addressed to me in the still room at Pygon's Farm.

*

Blum fiddled with his bottle of pale ale while I cross-examined him over the discarded postcard.

'Did you write anything about that lot? Sutton and Pye, Kav?'

'Blummin' eck! I've told you what I wrote!'

'You didn't put my name on it?'

'No! I wanted it anonymous, like.'

I sighed, 'Jesus...this address.'

I swigged at my bottle.

Blum said, 'He might not even find the postcard...'

Thoughts of an angry Pye smashing his way into Kitty's house, beating me to a pulp, or dragging me away at gunpoint for torture and judgement by Sutton, clamoured their way into my head, but I had to calm myself, think in a logical way.

'Did you rip it up when you realised you didn't have to send it?'

He shook his head.

'Where exactly did you leave it?'

'Look...'Blum started.

'Where?'

'Chucked it in the rubbish behind the door.'

I pictured that part of the still room. If Kav had broken in he could've missed it. He was looking for money, not postcards. I emptied my bottle.

Blum said, 'All this, it all depends if he's even found his way in there, doesn't it? No other bugger has -- even rat-face Clegg. For all we know Kav's got nowhere ...'

'What if he has? I don't want that bastard Sutton, or Pye, anywhere near here.'

Blum said, 'I haven't told you what Delly said, tonight's phone call.'

I looked.

'Delly got a visit from Pye. He said Pye put the poison in with Sutton about Kav. Told him he reckons Kav's been gabbin' about the hi-jack, or he was in with the scouse robbers.' Blum laughed, 'Anyroad, Sutton told Pye to get shut of Kav. He's out for good, no wages, blummin' nowt.

Pye warned Delly to stay away from Kav, or he'd get battered and no more driving jobs.'

I thought for a moment.

'So Kav's freelance now?'

'Yeah, he's after the dosh for his blummin' self -- must be, tracking me down like that.'

I opened another bottle.

'But he still doesn't know for sure we've got it, does he?' I said.

'He knows bugger-all, there's no proof, and we need to keep it that way. Are you still going away with Sandra?'

'We're sorting it out tomorrow.'

'You don't have to be back in work for a fortnight?'

I shook my head.

'Bob-on,' said Blum, 'Even if he turns up here, he's not going to get anywhere, not if we've blummin' disappeared.'

I began to feel better, 'He might not even find that postcard.'

Blum rooted in the satchel, 'Let's keep blummin' thinking that, eh?'

He pulled out a bundle of twenty pound notes bound with an elastic band, pushed it to me across the table. 'Here, you can take her anywhere you fancy.'

'I've told you I can't ...'

Blum raised his hand, 'I'm not arguing again. Just blummin' take it.'

I picked up the bundle, ran my thumb across the edge of the notes like a pack of cards. I'd counted it myself, a thousand pounds.

'I can't spend all this on a holiday.'

He pointed at me, 'You earned it. And that's on account as well, there'll be more to come. Do what you want with it. Buy a car...' He laughed, 'Move out of this place. You're always moaning how blummin' grotty it is.'

I laughed, waggled the wad of notes.

'Bloody hell, I could buy a little house up here with this.'

'Buy one, then.'

Blum asked if he could have a bath before he dossed down on the sofa. I made him beans on toast, dug out the thick plaid blanket I used on my bed in winter.

'Do I know you've got this job in Lancaster, in case Viv mentions it?'

He thought, 'You can tell her I told you tonight, on the phone.'

When he went to bed he took the satchel and shotgun with him. He never finished his single bottle of pale ale, a sign to me, that despite his optimism about Kav, he still remained vigilant.

I finished the rest of the pale, put the wad of cash in my jacket pocket with my holiday pay and what little was left from the pay-day before. It was more money than I'd ever had in my life. I had a bath and a shave, imagined Sandra and me dining in style at a country hotel; driving with her at my side, hood down, in a little frog-eye Sprite; finally, with her in a tiny cottage I'd bought on the road to Snapeback Fell, both of us lay across my big brass bed.

I had a thousand pounds and perhaps more to come. That cottage to share with her was a reality, not a daydream.

Chapter 40
Like Gold to Me

WHEN I GOT up later than I'd planned, Blum had gone. The plaid blanket was tossed aside on the sofa. Voices outside caught my attention. Thoughts of Kav reared up, I went to the bay window. I'd never seen Quinn Street as busy. Few who lived there owned cars, but both sides were chock-a-bloc with parked vehicles; cars, vans, motorcycle side-cars, squeezed between them all, other motorcycles. A stream of anglers lured by the £250 prize money, loaded down by rod bags, baskets, folding seats, keep nets, buckets and other gear, headed for the quay at The Packet.

I shifted to the other side of the window. Sandra's Mini was parked on the clinkered area by the wall and hedge of the quay, opposite Kitty's hedge. I hoped she'd slept, felt better now her work was almost done. Beside other parked vehicles, was an area fenced off in makeshift manner with old dado rails on bricks. The rails had lain under the hedge by Kitty's back gate as long as I'd lived there. I laughed aloud at a handwritten cardboard sign that read 'Private Parking.' I'd recognise Blum's scrawl anywhere.

I stood on tip-toe in the hope I'd spot Sandra, felt the familiar butterflies- in- the -belly sensation at the prospect, but all I saw were milling anglers. I anticipated the first leisurely day of my holidays with her and my friends. I picked up the plaid blanket, folded it. I was curious whether Blum had taken the satchel and shotgun.

I found the satchel stuffed into the bottom of my old-fashioned sideboard. It made me nervous having thousands of pounds here in my flat. I had to make an effort not to think of Kav forcing his way in with a gun, threatening me to tell him its whereabouts. The Signalman's gun, I couldn't find. Blum must still be on alert, wary, if he'd taken it with him to meet Viv and Fozzy.

I put the kettle on, discovered Blum had used the last of the milk. The last of my stale cornflakes had gone, too, along with the back of the packet, now doing service as a no-parking sign. I went to my jacket behind the kitchen door, took out my wage packet. I felt the wad of cash from Sutton's, wondered if that too should be hidden. I didn't bother, took the whistling kettle off the hob, left the house.

Yet again the air was heavy. The sun failed to break through the haze that covered the town. From here, most days, you could see the tops above the town, but this morning they were almost invisible. Heavy atmospheric pressure, Blum and others said, was good for fishing, usually ahead of a thunderstorm. I walked up to Dootson's corner shop. I had to dodge anglers who must've been parked on the top road, or were walking to the match, as they lugged their gear down the slope of Quinn Street. Even the shop was crammed with jostling fishermen buying fags, pop and all the bread, as a woman complained, while I waited to pay for my bottle of milk.

I left the shop, followed yet more entrants for the match. To the north-west the sky was darker. For Fozzy's sake, I hoped rain, or a thunderstorm, would hold off. I was halfway back to the flat when I stopped dead. Across the road, opposite me, was a green Corsair. My pulse rate rose. The car was empty. I forced myself to move back, had to apologise to a fat angler with a giant fishing basket who crashed into me. I stepped between two cars, into the road to see the number. It wasn't Kav's number plate. But what if he'd fitted a false one? Again, I had to push away ballooning anxiety.

I reached Kitty's front gate when I saw Sandra by the Mini. She raised a foot, toe-d the driver's door shut. She looked great in Levi flares and the yellow blouse I loved. In one arm was a bouquet of roses and astrantia in cellophane, over the other a paper carrier bag and a dress and jacket on a hanger. From her teeth hung the Mini's key on a leather fob. She hurried towards me.

She tried to speak in a hurry. It came out as gibberish. I laughed, took the key from her mouth.

'You were saying?'

She grimaced, 'That ladies' in The Packet, it's a right shithouse. Can I get ready in the flat?'

'I'll let you in...' I nodded to the flowers, 'They for me?'

'Sorry, no, our Mayoress, bless her...'

I ushered her through the overgrown front garden.

'Daddio says I've drawn the short straw, as he calls it, but I phoned her in the week, she sounds sweet. He calls her Dolly Daydream.' She turned to me, rolled her eyes, 'Do you know her?'

I laughed as we went into the porch, 'Daddio's being polite. Geoff Sillitoe calls her Dozy Doreen.'

'No?'

'Yep.'

She giggled, 'That's terrible.'

I pulled out my door key.

'Feeling better today?'

She gave me a sheepish look, nodded.

I opened the door, but put my hand against the opposite door post, blocking her. I leaned in to kiss her.

A double-beep horn, right behind us, shattered the moment. The Chev was visible between the tall unruly hedges each side of the front path.

Blum grinned from the open driver's window. In the passenger seat, Viv leaned forward to see. Fozzy gave me a thumbs-up from the rear window.

'See you down there,' I called.

Sandra looked back as the Chev slid away.

'Blum and Viv with Fozzy, I'll introduce you in a bit.'

I opened the door, relieved her of the bouquet and bag, followed her upstairs. She looked at her watch.

'Bloody hell! I'd better put a move on!'

She went into the bedroom.

I held up the bouquet, 'Don't forget Dozy Doreen's flowers?'

She laughed, 'Stop it! I won't be able to stop thinking that.'

I put the bouquet and carrier bag on the bed. She started rummaging in it straight away.

I held up the milk, 'Got time for a coffee?'

'Ooh, please. It'll have to be quick, though.'

She turned back to me, 'I will manage to sit down and talk to you today.'

I smiled, took the milk into the kitchen. I still hadn't tidied up. There were no cups or mugs left in the cupboard so I rinsed a couple, put more water in the kettle, put it on. While I did my best to bring some order to the place, putting last night's beer bottles by the bin for a start, I heard *Lay, Lady, Lay* from the bedroom. I smiled as I scraped the remains of Blum's beans on toast into the overflowing, whiffy pedal bin. I couldn't remember the last time I emptied it. I grabbed and pulled out the offending bag, but when I lifted it to tie the top, it ripped. Empty tins, toast crusts and teabags dropped on to the lino, knocking the beer bottles over.

'Shit!'

When I swung it to stand among dirty dishes stacked on the draining board, more rubbish rolled out of the tear, fell into the sink. I grabbed the bag and baked bean juice smeared the sleeves of my shirt.

I heard someone call hello. Or thought I did. It coincided with the whistle of the kettle. Then there was a knock at my entrance door. I tensed. Kitty would never knock without shouting, even if her legs allowed her up here. Was it Kav? Christ, Sandra was in my bedroom! How would I explain a visit from him? What could I do if he came in at gunpoint? What if Sandra was at risk?

I moved out of the kitchen on tip-toe. The entrance door was half-an-inch ajar. I glimpsed movement. There was another knock. I had to face him, try to get him away from here. I grabbed the knob, swung open the door.

Elaine, dressed her best, with full make-up, stood in my doorway.

She smiled, 'The front door was open, so I ...'

Fear gave way to a mixture of relief, then surprise, then, annoyance.

'Christ! What are you doing here?'

Her face fell, 'Well, that's a lovely welcome.'

The kettle whistled louder.

'What do you expect? You just turn up and...'

The Dylan record re-started.

'You got my message, didn't you?'

The kettle hit top note.

'What message?'

'I knew that stupid landlady'd get it wrong. Are you going to turn that thing off?!'

I hurried into the kitchen, my foot caught a rancid sardine tin, propelled it across the floor. I didn't want Elaine to come into the flat, but she followed. I took the kettle off the hob, turned to see her looking at the rubbish on the floor and draining board.

She pulled a face, 'How can you live in this...squalor?'

I wanted to man-handle her down the stairs, push her out on to the street, but took a breath, forced my temper down.

'Please, just say what you've got to say.'

She stepped forward, smiled, 'I got it.'

'What?'

'I got the Northampton job!'

'You've come all the way here to tell me that?'

'Is that all you've got to say?'

My voice was flat, almost sarcastic, 'Congratulations, well-done.'

She didn't pick up on it, 'But there's something more.' She bubbled, 'They're so keen to have me, they'll waive the twelve-month rule. I won't have to wait to get a subsidised mortgage from the bank. We can get a house straight-away.'

'Christ, I don't believe this'

She smiled, 'Fantastic, isn't it?'

'I mean what the hell's it got to do with me? We're finished. We broke up.'

She was airy, dismissive, 'That was weeks ago. We can't turn our backs on an opportunity like this just over a bit of a tiff.'

'You finished with me, remember? You said I didn't care.'

'I'd had a drink, we both had.'

I was incredulous.

She put a hand on my arm, 'Look, dad's outside trying to find somewhere to park. I'll tell him to go home without me, eh? We can have the day together. Talk it all through.'

I'd heard enough, 'There's nothing to talk about. We're finished, it was your decision.'

Behind her, Sandra came out of the bedroom in bra, knickers and a pair of tights. It was like an old Brian Rix farce.

Elaine said, 'All we need is a bit of time...

'Have you forgotten that coffee, I have to...?'

Elaine turned.

Sandra laughed, indicated her undress, unabashed, 'Sorry, just getting changed. You must be Viv...'

'No, I'm bloody well not.'

Sandra was startled, 'Oh?'

'Er, this is Elaine,' I said.

Sandra had no time to respond. Elaine's voice rose, 'Who the hell's this? Some scrubber you picked up last night?'

Sandra's voice was without any anger, edge, 'There's no need for that.'

But it was too much for me, I snapped. 'That's enough!'

I pushed Elaine out of the kitchen, manoeuvring her to the entrance door. I swung it open.

'Get lost! Don't come back!'

Elaine protested, 'You can't just...'

'Get out and stay away from me.'

'Who is she?'

'Get out!'

She stepped out on to the landing, turned to me, mouth open, but I slammed the door in her face, turned to Sandra, furious, 'She had no right to turn up like this. She finished with me, but now she's got that new job she thinks I'm going to drop everything and go back with her!'

'Have you told her you don't want to?'

'Yes!'

'You're absolutely sure?'

'I'm sure I'm sure! Christ Almighty!'

'Then go after her and tell her again, calmly and quietly.'

'What?'

'You threw her out like she's nothing, like a bluebottle in your kitchen. That's not like you.'

'She's just called you a...'

Sandra cut in, 'She's upset. Go and talk to her.'

I stared at her. Dylan was still singing. I could have looked into her eyes for a week.

Sandra put her hand against my chest.

'Go on. Make sure she's all right. Try and be kind to her.'

I opened the door, hurried downstairs. Through the open front door, framed by the hedges, Elaine was head-to-head with Viv on the pavement.

'Do you think I'm stupid? I know what's going on. You two were shagging behind your boyfriend's back when he was locked up. Admit it! -- It's been going on for ages, hasn't it?

Viv had her hands up, 'Elaine, that's not true.'

I hurried out to them.

'It's not true, Elaine. There's nothing like that with Viv and me.'

'What's she doing sneaking in here, then? Miles from where she lives?'

'You've got it wrong,' said Viv. 'He didn't even know I was coming here.'

I noticed two women watching from the gateway across the road. They were joined by a third.

Elaine pointed at Viv, 'Well you've picked the wrong time. He's got some other tart in there now!'

I looked to Viv, 'It's Sandra from work. She's just getting changed.'

'Don't believe him and his lies,' Elaine said, 'I've had them all. He doesn't know he's doing it.' She turned to me, even more upset, 'You said you wanted us to get married. All that rubbish about finishing your training, going to work in London. It was all bloody lies!'

I bit my tongue, remembered Sandra's bidding, 'I'm sorry, Elaine, but we don't get on anymore. If we moved away together it wouldn't work. Go to this new job, start again. You don't need me.'

Tears rolled down her face. Her eye make-up smeared as she swiped them away. Her voice was punctuated with sobs, 'I got that job for us. For our future...'

'I didn't ask you to do it.'

'You've made a fool of me, you lying bastard!'

Elaine started to sob.

A light blue Rover 2000 slid up from the bottom of the street, stopped. Ken Surridge, Elaine's father, got out, hurried round to Elaine, glared at me and Viv.

'In you get, love. I'll take you home.'

He opened the door, guided her into the passenger seat. He closed the door, took in me and my bean juice-smeared sleeves, 'You're just shit on her shoe, lad.'

I said nothing and he turned away. I watched Elaine, hunched, sobbing, as her father drove away. I felt Viv's hand on my shoulder, said, 'I didn't want it to be like this. Why can't she accept it's over?'

I turned to her, 'I'm sorry she accused you of all that... rubbish.'

She laughed, 'Well, it was a bit of a surprise. I only came to use your loo! Do you mind?'

I turned to the house, 'I'll show you.'

Sandra hurried out of the front door with the Mayoress's bouquet. She looked smart, summery, in a mini dress and cotton jacket.

Sandra came up to me, 'Did you talk to her?'

'She's gone home with her dad.'

Sandra nodded, 'Good. She needs someone with her.'

She turned to Viv, 'Sorry. You're the real Viv...I hope. Hello.'

'Yep. Hi.'

'This is Sandra,' I said.

Viv smiled, 'Pleased to meet you at last.'

'Sandra thought Elaine was you.' I said.

Viv laughed, 'God, talk about confusion. Did you know she was coming?'

I shook my head, 'She rang, but it looks like Kitty got her wires crossed over messages.'

Sandra looked at me, 'Were you kinder to her than you were upstairs...?'

Before I could speak, she turned to Viv, 'Was he?'

'Well...Er... I think he did his best.'

'She shouldn't have insulted you -- Or Viv.'

'It was only words. You saw how upset she was. She couldn't help herself.'

Sandra checked her watch.

'Sorry, Viv, but I've got to go.' To me, 'Before Dolly Daydream falls in the bloody cut!'

'You mean Dozy Doreen?'

She thumped me, laughed, 'Stop it.' To Viv, 'I'll see you and Blum and Fozzy in a bit.'

'Great.'

'I want to see how Fozzy gets on! I've heard all about his new place and the job and everything -- That was brilliant news from the specialist, wasn't it? What you and Blum did for him was really nice.'

Viv seemed taken-aback at this, 'Well... thanks.'

'Shit, I'll have to run,' Sandra looked at me, 'See you later.'

I watched as she hurried round the corner down to the quay, turned to Viv.

'I know,' she said, 'She's lovely.'

Viv had never said anything negative to me about Elaine. Though she'd spent time in her company, Viv had never risen to any of the snide remarks, the put-downs, but I'd always sensed Viv disliked Elaine. That a good pal like her said this of Sandra, two minutes after she met her, was like gold to me.

*

Viv waited while I cleaned up the rubbish in the kitchen. I tried to stop her, but she joined in, took it all out to the dustbin.

She laughed, 'Did Elaine see the state of this kitchen? I can just see her face. Bet she was mortified.'

'I think squalor was the word she used.'

'Pretty accurate – I can see why you call it the grotty flat.'

I told her I was on holiday and my plan to go away with Sandra for a few days. I couldn't mention the thousand quid, so qualified going away. 'I can only manage a couple of nights B&B, but we both need a bit of a break.'

This prompted her to ask if I knew Blum was starting a building job in Lancaster.

'Yeah, he phoned me.'

'What do you think?'

'He doesn't seem to have much choice. I didn't know the van business had gone slack.'

She was quiet for a moment.

'It worries me that he's hard-up. I'm scared there's more to it, him going away so quick.''

I looked at her.

'You know what I mean -- that he's up to something.' She shrugged, 'He says he isn't, but...'

I over-egged things, embroidered...

'He's just fed-up the business isn't doing too well. He told me the money was good, so...This is a bit of a knock-back he needs to fix, that's all, a few quid to keep things going, so he doesn't fail. Has he told you about setting up a haulage business one day?'

She laughed, 'Only about twice a week.'

'I reckon he'll do it. It's not in him to sit around twiddling his thumbs. He needs to work, so he's prepared to do some hard graft for good money, get him through this bad patch -- I'd be more worried if he was doing nothing, if you know what I mean.'

She nodded, 'I suppose so, yeah.'

I didn't want this conversation to continue. I chivvied her, 'Well...Are you going fishing, or what?' I displayed my stained shirt, 'I need to find something clean.'

Viv left to join Blum and Fozzy while I rooted out a presentable, not too creased shirt. Before I left I found myself at the front window looking up Quinn Street. Again, I checked the satchel was still in the sideboard cupboard, safe. I needed to relax, enjoy the day, get my worry over Kav out of my mind.

Chapter 41
One Man Down

DOWN ON THE canal the *Sentinel and Alumbrook Council Open Angling Match* had started. Anglers were in position at their pegs, which stretched right and left along the towpath from The Packet quay. The freeloaders, too, were in position and I saw a dozen town council faces already taking advantage of the bar in the marquee, where the canvas sides were rolled up to counter the day's mugginess.

I had Fozzy's allocated peg number from Viv and turned right along the towpath in front of The Packet. Many anglers had their keep nets in the water several caught small roach and bream as I passed. I spotted Fozzy first. He stood, rod in hand, looking frustrated. Blum knelt beside him, Viv sitting on the towpath grass, arms around her knees.

I joined them as Blum told Fozzy, 'You weren't quick enough.'

Fozzy protested, 'I was!'

'Don't be daft. If you had, you'd've blummin' hooked it. Get your line back in the same place. Get some more maggots chucked in and all. Quick!'

I joined them. Fozzy nodded as he scooped a handful of maggots from his bait box.

'Any luck, mate?' I said.

Fozzy smiled, 'I've had two bites.'

'That's good.'

He lobbed the maggots about five yards out.

'Ha. No good if he's too slow on his strike.'

I laughed, 'Give him a chance. It's his first time out.'

Fozzy cast out his float and bait.

'Not there! – The place you threw the blummin' maggots!'

Fozzy laughed, twitched his line back to the baited area.

'Where have I heard all this before?' I said.

'Yeah, we're not the only ones.' Viv said, 'Do what I do if he gets on your nerves, Foz, just tell him to belt-up!'

Fozzy laughed, turned to Blum, 'Are you always like this, fishing?'

'Every single time,' said Viv.

'Catching fish is blummin' serious. Wait 'til you come winter piking, not this tiddler-snatching lark.'

I laughed, 'Not that again!'

'We should've put a bet on it!' said Viv.

'It's blummin' true!'

Fozzy said, 'What's the biggest pike you've caught, then?'

'Fifteen pou...' Blum pointed to the water, 'Strike! Strike!'

'Quick!' said Viv.

Fozzy struck. 'Yes!'

Excited, he swung in a wriggling fish.

Viv stood up to catch hold of it. Blum dropped the keep net into the water.

'What sort is it?' said Fozzy.

'It's a little roach,' Viv said.

'About three ounces, well done,' Blum said, 'You just need to concentrate more.'

Blum watched as Viv showed Fozzy how to unhook the roach. He held and admired the little fish.

'You'll remember that for blummin' ever, nowt like your first fish.'

Fozzy slipped it into the net.

'Now get that blummin' line back in. Fifty more o' them and you'll be in with a chance.'

Blum chuckled and stood up, moved closer to me. 'You had a surprise visitor then?'

'I'm sorry poor Viv had to walk in on it.'

'So, that's it, then, you and Elaine?'

'"That's it" was bloody weeks ago in my book.'

'At least she's got the message now.'

'Yep.'

I watched Fozzy cast out, now more confident.

'Viv really likes your replacement, you know.'

'That's good.'

He grinned, 'She reckons you're smitten.'

I laughed.

'When do I get to meet her then?'

I pointed along the towpath, 'Any minute now...'

Blum turned, stepped aside.

What Geoff Sillitoe called 'the chain gang' were yards away. The Mayor, in his chain of office, accompanied by old man Henty, ambled towards us. Behind were Sandra and the Mayoress. At the rear was aldermanic hopeful, Councillor Harold Fairbrass, who finished a furtive pull at his hip-flask, tucked it into his inside pocket.

Henty was half-turned, attentive, to the Mayoress.

'What I don't understand, Mr Henty, is why you dry the flies you use to catch your fish? Why dry them when you're going to throw them in water?'

'Well...' said Henty.

The Mayor, cut in, 'Seems a reet malarkey to me, Arthur, every bit o' this angling business. Why bugger about with flies an' floats an' all the flippin' rest of it when us've got two damn good fishmongers in Standish Street?'

He laughed. His belly quivered beneath his waistcoat.

The Mayor glanced back at Fairbrass, 'No offence intended, mind, Harold.'

Fairbrass's face was blank. Sandra rolled her eyes at me.

Henty replied, 'I must beg to differ, your worship, catching a trout on dry fly at evening rise is a sublime experience.'

The Mayor turned to the Mayoress, 'Happen I feel the same when I get me battered haddock Friday teatime, eh, Doreen?'

The Mayoress piped up, 'Do you catch haddock with your dry flies, Mr Henty?'

Blum struggled to stifle his merriment as the chain gang progressed along the cut. Sandra peeled away, shaking her head.

'Blummin 'eck. Hear that? Haddock on a dry fly!'

I laughed, asked Sandra, 'How's it going?'

Sandra giggled, 'She's already dropped a bollock with the chairman of the angling club. She asked him if they were fed up of using fishing rods could they scoop the fish out with their funny nets. Hentypops' face was like bloody beetroot!'

I introduced Sandra to Blum.

'About blummin' time we had a look at you. Heard all about you, haven't we, Viv?'

Viv smiled, nodded at me, 'As much as he'd let on, anyway.'

Sandra faced Blum, 'I've heard plenty about you and all. Surprised you're even here.'

Blum's smile vanished, 'Eh?'

'You're encouraging a young man to go tiddler-snatching for blummin' money and silver cups!'

Blum's mouth opened. Viv laughed out loud.

Blum pointed at me, I laughed, 'Well, she needed to know!'

Blum laughed, 'Least I know you've all got the blummin' message.'

Sandra grinned back at him as she moved to Fozzy.

'How're you doing, Fozzy?'

'Three bites, but just caught the one.'

'Great stuff! Thought I might meet that talking magpie of yours?'

He shook his head, 'It's bit far for him, like.'

'And I bet he'd scoff all your maggots as well.'

Fozzy grinned, 'Yeah, he would. Never thought of that.'

'What's his name?'

In moments he was chatting with Sandra about Clicker, work, life with the Sharrocks. I could almost feel the warmth towards her from Viv and Blum. He caught another little roach, Sandra led the applause. 'Sorry, Fozzy, I'll have to go. Good luck!'

The Mayor's party had paused to talk to an angler about fifty yards on along the towpath. Sandra said goodbye to Blum and Viv. She touched my arm, voice down, 'You're not going off anywhere with your friends, are you?' She nodded along the towpath to the official party, 'I won't be stuck with that lot all day.'

'We're not going anywhere.'

She nodded, a quick smile, 'Got to go.'

I watched her hurry away to join the others.

Blum moved towards me, 'I like her an' all.'

His opinion had as much weight as Viv's earlier appreciation, 'Really?'

He nodded, 'I reckon Viv's right.'

I looked at his grinning face.

'You are blummin' smitten.'

*

Sunlight had failed to push away the haze, but it felt warmer and muggier. Fozzy had caught three more roach and a perch. I nominated myself to walk back to get us a few bottles of beer. The town's brass band blared through its repertoire and the quay was busier than I'd ever seen it. Guests had spilled out from the fake grass by the marquee. Curious locals and passers-by stood gawping at whatever they could see, most with drinks in hand. Anglers carried bottles from the pub to the canal bank. There was no sign of Sandra and the Mayoral group, but I spotted Kitty, dressed in a garish summer dress and hat. She'd already insinuated herself into the inner sanctum of the marquee bar and its free booze.

Not a single member of *The Sentinel* staff was flying the paper's flag or showing their faces, but as I approached the front door of The Packet, Geoff Sillitoe came out. He paused, tried to light a fag clicking his ancient Ronson.

I pulled out my matches, struck one, 'Try this, Geoff.'

Geoff looked up, 'Aye, aye, cocker. Ah -- thanks.'

He lit his fag, dragged the smoke deep.

'I thought you were fishing yourself?'

Smoke poured out of his nose and mouth, 'Last minute decision. Old Henty reckons it might be seen as unethical, as he put it, yours truly being *Sentinel* staff and all that.'

'That's a shame.'

He laughed, 'Scared stiff I'd win and cause a load of embarrassment, more like.'

He put a hand on my shoulder, he'd had a few.

'Don't want ter blow me own trumpet, but, between you and me, old cock, I'd've give some of them Yorkshire men 'ere a run for their money.' He waved his hand at the cut, 'Yours truly knows that watter backward, knows what's what...Let's get a drink.'

'I'm all right, thanks. I've got some friends back up the cut and...'

'Come on, just a quick 'un.'

I hesitated.

'It's on the rates -- and out of Henty's profits, the sweat of our labour,' he laughed, lowered his voice, 'I'm telling yer, cocker, it'll taste all the better, like fuckin' nectar, no less.'

I agreed to a quick one and we entered the fake grass area. Geoff nodded to the burly British Legion man in uniform posted to deter gatecrashers, and we arrived at the bar. While Geoff waited to be served, I looked around for Sandra, but there was still no sign of her, or the Mayor's party. I knew from endless meetings the mayoral car would pick them up at Carus Bridge, chauffeur them back to the quay to await the weigh-in of fish caught.

Two sausage rolls financed by Henty's profits and the ratepayers were crammed into my mouth in lieu of breakfast. I'd just spotted Sandra's father out on the quay with a group of men when Geoff came back, thrust a tumbler of whisky at me. It had nothing in common with any pub measure.

'Oh...Thanks.'

Geoff raised his own drink, 'Yer've earned it, cocker, that syndicated publicity stuff you put together did the trick.' He tapped his nose, 'Little secret. That many late entries this a.m. the angling club lads had to nip out and bang in another load o' pegs, both ends. Next year, it'll be bigger. We'll pull 'em in from the Midlands, the North-East, all over, and I'll be ear-bashin' the Town Hall and Henty ter double the prize money.'

Geoff rambled on, while I looked for a chance to escape back to my friends.

'Summat else to keep under yer cap,' he said, 'Mo Crowcroft, you know, the match pro from Doncaster I was on about, proper maggot maestro. He's seen my pieces for *Angling Times*, guess what?' He poked his fingers into my collar bone, 'His wife's old feller only owns that magazine, *Tight Lines*. Mo's asked yours truly to bang in a few features -- says he'll see me right with the fatha-in-law.'

'Hey, that sounds good.'

'Even better, old cock, I heard him telling someone they'll be looking for a new editor inside twelve-month, or so, summat ter do with a new investor.'

He winked. It came to mind the benefits of this occasion could be more about Geoff Sillitoe's ambitions in the angling world than the noble civic and community guff attributed to Councillor Fairbrass, mostly fabricated by me.

Geoff winked again, finger to his mouth, 'Tight lips about *Tight Lines*, eh?'

He then switched to Saint Maurice Crowcroft's ground baiting technique, I was relieved when one of the local angling hierarchy interrupted. I slid away, to be waylaid by the town's only Liberal councillor. Rather than dump my free whisky, it diluted the tedium of listening to the earnest history teacher, who slurped a large, free gin and tonic, whined about town hall profligacy. It took ages to escape.

It was a scrum inside The Packet. I couldn't get inside the side door for off-sales. I doubted the pub had been as busy since VE Day or the Coronation. In the main bar I bought four pint bottles of pale ale. Outside, I looked again for Sandra. I was just about to head back to the others when I spotted Denny Barwise, the estate agent. He was wearing cricket whites, a jumper over his shoulders.

I moved to intercept him. We were both obviously 'off-duty,' but it would be something for Blum if the estate agent could come up with info about buying Pygon's Farm before he left for the Lake District.

'Hello, there,' I said.

He smiled, 'Oh, hello. You here to write-up this extravaganza?'

'No, thank God, I'm on holiday.' I nodded to his whites, 'Looks like you've got the day off as well.'

'I wasn't due to play, but we've a fixture over at Leyland and the First Eleven's one man down. What can you do?'

I laughed, politely, 'I tried to phone you yesterday? For a bit of advice, a property matter.'

'Oh? Professional, or private?'

'For a friend. He's interested in buying an abandoned farmhouse.'

I'd piqued his professional curiosity and he listened as I told him what I knew. I told him my friend had come into a sum of money.

'We get this situation quite often. I've dealt with farms on the tops that were abandoned back before the First World War. He'll need a solicitor, eventually, but tell your friend to get in touch with location details and anything else he has and I can make some preliminary enquiries; call it a favour.'

'That'd be great, but he's away at the moment. Could I see you instead? I can get the details by phone. See you on Monday perhaps?'

He frowned, 'Could it wait a week?'

I supposed it could, 'Yeah, no rush, thanks.'

'I'll be away myself, in Paris from Monday.'

'You said you wanted to expand, but Paris is pretty ambitious!'

He laughed, 'I'm taking my fiancée. Well, she will be by then. My parents are having a bit of a celebration do tonight, mark the engagement and all that.'

'Congratulations.'

'Thank you,' he said, 'Must dash, if you'd excuse me.'

He left me as I saw Sandra approach her father who was talking to old man Henty. I was surprised to see Denny move to head her off. Sandra saw Denny.

She seemed surprised, 'What are you doing here?'

Then she saw me.

She was torn between looking at me, or Denny.

'They're a man down for the match. I might be a bit late picking you up for the do.'

Now she looked shocked.

'Just thought I'd come and tip you off,' he laughed, 'Avoid any panic. We won't be late for our own engagement, promise.'

Sandra switched her eyes between both of us.

Denny said, 'Is that all right?'

She forced herself to look at him.

'Fine, fine.'

'Are *you* alright?'

'I'm fine. Busy.'

'See you later, then...'

He kissed her, a peck on the cheek.

Then turned and walked away.

The blare of the brass band diminished. Everything around me seemed to shrink away. I felt the four bottles of pale ale slip from my grasp. It was as if the universe had contracted to just our faces; our eyes, staring at each other.

I heard old Henty's voice, 'Sandra, love, come and tell Betty about your engagement.'

Henty's arm came around her shoulders. I wanted to shout her name, but nothing would come out. I was paralysed. Her face and eyes move away. I tried to pull meaning from the expression in them. I didn't know if it was shock, or guilt, or pity; or all three. I felt as though an unseen force had torn out my insides.

Then Sandra had gone and I was aware of tears and snot on my face, lost beer and broken glass in the dust, and I wanted to flee, to hide.

Chapter 42
Tears, Anger and Fear

I PUSHED PAST groups of people still turning up on the quay, hurried to Kitty's front door.

I couldn't believe what had happened, what she'd done to me. I hadn't had a single clue Sandra was involved with anyone else. I was sure she'd never, ever slipped-up while talking to me. And I'd never, ever, had cause to suspect anything like this. Was that why she was so tolerant of my on-off relationship with Elaine? All our hours and days and nights together; all those intimacies, the laughs, the joy, the affection, the passion; was it all gone? Was this chance revelation of her other life the end of everything between us? Was all I saw in her and wanted never reciprocated by her? Was it all an act, a performance? But why? What did I mean to her? Had she in some way used me?

I rooted in my jeans pocket, pulled out my key. With it came the key to her Mini. I stared at it. My last thought was the only answer. She'd used me. That was it. Used me as some sort of entertainment, an amusement, while all those months she'd been laughing, sharing things, having sex -- everything we'd done together -- with a man she was now going to marry; the rotten, using bitch.

I opened the front door, pounded upstairs.

I went straight to the bedroom -- the place where we'd spent so much time. Cold winter nights and warm sunny afternoons, excited helloes, muted, lingering goodbyes; episodes of passion and long, indolent conversation; the exploration of the things that interested, amused, mystified and delighted us. The place where together we'd built what I thought could, and would, go on forever. The place she used me.

I snatched up the paper carrier bag. Into it I stuffed her Levis and that yellow shirt I liked so much. In went the shoes she wore that morning. Then I found her hairbrush, make-up things and purse. I pulled open the second drawer of the old chest, pulled out a scarf and spare underwear. It all went in the bag along with an historical novel of hers. I took the bag to the bathroom and grabbed her toothbrush, toothpaste, soap and other items of make-up, a packet of tampons. Back in the bedroom, I whipped the Dylan record off the turntable, tried to snap it in half, but it only bent. I pushed it down the side of the bag, ran downstairs, out through the still open front door.

The Mini key was still in my hand, but the driver's door was unlocked anyway. I swung it open, tipped out the carrier bag on the seat.

I heard my name called, ignored it, dashed her belongings across into the passenger seat and foot well, slapped the key on the seat, slammed the door.

'What the blummin' eck are you doing? Where've you been?'

I felt tears on my face, turned away from Blum, but he grabbed my shoulders, forced me to face him.

'Jesus, what's happened?'

'She's getting engaged to someone!'

He looked incredulous, 'Sandra?'

I couldn't believe I was crying in front of Blum.

His questions poured out: Are you sure? When did you hear this? You didn't know anything about it?

I couldn't answer him.

'Blummin' eck, let's get you back to the flat.'

I allowed myself to be steered upstairs. He sat me at the kitchen table, took out his cigs and matches. He lit one for me. I took it. Didn't smoke it, held it.

He squatted down to my level, 'What did she blummin' say?'

I tried to explain, but I was losing control. My shoulders started to heave. I couldn't stop sobbing. Even in this state I sensed my friend's unease.

'I'll have to get Viv. Where's your key? The front door's wide open.'

I felt him checking my pockets, retrieving the key.

He squeezed my shoulder, 'Won't be long. Stay put.'

Quick steps going downstairs and then the bang of the front door.

I sobbed until the cigarette burned my fingers. I dropped it in the filthy ashtray, sobbed more. I kept going over and over the times Sandra and I had been together. How could we have been so close, how could she have been so intimate, so passionate, so full of fun when all the time she was planning marriage with Denny Barwise? I couldn't answer. It seemed so cold, callous, so unlike Sandra.

I stared out of the window at the rooftops of the streets behind. The brass band played ragtime and I searched my memory for anything in two years that may have indicated there was someone in Sandra's personal life apart from me. I was unaware of Blum's return with Viv until she sat opposite, put her hand on mine.

She questioned me. The questions Blum asked and those I'd asked myself in past minutes. She'd seen for herself how together we were that morning; how close, how happy, or so I thought.

I pulled my hand from Viv's, stood up, 'I've got to see her. I need her to tell me herself.'

'Not now,' Viv said.

'I can't just sit here and let this happen. I've got to...

'Now's not the time. You're upset, in shock. You need to stay calm.'

'She's getting engaged to him tonight. I need to...'

Blum plonked an open quarter-bottle of whisky and glass on the table.

'Do what Viv says. Have a sup o' that. Settle yourself.'

Viv carried on, 'Getting engaged isn't getting married, is it? It's not...not final. You'll have your chance to talk to her. Hear what she's got to say? But not today, not in this state.'

Blum poured the whisky, passed me the glass. I drank some, sat down.

'It might help if you went home for a day or two. We can take you, can't we Blum?'

'Aye, if he wants.'

'What time do you have to be in Lancaster?'

'Er...said I'd meet up with them at seven.'

She turned to me, 'So we've got time to get you to your mum and dad's.'

I didn't want to be in Lydiate, nor did Blum, not as long as there was still a chance Kav, even Pye and Sutton, might still be waiting, watching.

'No, no, I'll stay here.'

'Are you sure about that?'

I nodded, drank the whisky.

Blum moved the bottle towards me. 'Have some more.'

I splashed whisky in the glass, drank half of it in one mouthful.

Viv showed her professional side. 'Too much of that won't help either. You'd be better off with a sleep. You've had enough shocks for one day.'

I held up the glass, 'When I've finished this.'

'Right,' said Viv.

I nursed, sipped it, while Blum and Viv talked practicalities. By now the fishing match would soon be over. Blum and Viv were committed to taking Fozzy home. Viv wasn't due back at work until tomorrow evening

She put her hand on my shoulder, 'Will you be all right on your own?'

I nodded, 'I'll have a lie down.'

'We'll come back before we run Foz back.'

My answer was genuine, 'No! I don't want him to see me like this.'

They swapped a look.

Viv said, 'I can phone you later on then, see how you feel.'

I nodded, 'Thanks.'

Blum again squatted down beside me. His remark was pointed 'I'll talk to you as soon as I can, eh?'

I knew when he'd said his farewells to Fozzy and Viv at the Sharrocks' he'd be back here for the money then away to The Lakes. I didn't want my shock, upset, to alter his plans. I picked up my glass, stood.

'I'm going to get some kip.' I swallowed the rest of the whisky, put the glass down. 'I'll be alright.'

Viv gave me a hug, reminded me she'd ring later, 'I think she owes you an explanation, but you need to be in the right frame of mind to talk. Don't chase after her, give her time.'

'She's going to Paris for a week -- with him!'

'A week's nothing. The little bit of Sandra I've seen, she's not what you might think she is right now. She'll be in touch. I'm sure of it.'

I stood on the landing as they left. Blum turned back. Unseen by Viv, he memo-ed the words 'See you later.'

The brass band was now silent. The house too. I went into the bedroom, lay down. In that silence, the shabbiness, the grubbiness, the stale odours, seemed magnified. When Sandra was here these material faults didn't matter. Her presence, its anticipation even, would sweep aside these imperfections like crumbs from a table cloth. That it would never again happen crushed me, I cried myself to sleep.

*

I woke disorientated. It was still daylight. Those moments by The Packet with Denny, Sandra and I bled back into my consciousness. Emptiness turned to anger. Why hadn't I dragged her away from Henty, her father, everyone on the quay? I had to challenge her -- see her face to face, demand an explanation. Viv's advice, its commonsense, no longer mattered. I rolled off the bed, went straight to the kitchen. I wanted a drink. I strode to the table, reached over to snatch up the open half-empty whisky bottle, but my foot kicked the flimsy table leg. The bottle fell over the side. By the time I'd pushed away the chair, the spirit was a spreading pool on my dirty lino. Anger at the table, the bottle, my clumsiness raged through me, but focused on Sandra.

I dropped the bottle, left the house, slammed the front door behind me. Anger propelled me to the quay through straggles of home-going anglers. I headed for the marquee, stopped at a distance, looked for her. Hard-core freeloaders still drank free booze on the fake grass while council men loaded potted plants into a van. I turned to The Packet. Anglers laughed, drank, smoked, tackle and gear piled beside them; the pub still crowded.

I'd drag her out of there, I didn't care. I pushed my way through the drinkers. One or two protested, but I didn't acknowledge them, all I wanted was to confront Sandra. I searched the faces. All strangers. I went to the taproom, then the best room. I stopped at the entrance. Geoff Sillitoe was with a group, including Fairbrass and Kitty, who stood to take a fresh drink from one of the party, 'To you, good health, *cariad!*'

I checked the room, hidden by the door jamb. No Mayor, Mayoress, *Sentinel* bosses. No Sandra and nowhere else to look. By now she might be at Denny's parents' home; a cosy celebration. A diamond ring displayed to her future in-laws; Denny's proprietorial hand on her waist, his hip against hers, their future each other's; my future, our future, of no concern, forgotten. Anger and frustration fluxed and bubbled up inside my chest, my shoulders heaved.

Fear of public tears propelled me outside, barging through, like a lout. I gasped in the heavy warm air, now aware of the black clouds on the skyline, headed back. I saw the Mini had gone. A dozen yards from my front door and she'd driven out of my life without a thought for me.

I stood, lost, not knowing what to do. To regain control all I could think of was drink. I checked my pocket for my wage packet, walked up Quinn Street, still full of parked vehicles. Anglers packed away their gear, talked, shouted farewells. I turned at Dootson's shop on to the top road. More parked vehicles. I went in to Ashe & Nephew's wine shop. Most of the customers were match fishermen buying cigs, chocolate, cans of Bass and Double Diamond. I bought forty No 6, dithered over a quarter or half of Bells, chose a full bottle.

I'd almost reached Dootson's corner when I saw the green Corsair. There was no mistake. It was Kav's car. The number plate confirmed it. I saw his face, framed with lank, greasy hair, half-turned, as he tried to reverse into a space between two cars.

A shaft of fear shot through me. He'd found the postcard. He'd come for the money.

He was obstructed by two anglers loading a pile of tackle into the boot of one of the cars. While his eyes stayed on his wing mirror I turned my face away, hurried past him to the corner. I looked back. Kav was still waiting to park the Corsair.

I ran the length of Quinn Street, my heart hammering, as distant thunder rumbled. I reached the front door, dug in my pockets, swapping fags and whisky, from one hand to the other, to find my key. Christ! No key. Then I remembered -- Blum had taken it. I moved to the gateway to the front garden. I looked out, afraid I'd see Kav come down Quinn Street, his hand already on the pistol in his pocket, but there was no sign of him. I sprinted round the corner to Kitty's back garden gate, hurried through her kitchen, upstairs to the flat. I had no lock on my entrance door, only a small bolt. I pushed it across.

I felt paralysed by tumbling thoughts, indecision. Should I run downstairs and bolt Kitty's back door? No, locking her out wasn't practical. Should I grab the satchel of cash and run? But where would I go? Kav had a car, I hadn't even a pushbike. I went to the front window and looked out from behind the curtain. I couldn't see him. I needed to sit tight, wait for Blum. We could take the Chev, go anywhere we wanted when he... Shit, I had to warn him.

I rushed to the kitchen and got my contacts book from my jacket to find the Sharrocks' phone number. Thunder rumbled again. The air in the house was hot, heavy. I put the whisky and fags on the draining board, hesitated. I needed to calm down so I unscrewed the cap, swigged from the bottle. I scrabbled open a packet of fags and lit up, drew deeply. In moments I felt that glow from the spirit, then the feeling of confidence, of control.

I rooted out some coins and hurried downstairs to ring the Sharrocks' place. It rang for ages before Glenys answered. I asked for Blum.

'I'm sorry, love, he's just this minute gone. Peter and Viv went out to see him off.'

'Are you sure he's not still there? Can you go and see?'

'I'm pretty sure he's left. I've just heard Peter in the back hall.'

Christ! Why didn't I ring him the instant I got in?

'Viv's staying for some supper, I'll go and get her...'

Jesus, not now, I can't talk to Viv...

'No, no, never mind. It's alright. Thanks, Glenys.'

'Bye, bye then.'

I put the phone down, retreated to the flat, slid the bolt on the entrance door. From the sideboard, I took the satchel, went to the bedroom and tossed it on to the bed. The thought of Kav with a gun was horrifying. If he got in here, how could I even attempt to repel him, defend myself? I went back to the living room, looked for the Signalman's gun. I couldn't find it anywhere. Blum must have taken it in the Chev. Damn! Then I laughed to myself. I'd forgotten Blum's haul of guns from the still room. I'd not thought about them for weeks. I went to my wardrobe, heaved out the double-sacked bundle of firearms.

Past, idle talk between Blum and me had covered the hypothetical merits of close-quarter gun fights between fighters armed with pistols and shotguns. Blum was adamant the best choice was a shotgun. I had no experience of the single bullet from a pistol, but I'd witnessed the devastating close range impact of a shotgun discharging two-hundred plus pellets into earth, or a sack of horse manure. My hand grasped the barrels of a 12-bore as I realised I'd no shotgun ammunition, only the chocolate box of pistol cartridges. My only choice of weapon was one of Blum's five pistols.

I shoved my hand into the sack, pulled out the Beretta automatic. I groped for the chocolate box. It was empty; all the ammunition had spilled into the bottom of the sack. I trawled up as big a handful as I could, tipped them on the bedspread. It took a minute to work out how to remove its magazine for loading, but when I tried the cartridges wouldn't fit. I swore, dropped it back into the sack, found one of the Webley service revolvers. It was heavier than the little Beretta, but it was easy to load six fat cartridges.

I took the Webley with me to the kitchen, collected the bottle and fags, returned to my bedroom. I clicked on the bedside lamp and sat, back to the bed head, the pistol on my lap, had another swig from the bottle. I pulled the satchel of cash towards me; tried to estimate how long it would take Blum to drive from Tarleton. If I heard the Chev outside I knew I'd have to go out to meet him. I dreaded it, but at least I'd be armed, a deterrent, if Kav was watching the house. I took another swig.

I was startled when the phone on the stairs rang. There was no way Kav had the number. It could be Blum, but he was on his way back. It had to be Sandra. Anger surfaced again. I was damned if I'd discuss anything on the phone -- I wanted to see her face-to-face. I hurried to unbolt my entrance door. I still had the Webley in my hand, decided it would go with me. For all I knew, Kav could've sneaked in through Kitty's back door. I went down holding the heavy revolver in two hands, one to steady the barrel, as if it were a sawn-off shotgun, ready to fire from the hip. I snatched up the phone, sat on the stairs, the Webley resting on my upraised knee, its barrel pointing through the turned spindles of the banister, aimed at the spot anyone coming from Kitty's quarters would appear.

My breath was irregular, my whole body trembled, 'Hello?'

Chapter 43
Drunk

'IT'S VIV, ARE you alright?' *Viv! I should've known she'd ring back, ask why I wanted Blum.*

'Yeah.'

'Are you sure?'

'Yeah,' I said, 'Fine.'

'You don't sound it. Have you had more of that scotch?'

I lied, 'Just a bit, yeah.'

'Glenys said you were in a bit of a state. Have you seen Sandra, phoned her?'

'I thought it was her -- when the phone rang.'

'Oh, God, sorry...'

I had my left eye closed as I looked along the barrel of the Webley, my finger on the trigger. I was straining with my free ear, alert to any possible sound made by Kav.

'...You haven't tried to contact her?'

'I wanted to, but...'

'I know it's hard, but I meant what I said, I'm sure she'll explain when she can. It's best to wait.'

'I still can't believe it.'

'I know...Blum and me, I know we only met her today, but we can't either.'

I said nothing. I wished things were normal; that I could sit, talk properly to Viv; tell her everything I felt about Sandra. Then I heard a noise, but couldn't tell where it came from.

'Are you still there?'

'Yeah.'

Viv said, 'Glenys said you wanted to talk to Blum?'

'Oh... yeah...'

What the hell could I say?

I heard the noise again; hushed, whispers between two people.

'I just wanted to...I never wished him good luck in The Lakes.'

'What?'

Christ, no!

'I mean, in Lancaster... I didn't wish him good luck...With the building job.'

I realised the noise was outside. Two people laughing, drunks from The Packet, not Kav.

Viv said, 'He promised to ring me as soon as poss. I'm sure he'll phone you as well.'

'Yeah.'

'Would it help if I came over? Would talking help?'

'No... No, it's alright.'

'I'm not working 'til tomorrow night and it won't take long on the bike...'

I had to put a stop to this. Sincere as she was, she might just relish a fast ride from over there.

'No, it's...Thanks, but I'll be alright. I'm dog tired. I think I should go back to bed.'

'Well, if you're sure. You will ring at the flat if I can help?'

'Thanks, Viv.'

'I'll call you soon, eh? See how you are?'

'Thanks.'

I felt guilty when I put the receiver back. Like the friend she was, Viv had tried her best to make me feel better over Sandra, while, behind her back, I was involved with Blum in this deceit, lying to her as I'd done before; like Blum had done so often. How I wished I could accept her kindness, her genuine concern, in that unselfish offer to talk. But I had no time to dwell on it. Kav was here, probably only yards away, and Blum should've been back by now. I started at another, louder rumble of thunder. I went back upstairs, the Webley covering the stairwell.

I bolted the entrance door behind me. Then I realised I'd have to get out fast when the Chev arrived. I left it unbolted, sat on the bed, back against the bed head, the big pistol ready to intimidate anyone who came through the bedroom door, which was ajar. I was about to light a cig when I heard knocking on Kitty's front door.

It had to be Blum. But I hadn't heard the Chev. I snatched up the Webley, grabbed the satchel. It would be best to bundle Blum back in the car, get away for the night, up on the moors, anywhere. I reached the top of the stairs, heard another rumble of thunder. The knocking changed to urgent rapping of metal on glass. Jesus Christ, was it the sound of Kav's pistol muzzle on the stained glass panels of Kitty's front door?

I crept downstairs, heart racing, the pistol ready, and reached the half-landing. I leaned over the banister, the Webley now aimed at the front door. I shifted for a better view.

It was Geoff Sillitoe tapping his car key on the glass.

I had to get rid of him. The only time he'd visited before was about a work matter. It'd taken almost an hour of office politics, while Sandra hid in the bedroom, before he left.

I laid the pistol in the corner of the half-landing, covered it with the satchel. With a backward glance towards Kitty's quarters, I went to the front door, swung it open. Geoff fell forward, saving himself from going down full length by grabbing the door post. He hung from his supporting arm, his legs bowed. I almost laughed. He looked like a chimpanzee.

He thrust his car keys towards me, slurred words running together, 'Keys-keys-can't-drive-cock-too-pissed-change-gear.'

Christ, this was the last thing I needed, 'I can't bloody drive you home.'

'Na-na-na-na-can't-go-home-Rita-bloody-kill-me-this-state,' he slurred, jiggled the keys at me, 'Take-keys-don't-let-drive-got-sleep-off.'

I was trapped. I couldn't turn him away, not drunk and incapable.

I took his keys and he found the strength in his legs to lurch into the hallway. I peered outside then shut the front door, turned to see him reel towards Kitty's kitchen. I rushed to grab him.

'Whoa, mate!'

I steered him back to the stairs.

'Upstairs.'

I got him across the half-landing to the longer flight of the stairs, 'Stay there a sec.'

He clung to the banister like a shipwrecked sailor while I picked up the satchel, put one of the straps over my shoulder.

'Wha-yer-doin'?'

I glanced to check if he was looking, snatched up the Webley.

'Hang on, Geoff.'

I dithered a moment, pushed it down my belt at the small of my back.

'Nee-a-pissss.'

To get him in and out of the bog must've taken ten minutes. All the time I was tense, telling Geoff to be quiet, my ears alert for any sound of entry by Kav, or Blum's arrival. I got him to lie on the sofa face down. He was asleep in seconds. Despite the closeness in the room, I covered him with the plaid blanket, rushed to the kitchen. I tipped dirty dishes from the washing-up bowl, put it by him in case he vomited.

I still had the satchel over my shoulder, the Webley in my belt. What if he woke up, saw them? And if he didn't, could I leave him here when Blum and me drove off to lie low? I went back to the bedroom. Where the hell was Blum? I had a longer slug of whisky, sat on the bed, leaned back against the bed head.

My thoughts were all over the place. With the Webley across my knees, I thought about Sandra. What was she doing this minute? What would she do with Denny in Paris? When was the wedding day? I wanted to cry, resisted it. Then, abruptly, I found myself euphoric about the money we'd stolen; the thought that after all her worry, Blum's mam could have a new life. Then I thought of Kav, waiting, watching. How I hated him that first night at the Soldier. That hatred fermented inside me now. Did that greasy-haired bastard, that scum, deserve even a ha'penny of that money? Money that gave Blum's mam a future future?

Christ knows how, but I dozed off for a minute or two. The clunk of the front door as it closed jerked me awake. I hadn't heard the Chev. Was it Blum? Or Kav? I sat up, gripped the Webley. My hand reached for the satchel. I heard Blum's voice, muffled; another voice, Kavanagh's.

Footsteps sounded on the stairs. I switched off the bedside lamp. There was a crack and rumble of thunder that blocked their voices a moment or two.

'I've told you, we've got no blummin' money.'

Then Kavanagh, 'Where's that mate of yours?'

'Don't know, but he hasn't got owt either. You've got it wrong.'

'I'll have to fuckin' look for it meself, then. Gerrin there.'

Blum's voice was much louder as I heard my entrance door open, 'You don't need that blummin' gun.'

It was a warning for me, I was sure of it.

'Just remember I've fuckin' gorrit, eh?'

I stood, took a step towards my bedroom door. Everything was in semi-darkness. My entrance door was pushed opened. I was still, the pistol in both hands, pointing at the bedroom door. The entrance door didn't close. Then light showed around the edges of the partly open bedroom door as the living room light clicked on.

'In, you. Gerraway from the door...Fuck! Who's he?'

'Never seen him in me blummin' life.'

'That bowl. Is he fuckin' drunk?'

Christ, I hoped Geoff didn't wake up, witness this.

Blum's voice was loud, 'How would I know? I told you. I don't know him. There's all sorts stopping here.'

'Like you and yer mate, hiding out before you spend the money? Eh?'

Blum laughed, 'What money? We're here for the weekend, that's all. We're starting blummin' building jobs on Monday. We're skint.'

'Like shite, yer going to The Lakes. Think I'm fuckin' soft?'

Blum laughed, 'Ha!'

I swapped hands on the Webley and wiped sweat on my jeans, re-gripped it, took another step towards the door.

'Look, put that blummin' thing away. We know nowt to do with anything in Scarisbrick. Even that feller with you said that.'

'He was fuckin' wrong.'

I used my left hand to open fully the door. I looked out, to my right, saw Kavanagh's back. Beyond him, Blum's shoulder was visible. The sight of that bastard Kavanagh increased my loathing. My legs began to tremble.

'I've been ter that ould farm,' Kavanagh said, 'I've seen yer hideout with the safe an' that. Seen yer fuckin' van outside...'

I stepped soundlessly out of the bedroom, the Webley pointed at Kavanagh's back. His left hand pulled something from the back pocket of his jeans.

'...Found this with the address fer this place. You wrote it, didn't yer, eh?'

I stepped forward, the pistol pointed at Kavanagh's back. His left hand held up the crumpled postcard. He stuffed it back in his pocket.

'Don't know what you're blummin' on about.'

'Know worr else I seen an' all? Two green boiler suits, two ballys, two women's fuckin' stockin's. Stuff I know them robbers was wearin'. You an' that smartarse mate aren't that fuckin' clever, are yis?' He snarled, 'Youse robbed that fuckin' money! I wan' it now!'

I could see Blum, knew he could now see me, but his face was impassive, no eye movement.

Blum was calm, 'There's no money. We've robbed blummin' nowt.'

'I'm not scared to use this. One in the leg and yer'll soon hand it over.'

I took another silent step forward. I raised the gun to the level of Kavanagh's head. My hatred focused on his filthy hair, only eighteen inches from the Webley service revolver, its fat lead bullets. I could even smell the bastard; dirty hair, unwashed armpits. I could do away with this insect, this cockroach, in a second. It would be so easy; one sharp pull of my finger and he would cease to exist.

Kavanagh's anger, frustration, rose, 'I'm tellin' yer, give it 'ere now, or you'll fuckin gerrit!'

How dare this bastard demand that money? It was Blum's money, for his mam, nobody else's. I wouldn't allow Kavanagh to take it. My friend sweated, spent sleepless nights trying to secure his mother's future. I'd sooner splatter Kavanagh's stinking blood and brains across my walls than let him have it.

He shouted, 'Get the fuckin' money!'

Geoff grunted, shifted on the sofa. Jesus! I seized the chance, took a half-step forward. Geoff muttered, went back to sleep.

My finger rested on the trigger. I pushed the muzzle against Kavanagh's head, 'Put it down, you shit, or I'll blast your head to bits.'

Kavanagh stiffened.

'Bend down and put it on the floor.'

He didn't move.

Thunder cracked over Quinn Street.

I drew my elbow back, stabbed the steel muzzle hard into his skull. He almost collapsed with the impact, but staggered a step, regained his balance, dropped his automatic pistol on my threadbare carpet.

Chapter 44
Yer 'Aven't Got The Arse

BLUM STEPPED FORWARD and snatched up the small flat-sided pistol.

'Get away from me,' I told Kavanagh, 'In the middle of the room.'

He moved away, hands away from his sides, not looking. Blum backed away, checked the automatic. He clicked the safety catch, pushed it into his jeans pocket.

I aimed the Webley at Kavanagh's back, 'Put your hands on your head.'

He did as he was told. His fingers massaged his greasy scalp where I'd stabbed the Webley's muzzle.

'Fuckin' Sutton an' Pye'll be all over yous for this. Yer won't gerraway with that cash.'

Blum laughed.

Yet again, I felt calm, despite this tense situation. Smashing the shotgun into Sutton's temple flashed across my mind. Like then, my legs had ceased to tremble. Whisky streamed through me. I felt in control.

'What do we blummin' do with him now?'

I wanted to confuse Kavanagh.

'You get the satchel and go. Don't bother with The Lakes job. That can wait.'

'But...'

Kavanagh turned, cut in, 'I fuckin' knew you done it. Who told you about Sutton's money, eh?' He sneered, 'That fuckin' gobshite, Delly? Yer ould mate from 'Avvy?'

Blum laughed, 'That clown? Nah, you need to look a bit closer to Sutton than blummin' Delly.'

Kavanagh's expression told me he was thinking.

'Not fuckin' Pye? Is that why he...? You're in on it with him?'

Blum laughed, imitated Pye, 'Not that f'ckin scouse knobhead. Yer jokin,' aren't ya, bollocks.'

What was Blum up to? I knew he'd protect Delly by denigrating him, but why miss a chance to put suspicion on Pye? Or taunt him with the scouse voice, the admission of our involvement? Was it a stupid boast?

Kavanagh sounded desperate to know, 'Who?'

I kept the gun aimed at Kavanagh, told Blum, 'Never mind all this, just get the satchel and go.'

Blum protested, 'I can't just...'

'Go! I'll leave this dump tonight as well. You can get a message to me at that sentinel place. Ask for Geoff Sillitoe. I'll ring you back.'

'What about this pillock?'

My mind raced. I took inspiration from Blum's encounter with Delly at his home. I bluffed.

'He wants the money. If it's gone what can he do? He can bugger off tonight and I won't tell the others he came after the money,' I adjusted my aim on Kavanagh, 'Or if he wants to cause trouble I will blow his head to pieces. It's up to him.'

Kavanagh glanced at Blum, then back to me.

'This is shite, the fuckin' lot of it.'

Blum said, 'Should I phone Karen?' He pointed at Kavanagh, 'She might want you-know-who to see to him if she knows this bog- rat came after her money.'

Kavanagh looked to Blum, then me, for an answer, 'What's this? Who's she?'

Blum chuckled, 'Sooty's daughter. Told you to look blummin' closer, didn't I? She planned it. Karen and her feller's not happy with what Sutton's doing in Southport, thinks they'd make a better job if they took it all off 'im.'

Kavanagh looked rattled, uncertain. There was sweat on his face. I saw a chance to increase the bastard's confusion, add to his fear; that he might now believe he was trying to rob people more powerful, more dangerous than he'd imagined.

I took Blum's lead, embroidered, 'Karen and Mick are out to destroy her old feller. That thing at Scarisbrick was just the start and we're getting well-paid. Mick's lot from Manchester'll be on you like a ton of bricks if they know you've come after their money.'

Kavanagh was quiet for a moment, then. 'They wouldn't use fuckin' woolly-back no-marks like yous. Why the fuck'd they wanna do that?'

I was at a loss. Blum pointed at me, 'Mick's his blummin' brother, that's why.'

Kavanagh's face fell.

'Right,' I said, 'Get the satchel and go. Ring Karen. She can ring me here if our Mick wants to get someone to see to this. I'll watch him. Go on.'

Blum made a move for the sideboard.

'It's in the other room.'

Blum left for the bedroom. I adjusted my aim on Sutton, glanced to check Geoff was still passed-out. Kav shifted his feet.

'Stay still!'

Blum came back in with the satchel over his shoulder and the little automatic in his hand. He moved to the sideboard, reached behind it, drew out the Signalman's folded shotgun. It had been there all the time, stood on end.

'Is that pistol of his loaded?' I said.

'Yep. Checked it.'

'Leave the shotgun then. I'll bring that.'

Blum handed it to me. I put it on the armchair.

'You've still got the key for this place as well.'

Blum pulled it out and I stuffed it in my pocket. The Webley was still aimed at Kavanagh.

Blum lingered. I glanced at him. I knew he was concerned at leaving me, but I was confident with Blum gone, the cash gone, Kavanagh was unsure enough, scared enough, to walk away, run away. I held Blum's gaze for a moment, before I looked back to my prisoner. Let Kavanagh make of this what he would. I didn't care about him. It was for Blum, to make him leave. 'I told you why I came in on this. It was to stop all the worry, give her a new life. I don't want anything messing that up. Right?'

'Don't be daft.'

'I promised, remember? Just go.'

Blum hesitated, pulled the satchel higher on his shoulder. Then he nodded.

I looked back to Kavanagh. His eyes were on the satchel with the money he lusted after, but it disappeared from view as Blum left, thumped downstairs.

Kavanagh stared at me. I listened for the front door, but it didn't open, or close. He must have gone out through Kitty's.

'I need a slash.'

I looked at him. My loathing of this parasite, was even more intense, 'I couldn't care less if you pissed yourself.'

I heard the Chev turn over. You always had to try twice before it caught. But there was no second attempt from Blum. What the hell had happened? -- I wanted him away from here. Moments passed.

I turned my head towards the window, strained to hear. Kavanagh shuffled a step towards the door. 'Sounds like it won't fuckin' start, eh? Like he's stuck 'ere.'

I took a step closer, poked the Webley at him, 'Don't move!'

He sneered, 'Yer drunk.'

'Stand still!'

'I can smell yer breath from here. Yer fuckin' rotten.'

He took a step sideways to the door, then another.

I felt the whisky pile in on me. Sweat ran from my armpits, down my back.

'Stay there! I'll shoot!'

He took a small step towards me, 'You 'an 'im, it's all play-actin' -- Yer 'aven't got the arse.'

He grinned at me. I hated him, despised him, every single thing about him.

I raised the muzzle of the Webley to his face.

'I mean it!'

'Losing yer arse good-style, aren't yer? It's you that's pissin' yerself.'

He laughed.

'Yer shit-scared! -- Fuckin' bevvied off yer 'ead!'

There was an eruption inside me. Everything that happened today: Sandra's betrayal, Kavanagh's arrival, his invasion of my flat, his attempt to rob Blum of the money; now this. A searing lava stream of hatred rose up inside me as this worthless vermin ridiculed me, laughed at me, humiliated me.

I jabbed the revolver at the bastard's face, pulled the trigger.

The muzzle blast was terrific.

I wanted his brains dripping off my ceiling, but Kavanagh was alive, intact, still as a statue.

The big bullet had gone past his head through the open living room door, the entrance door, hit the wall across the landing.

The sound died and I heard the Chev turn over. Then a second time as the engine caught. Kavanagh launched himself at me, wrenched the Webley from my hand, pushed me in the chest. I fell backwards against the edge of the armchair, down on my backside.

Thunder crashed.

Kavanagh ran out of the room. I was furious. He had a car, now another gun. He was after Blum, after the money. I was damned if I'd let him win, ruin everything for Blum.

The front door slammed.

I jumped up off the floor, snatched the Signalman's gun from the armchair. I had a single need in my whole existence -- to kill Kavanagh. My next shot wouldn't miss.

I checked the cartridges in the open breech, pressed the button and snapped the barrels into place, hurried to the door.

'Woz-goin-on?'

'Thunderstorm. Go to sleep.'

I clicked off the light, legged downstairs, crashed my shoulders against the walls as I rushed, drunk, through

Kitty's kitchen and garden out on to the ground between the house and The Packet's car park and quay. Big drops of rain fell. I heard the Chev going up Quinn Street. Where the hell was Kavanagh?

An engine revved. Headlights came at speed up the ramp from the pub. I saw the number plate, the green Corsair, Kavanagh at the wheel. I was too high up for a shot. I dropped to one knee and as the full beams swept away, I saw his profile, swung the gun barrels from behind, through and ahead of his face, as if shooting a pigeon, a rabbit, pulled the trigger.

Shit!

I hadn't thumbed-back the hammers to cock it.

In impotent rage I staggered upright, ran to Quinn Street to see the Corsair turn out right on to the top road, only moments behind Blum.

Shit! Shit! Shit!

I staggered to one side, leaned against a car with one hand, the other holding the shotgun. The rain was heavier. It was Geoff's car. A Cortina 1600E; a company car, once the property of Sandra's father, but handed over for Geoff's use when Daddio got his Rover. I'd heard it was a sweetener to smooth potential in-house friction between *The Sentinel* and the journalists' union. And his keys were in my pocket. I didn't hesitate. All I wanted was to get Kavanagh, to destroy him.

I threw the Signalman's gun, muzzle down, into the passenger foot well, got in. I wasted time finding the lights and windscreen wipers. I started up, reversed so I could drive out on to the street. I kangaroo-jumped the unfamiliar clutch, but didn't stall. Rage drove me up the street to turn on to the top road. There was no sign of the Corsair, or Blum's Chev. I shifted into top gear, jammed my foot down, hunched over the wheel, stared into pelting rain, full of rage, drunk.

I kept on that road, covered more than a mile before I saw the red lights of two cars ahead, both travelling fast, as the town was left behind. It was hard to keep them in sight in the rain; oncoming headlights dazzled me.

When I said Blum should abandon running north to The Lakes, I didn't expect him to head south. But his direction now was due south, to Bolton, perhaps ten miles away, not south-west and home. Where was he heading? If I were him, where would I go? Pygon's Farm was no longer a refuge from Kavanagh and he wouldn't bring danger to his mam at May Bank View. Nor would he risk going to Viv's, not if it would endanger her, not if it meant explanations.

Brake lights showed as first the Chev, then the Corsair, slowed then turned right off the main road. The direction of the Chev was now due west. As the crow flew, it would lead to the Tarlscough estate. I knew he could hide there, stash the money. He'd known those sprawling acres since he was a kid. But there were no main roads from here to Tarlscough. It was all cross country, tortuous, about eighteen miles. I braked to turn, but had to wait for oncoming traffic to pass. I stalled as I set off. Then I had to wait for another vehicle.

I was terrified I might lose both cars. I had to catch up. I turned and went up the gears. I had to brake hard when, instead of switching the headlights to full beam, I fumbled and switched them off. I lost more time as I panicked and groped to get them on again. I had to get going, I had to kill that bastard Kavanagh and I didn't care how I did it. With the Cortina's lights on full, I accelerated.

I powered up a hill through woodland. Heavy rain slackened at the summit as the road fell away. To the right, the woodland stretched ahead, left was open land, house lights below in a small valley. Two hundred yards on the rear lights of the Cortina and the Chev were moving at speed. I put my foot down. If Blum hadn't realised he had a pursuer, he must know now. The Corsair was only yards behind him. Kavanagh planned to run Blum off the road. I knew it. I accelerated harder. I understood what I had to do. I increased speed. There was a curve in the road ahead of them. I'd ram the Corsair on the bend, send that scum to his death.

All my drunken concentration was directed at the offside end of the Corsair's bumper. I had to gauge its relationship to the oncoming bend, then ram and maintain the pressure, for moments only, before correcting my trajectory around the bend.

It all happened so fast. I reacted to the burn of brake lights from the Chev, followed by a flash from the Corsair's. I braked. Kavanagh's Corsair's back end slewed from side to side then shot off the road. One moment I saw the red lights of the Chev dance in the darkness, the next they'd gone. I managed to stop. In my full beams I saw the drift of fine mud scarred by wavy tyre tracks, washed down through the steep slope of trees on my right, moving imperceptibly over the tarmac and away; not as viscous as oil, yet just as treacherous.

For moments I was still, stunned; in a state of disbelief.

Then I got out, hurried to the edge of the road. Fifteen feet or so down a slope of grass and weeds was a post and wire fence that edged a pasture. It was wrecked. Across a tapering strip of pasture were head and tail lights against the edge of a belt of trees, perhaps thirty-five yards away. To my right, further along, were another set of red lights and headlight beams shining into, across wet grass.

It was the Chev.

I couldn't leave the Cortina here. I got back in, started up, crawled it off the bend, clear of the mud. I left it on the right edge, half off the road under trees, I grabbed the Signalman's gun and re-crossed the road. I went down the slope, jumped the wreckage of barbed wire fence, legged down the slope to the Chev.

It was on its roof. The driver's door was wide open. In its angle, Blum lay half-out of the car, his legs on the headliner.

'Blum! Blum!'

Thank God he'd been thrown clear. I dropped the shotgun on the grass, took hold of his head, turned his face towards me. His eyes were open. 'Are you alright? Can you move?'

He blinked rapidly.

He was alive.

'Can you get up? Can you stand?'

He said nothing. I could see his eyes strain, to focus, to see me.

'I'll go for help, but it might take a while.

His hand moved. I touched it, cold.

'Did you hear me? I'll go for help.'

His mouth moved. I willed him to speak.

'Go on!'

His voice rasped, 'Money for mam. In the Chev. Get money for mam...'

His body convulsed, he coughed. Pink, foamy blood appeared across his lips. He coughed up a gout of it. Then bright blood ran fast from the corner of his mouth.

His eyes turned to me, but the light in them vanished.

'Blum?!'

I shook his shoulder. Put my hand and ear on his chest.

'Blum!'

I pressed my forefinger on the inside of his wrist.

'Blum!'

I was alone in that wet field. Only the ticks and creaks of his overturned car made any noise.

Blum was dead.

Chapter 45
Christ, it's You!

I STARED AT HIM in the quiet of the field that smelt of petrol and oil, wet earth and leaves. The blood running from his mouth moments ago had stopped. His eyes stared, fixed, blank.

I thought of his mam, of Viv.

Blum's mam left with nobody, for the moment still only worried he was working away, perhaps. Then Viv, lying in bed, missing him, thinking him safe and well in Lancaster; both women yet unaware of the terrible shock to come.

I had to cover this up. I had to get the money and go. Drunk as I was, my mind raced. What was here to reflect badly on Blum? Neither his mam, nor Viv, nobody, must have even a glimpse of the events that lead to all this, his death. Anything connected to his criminal acts had to be eradicated. His reputation in death must be unblemished, untarnished by any of it. He must keep his secrets. My drunken mind locked on to this single imperative.

I tried to make a mental list. To lie in the wet grass, sleep and never wake, was what I wanted, but I had to concentrate, do what was necessary, now. I had to take away anything that invited further investigation. I needed the money and the automatic pistol Blum took from Kavanagh. From the Corsair I needed to recover the Webley service revolver and that damn postcard.

I wriggled my fingers into the right pocket of Blum's jeans, took out the little automatic, stuffed it in my pocket. I leaned over his body, peered into the upside down Chevrolet. Fag packets and cigarette ends littered the car's headliner that was now the floor. I crouched, shuffled inside, reached up to feel the underside of the seat, now inverted, groped for the satchel. I had to go right inside, squatting, as I covered the length of the bench seat. There was nothing. I twisted round, opened the glove box. Litter cascaded down, but there was no satchel.

I backed out and stepped, reverently, over Blum. The back seats were boxed in, so the money couldn't be there. I had to check the boot. I moved to the back of the car.

A dull thump, a whoosh, the instant creation of a ball of flame, blew me off my feet as the Chev's fuel lines and petrol tank exploded. Intense heat forced me to scramble clear. The fire was furious. I couldn't leave Blum exposed to this and I hurried to his body, put my hands under his arms, pulled him away from a heat that seemed fierce enough to boil my blood. I had to go back, snatch the shotgun, its barrels gleaming, hot to the touch, in the light, the heat, of the blazing car.

I needed to get away from this light. Somebody, soon, would become aware. And I had to check Kavanagh's car'.

'Webley and postcard, Webley and postcard...' Over and over, I said it, hurried to the Corsair.

I stopped.

'Webley and postcard...Webley and postcard...'

What if he was clear of his car? Alive? Was he watching, waiting, the Webley ready? I pointed the Signalman's gun, hammers cocked, prepared still to kill him, the desire for vengeance now burning inside me. Flame from the Chev made it easier to see. Kavanagh's car was smashed into the trunk of a sycamore. The buckled bonnet skewed skyward. The front of the car was compressed. I peered inside the driver's window. The steering column was forced back by the impact. Kavanagh's body was a broken doll crushed between the wheel and seat back, his head and face a bloodied mess, part of his right cheek ripped aside to reveal gums and teeth, arms hanging loose and useless, dead.

I turned away, forced back vomit, 'Webley and postcard...Webley and postcard...'

I had to do it, search inside. I dropped the shotgun, pulled at the driver's door. It was jammed. I panicked, heaved on it, terrified the crash had sealed it shut, put the postcard and gun beyond my reach. I heaved again.

It opened.

Kavanagh's clothes were sodden in blood, so much I could smell it. The Webley was between his thighs, ready to threaten, even kill Blum, only minutes ago. I picked it up, felt the stickiness of his blood. I turned and rubbed the pistol in the wet grass and, for the second time that night, stuck it down my belt at the small of my back. I knew the postcard was in the left side, back pocket of his jeans. I hesitated at what its retrieval entailed; sickening contact with his blood, that same blood I wanted to spill seconds before.

I tore at my left shirt cuff, pulled it back up my arm. I had to insinuate my hand and forearm under his corpse. I turned away from him as my hand, fingertips, pushed and struggled to reach the pocket. I strained to keep my body away from the mess of his. I felt the postcard, drew it out, checked my address in Blum's scrawl, now defiled by Kavanagh's blood. I wiped it in the grass and pushed it into my pocket. I stepped away, wiped my hand, then arm, in wet grass; kicked the door shut on him.

The Chev burned, less bright now. Blum's money had gone. I wanted to take him with me, but it was impossible. I picked up the shotgun, made it safe, folded it, and half-ran, half-crawled up the pasture slope back to the road. While I gasped for breath, I checked both ways for headlights, scurried across the tarmac to Geoff's car. I threw the three guns behind the driver's seat, did a three point turn, drove back the way I came.

I had no problems with the Cortina's gears, clutch, but my judgement of speed, sense of space, distance, was shot by drink. Twice I ran over kerbs. On the main road back to town, double-vision struck; the single white line became two, as did oncoming vehicles. I had to close one eye to return them to a single image, cut my speed. My objective remained clear, though – I had to dispose of everything.

I left the Cortina where Geoff had abandoned it, let myself in at Kitty's front door. Her drunken snores filled the house and, at the top of the stairs, were complemented by Geoff's version. I stepped on something, groped along the wall to click the light switch. Fragments of plaster covered the thin carpet, blown out of a saucer-sized crater in the landing wall by the bullet I wanted to destroy Kavanagh.

I had to tidy up.

In the kitchen, I found my brush and pan, swept up as best I could. I found the bullet, a flattened lump of lead, in the debris, put the fragments in the bin, but there was nothing I could do about the crater.

In my bedroom I switched on the light, stood at the mirror on the wardrobe door. Blood smeared the front of my wet shirt. My jeans were soaked, but I found no blood on them. I balled-up the shirt, threw it under the bed, hurried to the bathroom. I checked myself from the waist up, cleaned Kavanagh's blood off my chest and arm. I found a jumper, put it on. I was desperate for a smoke, took fags and matches from the bedside table. I looked at the whisky bottle, now half empty. The urge for more, to block out everything, to drink myself into oblivion, was calling, but I had to keep on.

I was tired and it was an ordeal, to get the double-sacked bundle of shotguns and pistols down to the Cortina. I scanned and re-scanned the street, terrified of watchers. The boot was too small, unless I took the shotguns to pieces, so I lay them behind the front seats. I took the Signalman's gun, put it in the sack with Kavanagh's automatic and the Webley.

I set off. There was no confusion in my mind over destination. I kept to the speed limit, glad I'd not had more whisky. Outside town, I risked more speed, drove on. I saw only two other cars. The air was fresher now and I wound down the window, lit up.

I didn't see the flashing blue light behind me until I made my planned turn right.

I didn't stop until the police car swerved past me, cut me off.

Oh, Christ! It ran through my mind: no driving licence, no valid insurance, drunk driving, taking a car without consent, possession of pistols and ammunition without a firearms certificate; all that was legal about me was my possession of shotguns – and my certificate was back at the flat.

I saw the burly shape as a policeman approached.

'Had a drink, have we, sir? You failed to signal…'

I looked at him, aware my jaw had dropped. Neil Posset spoke first, 'Christ, it's you!'

I greeted him, 'Alright, Neil?'

'No, it's not alright.'

I heard the crackling of the police car radio.

'You stink of it. How much've you had?'

I shrugged, 'Just…Not much.'

'Is this your car?'

He didn't know if I had a car, or not, but he could check.

'Geoff at work, he lent it me for a day or two.'

'What are you doing up here?'

The police radio voice gabbled.

'Had a bit of a shock…My girlfriend…'

'Thought you two were going away…?'

'Thing is, she's got engaged to someone else and…'

'That boss's daughter, the blondie?'

'Yeah.'

'Bloody 'ell. How long have you been together?'

A voice shouted, 'Neil!'

He looked away. A second copper was out of the passenger side of the Panda car.

'Our shout, mate -- serious disturbance, Acregate Lane Labour Club.

Neil hesitated, as if torn. He wanted my story of Sandra, but he faced urgency he couldn't ignore. He pointed at me.

'Just turn round now and go straight back to your digs, do you 'ear? Nowhere else, right? Be bloody careful.'

I nodded.

'If I catch you behind the wheel like this again, I'll fucking do you. Have you got that?'

I nodded.

Neil hurried away. He swung the police car round while I turned the Cortina to follow. He glared at me through the window. I drove the few yards back to the main road. Blue lights still flashing, the police car sped away.

I wrenched the wheel to the right, drove up the lane that led to Snapeback Fell.

*

Above the reservoir the sky was lighter after the thunderstorm, the air fresher. I worked in the shadow of the fell, yards from the long rule on the pump house wall that put the depth of the reservoir at 30 feet.

First into the black water went Blum's three Webley service revolvers, the Beretta and Luger, as well as Kavanagh's automatic. I tossed the shotguns and the set of barrels, one at a time, out of my possession. I put aside the Signalman's four-ten gun, tipped the pistol cartridges out of the inner sack and used the Terry's chocolate box to catapult them across the water.

I snapped the barrels of the Signalman's gun to full length. Blum loved the pretty little double-barrel. I was there when he stole it; the first time he showed true, reckless criminality. He'd used it to intimidate a farmer who caught us poaching, to frighten Delly, to rob Sutton. And I'd used it to club Sutton unconscious. And I hated Kavanagh enough to use the gun in my drunken attempts to murder him. For a moment, I wondered if it was cursed, evil. I took hold of the muzzle, hurled it out as far as I could, watched it splash, disappear.

I sat, lit a cigarette, then burnt the picture postcard in the Terry's box. I was still drunk, in shock, I supposed, but I'd done what had to be done. My mind flitted from thought to thought, to and fro, from past to present; years ago to the past few hours. I stared at the water. Reality coalesced in my mind: my friend Blum was dead, gone forever; the girl I loved had deserted me in a heartbeat, gone, I was sure, forever.

It all found voice in a raw and primitive howl of complete distress, grief and loss that tore across acres of water, echoed back to me, as a flock of startled lapwings rose, wheeled and cried in empty air.

Chapter 46
That Sunday...

I HAVE NO memory of my drive back from Snapeback Fell.
Nor any recall of my return to the flat. Yet those moments of
waking, a few hours later, have never gone. A full bladder,
indistinct noises from the bathroom, drew me back from
blackness to a rushing, stark recall of yesterday's hellish
events, no memory gaps, bar my return from the reservoir.

Blum's death, my attempts to murder Kavanagh,
Sandra's betrayal, streamed back, swamped my
consciousness with the inescapable pain of grief and loss.
The hangover was no more than background to my agony. In
those moments I might've embraced my own death. But I
had to cope, function, protect Blum's reputation. Geoff was
still here and I expected that inevitable call with news of
Blum's death. It would come from Viv. I had to face the
realities of today, the days ahead.

The bog flushed, church bells rang, and a knock at my
door came soon after.

'Hang on, Geoff.'

I scrambled off the bed, still clothed. I pulled off filthy
shoes, still wet jeans and jumper, grabbed my tatty dressing
gown from the hook on the door. In blistered varnish, a
burned-out fag lay on my bedside table. The level of whisky
in the bottle was a few gulps lower. I tied my dressing gown
belt, went to find Geoff.

He was at the bay window, looking out. The plaid blanket
was folded on the sofa. He dragged on an Embassy, looked
nervy, anxious, a man with a grade one hangover. His clothes
were creased, pocked with lint and fibres from the blanket.
He turned, embarrassed.

'I were just off, old cock.'

I nodded, 'Sleep alright?'

'Grand,' he said, 'Sorry ter barge in on yer like that. Can't believe I were that arse'oled I couldn't drive.' He added, 'Hope I didn't mess things up for yer, Sat'day night an' that, yer holidays.'

I shook my head, 'I had an early night.'

He nodded.

Here, in these circumstances, we had nothing more to say.

'I'll see meself out then...'

'Right...'

'I did give yer me keys, didn't I?'

Christ! Was Geoff's car damaged? Had I scraped a dry stone wall, a parked vehicle, anything? I felt drunk again.

'Well, if yer could...'

In my anxiety, trying to remember, I forgot my boss wanted to leave.

'Sorry... Er...in the other room.'

I retrieved the keys, checked for blood, handed them over.

He patted my shoulder.

'Many appreciated, cocker. Enjoy yer hols, eh?'

He went downstairs, out. I hurried to the window, my bladder an urgent distraction. He wouldn't be sure exactly where he left the car, nor was I. Blood on the steering wheel, seats, damage to bodywork, an overlooked gun, a stray pistol cartridge, were my real worries.

Kitty's hedge blocked any view of Geoff and his car, but there was no delay before the Cortina reversed and he drove off up Quinn Street. If anything was amiss I'd need to wait for news of that as well.

I went straight to the bathroom. I wanted to go to bed, to sleep, but I forced myself to wash, shave. No bath in case the phone rang. I collected my bloodied shirt, jeans, socks and underwear, cleaned my shoes. I dug out fresh clothes, made a cup of coffee, too anxious to drink more than a mouthful. Food had no appeal; not the stale bread, cheese or sardines I had in. I couldn't settle, resisted the idea of a whisky. I tried to read, but it was impossible.

Kitty went to the pub and I sat on the stairs, watched the payphone, thinking, remembering, and waiting.

Viv rang at twenty-to-one.

Such is my shame at what Kavanagh might've called my 'play-acting,' most details of our conversation are long blotted out, filed in my subconscious. I know I acted shocked, mystified and ignorant, why he'd died near Brinscall when his stated destination, to Viv and his mam, had been miles to the north, in Lancaster. To take news of the death of her boyfriend, my best friend, to deliver lines like a character, an actor, shocked and upset, when, all the time, I'd been present at the scene hours before, knew everything, was truly shameful. When the other party was my friend, Viv, it seemed, and still seems, to compound the most sinful act I ever committed.

I told her I'd come home straight away. She'd anticipated me, despatched her brother Tony to drive me back to Lydiate. He was on his way to Quinn Street now. First I rang my mother to tell her Blum had died, avoided detail, told her I'd see her later. Dirty washing went in my old cricket bag with a change of clothes. The bloodied shirt, wrapped in newspaper, I buried in the dustbin. My holiday wage packet was retrieved from the wet jeans and I put my jacket on, made myself presentable. I would've gone to The Packet to tell Kitty I'd be away, but I craved a drink, gave it a miss. Tony found me on the pavement, clutching my cricket bag like a shell-shocked soldier.

Tony was polite, solicitous. I asked for details he'd expect me to ask, but he knew little; he was there only to help his sister at a time of need. Our journey was near silent. I slipped into thought.

Everything since Blum set out to save May Bank View had been a waste of time, of effort and Blum's optimism. His mam still faced eviction and he was dead. A satchel of money that meant so much in terms of his pride, in being provider and honouring his dead father; all that could have saved Nancy Gatley's future, her freedom from worry, a new happiness, had gone. All lost in the happenstance of a robbery's aftermath; pursuer, thunderstorm, slurry of mud and an overturned car. For so long she'd faced relentless worry. Now, she'd lost her son, her only child, the tangible gift of a short, happy marriage. I yearned to find some way to help her, but had no answers.

Tony dropped me at May Bank View, told me Viv must ring if she wanted anything at all. There was an Austin Maxi on the drive I didn't recognise. Viv opened the back door, hugged me, even before I'd put down my bag.

'I'm sorry, Viv,' I said.

She nodded, 'I'm glad you're here.'

I followed her into the back parlour and she told me of her shock when a policewoman rang her at the flat from May Bank View, woke her. She'd phoned Tony, who drove her to find Blum's mam, also in shock, two police officers making tea.

'How is she?'

Viv perched on the arm of Walter's chair, 'A bit better now, she's in the front room with some friends, Mr and Mrs Sykes, is it?'

'He used to be the church warden; she's known them for years.'

Viv told me she'd asked Blum's mam who she should phone. Ted and Marion were contacted as well as people from church, a message left for the vicar. She apologised for taking so long to call me, but Nancy Gatley had become upset, several times. Viv's offer to call Dr Grey, for a sedative, was declined.

'And I wasn't sure how you'd be... About Sandra...Have you heard anything?'

I shook my head, didn't want to talk about her, not now, not here.

She touched my arm, 'Sorry.'

My need to get through details of Blum's death and its circumstances, get past them, surfaced. I had to consider any questions from Viv with care, not to reveal anything unknown to her and Blum's mam, no blunders.

'Where is he now?'

'Chorley, at the hospital mortuary, they said. There'll have to be an inquest.'

She told me it had been arranged that Ted would go to the mortuary to make a formal identification of Blum's body.

Her voice cracked, her first sign of emotion in my presence, 'I didn't want his mum to have to do it and I couldn't.'

She composed herself. I pressed on. 'What else did they say? How did it happen?'

'They didn't know much, but the Chev went off the road in the thunder last night, there was another car. The other driver died as well.'

Her voice cracked again, she rubbed one eye with a knuckle. I wanted to hold her, comfort her, but I couldn't, not while I had to continue this charade.

'Why Brinscall, though?' I said, 'What the hell was he doing there?'

'I've never heard of it before. Do you know it?'

'I've only been the once, to some pub with Sandra.'

Apart from last night, that was true.

'Does Blum know it?'

'He's never mentioned it, I'm sure.'

'Is it far from yours?'

I shrugged, 'Five or six miles.'

Her eyes met mine, 'Did he come back last night, to your flat?'

I looked into her eyes and lied, 'If he did, I didn't see him.'

'You went to bed, you told me. Do you think you might've missed him?'

'I drank all that whisky, I was so knackered and...'

'He could've gone to yours, got no answer, and then headed back here.'

'But why? Why come to the flat?'

'He was worried about you.'

'I was fine.'

'You were a mess. God, he told Glen and Arnold, said he'd never seen you like that.'

'Why go to Brinscall, though?'

'I think he might've changed his mind, about the job in Lancaster. He was on his way home, but got lost in that thunderstorm, took the wrong road, or something.'

She'd created an explanation and it suited my purpose, nothing to damage Blum's reputation in the eyes of his mam, or anyone else, not Viv's either. 'He needed the Lancaster work, though. He told us.'

'He hated the idea of working away. When he got out of Havershawe, I suggested it and he wouldn't even think about it. Suddenly, he says he's off to Lancaster...I don't think he wanted the job. I think he changed his mind, came back.'

Interrupted by the Sykes' departure, it was left there.

'I've told Nancy, I'll call tomorrow,' Dolly Sykes told Viv when she showed them out, and it was my cue to see Blum's mam, offer condolences. She patted the sofa beside her, urged me to sit with her, declined more tea. I told her how sorry I was, how I'd miss him, that I couldn't believe he'd gone. We talked of his past, his childhood, how difficult he could sometimes be; my first untainted conversation that day.

'They say a mother's worry's never done, but I'd've been happy to fret over me-laddo for a few years yet,' she said.

It was a comfort, she told me, that Blum, Viv and I spent time together that final day. 'Poor Vivien,' she said, 'She's been so good, so helpful since the police came, but I know her heart's breaking. She says she wants to go to work tonight, but she should rest. Will you tell her?'

I nodded.

Next to turn-up were Ted and Marion, back from the mortuary, Ted, in a dark suit, out of place to me without his working clothes. It was so obvious Marion was upset, the redness of earlier tears in her eyes, on the verge of more. She hugged Nancy and me.

I left the Crossmans with her. Ted joined me later, smoked with me on the bench by Blum's father's yew hedge. Unlike the usual Ted, he was silent for minutes. He blew on the tip of his roll-up, plucked tobacco from his lip. 'The missus has taken it bloody bad. Like her own bloody son to her was our Davy.'

In years I'd never noticed that truth, didn't doubt it now, their marriage was childless. With calloused fingers, Ted crushed the burning butt of his fag, stood, 'Christ!' he said, 'Twenty-bloody-one, no bloody life, none-a-bloody-tall.'

He threw his fag-end to the ground.

'I'd jump in me bastard grave this fuckin' minute if it'd bring that boy back for Nance, for Marion.'

He moved away, along the hedge, and I could tell he was crying. So was I.

*

Five or six others turned up to offer condolences, Dr Grey, included. Marion insisted her cousin should see him and he arrived in his sports car, wearing his RAF blazer, as well as his trademark moustache. Nancy Gatley promised Marion she'd take the Doctor's sedative come bedtime if she needed it, not before.

Viv was dead beat when I insisted I take over her tea-making. She was adamant she'd clock-in for her night-shift. I knew it was useless to argue, but I told her she needed food and rest before work. She rang Tony to collect her.

I'd not eaten since those sausage rolls at the marquee, needed food. I left Marion making a snack for the three of them and said I'd look in later. When I left May Bank, the vicar arrived in his Austin 1100. He smiled at me as he pulled onto the driveway.

Blum's van wasn't there. Had Viv noticed?

Chapter 47
Christian Charity

WHEN I ARRIVED at my mum and dad's I was agitated over Blum's van. I knew where it was, but its absence niggled. My mum's fuss, her natural concern over my first personal experience of the loss of someone close, was a distraction, it irritated me. She was all for packing me off to bed. My dad sided with me and I apologised to both for my snappy response. Before I ate the plated and warmed-up savings of Sunday dinner, my dad poured me a glass of the whisky he never touched, but I couldn't finish it.

Of course, they wanted details of the accident, and I gave Viv's version; it was an accident in a storm, nobody knew why he was on a country road near Brinscall, Viv thought he might be lost; no I was sure he'd not been drinking. My mum said an early night might be better than going out, but I'd promised to see Blum's mam, I said.

On the way to May Bank View, Ted and Marion's van drove towards me. I waved, but they stared straight ahead, the hurt in their faces still. I changed direction, to Pygon's Farm.

Darkness was close when I climbed over the still padlocked gate, walked down into the yard. Blum's van was in the usual place, but the corrugated iron sheets that hid the still room door were pulled away at one end. The door was ajar, the wood around the lock smashed, splintered. I felt along the shelf for the tin lantern, lit it.

The remains of the Daltry's stuff were still there as well as evidence of Kavanagh's search for the cash. The boiler suits and balaclavas were thrown on the table. The safe door was open, key in the lock, where Blum left it. The German rifle had been moved, now lay across some boxes. I blew out the lantern, withdrew. I had to deal with this storeroom. Some items had markings to link them to Daltry's, connections could be made, but I couldn't do it now. I pulled the damaged door shut, pushed the corrugated iron back in place. Inside the van, I took the spare key from the split in the seat and five minutes later pulled up on the driveway at May Bank View.

No answer to my knock at the back door, so I went in, called hello. She was nowhere downstairs, so I called upstairs, no response. Outside I checked the bench by the yew hedge, nothing. In the dusk I found her sitting at the top of three shallow steps that led from a lawn down into the orchard.

'Hello?' I said from a distance. I didn't want to make her jump. She turned, smiled, turned away. I reached the steps, 'Are you warm enough out here?'

'You don't feel the cold when you've a garden that always needs work.'

I sat beside her.

'I saw Ted and Marion going home.'

'She was all for staying, but I wouldn't let her. Ted'd sit there and curse his head off while the house fell down round his ears, if Marion wasn't with him.' She laughed, a moment, 'Poor Marion, she was so fond of our David. They both were.'

It'd been a long time since I'd sat on these steps. Blum's father planned them before his death, even got in the old setts, from the yard at the old Maid of Erne pub, long gone. A few years after, a driven Blum, with me as assistant, built them one Whit holiday, a sort of memorial to his dad, I supposed.

'Remember the song and dance he made when they were finished?' she said, 'He was so proud of himself, finishing the job.'

'I remember you having to walk up them for the official opening. Do you remember us having to make a toast with dandelion and burdock?'

She nodded, 'I remember everything, love. Twenty-one years of it.'

She sat silent for a few moments, darkness came.

'Time to go in. Will you stop for a drink?'

'Please.'

I expected tea. I was surprised when she brought in a bottle of wine and two glasses, poured it out.

'Our Walter had nowt to leave anyone, but he didn't get through his plum wine, never would at a glass a week after Sunday dinner. I got fed-up tipping it down the sink, wasting it. Must be a hundred bottles in the washhouse -- I like a glass or two if I can't sleep.'

I imagined her nights of worry.

She indicated her glass.

'Don't fret, love, those pills of Dr Grey's are in the drawer. I won't take any with this.'

She had two glasses, I had three. I told her I'd brought the van back, said my dad had borrowed it to collect flagstones for a patio he wanted to build and we talked about her husband and Blum, the decline of her work as a seamstress, the financial blow when she lost her housekeeper's job.

She brought the conversation around to her future without Blum. It all came out.
The lease, the eviction timed for the New Year, the loss of her home, the garden, she'd tended, loved, since her marriage. There was a resignation in her. How trivial it all seemed compared to the loss of a son, she said. She cried and told me she had so little money, nowhere near enough for a funeral.

'The vicar gave me some dates and times, but I didn't know what to say. In the end I had to tell him I'd no money.'

She wiped her eyes with her hanky.

'What did he say?'

'Oh, I don't know, I was upset. Said he'd look into it, exceptional cases, parish funds, I don't know.'

I asked if Ted and Marion might be able to help, but she said she'd never ask. I got the same response when I suggested Dolly and John Sykes, who were well off, their farm the biggest in the parish. I wondered aloud if Viv might have some ideas.

'No,' she said, 'Vivien's a good girl, but I don't discuss our business outside of family.'

I remembered similar responses from Blum. Family, now, was her alone.

'But she might be able to help if she knew,' I said, 'And you've told me, haven't you?'

'That's different, we know you.'

I took it as a signal of trust and she said nothing more.

She announced she was off to bed. I said I'd call next day.

I walked home, touched the wad of cash in my jacket pocket, the thousand pounds Blum gave me forty-eight hours before. I knew what I had to do, but how? If I handed it to her, she'd refuse to take it. To feel beholden to me, no matter how trusted, known, would be unacceptable to her, I was sure. I could give it to the vicar to pass on, but he didn't know me, only my mum. And I couldn't risk even a private word between them. I supposed I could just stick it through the letterbox at May Bank View, but she would worry about it, perhaps be afraid to use it. How could I do it?

My family had gone to bed and I drank my unfinished glass of whisky. The bottle was still in the kitchen, so I had another. Like so many times before the alcohol spurred clarity of thought; an illusion, maybe, but to me often useful. I went to the bookcase in the front room, found the unread 1930s dictionary of Biblical quotations, there as long as I remembered. I got out my Olivetti portable and a sheet of paper, flicked through the dictionary.

It was difficult to understand the Biblical language of the quotations, the opposite of the direct prose I strove to master for work. Frustrated, I chose one at random from the section on charity and alms, typed the words 'From a well-wisher of St. Thomas's Parish.' Underneath, I copied the quotation, *'That thine alms may be in secret and thy Father which see-*

eth in secret himself shall reward thee openly.' Whatever it meant, it would do.

I wrapped the sheet around the cash, sealed it in one of my mum's envelopes. Fifteen minutes after, in a light drizzle, I dropped it through the letter box at May Bank View.

*

When I returned next day Nancy Gatley was on the drive talking to an older couple. She smiled. 'Hello, love, Vivien's made a start on the damsons.' I walked past the van and Viv's Norton. I looked back when I heard another voice. Dolly Sykes joined them on the driveway.

Viv poured a basket of little blue-black plums into a wooden fruit box, one of many I'd used to help Blum and his mam harvest their autumn fruit. The familiar high stepladder was next to the tree.

'Shouldn't you be getting some sleep?'

She looked, 'I wanted to help.'

'Are you alright?'

She looked drawn, tired. She nodded, 'How about you?'

I shrugged, 'Alright. Don't know if it's hit me yet,'

'Don't think it's hit his mum yet, either,' she said, 'I talked to me dad. He said there's loads we should be doing. Funeral arrangements, release of his body, all sorts, but she seems more interested in damsons.'

'Her way of coping, I suppose.'

'I still think we should be doing something.'

I took a pail, started to pick what I could reach. Viv mounted the stepladder, 'It's like she's hiding from reality.'

We worked in silence a few minutes.

'I see the van's back.'

I froze.

'Sorry?'

'Blum's van. It wasn't here yesterday, now it's back.'

'I brought it back last night. My dad borrowed it for the weekend.'

I looked up, un-nerved to see she was staring down at me.

'He was shifting some flagstones, he's building a patio,' I said, 'I suppose we should sell it now, she might welcome the money.'

'You're not keeping it?'

'Me?'

'He hasn't paid you back -- What you lent him to buy it.'

Christ, I'd forgotten the lie Blum told her.

'I know, but...Well, it's ...It was Blum's, it's hers now, surely? I can't be asking for it back. It's not right.'

Her eyes stayed on me.

'You're out of pocket on the Chev as well. You bought that and never used it, now it's a write-off, burnt-out, that policewoman said – It's a lot of money to just lose.'

Jesus, what could I say?

It was an acted line, straight from the television plays I watched when I was home, 'I don't care. It's only money. It won't bring him back. Not for any of us, will it?

I turned away from her. I pretended I was upset, put a hand to my face.

'Hey,' she said. I heard her come down the stepladder. Felt her hand on my shoulder, 'Hey, I didn't mean to upset you.'

I shook my head.

'It's alright.'

I kept my back to her, didn't trust my face. I shouldn't have trusted my mouth. Out came false anguish, a liar's smokescreen, 'Blum dead...Losing Sandra like that...'

What I felt about Sandra two days before, that violent urge to confront her, to demand an explanation, to pillory her for using me, was no longer there; my anger, my condemnation of her, all evaporated. There was only numbness, a longing; and now the shame I'd used her, the girl I knew I loved, to embroider this false emotion in front of Viv, to cover mine and Blum's criminal behaviour. It felt like my own betrayal of her. Tears came, genuine ones.

Only then did I face Viv, let her see the tears. Hiding Blum's activities before his death was for her ultimate benefit, her memory of him, as well as his mam's. But inside I felt the weight of shame, guilt, at what I'd done.

*

When Dolly Sykes had gone, Nancy Gatley brought out mugs of tea and we sat on the steps to drink it. Viv and I had spoken only mundane, practical words since my tears. Blum's mam told us Dolly had rung her husband, one of their farm lads would pick May Bank View's fruit, it would be a help.

'We need to make arrangements for David's funeral', she said, 'He was like his father when it came to church, but I'd still like him buried at St. Thomas's, with Eric.'

She'd already phoned the vicar. The service would be at the church, interment to follow. Refreshments would be at May Bank View. I was grateful and relieved she'd accepted the money.

Viv was keen to help with the arrangements, but Nancy Gatley was insistent, she must go home to rest. 'Would our David want you tiring yourself out?'

In the back parlour she sat at the table with the telephone directory, looking for an undertaker. I asked if she was alright to make funeral arrangements, what about money? She opened the sideboard drawer, took out the torn envelope. 'Look at this.'

I examined it. She told me it added to a thousand pounds. 'Anonymous? Just this verse?' I said.

She nodded, 'If you ask me it's from the vicar. He'd sooner bring it in the night than embarrass me face-to-face. He's a decent man, it's Christian charity.'

That was good enough for me.

I used Blum's van to drive her, with the money, to an undertakers in Ormskirk and I was relieved they'd handle everything with the coroner's office in Chorley; release of the body, transport back to the funeral parlour, many other details. We put a death notice in the Thursday *Advertiser* and I stopped at the council offices and got an application form for her to join the list for a council house. I helped her fill it in and she cried over the loss of May Bank, but I told her she now had no choice, she had to find somewhere to live. Funeral costs would, I knew, take up most of the money. To keep her and May Bank View going, I needed to raise as much cash as I could. Next day I told her I'd sell the van. With the Chev destroyed, she urged me to keep the proceeds for myself, but I refused. I took the Bedford's log book, drove to the farm. I removed labels, anything I thought might link goods to Daltry's, and loaded the van with Blum's stolen gear. Captain Westbrook's German rifle went in as well. Weeks earlier I'd looked up specialists in antique arms and armour and took it to a dealer at a house in Lostock Hall. I told him what the Captain told Blum of the rifle's history, sold it for £150.

Using the name Richard Seddon, Pygon's Farm, the farmer who hanged himself, I left the van's contents for auction, divided between two salerooms in Longridge, with confirmation I'd collect the proceeds in cash. On the drive back I sold the van for £180 at a back-street garage in Ormskirk, caught a bus to May Bank View. I handed over the money to a grateful Nancy Gatley and told her I had to go back to the flat next day. I hadn't paid my rent.

Chapter 48
Please Don't Hate Me

I WAS TWENTY yards down Quinn Street and stopped dead at sight of the police Panda car outside Kitty's. Why was it there? What information did they have about me? Could it be Neil the copper, checking up on me? It was days later, but had someone reported that shot from the Webley revolver, or seen me loading guns into the Cortina, witnessed me trying to fire the shotgun at Kavanagh?

I walked down to the house, tried to look nonchalant, but my heart raced. I stopped between the Panda car and the gap between the hedges. Kitty's front door was ajar. If there was a search in progress, thank God those pistols had gone. I didn't linger, moved on, round the corner, towards The Packet.

An ambulance was parked by the back gate. A uniformed constable stood by as two ambulance men stretchered Kitty out of the back gate. Her next-door neighbour, Mrs O'Carroll, followed her out. Images of violence invaded my mind. Before his death, had Kavanagh shared this address with Pye, or Sutton, in the hope they'd take him back? Had that lout Pye beaten Kitty in his search for the money? I wanted to see her, to check.

The ambulance men turned the stretcher to manoeuvre her inside their vehicle, Kitty spotted me, 'Bloody rent, *Bachgen*, missed again, isn't it?!'

My relief made me eager to please.

'Sorry, Mrs Williams, got it here. I'll pay today, two weeks.'

She pointed at her neighbour, 'You make sure he does, Maggie, no buggerin' off, not payin'!'

I told the copper she was my landlady, 'What's happened?'

Before he could speak Mrs O'Carroll barged in with her version. Despite her name, her local accent was one of the broadest I ever heard. She said she let herself in for their late-morning cup of tea to find Kitty on the floor in her living room, fully-dressed. Kitty was too angry, frustrated, to confirm or deny her fall happened after the pub, or when she got up. The ambulance men suspected cracked ribs, likely a fractured hip.

The copper got a chance to speak, 'They'll take her to Queen's Park, Blackburn, sir.'

'Tha'll 'ave ter shift piggin' Packet ter th'end o'er bed ter kep 'er in th'ospital,' said Mrs O'Carroll.

When the ambulance and Panda car left, I followed Mrs O'Carroll inside, helped put back furniture moved by the ambulance men. I showed her my two weeks' rent money. She collected items Kitty might need, said her son-in-law would drive her to the hospital later. I told her I'd visit as soon as I could and to lock the back door behind her, I'd be away.

I took my rent book from the drawer in the hall table and put the money inside, replaced it and shut the front door, where Mrs O'Carroll had admitted the copper.

A violet- coloured envelope had been pushed back by the door. I picked it up -- my name and address, postmarked Monday, Sandra's handwriting. I sat on the stairs, tore it open.

I can't tell you how sorry I am you had to find out the way you did yesterday. I know I've hurt you. This is all my fault and I should have told you months ago, but there are reasons. Yes, I will be marrying Denny. I've made the decision now and told him, but it was so hard. But now it's made and I'm engaged I can't see you like we did before and I'm so sad it has to be like this.

Denny and me have known each other since we were little. Our parents are best friends and have been nearly all their lives. I've grown to love him over a long time. It might

*seem strange, but he's very old-fashioned. He believes in
waiting till marriage. I tried to make him change his mind,
but he's always stuck to his belief. I have been with other
lads just for curiosity more than anything, but none of it was
important, not at all. But you were so different and I meant
what I said at Snapeback -- it really is the truth.*

*I wanted you the very first day I saw you and those
feelings have never gone away and I still think you're the
kindest person I've ever known. I started to love you as well
as Denny, but in a different way. I did want us to be our own
"lovejob" like your friends Blum and Viv, but you never said
anything. I was so scared if I told you how I felt you'd stop it
all because it wasn't what you wanted and I was never sure
about you and Elaine, that's why I never asked you to give
her up.*

*Denny asked me to marry him last Easter and both sets of
parents seemed so happy and excited, but I kept him waiting
for a long time while I waited for you to say something to me.
I thought you were going to tell me that night on the river at
Mitton, but you didn't, even when you told me it was
definitely all over for good with you and Elaine. When we
went to Snapeback on Friday Denny was still waiting for me
to say yes, but I didn't because I thought being up there you
might say something. I decided if you didn't I would tell you
there and then what I've told you now. Please forgive me for
not having the courage to tell you then and spare you what
happened next day and how horrible it must have been.
Believe me I would've told you in person at the canal on
Saturday and I'm so sorry again how you found out.*

I turned over the single sheet...

*Tho' I have decided to marry Denny I would've told him
no if you'd said something. I'd decided I didn't care what our
parents would think if you told me you loved me. But I was
frightened as well. I know it will last with Denny because
we've known each other so well for so long. With you things
were so lovely and right from the very start that I would
always be terrified that one day everything would just fizzle*

*out and even thinking about that frightens me to death. I hope
you understand all this. I think this is for the best tho' I'm
crying now.*
Please don't hate me.
Sandra

I read it a second time. Then read it again.

*

Talk and laughter combined in a roar. Fag smoke fought
with air. I was drunk. I dropped a coin in the jukebox, went
back to my corner of The Chapmen's Arms, my double
whisky and glass of bitter. Dylan's *Lay, Lady Lay* started to
play for the fourth, or fifth time, I didn't know. I took out the
single sheet of notepaper I'd read a dozen times.

Why? Why did I never say it? Why did I never tell her I
loved her? God knows, I'd thought it often enough, but what
held me back? I'd never been close to it with Elaine, never
even thought about it. With her, there was a sort of
presumption on her part, as if a relationship had survived x
amount of time, it could mean only marriage and, one of her
favourite's, 'settling down.' She never, ever said the three
words to me. Why the hell didn't I finish it all with Elaine
when I knew I'd sooner be with Sandra?

Had I taken Sandra for granted? Were some of the
elements of my character, the part of me that was happy to
drift along with Elaine, present with Sandra? Then there were
the times I'd forgotten what I'd said to Elaine, or she'd
tripped me up on a lie; it always resulted in a row, even one
of our many break-ups. Had my frequent attempts to try not
to lie to Elaine, then my vow never to lie to Sandra, broken
only that once, somehow made me shrink away from telling
her? Was I afraid of being accused of lying by Sandra? I
couldn't have blamed her for thinking so when I continued to
see Elaine.

Or was it to do with drink? Those times I'd believed I
loved Sandra, when I added small moments of our time
together to my mental list, had they been the complacent,

379

mellow fantasies of a drunk? Or were my additions to an endless list a way to avoid, postpone, telling her I loved her simply because I was too frightened to say so first?

I looked at her letter again.

That night at Mitton, I should've told her. Her mood then seemed to me to be about avoiding conversation, the way she'd started back to Edisford without me. Instead it was disappointment I'd not said anything about us. To me it was all about confirmation Elaine and I were at last finished, my desire not to be seen as a liar about that. I'd put Sandra's quietness down to her weariness, overwork. That same concern had influenced our short visit to Snapeback Fell. There, pre-occupied with her tiredness, too quick to blame that stupid fishing match, too stupid to give voice to that feeling of one-ness with her I'd felt up there. Why the hell hadn't I told her? Christ, what a fool I was. Had I voiced my feelings it could've, would've, changed our lives.

I threw the whisky back, washed it down with the bitter, bought the same again, dropped most of the whisky in a gulp. The jukebox fell silent, so I went over, took out coins.

I reached for the buttons to play Dylan. A hand came down on mine.

'Fuck off, we've 'ad enough o' that shite.'

I pulled my hand away. He was my size, similar age.

'Leave me alone!'

I turned back to the jukebox.

He pulled at my left arm, 'I said no more sh...'

It was only a moment, yet enough to spark anger, rage, instant, violent hatred. I twisted my body, moved my feet, hit him as hard as I could. Bone cracked when my fist struck between his eye and nose.

Before I could move, two other lads came at me. One grabbed my shirt front, butted me in the face, I dropped. In seconds, they kicked me in the back, chest and guts, then all three burst out of the pub door, away.

When the landlord confirmed I could walk he pushed me out on to the street, ignored my loud claims of self-defence. I cursed him back into his pub, threatened him with catastrophic bad publicity in my capacity as a *Sentinel* reporter. In bed for thirty-six hours at the grotty flat, I slept a lot, ignored calls on the staircase phone, rationed myself sips of whisky from Saturday's bottle until it was all gone.

*

When I walked into the first of the salerooms in Longridge on the Friday, I was nervous. The bruised eye didn't help my intention to appear ordinary, forgettable, but the proceeds from half the remaining gear Blum stole from Daltry's was waiting for me, £196 in cash. In the second, I was asked to wait and the woman went into another office. Twenty minutes of anxiety passed while I worried whether items had been identified, enquiries made, police informed. Instead I was handed £220 cash and an apology for their slowness settling my account.

Earlier, I'd stood in front of the wardrobe mirror, examined myself. Bruises covered my ribs, but the pain, stiffness, had gone. By now I should've been with Sandra in the Yorkshire Dales. I imagined what she might be doing in Paris, but forced it aside. I did the same when I thought of Blum. Without Kavanagh's interference, he'd be alive, safe in The Lakes, perhaps in a job, anything to save using his mam's money, the means to buy Pygon's Farm. But it was pointless to dwell on things that never happened. I had to keep on, do what had to be done.

I added a third week's rent to the money in my rent book, put it in my pocket. I walked to the bus station cafe and ate a fry-up breakfast with toast and jam, caught the bus for Blackburn. On the walk to Queen's Park Hospital, I looked at a fruit shop display for something I could take-in for Kitty. I'd never known her eat anything other than bacon and eggs so I rejected grapes, bought a quarter flask of Bells whisky at a pub off sales.

Kitty, propped up in bed, fag in hand, greeted me more genially than I anticipated, even more so when she saw my gift. She told me she wasn't allowed booze, cackled at her

381

disobedience, asked me to put it in her bedside cupboard.
There was a similar bottle inside. She welcomed three weeks'
rent, she was low on Senior Service, and signed my rent book
without comment. Her good mood disappeared when she
confirmed her hip was fractured and I asked how long she'd
be kept in.

'Four to five weeks -- five weeks! Too bloody busy, I am,
to be lying here, weeks on end.'

Mrs O'Carroll had visited her each evening, but Kitty
berated her in her absence for her failure to bring in the right
items, forgetting others. I told her I had to get back to work
and left with three letters the maligned Mrs O'Carroll forgot
to take. I promised to visit soon and post her letters, two I
presumed were for relatives in Caernarvon and Llangefni, the
other to Joe Proctor, a widower and retired railway man, who
drank with her in The Packet. I posted them in the first pillar
box I passed.

To save money, I walked north east, thumbed for a lift. I
headed towards Wilpshire with the hope I might reach
Ribchester, then on to the salerooms at Longridge. It took the
best part of an hour, but I was lucky. A farmer from Chipping
in a muddy Landrover had to detour to Longridge to collect
poultry equipment for his wife and dropped me yards away
from the first saleroom on Berry Lane. He talked non-stop,
but didn't ask me a single question.

Pleased with the £416 raised, I pushed my luck as a hitch-
hiker, walking while thumbing, but reached the White Bull at
Alston, on the Preston road, without a lift. Inside the pub I
ordered a pint, took it to a corner. I was the only customer, so
I merged the two bundles of cash without being seen,
checked it, and tore paperwork from both sales into tiny
pieces I dumped in an ashtray. I couldn't present the
proceeds of Blum's theft to his mam; the only solution was
another anonymous envelope, a random line from the
dictionary of Biblical quotations, another act of Christian
charity.

Even as I swallowed the last of the pint, I was on my feet, ready for another. Nothing unusual, but this time I paused, sat back on the bench, stared at the empty glass in my hand. If I hadn't been drunk I wouldn't have punched that lad in the Chapmen's Arms. Nor would I have lost control and tried to shoot Kavanagh in the face and, later, that other attempt to murder him with the shotgun. Drink triggered, drove, the rage that made me give chase, urged me to run him off the road at Brinscall, determined to try to murder him a third time. Even worse, my drinking contributed to Blum's death. I opened a bottle of whisky when I should have phoned the Sharrocks' and caught Blum in time, stopped him driving back to the flat, into Kavanagh's armed ambush. And when he did return, it was me who was too drunk to manage the armed custody of Kavanagh, to enable Blum to get clean away, to save his unnecessary death, even Kavanagh's own life. The seriousness of what my drinking had caused was only now in my consciousness. Even if Blum hadn't died at Brinscall, got away with the satchel of cash, I might now be in custody for murder, my only prospect life imprisonment. Christ.

My drinking affected my relationships as well. The times with Elaine I drank to anaesthetize myself into not showing irritation, not starting ridiculous arguments: other times when drink produced exactly those results. It fuelled my deceptions, my easy lies, my carelessness; that absurd drunken suggestion of marriage, forgotten the next morning. With Sandra, there were no lies, and though I lived for our times together, I wasn't often sober in her company. Through drink I forgot I told her about that marriage thing with Elaine. Did the drink compensate for the flatness I so often felt on days I couldn't see her? Did it enhance my delight, my pleasure, when we were together? Was it the reason I never questioned her about anyone else in her life, content to bowl along, drinking myself into contentedness; happy to live in the moment, ignorant and careless of how she might feel?

Had my drinking dulled and flattened my emotions so much I couldn't function in a normal way?

These thoughts impelled me to go to the bar, buy more drink to wash them away, but I resisted, put my glass on the bar, left the pub. I didn't want to drink anymore. For the first time, I was frightened what it could do to me. I stuck out my thumb ahead of approaching vehicles, hitch-hiked into a sober life.

Chapter 49
Worry and Tests

DRINK, OR MY drinking, surged to the top of my mother's agenda when I reached home early evening and she saw my black eye. I didn't tell her I struck the first blow in drunken rage, but admitted I'd been in a scuffle over my choice of pub music.

'I know how upset you must be, but drinking isn't going to help. Fighting in pubs won't either.'

I let her pillory me a bit longer before I announced I'd not be drinking anymore. She agreed it was a sensible action, moved on to her next item.

'We've been worried about you.'

I was away most days of the year, couldn't see three days being significant. 'You don't usually worry.'

'It's not just me. So were Mrs Gatley -- and David's girlfriend.'

'Viv?'

'She phoned your flat and didn't get a reply, so when she'd gone, I rang too. Time like this, you can't blame us for wondering where you were.'

'Viv came here?'

'I'm sure she's better things to be doing, but she was worried about you.'

'How was she?'

She told me how tired Viv looked, how she was still at work, even before the funeral. 'She's a trooper, that's for sure. She helped me to cut the back hedge, wouldn't take no for an answer. Even though she's trying to help Mrs Gatley,' she paused, added, 'Like you were supposed to be doing.'

She relented when I told her about Kitty's fall, my time in bed after being battered, visiting the hospital in Blackburn. While she made the tea, I had a bath, chose another Biblical quotation to type-up, to go in an envelope with the cash from the salerooms.

It was in my jacket pocket when I arrived at May Bank View where Viv stood beside the Norton, putting on her biker's jacket.

'You're back then?'

She saw my eye, 'God, how did you get that?'

I told her what I told my mother.

'Couldn't you have posted the rent money? Better than getting duffed-up and going missing.'

'My mum said you'd been round. Sorry you were worried.'

She nodded back to the house, 'Not just me.'

Her eyes on mine, made me feel like I was lying as I related Kitty's accident, the visit to see her hospital.

She zipped-up her jacket, 'I went up there when I couldn't get you on the phone.'

'To the flat? When?'

She held my gaze. I felt uncomfortable.

'After my shift this morning, must've been after nine.'

'You missed me. That'd be after I got the bus to visit Kitty. There was no need to trail over there.'

'Well...I *was* worried. I thought you might've...I don't know...You going missing, that it was something to do with Sandra?'

'As far as I know she's still abroad.'

'Oh, yeah, of course.' She paused, 'No message, though? A postcard, or something?'

The content of Sandra's letter felt too personal to discuss, even with Viv. And the way she stared at me, forced me to hold her gaze, made me feel she was probing, suspicious.

I shook my head. I expected sympathetic words, perhaps a re-iteration of her belief Sandra would explain all, in time, but nothing came. She left for work.

Nancy Gatley added to my unease over Viv. When I'd explained my black eye, the extended stay at Quinn Street, I apologised for worrying her.

'Oh, I wasn't worried, love. I thought you might want some time to yourself. It was Vivien doing the worrying, asking if you'd phoned, if I knew what you were doing?'

Not what Viv told me. And it sounded like she'd told my mum the opposite as well.

'Poor girl needs time off before the funeral in my opinion. Though I remember after Eric died, what do they call it? -- Yes, I threw myself into work.'

She said no more and I helped her in the garden until it went dark She told me Blum's funeral was confirmed for the following Tuesday, showed me the brief report in the Thursday *Advertiser* of the deaths of motorists David Gatley, aged 21, of Lydiate, and Stephen Kavanagh, aged 26, of Burscough, at Brinscall.

I watched television with her, to keep her company, and my first test as a non-drinker arrived with a bottle of Uncle Walter's plum wine. I made a joke of my abstinence, the fracas in the Chapmen's Arms, the need to leave it alone. 'All things in moderation,' she said, but I declined the wine. My second test as a non-drinker came when I left. I had to kill at least an hour to make sure she'd fallen asleep before I could deliver the envelope. Any other time, I'd've looked for company in the Soldier, the Plough Horse, had a few pints. I could've gone home, but going out again would attract comment. The prospect of lemonade instead of beer was unattractive and I walked north, passed the Soldier on the other side of the road, then east along the lanes towards the old Waggon and Horses, turning to join the canal at Downholland. Walking under a full moon along the towpath, invoked memories of Blum; all our lives, this waterway that divided the parish, had been our favoured, discreet route, to move from north to south, whatever we were up to, night or day.

An hour later there were no lights on at May Bank View and I pushed the envelope, containing the random quotation and £416 pounds, through the letterbox. I'd do everything I could to get Nancy Gatley a council house, but I'd run out of ways to raise any more money for her.

*

The third test of my sobriety was Blum's funeral. It was the first I'd attended for someone I knew well. Every new reporter on *The Sentinel* was sent to funerals to record the names of all mourners for publication. It was a two-fold exercise: to sell papers to those who wanted to see their name in print and an exercise in accuracy and name-spelling for young reporters. Complaints over a single omission, a misspelt name, meant a stern, personal memo from old man Henty. I'd spent fearful hours waiting inside churches, at wakes, often drinking, struggling to double-check names, searching for stray mourners. I disliked funerals.

Had I drank too much, anything at all, I might have made a comment to upset those who gathered. For like so many funerals, I'd witnessed, Blum's seemed inadequate.

With Ted, Neville the under-keeper, John Sykes, and two male neighbours of Nancy Gatley, I was a coffin bearer. Nancy Gatley sat in the front pew with Ted and Marion. Behind them were Viv, Fozzy, my mum and me. Arnold and Glenys Sharrock were at the back. I was cheered to see one or two faces from the workforce at Daltry's, a handful who were at the church school with us, and a number of farmers and growers I knew by sight. Had any of them had bought Blum's stolen goods?

I gave the traditional reading from *Ecclesiastes* at Nancy Gatley's request, but I should've given the eulogy. The Vicar's version was well-meant, but bland; a scant, factual record of his short life. Yet if I were to have given it, what could I have said? I knew more about him than anyone in church, his mam included, but the events of the past two years, those of recent days, in which his desire to change his mother's life, whatever it took, in my opinion a shining goal, could not be revealed. It was better he was left to rest in peace; his reputation intact, his most admirable action in life to raise that vital money, remaining unknown to anyone but me.

Back at May Bank View, my mum helped Viv and Dolly Sykes to make sure mourners had their cake and sandwiches. In contrast to Walter's funeral on a bitter winter's day, mourners spilled out into a garden washed with warm, autumn sunshine. It was the sort of October day in Blum's favourite season that might've seen us beating on a Tarlscough partridge shoot, or fishing for elusive big perch; stopping off for a pint or two to round-off the day.

Nancy Gatley offered bottled beer, whisky and plum wine. Only Viv queried my choice of orange squash. Other times she would've made a joke at my explanation I was taking a break from drinking. Of course it was her boyfriend's funeral, her mind was elsewhere, but she only nodded, said, 'Oh, right.' There was no contact between us the rest of the day, almost as if she were avoiding me. Though I didn't go out of my way to talk to her, or to mingle; spent most of the time on the edge of the company, remembering times gone with Blum. A few times I was aware of her, watching me, or so it seemed. I left when Marion and Ted said they'd sit with Nancy until bedtime, glad to be away.

In the remaining days of my time off, I even went fishing, found myself sobbing for an hour or more at Hill House Pit when I realised I'd never, ever, cast a line without the presence of Blum, never would in future. Most of those days were spent helping in the garden at May Bank View, arranging for boxes of fruit to go to a greengrocer's in Aintree, always a responsibility of Blum's. On my last day I gave Nancy Gatley my numbers at Quinn Street and *The Sentinel*, in case she needed me, told her I'd visit as often as I could. I wished I could be more optimistic for her, but promised her I'd do my best to help find her somewhere to live. That hopeless promise was to intrude on my sober sleep.

I didn't see or hear from Viv before I had to go back to work.

Chapter 50
Jigsaw and Verdict

I COULDN'T FACE passing the door of the advertising department on my first morning. I couldn't cope if I came face-to-face with Sandra. For days I used the back stairs from the print hall up to the compositors' room to reach our newsroom, or to leave the building. I had to stop myself more than once when I went to check under my typewriter for a note. I made a decision to avoid her, to try to put the loss of Blum and Sandra out of mind, my energies into work.

I thought Geoff might still be embarrassed over his drunken visit to the flat. He was business-like, no banter, when he despatched me to cover the Magistrates' court; no mention of that night at Quinn Street, or what I'd done in my holidays. It wasn't until evening when, about to knock-off, he asked if he could have a word. He looked serious.

My first thought was he'd found his car was damaged, evidence of blood, something to show the Cortina had been used. My only option was to lie, deny all knowledge. I was relieved, then surprised, when he told me he knew about the fracas at The Chapmen's Arms. And, more to the point, my drunken threats to the landlord about bad publicity in *The Sentinel.*

He asked me for my version of the story. I said it was self-defence against an aggressive yob. I told him I couldn't remember my threats; I was too drunk, upset about other matters.

'Fuckin' 'ell, it's a good job old Henty were off fishing in Yorkshire, an' he were put through to yours truly. Ron Atherton worked here as a comp before he went into licensed trade. His old man and his grandfather were printers here, the Athertons and Arthur Henty go way back.'

He lit an Embassy, 'If Henty'd got wind of all this yer'd've 'ad no job this morning. As it is, think on will yer. I've squared things with Atherton, but no matter how arse'oled yer might get in future, no daft threats; no bringing *The Sentinel* into it, eh? And stay out The Chapmen's for a while.'

I apologised.

'Anyroad, cocker, what were yer so upset about?'

I told him my best friend at home was killed in a car accident. I didn't want to point towards Sandra, give any clues, said my girlfriend had chucked me for someone else as well. Straight away, he was supportive. I thought he might suspect fibs, like the one about my gran's funeral, but typical Geoff, he asked my friend's name; then made a connection, 'Brinscall. We carried a couple of paras on it; Tuesday paper, front page, week before last. I noticed one of the lads came from that place yer from.'

He pulled the edition from the pile on the side desk, let me read it. It was brief, factual. I pushed it away. He stood, put on his jacket, 'Well, yer've had yer official bollocking, me old cock. Fancy a flyer at The Boot?'

I told him I was giving drink a rest.

'Wish I had a quid for every reporter told me that. Mind yer, seen a few newspaper careers flushed down the shitter with booze.' He laughed, 'Pot calling kettle, eh? Promised Rita I'd cut back after I had to stay at yours. Thank God for fishing, eh? Reckon the pair of us'd best get straight home.'

If I'd not kept out of The Boot I might have heard the news about Sandra earlier. Two girl colleagues were talking about her when they came back from lunch. Sandra hadn't returned to the paper after her time off – she'd gone to work for her new fiancé at Barwise and Son, no notice served, no leaving do, nothing. 'Good on 'er,' said Christine, 'She won't have to do a tap when she's wed, that Barwise lot are minted.'

For a few moments, the remark made me uncertain, angry, with Sandra, but I knew better than the gossips and believed what she'd said in her letter was sincere, truthful. An urge to go out, to drink, surfaced, but I quelled it. It was my fault Sandra and I were no longer together. I'd have put money on my belief her move to Barwise's estate agency wasn't solely for her own benefit.

*

Weeks passed and I worked hard. I took on more night jobs to bolster my requests to Geoff for clear weekends so I could go home, look-in on Blum's mam, help as much as I could at May Bank View.

Without Blum what spare time I had during the working week was flat. I missed his phone calls to the office and Quinn Street, missed him full-stop. Sandra's absence was close to depressing. No notes, no clandestine meets, no returns to a chilly flat to find her snuggled up in my bed, full of fun and gossip. The times when I wanted to drink myself to sleep, into unconsciousness, were more than I'd anticipated, but I refused to give-in. Since I was a boy, I'd known several drunks. I didn't want to end up alcoholic like Kitty, any of them; though when I visited her twice a week, most times I took her a quarter of Bells. Other evenings, I resisted the call of the pubs, read more books than I had in two years, but sometimes found myself staring at the grubby walls of my flat. I now hated it. I started to check *The Sentinel* small-ads for a new place to live.

A new place for Blum's mam was never far from mind. I rang the council housing department, but without any success, the queue was long. I signed up with estate agencies at home, had rental details posted to me. Those with large gardens were far too expensive. It looked like she'd have to settle for an emergency let when she was formally homeless, most likely to be a flat with no garden, in another neighbourhood.

In this time, I never saw, or heard from Viv. I could've phoned her, but her behaviour, her staring at me, her distance at Blum's funeral, her apparent suspicion, made me uneasy. Then one Saturday afternoon as I walked towards May Bank

View, she turned out of the driveway on the Norton. I put my hand up, but she rode past me, accelerated. She may not have seen me, but I doubted it. When I asked Nancy Gatley if she'd heard from Viv, I discovered there'd been one phone call since the funeral; today was her first visit.

I helped her remove soil from a mass of unearthed dahlia tubers. I said, 'She could've managed to look-in a bit more often.'

Nancy Gatley was dismissive, 'She's got her whole life in front of her, love. Best she looks forward, no hanging on to the past.'

When I told her Viv hadn't been in touch with me, she said, 'The three of you spent a lot of time together. Perhaps she doesn't want reminding, love. I wouldn't worry about it. Life changes -- you need to look forward yourself.'

'What made her turn up today?'

'To see if I wanted her to take me to the inquest. It's on Thursday. She has to be a witness.'

*

I caught a bus to Chorley on a foggy November morning to attend Blum's inquest.

Blum's mam had turned down Viv's offer to drive her there in her father's car; said she'd seen enough of such things on television to want to listen to officialdom going over the awful details of her own son's death.

Viv's attendance as a witness might have un-nerved me, but I knew about evidence. She might have suspicions about events before Blum's death, but that wasn't evidence. I'd covered maybe a dozen inquests since I started at the paper. Most were easy-going, almost informal, compared to the point- scoring, combat of a trial in a criminal court. What could Viv tell the coroner? -- Nothing that might reveal our robbery of Sutton, the devastating interference of Kavanagh, the true reason for the location and cause of Blum's death.

When the inquest date reached Geoff Sillitoe's attention, he asked if I needed time off to attend. I told him I'd be going, so I might as well cover it. 'Up to you, cocker, but no disrespect to yer mate, it'll go on the spike if there's no local angle.' He told me to take the day off anyway.

The coroner's court was housed in an old-fashioned single-storey, red brick and stone building, set among lawns and shrubberies. A uniformed copper stood on the lawn, smoking. Inside, I looked for Viv, but she hadn't arrived. A few people were sitting in the hallway, others talked to an usher. I went into the old-fashioned coroner's courtroom where the Press bench was occupied by another, older reporter, introduced myself. He worked for a press agency from Bolton.

Viv arrived, wearing her biker leathers, moments before the coroner entered and took his seat. Our eyes met. I nodded to her, but there was no smile, no return nod. That could've been due to a teenage girl anxious to sit, who hustled Viv along the public benches, but I wasn't sure.

The first of the two inquests listed didn't take long. An old man found dead on his sofa was found to have died after choking on a sandwich, the presence of a half full bottle of rum and his blood alcohol level suggested he had attempted to eat while lying drunk, listening to the radio.

The inquest into the deaths of David Gatley and Stephen Kavanagh were outlined by the coroner, a distinguished man with a kindly face, gleaming bald head, a crimson bow tie. First evidence came from a lady hospital pathologist. Blum and Kavanagh both died from multiple injuries consistent with their cars leaving the road at speed; neither had alcohol in their bodies at the time of death.

The uniformed copper described his and a colleague's attendance. He said both cars left the road at the same downhill bend in poor weather conditions. Questioned by the coroner, he said it was impossible to say whether that had happened at the same time, there were no witnesses. The coroner asked if there was any evidence the young drivers may have been racing, there'd been recent incidents. The copper said there was no evidence, or witnesses, to suggest that, none to show the two drivers knew each other. The coroner questioned him about the accident report, his evidence of mud on the road. The copper said it was his opinion the mud on the road resulted from the thunderstorm, that it caused both drivers to lose control. When the coroner turned to why the drivers were in that area at the time, he called Kavanagh's mother, Elizabeth. She said she'd not seen her son for two weeks, had no idea if he worked in the Chorley area, or had friends there. The careworn Mrs Kavanagh returned to her seat, wiping her eyes, to be comforted by the teenage girl I guessed was Kavanagh's sister.

The coroner called Viv, referred to a statement she'd made. Questioned, she gave the same theory she suggested to me after Blum's death; that he'd changed his mind about the job in Lancaster, possibly gone to visit a friend, lost his way in the thunderstorm. Asked if she had any idea of his destination, she said she hadn't. Her voice cracked, 'I'd like to think he was coming to see me. To tell me he wasn't going to work away.'

While the coroner started his narrative of findings, I sensed Viv looking at me. When I looked up from my shorthand, she turned away. I felt for her, for Mrs Kavanagh, who had a crumpled hanky to her eye, but I told myself yet again it was best Blum's death remained untarnished in Viv's memory. And I imagined Elizabeth Kavanagh would prefer the remembrance of her son's death unsullied by the truth of his activities in life.

The coroner recorded a verdict of accidental death on both men, offered condolences, and with a glance at the press agency reporter and I, an unspoken request for publicity, said he would write to the county highways surveyor requesting urgent investigation into the cause of mud on the road at Brinscall. He asked to see us when the court rose.

I didn't want to see the coroner. I wanted to see Viv; to ask why she was keeping her distance from me. But it wasn't acceptable in local newspapers to snub such a request. Viv left with the others from the public benches. The coroner wanted to push county highways over the dangerous mud, so we agreed to angle our reports along that line. It was ten minutes before we got away, everyone had gone.

I declined the agency reporter's invitation to have a pint. We parted at the front gate and I headed for the bus stop, my afternoon free. I'd already decided to use it to find another, less grotty flat, or bedsit.

I stopped when I saw Viv. She was sitting side-saddle on her Norton, a fag in hand, her outline unclear at thirty yards in the mid-day fog. I walked towards her, thinking how to broach her distant behaviour. She slipped off the motorbike, tossed the cigarette to the ground, took a couple of steps towards me.

She knocked me off-balance straight away.

'Did you enjoy that?'

'What?'

'Seeing me give evidence I know wasn't the truth? – Why he was in that Brinscall place?'

'Sorry…'

She took another step forward.

'You and Blum lied to me for months.' She jabbed her finger at me, 'You've been lying your head off since he was killed.'

I forced a laugh.

'What are you talking about?'

'He was up to something. And you were in on it, weren't you?'

'That's ridiculous. I wasn't in on…'

'If you weren't, you were covering up for him, still are.'

'Viv, I'm not.'

'He told me he was staying at his mother's the night before the fishing match, but he wasn't there. I checked with Mrs Gatley. He was with you, at your flat, or somewhere else, wasn't he?'

Telling the truth wasn't an option. I had to lie.

'No, he wasn't.'

She stuck her hand inside her leather jacket, pulled out a piece of cardboard, held it up, across it were the handwritten words PRIVATE PARKING.

'How do you explain this?'

Like the last time I saw it, despite the ink smudged by rain, I recognised Blum's scrawled block capitals.

I shrugged, feigned puzzlement, 'What about it?'

'I found it under the hedge at your flat, that morning when I went there, the time you did your disappearing trick. Recognise the writing?'

I shook my head, 'No.'

Her face was ugly in its contempt.

'You knew him years longer than me and I'd recognise it anywhere. It's Blum's. The three of us turned up for the fishing match and he'd saved a space for the Chev. I didn't think at first, but it came to me when I was thinking about our last day.'

Why the hell hadn't I realised that danger at the time? Why hadn't Blum?

'To put this sign up, he must've been at yours before he picked up me and Foz in Tarleton. I reckon he was with you the night before.'

I lied again.

'Anyone could've made that sign – the neighbours were worried about cars blocking the place up for the fishing match.'

'No, you can't get away with that. I helped to clear the rubbish out of your kitchen that morning, remember…'

She turned the cardboard over, showed me the print of a cornflakes packet.

'…and put it in the bin. There was a cornflakes box with the back torn off, just like this.'

Christ, what lengths had she gone to with her suspicions?

'This is stupid. What are you trying to get at?'

'I looked in the bin by the back gate.' She waved the cardboard, 'The same torn box was still there. And this bit matched like a bloody jigsaw. It came from your flat.'

I shook my head, blew out, as though I were listening to someone insane.

'There's the van as well? Not there when I turned up to meet the police at May Bank at six o' clock on the Sunday morning, but you brought it back that night.'

'I told you about that.'

'Oh, yeah, your dad moving flagstones for a patio?'

'Yeah.'

She laughed, 'Did you know I helped your mum to cut her hedge? I told her a patio'd look good in the garden. Know what she said, eh? "That's a good idea, never thought of that. Perhaps next summer..." Not a word about moving flagstones. Not a flagstone in sight.'

I was desperate, 'I didn't mean a patio at ours. It was for a mate of me dad's.'

'You're doing it now! It's one lie after another, isn't it? That's not all about that van. You couldn't get shut of it quick enough. And you gave Blum's mam the three-hundred-and-thirty- quid you said you'd got for it. It doesn't ring right with me. You'd lost the Chev, then you give up the van.'

I still felt that terrible shame when I said, 'I told you my feelings on that.'

'You've moaned about trainee reporters' wages since you started that job, but you didn't bat an eyelid about losing over five-hundred quid on both motors. I'm wondering if you did buy the Chev yourself, if it was all lies from Blum that he borrowed from you to buy the van?'

I came straight back at her, 'That's a rotten thing to say. You know I wanted his business to be a success, to get him on the straight and narrow after being done, getting sent to Havershawe.'

Her eyes were on mine.

'I don't believe you. Nobody who cries poverty'd let him get away without paying back anything for a year. You know what I think? – I think you and him have been up to something for ages; something that's brought in money for both of you. You didn't lend him money. You and him already had it, didn't you?'

I could feel my neck, face, flush, hoped it looked like anger at a wild allegation.

'Christ, Viv, this is all in your imagination.'

She bristled, anger not far away, 'Well, I know what's not in my head. I know about cars, second-hand ones most of all. That van, that year, the wear on it. You'd get one-fifty to one-eighty for it, not three-hundred and odd. I checked with me dad, he knows the trade inside out. He agreed with me. Where did the extra cash come from?'

She meant the money from the sale of the German rifle, I bluffed, 'I can tell you where I sold it, you can check.'

She ignored that. 'Just tell me what was really going on? That weekend he died?'

'For Christ's sake, nothing!'

'And why did you disappear for a couple of days? Don't give me that balls about paying your ...

'Jesus, it's the truth!'

'What were you really up to? Why did you really get beaten-up? Who have you upset, eh? Who have you crossed? Is that why Blum got killed? Was he being chased by that Kavanagh feller when they skidded in that bloody mud?'

'I told you. We weren't up to anything. I don't know why he was there? For all I knew he was in Lancaster!'

'I don't believe all that stuff about Lancaster either. It was too sudden, Blum telling me right at the last minute. You said you were going away with Sandra an' all. I don't believe that, I reckon you and Blum were running away from something – something that happened when he didn't stay at his mum's place, when the van was missing.'

'I think you're...all wound up over Blum, you're grieving, not thinking straight.'

Her face showed her contempt, but she kept on. 'What about that phone call to the Sharrocks' after the upset over Sandra? I keep remembering what you said. Glenys said you were in a right panic to talk to Blum, wanted her to chase outside and catch him. When I rang you back you said you only wanted to wish him luck in The Lakes. Not Lancaster, The Lakes…'

I'd almost forgotten that.

'Jesus, it was a slip of the tongue, that's all…'

'Was that where you two were planning to hide away from whatever you'd done?'

Close as she was to the truth, I shook my head, as though in complete disbelief.

'I know Blum sometimes told me lies, small things, but not like this, not like I've proved. You're a bigger liar than he could ever be. Elaine called you a liar. That was her biggest complaint about you...'

Her tears started to come

'I believed you weeks and weeks ago when you damn near swore on the Bible you'd stop him if he was going to risk prison. I was stupid enough to believe you and all along it was lies and now he's dead. That's what hurts. You knew, but you didn't stop him! You were in on it yourself.'

'Viv, Viv…'

'You're a liar.'

I made a move towards her, to try to mollify her. She slapped me hard across the face with her gloved hand.

'Elaine was right – you lying fucking bastard.'

I stood, shocked, my face stinging.

She turned, strode back to the Norton, threw the piece of cardboard aside. She swung her leg over the motorbike.

She shouted, 'I wish to God I could prove what I think, but I can't and you know it.'

'Viv, you've got it all...'

'I don't want to see you again –Ever.'

She kick-started the bike, swung it around, accelerated away, into the mist. Exhaust fumes from the powerful engine lingered for moments; then mingled with the fog, disappeared, like that friendship with her I didn't want to end.

*

I stared at the livid patch on my cheek, reflected in the bus window, like a mark of shame. Viv was right, had I tried I could've stopped everything that lead to Blum's death. But drinking hard, craving the thrill of taking risks, spurred by Blum's drive to steal the money, I didn't. How different things might've worked out had Blum, from the start, put his pride aside, shared the problem of May Bank with Viv. How different if I'd refused to go along with him, perhaps took a risk on our friendship, and told Viv of his problems, his plans.

The bus passed a sign that pointed the way to Brinscall. I never wanted to go there again. It would remain in my past. Like I would remain in Viv's past; a bad memory, something to be pushed further away as days passed.

I regretted the loss of Viv in my life. From the start of Blum's romance with her I never felt like I played the gooseberry. We spent a lot of time together, I liked her, was sure she liked me. Through Blum's time in Havershawe, we saw a lot of each other. I even saved her life, as Blum would have it. She was a decent person, a friend I should've valued. How long after Blum's death might we have kept that friendship, but for my lies? Yet like Nancy Gatley said, she might be better off not reminded of the past. Life does change, as she said, perhaps Viv and I both should look forward.

My first step was a new place to live, somewhere with no memories. I toured the town centre and the shops I knew that displayed postcards offering rentals in their windows. I chose one, called round and used most of what was left of my wages to pay a small deposit. It was a similar set-up to Quinn Street, but not as big, a 1930s house. My future landlord, who lived on the ground floor of the house, was a long-distance coach driver, a widower, but the place was immaculate, the rent a pound a week more than Kitty charged -- and it was a long walk to the nearest pub.

Kitty was due home the following week. In the back of my mind was a dread that while she regained her health, it might be too easy to become reliant on me. I hated my imagined image of her wheedling for me to walk her to The Packet, then escort her home; over time to become some old retainer, her bloody butler. Next time I visited Queen's Park Hospital, I'd give her a week's notice on my tenancy.

Walking back to Quinn Street, I wondered if she might be awkward over my returnable key money, held against damage. There was a stain on the carpet from a glass of British port Sandra once knocked over. I still hadn't tried to repair the fag burn on my bedside table from the night of Blum's death. And the bullet crater in the landing wall needed to be fixed. I stopped off at a hardware shop, spent the last coins on sandpaper, a bag of Polyfilla and a tin of varnish.

The fag burn was easier than I thought. Ten minutes with sandpaper and it looked presentable after smearing varnish over it with a pad of bog paper. The stain on the carpet was impossible. I moved the armchair to put the stain in shadow, hoped it would pass any inspection. The crater took longer. I had to wait for it to dry, build up it up again with more filler. When it was dry, I sanded it smooth. The problem was paint. How could I match it in with the landing and stairs colour Sandra called 'loony bin green?'

I found a candle, went downstairs, out to Kitty's garden shed. I struck a match. I'd seen a lot of old paint tins there when I liberated the parrot cage for Fozzy's magpie. In the light of the candle were a dozen or more tins on a bench piled with neglected garden tools, old bathroom tiles and other junk. I pulled away a pair of moth-eaten curtains to reach them. I held the candle up, searching for telltale pale green drips around a tin that might finish the job.

I could so easily have missed it. It was pushed between the paint cans and the wall, a leather schoolboy's satchel. I leaned over, dragged it out, scrabbled open the buckles with one hand, while holding the candle. Inside were the bundles of banknotes Blum and me robbed at gunpoint from Sutton.

Paint forgotten, I legged upstairs with the satchel, counted and recounted the money on my bed. In twenties, tens, fives and pound notes, there was £17,860. I stared at it, now rewrapped with elastic bands. Clever Blum hid it during those tense moments when I had Kavanagh at gunpoint, when I thought the Chev wouldn't start; that Blum was trapped. He wanted to ensure the safety of the money, his mam's future, more than anything else. I almost laughed over his words to me in that wet field moments before he died, *'Money for mam. In the Chev. Get money for mam...'* Not 'In the Chev,' 'In the *shed.*'

Blum lost his life as a result of the robbery of that money. I took on that job for kicks, but also for Nancy Gatley, because Blum was my friend. Now it was my duty as his friend to finish the job.

It would be a bigger part of my life than I could imagine.

*

For years I kept track of people I knew at the time I worked on *The Sentinel*. I even had a subscription to the paper until it closed in 1996.

Elaine became area manager of a different bank in the East Midlands. Her work friend, Pete, became her husband and the financial director of a national charity. They had two children. He was her type, after all.

Viv left to live in Australia within a year of Blum's death and, as she wished, we never saw each other again. When the internet arrived I contacted her through *Friends Reunited*, not expecting a reply, but I got one. 'Please don't ever try to contact me again.' From her entry, I learned she was married with a son, trained nurses in Melbourne. Had she sent a different reply, I believe I would, at last, have told her the truth.

Sandra had two sons and a daughter from her marriage to **Denny**. She helped create a successful property company that brought new life to old cotton mills. I once saw a photograph of her daughter in *Lancashire Life* magazine; my heart jumped, she looked so like her mother at the same age.

Sandra died of breast cancer in 1992 at the age of 42. I heard too late to attend her funeral, but days later visited the churchyard in her home village, said my own goodbye at her grave; watched the glow of sunset across Snapeback Fell and cried for the loss of a lovely girl. I understand why Denny never remarried.

Geoff Sillitoe became the editor of *Tight Lines* and was at the vanguard of VHS angling personality videos. When he's not fishing and filming in the Caribbean, Australia or the Far East with **Rita**, he wets a line on the cut, still organises SACOAM. He is the owner of the *Yours Truly, Geoff Sillitoe –Angling Adventures*, the YouTube channel, with several million subscribers. We keep in touch, but I've never told him the story he slept through that night after the fishing match.

'Caernarvon Kitty' Williams died of exposure after a fall in deep snow one night in 1980 on her way back from The Packet. I learned from *The Sentinel* she once travelled the world as a stewardess on ocean liners. Her husband had been a hero of the Atlantic Convoys, later a captain with Cunard, information she never disclosed to me.

Neil Posset had a successful career in the police. Before retirement in Lytham St Annes, he was a Detective Chief Inspector with the Regional Crime Squad, a proper copper. He hunted war criminals in the former Yugoslavia. I never saw him again after that night when a call of duty saved me from certain imprisonment. He married a girl from the town where we both worked.

Alan 'Delly' Delamere served numerous prison sentences. His last venture was a bungled off-licence robbery in Southport. He was murdered by suffocation in Wymott Prison, Lancashire, in 1995. A senior detective contact told me he was a police informant.

Bert Travis died alone in a Blackpool bedsit in 1988, undiscovered for two weeks. He was due to appear in court for stealing sausages and beer from the local Spar shop. He committed suicide. **Mrs Travis** re-married, to a bookie from Morecambe.

Peter 'Fozzy' Foster became the joint owner, with **Paul Sharrock**, of the expanded Sharrocks' growing business after the deaths of **Arnold** and **Glenys**. Between them they established a horticultural company near Amsterdam. His proudest moment was when he sent Arnold and Glenys on a Mediterranean cruise to mark their retirement. I still see him and his wife and daughters, but he lost touch with Viv.

Ted Crossman died in **Marion's** arms in the pub after a shoot in 1983. The roll-ups, booze and his over-excitable nature caught up with him in a fatal heart attack. Marion told me he was blathering in full flow with a glass of Cutty Sark in his hand when it happened. He died surrounded by friends he'd known all his life. Marion had to leave her home, but Tarlscough Estate's owner, Sir Julian Leggat, provided her with an annuity and a bungalow for life in her native Fylde. Each Christmas and Easter before Marion died, I drove Blum's mam to visit her near Weeton.

Nancy Gatley became a friend.

My wife, **Anne,** clicked with her as soon as they met, in part because of their shared passion for gardening. Anne took on the heavier work when Blum's mam could no longer manage.

For more than 30 years between Blum's death and Anne's discovery of her body in her greenhouse, Nancy Gatley never knew her Victorian semi-detached house, not a mile from the former May Bank View, was owned by me.

Nor did Anne.

It was bought on my behalf anonymously in early December 1971 by a back-street solicitor in Preston for £5,250, my name on the title deeds, stored by him. Then, before computers, money-laundering regulations and invasive data collection, it was easier to cover your financial tracks. My last criminal act, to retain my anonymity, was to avoid a normal estate agent's viewing of Nancy Gatley's new home. Instead I sneaked up from the canal bank, crossed two gardens, and broke into the empty house.

It was a frantic period for me. I knew little of house-buying and finance and all my spare time was spent researching the subject. At more cost I managed to move Nancy Gatley into her new house, with a largish garden, sheds and greenhouse, ten days before the lease on May Bank View expired. I told Nancy a mate was doing me a favour, but employed a landscape gardener to transport and replant shrubs from May Bank at the new place.

The whole venture involved more lies. Blum's mam was delighted with the new house, but curious about her low rent. The back-street solicitor set-up a company called C and E, her new landlord. I told Nancy it was a church charity that dealt with hardship cases for C of E parishioners. All contact between her and I was conducted on headed notepaper, via a PO Box number. Forgery and false names were all part of it. Her modest rent cheque went straight back into C and E's account. Only when she found a job in a shop, with it new friends, more dress-making work, did I increase, for appearances, the monthly sum. Whether she ever suspected me and my close attention to her housing matters, always ready to talk, write, to her landlord for her, I never knew.

Meanwhile, I left *The Sentinel* after eighteen months. I needed to be home in Lydiate, closer to Nancy Gatley, to continue my duplicitous life. Sometimes that life was complicated. Before I met and married, Anne, I found a job at the Thursday *Advertiser*, stayed the rest of my working life.

High interest rates until 1990 kept the balance in the C and E accounts healthy, but rates, then council tax, maintenance and improvement costs were a drain on remaining funds. I dipped a toe into investments. I was never rash, but the proceeds were steady and sufficient. Nancy's funeral costs and headstone work all but exhausted the last of the money.

In those days before her funeral and Anne reading my account of Blum's last two years and my involvement, our discussions, rows, over the kitchen table went on for hours. She didn't want to benefit, by residence or sale, of a house bought with stolen money, but now worth an enormous amount more. How could I have spent so much time and effort investing and dealing with thousands of pounds when we'd had such a struggle to buy a tiny terraced house not far from Nancy's larger home? Much of this discussion went off on tangents; how could I rob someone with a gun, attack them, try to murder people? And why did you fall for that bitch, Sandra, or believe what she said? She was a tart, she used you.

I feared for our marriage.

The breakthrough that led to us and our two children going to live in the house I owned was simple. I told Anne of a conversation I had with Nancy Gatley a year before her death. We were in the garden, drinking coffee. 'I'll always be grateful you found me this house,' she said, 'I only wish when I'm gone you and Anne could live here and look after my garden.'

It was the truth.

Now and then I feel guilty I benefited from that venture half-a-century ago. Then I revisit old haunts. Like Pygon's Farm, another man's dream, now restored by a wealthy solicitor; or the vanished May Bank View, now homes for people with no knowledge of those who breathed, walked, lived and loved, on that patch of land. Or, to save my legs, I go to one of the bridges along the canal, so much a part of mine and Blum's young lives. I rest for a while, fancy Blum is with me still, and I hear his voice. And his reassurance comes, 'Don't be daft...'

If you enjoyed this book, look out for *The Signalman's Shed, the Blum Gatley Stories.*

The 1950s and '60s...Blum Gatley, young thief, practical joker, master of revenge and future criminal, meets his best friend and co-conspirator as times change in their community outside Liverpool, where farmland is giving way to new housing estates. It's a friendship that will map their futures...
    What secret did The Signalman's shed hide? And what was Blum's retribution on the man who owned it? How did Blum uncover the mysterious disagreement that caused a life-long feud between two drunken farmers? How does Blum take revenge on a man who once tried to land his dead father in serious trouble? And who better to engineer the costly downfall of a lay-preacher and sex offender? Or, to insult and humiliate the Home Secretary?
    Nine stories of a lost time and an 'apprenticeship' that one day will have consequences – Blum Gatley's life before *Friends, Lies, Booze... and Magpies...*

BARRY WOODWARD was brought up in Lydiate in the 1950s and 1960s and those times and place inspired *The Signalman's Shed, The Blum Gatley Stories*, and *Friends, Lies, Booze ...and Magpies.* He worked as a reporter, a news editor, a freelance advertising copywriter, a press officer and as a jobbing scriptwriter on TV programmes like Channel 4's *Brookside, Hollyoaks* and *The Courtroom*, Yorkshire Television's *Emmerdale* and *Heartbeat*, Thames Talkback's *The Bill* and Granada Television's *In Suspicious Circumstances*, as well as plenty of futile and aborted projects for film and TV. He wrote many articles and had more than 500 scripts produced, some broadcast in more than 50 countries. He once had a *Writer's Guild* nomination, but lost the certificate. He lives near Preston in Lancashire with his wife, Anne, and their cats.

You can contact him at BWlydiateseries@gmail.com

Printed in Great Britain
by Amazon

36176771R00246